PAND

Ellen could n~~~~~~~~~~~
vision of the un~~~~~~~~~
During the next t~~~~~~~~~
brought up the temporo-spatial model. Before she'd just
deleted one rule, the sequentiality of time; now she added
ambiguities. Because KNEE was intended to handle the
notorious ambiguities of natural languages, it was possible
to qualify rules as simultaneously true and not-true, depending on context. She did that to the sequentiality rule, then
stared for a while at the resulting rule set. It wasn't enough.
You had to add something. *Kit*. She created an atom and
called it KIT_STRUC_KB and added a rule which said that
the presence of KIT_STRUC_KB in any net would cause
the sequentiality rule's truth value to change. It was a crude
approximation, but she needed *some* way to factor in the
presence of someone whose brain held all the understanding they were trying to give to KNEE.

This time, the simulation program did not produce the
old elegant dance of interlocking and unfolding, overlapping and separating spheres, that Ellen had produced every
other time she altered the temporal rules. Instead one sphere
folded and collapsed as if it were being drawn inside out.

"Where did I go wrong?" Ellen muttered. "This *can't* be
right. It looks as if time were collapsing in on itself, as if all
times were becoming one. And that is obviously *not the case*."

* * *

In the shady lanes around Greenholt, gravel and asphalt
disappeared in some places to be replaced by deep muddy
ruts. The neat fences of a neighboring farm were overgrown
all in a night by white-flowering brambles that smelled sweet
and winey. Clouds and sun made a patchwork of light and
shadow over the high grassy Downs, and in the shadows
there were forms of air blurring together, and in the golden
sunlit grass there were twisting lines of sharper, clearer light.

Baen Books by Margaret Ball

The Shadow Gate
Flameweaver
Changeweaver
PartnerShip (*with Anne McCaffrey*)

MARGARET BALL

A Baen Books Original

Baen Publishing Enterprises
P.O. Box 1403
Riverdale, NY 10471

ISBN: 0-671-87633-3

Cover art by Newell Convers

First printing, December 1994

Distributed by Simon & Schuster
1230 Avenue of the Americas
New York, NY 10020

Printed in the United States of America

The masque began as no more than a pleasant evening's entertainment. But halfway through it changed. The pattern of song and music and dance Kit had devised summoned the deep magic he sought; Eleanor could sense it like an invisible curtain of ice that divided them one from another.

Where the pattern of moonlight and torchlight and writhing shadows fell upon her, she felt a net of fire and ice. Raising her eyes, she saw the branching horns that crowned Kit's head, silver and glimmering with light like the apple branch within her hand.

The musicians struck up the lively tune that was the prelude to the commoning. Her fingers opened, let the silver bough fall. No sound of ringing bells followed; she looked down and saw the branch falling down into a mist that had risen above the floorboards— and farther down, into stars that swirled and danced in dizzying patterns beneath her feet. She looked up, and the same stars danced above her head, as though the roof of the Long Gallery were no more than a whisper of summer breezes. Lights above and lights below drew closer, joining here on this stage the spheres that had been so long apart.

"A dance, a dance!" cried a boy's shrill piping voice, and all at once the whirling lights were the jewels on the masquers' vizards, and the stage was filled with the Nymphs and Hounds—too many of them, far more than there could possibly have been. Eleanor could not recognize Jane's merry smile beneath any of the Nymphs' glittering vizards.

They were like a rushing stream of stars between her and Kit. Eleanor stepped back, behind the painted scenes. She did not fall into the skies that glittered above and beneath her; here, in the center, the natural sphere of mankind still kept its shape.

Or did it? The painted trees about the gallery trembled in the darkening air, now that the masquers had carried all the torches into their wild leaping dance. Eleanor laid her hand on a canvas scene-cloth. It was rough as bark, cold as night air, and it seemed to curve in the shape of a tree trunk under her fingers. Beside the rough rounded bark, her questing fingertips found only air and darkness, then another green growing tree springing to life where there should have been only painted canvas. She reached forward and felt only air and darkness. She could still see the stage and part of the hall, but they were like a distant image, a painted picture that moved by unknown art.

While Eleanor watched from her starry prison, the two choruses of masquers, Diana's Nymphs and Actaeon's Hounds, set their torches in the wall brackets and mingled with Kit's nobly-born guests. Beneath the jeweled vizards their faces seemed pearl-pale, unfamiliar, and their eyes glinted brighter than jewels in the torchlight. A cool shadowless light of their own, like the brightness shared between moon and sea, illuminated the hall where they drew the visiting gentlefolk of the West Country into a stately pavane. The pure sexless voices of children, or angels, or spirits, sang what Kit had written for the masquers. The Nymphs and Hounds took hands with the gentry and danced in silence through the high clear words and their answering echo from the far end of the gallery, where no singers should be.

Circe bids you come away,
Echo Come away, come away.
From the rivers, from the sea,
Echo From the sea, from the sea.
From the green woods every one,
Echo Every one, every one.
Of her maids be missing none,
Echo Missing none, missing none.
No longer stay except it be to bring
A med'cine for love's sting;
That would excuse you and be held more
  dear
Than wit or magic, for both they are here.
Echo They are here, they are here.

It was Eleanor's cue to enter as Diana, but she could not move back into that world of light. Darkness surrounded her, and the cool damp air of a night wood. The moon that had shone so brightly to welcome Kit's guests to Greenholt gave no light to this wood of troubled air and spirits. An owl hooted, and leaves brushed her cheek, invisible fingers of darkness and mist. Where was the crescent moon now?

That question was answered as she gazed at the

distant figures dancing in the hall. One moved among them crowned with moon and stars. It was she—the Dark Lady of the wood. She had taken Eleanor's place in Greenholt, and Eleanor was trapped in the Ladyswood. She had taken all the lamps of the night to light her dance. Kit had claimed he would join the spheres of this world and the next, would draw down spirits with his music. Was this his success?

She could not even call to them; her throat was filled with darkness. She could only watch as the dancing came to its ceremonious end and the masque resumed.

Where she should have appeared as Diana, the Lady clothed in pearls and moonlight stepped forward to meet Actaeon, and the vizored nymphs welcomed her. Kit came forth, his lean dark face cast half into shadow by the high branching horns that crowned his head: Actaeon made less than man by Diana's retribution and the relentless pursuit of his own hounds.

The dance that followed, the songs and speeches tended only towards one end. She watched, helpless to interfere, as Kit sealed his bargain with the one who had taken her place in the masque.

As the last notes of music died away, the Dark Lady raised her branch of silver apples over Kit's head. The crown of horns dissolved into a dazzling mist that drifted slowly downwards, transforming Kit as it moved. Instead of Kit's lean intelligent face, his sober black doublet and trunk-hose, Eleanor saw a form made all of moving shadows like the Dark Lady's own. And like her, he now gave off his own ghost-pale radiance, as if the two of them burned in a cold fire impalpable to mortal touch.

Kit's voice mingled with the clear purity of the Dark Lady's song and the cold music of her silver bells. Together they sang the words that should have been his duet with Eleanor.

A day, a night, an hour of sweet content
Is worth a world consum'd in fretful
  care. . . .

That dark wood held her mute, a spiderweb of branches and leaves that had never flourished under any earthly sun, and Kit knelt to sing his worship to the Lady whose face was a shadowed mist behind her dazzle of moonlight radiance.

Time stands still with gazing on her face,
Stand still and gaze, for minutes, hours
  and years to her give place.
All other things shall change, but she
  remains the same
Till heavens changed have their course,
  and Time hath lost his name.
Cupid doth hover up and down blinded
  with her fair eyes.
And Fortune, captive at her feet,
  condemned and conquered lies.

Then they were gone, and never a hint of the creaking ropes and pulleys that should have managed their magical ascent into Diana's starry heaven: only two cold pale flames that burned a moment beside Eleanor, amidst the trees of the Ladyswood that had against all reason replaced the painted scenery of the hall. And then—nothing, no trees, no flames; only the waves of human voices murmuring, shouting, crying aloud in surprise, crashing against Eleanor's ears and drawing her back into the room full of guests and masquers.

The dark wood was only painted canvas again. She could not find her way back into the place where Kit had disappeared to; she was fixed in the hall again, locked in mortality. The smell of burning tallow and bodies crowded into a small space and rushes too long unchanged assaulted her. Kit's guests stirred and muttered, and a man pushed forward from the back of the gallery. It was Raleigh's pet priest-hunter, Richard Topcliffe. "An end, an end, an end!" he shouted, brandishing the warrant from the Privy Council.

The Nymphs surrounded Eleanor. They were warm and human and stank reassuringly of sweat and paint, and there were only the three of them, not the multitude of inhuman masquers who had commoned with Kit's guests. Jane smiled tremulously at Eleanor and attempted to lead their final chorus.

> *Come away, away, away,*
> *See the dawning of the day,*

she sang, before Topcliffe's voice overpowered hers. "The villain's 'scaped us! Search the house!"

> *The morning grey*
> *Bids come away;*
> *Every lady should begin*
> *To take her chamber, for the stars are in.*

A mocking voice, pure as moonlight and accompanied by a chime of silver apples, rose over the shouting of Topcliffe and the other men come with their warrants for Kit.

> *Live long the miracles of times and years,*
> *Till with this hero you sit fix'd in spheres.*

2

Saturday, May 7, 1994

Fair in a morn, O fairest morn, was ever
  morn so fair,
When as the sun, but not the same, that
  shined in the ayre,
But of the earth no earthly Sunne, and
  yet no earthly creature,
There stood a face, was never face, that
  carried such a feature.

As always, the dream stayed with Ellen through the misty moments of first waking, a grey root-skein of tendrils whispering through her head while she boiled water for that first, vital cup of coffee. Steam rose from the kettle. Ellen scraped at the last dried crumbs of instant coffee and gave it up as a bad job. With the action, the last cobweb tatters of the dream dissolved into common daylight reality: a dripping faucet, linoleum beneath her feet worn smooth by many tenants, instead of— what *had* the dream been? Now that she was safe in the morning sun and the ancient kitchen, Ellen could remember little beyond the pounding of her own heart and the terror that always woke her, clammy with sweat but quiet. Quiet. At least that was a blessing. If she'd been one of those who screamed with nightmares, she'd never have kept a roommate, in college or afterwards.

But now, remembered in shreds that dissolved as she called them to mind, there was little enough of nightmare in the dream. Something about a play that went all wrong; then there were green lanes through which she ran, mired to the knees in heavy long skirts. The sound of water trickling just out of sight. And somewhere ahead, a grey place where all light, all change, all time became one and died. And there—

A grackle squawked from the windowsill. *One for sorrow*, Bethany would have said forebodingly if she'd been awake, forgetting that where one grackle came several hundred more were likely to follow. "Although several hundred grackles may count as sorrow enough," Ellen murmured. She shook her head and stepped out onto the sagging front porch to face the day. Not such a bad day, really, if you discounted the dream. The May sun held a promise of the baking summer heat ahead, but it wasn't really bad yet. It was Saturday; she could take her own slow pace through the morning, beginning with scones and coffee at the Hyde Park Bakery. She paused on the porch, savoring the reality of sun and grass and weathered wood. May, and in between spring rainstorms Texas was bursting into life. Even the featureless grey surface of the parking lot next door was split and cracked by hundreds of resolute little green weeds.

The squirrel who inhabited their spreading pecan tree leapt to the ground, bounced up to the porch, perched on the railing, and chittered hopefully at her. "Not a chance of crumbs until I've been to the bakery," she told him, and with her first step he skittered back to the sheltering tree. Ellen noticed out of the corner of her eye that he had acquired a companion, a remarkably handsome sleek grey squirrel with fur so smooth it gleamed like silver in the morning sunshine.

Down the street, Ilena Swenson's herb garden beckoned to her with bees and sweet smells and the bright colors of the larkspurs and marigolds that fought for space with the useful mint and lavender and rue. Ellen set off for the bakery, almost—but not quite—humming under her breath. She could sing almost anything without disaster, just as long as she stayed away from the Elizabethan songs that reminded her too strongly of the devastation of her sophomore year. But the music was always there, in the back of her head, and sometimes nothing else would do. And with the dream fading into memory, with sun and spring and noisy grackles all around her and the promise of coffee in a minute, she felt safe enough to let a little of it out. Just to remember a line or two of the songs she had loved better than anything else, without letting herself think about what had ended it. *Harke al you ladies that do sleepe*, Ellen didn't quite hum in her throat, and her memory added the lutenist's accompaniment.

Behind her, the new squirrel ran a short way down the cracked sidewalk, then scuttled into the safety of a low-growing juniper tree. A moment later, a slender young man with buttery-yellow hair pushed

aside the stinging sprigs of juniper and followed
Ellen down Avenue F.

Old Mrs. Swenson was pinching the herbs as Ellen
passed. The mingled scents of fresh mint and lavender
spiraled through her head. The sidewalk beneath
her feet was a labyrinth of cracks where underlying
roots had forced their way to water; maze, roots,
water, mint caught her for a timeless moment. When
the noise of traffic broke the momentary spell, she
was crossing 43rd Street, a block from the Swenson
house. And she couldn't remember the last three
minutes. Had she even said good morning to Mrs.
Swenson, or had she walked past in a waking trance?

Oh, it was too much! Didn't she know her danger
spots? Wasn't she careful to stay away from anything
that might make her space out again? She didn't
even sing any music that would remind her of that
devastating semester when everything fell apart.

But the list of danger spots seemed to grow longer
every year: the songs she had once loved, poetry, a
certain shade of light on the side of a green hill,
and now just the smell of herbs in the sun. . . . Ellen
shook her head until her long fair braid bounced
from shoulder to shoulder, pushed open the blue-
painted screen door of the Hyde Park Bakery, and
entered upon a world of sensation that had always
been safe for her. She loved coffee, and unlike so
many other scents and tastes, the smell of fresh coffee
seemed to anchor her firmly to the everyday world.
For a moment she stood before the display case of
baked goods, loving the sun on the floor and the
reflections in the window case and the smell of coffee
and new bread—all the little ordinary things that
made a real day, that chased away the grey maze.

Then one of the reflections moved slightly, shimmered, coalesced into the shape of a young man standing just behind her. Strange how she hadn't noticed him before. He must have moved closer, becoming impatient while she daydreamed in front of the bakery case. Ellen paid for two currant scones and a cup of coffee, moved aside and set down the paper bag of scones while she cooled her coffee with milk from the open carton that stood among half-melted ice cubes in a tin pan. Just above the table would be the current show of art for sale, something Ellen always enjoyed looking at.

Not today. The usual display of slashing modernist paintings and amateurish fields of bluebonnets had been replaced by a bunch of worn travel posters. Ellen looked up into a green valley like a cup, ringed round with woods and hills that walled in a village of golden stone.

The hot coffee splashed over her wrist and gave a perfectly good excuse for her small gasp.

"What is the trouble?" A strange hand mopped up the spill with a wad of paper napkins; the young man who'd been waiting in line behind her. Ellen looked into his face for the first time and glanced away quickly. Some people were too handsome to be real; this one shouldn't have been allowed out on the streets without some small disfigurement, a dueling scar perhaps, or smallpox pits. What a strange thing to think—people didn't duel these days, except for mock fights in the SCA, and wasn't smallpox just about eradicated? Well, chicken pox, then. Something was definitely needed to dim the glowing effect of that face.

"Nothing's wrong." Her tongue felt thick and clumsy. "Thank you. I'm sorry— I—"

"The pictures displease you?" He sounded hurt. Perhaps he was the one who'd put them up.

"They're very nice," Ellen said. "I have to go now. Excuse me."

"You have hardly seen them." He pointed out the central poster, the image of the Downs ringing a village of golden stone. "There is Emminster, in Dorset; and above the village, see, Greenholt still stands."

The image that accompanied his words was far too detailed to match the tiny golden blur in the picture: a Tudor house, cross-beamed and sparkling with many tiny panes of glass in the new style, with sheep meadows stretching below it to the village, with a dark copse of ancient oaks and beeches above it at the edge of the Downs. The dew would sparkle in the morning sunlight, and cool misty days would succeed one another. . . . Ellen shook her head again, shook the imagined pictures away. What was he trying to do, pick her up or recruit business for a new travel agency? Certainly not the first. Any man as handsome as that probably had to fight girls off with a stick. "I—I'm sure it is a lovely vacation spot," Ellen agreed. "Unfortunately, I don't make that kind of money."

"Money?" He sounded puzzled, like someone who'd never had to consider such trivial problems. He looked in her eyes for a moment, as though he could read a translation there. "Ah—you need gold?"

"Folding green stuff would do nicely. Haven't you noticed what airplane fares across the Atlantic are like these days?" Good practical subject. She kept her mind on the ruinous costs of airfares and her eyes away from the poster that had by some terrible chance reminded her of the safe green place she sought in endless dreams.

"Air Plane," the man repeated as if it were a foreign phrase.

"Well, really. What kind of a travel agent are you?"

A quick smile flashed across his thin face, lighting and warming all those eerily perfect features. For a moment he looked more like a real person than like some impossible dream from a catalogue of male actors. "Not very good. But I can learn quickly enough. Tell me about air pairs."

"Fares. Sorry. I really do have to go." There was a limit to how long she could stand next to that picture and not look back at the perfect golden village in its sheltering ring of hills.

Somebody called after her as she left the bakery, but she walked on, wading through sunshine as hot and sticky as melting asphalt, concentrating on the plain facts that anchored her to reality and kept the grey maze of nightmares away. No cool mists or green hills in this sunny Texas town. Her name was Ellen Ainsley. She lived in a rented house in Hyde Park. She had a B.S. in computer science and a good programming job at GIC. She didn't forget things anymore—not who she was, nor where she was going, nor even—

"Damn," Ellen said aloud. The scones. She'd left her paper bag on the table next to the milk and napkins. Go back? Not likely. Anybody could forget their scones once in a while and not be considered crazy. But if she went back, that annoying man would want to talk to her. About that place in the poster. That village where she had never been, and never intended to go, and which for some reason had come very close to setting off another of her bad spells. Never mind; she still had her coffee. That was what

she needed. She wasn't haunted; she was just suffering the headache and the vague fuzziness of caffeine deprivation. She decided to sit down right where she was, on the low stone wall that bounded the Elizabet Ney Museum, and take care of that little problem.

There was no sidewalk here. Ellen set down her paper cup, kicked off her sandals, and wriggled her toes in the soft grass. The wall was a grey island in a sea of flowers, gaudy undisciplined iris planted by somebody who loved color more than coordination: yellow, purple, apricot, mauve, blue, a riot of jellybean colors.

And across the street, perched precariously atop the playscape that dominated the south side of Shipe Park, was a young man whose butter-yellow hair gleamed in the morning light.

He didn't have a lute in the bakery. And that was all Ellen had time to think before the sweet melody and the words as familiar as her own breathing caught up with her.

> *Descend,*
> *Descend,*
> *Though Pleasure lead,*
> *Fear not to follow;*
> *They who are bred*
> *Within the hill*
> *Of skill*
> *May safely tread*
> *What path they will;*
> *No ground of good is hollow.*

But the hills opened beneath her feet, and they were hollow, empty as a grave ransacked centuries past, and at the same time so full of stifling grey fog that she could scarcely breathe.

Somewhere, always, the sound of water trickling.

A lute, the strings plucked idly, drops of pure music that caught her wandering thoughts and carried them deeper still.

Grey misty light. The ground changing beneath her feet; a deep drift of oak leaves, a thicket of bare trees, their black stems tangled against the grey and sourceless light.

A flight of black birds exploding upward from the trees: one, two, three, four, five, six, seven for a secret that's never been told.

Salt tears running down her face and trickling into the corners of her mouth.

"Here is none weeping, nor laughter neither," warned a voice like the chime of silver bells.

The stone of grief and loss in Ellen's heart melted. The tears dried on her face. Why was she weeping? What was she searching for? What was there to search for? All was here; the world was one, a seamless grey unity that encompassed her. Feeling, movement, speech, music drifted away like the ghosts of memories. Only the moon-pale light and the enshrouding mist remained. She herself was a ghost, light enough to blend with the mist, to dissolve and escape all the memories that bit at her like pursuing hounds. No need for that now, no need, no need for anything . . .

"Well, are you going to come in, or stand on the porch all morning?"

The mists cleared and Ellen could see Bethany standing before her. She put out an unsteady hand to grasp the porch railing; weathered, uneven wood, warm and hard and real beneath her fingers.

And beside her, the unnervingly beautiful young man who'd put up those posters in the bakery.

"What are you doing here?"

"Ellen," Bethany reproved her. "Is that any way to talk to Payne, when he was kind enough to walk you home?"

The young man's smile made Ellen feel weak at the knees. He bowed with the grace of an acting student and handed her a crumpled white paper bag. "I cannot claim the honor of having accompanied your friend," he told Bethany, turning the radiance of his smile on her. "She forgot her scones; I came after her to give them back, and she seemed— confused—so I thought it would be best to see her safely home." He regarded Ellen again with that look of grave concern that was somehow as winning as his smile. "Are you feeling better now?"

Surreptitiously, Ellen checked out the cluttered contents of the porch behind this Payne. Two rusting metal lawn chairs, a box of odds and ends for Goodwill, the table she and Bethany had rescued from a vacant lot just before the bulldozers flattened everything there.

No lute.

No lute case.

You couldn't hide something as bulky as that, could you?

The whole thing had been one of her spells. One of the worst she'd had in the six years since she made the sensible decision to give up Renaissance music and major in computer science.

"A touch of the sun," Payne suggested, excusing her. "Anybody could become momentarily dizzy in this intense heat." He took her hand and gazed into her eyes until Ellen did begin to feel dizzy. She snatched her hand away and glared at him.

Payne sighed. "It's not working, is it?"

"I don't know what you're talking about," Ellen said, "but it's not that hot." Spring in Texas was warm enough, eighty degrees today; but you didn't want to think of that as hot weather, or the hammer-blows of June and July and August would beat you down entirely. "You think this is hot, just wait for summer," Ellen told him. "Where do you come from—up north somewhere?"

"You might say that. A much . . . gentler climate." Somehow he'd taken Bethany's hand during this exchange, and was gazing into her eyes with the same look of tender interest he'd just turned on Ellen. "I do not know this land well. I would be most grateful if you would help me. . . ."

"I'm sure Bethany will be delighted to do just that," Ellen said. In all the years since she and Bethany had met as freshmen in the UT dorm, she'd never known Bethany to pass up a chance to hold hands with a pretty blond young man. Bethany was good at batting her eyes and concealing her intelligence behind a line of New Age psychobabble, too, which the pretty young men seemed to like. How anybody who'd graduated magna cum laude and Phi Beta Kappa could actually *believe* all that stuff about crystals and auras was one of the mysteries that kept Ellen fascinated with Bethany. "Now, if you'll excuse me, I really do have to get over to the office."

"On *Saturday*?" Bethany protested.

"We're having some problems with the temporo-spatial module. And practically everything else in KNEE depends on that one. I've got to get it fixed so people can work on the higher-level inference modules." It happened to be true; but even if it hadn't been— Ellen thought with longing about the safe place she had made of her cool white cubicle at GIC, windowless, featureless, with no pictures or cartoons or plants on the walls to catch her mind in traps for the unwary.

"Knee?" Payne repeated.

"KNowledge Epistimological Engine," Ellen translated.

"I never *have* understood Ellen's work," Bethany said plaintively.

"Well, I suspect they just picked the name to make a cute acronym. You wouldn't believe the scuzzy puns some of our technonerds come up with. They've called the predicate calculus interpreter—"

"I'm sure it's very interesting work," Payne said. "You must tell me all about it some time."

Ellen was used to that tone of bored superiority from young men who assumed that she couldn't possibly really be doing anything as complicated as basic work on the major artificial intelligence project of the decade. They assumed she was a secretary or a flunky programmer trying to make herself sound important.

She knew exactly what to do about it, too. "Yes, it *is* interesting. We're trying to solve the problem of intrinsically brittle software by building a platform of independent knowledge and reasoning abilities. The first-pass research involved a basic ontology of matter, topological space, metric space, causality, and temporality. Then we extended the epistimological model for fuzzy concepts: ambivalence, negation, point of view, objective, and so forth."

Payne nodded and looked intelligent. Ellen sighed to herself. Usually people's eyes were glazing over by now. She decided to let him have it with the other barrel.

"To put it another way, we have designed a basic ontology, a language to express the epistimological level, a collection of unique data structures and inference algorithms. Now we're testing the coherence of the system as we enter information about the real world and let the internal neural networks apply their heuristics to generate subclass world-models based on the rules they've been given. So far we've entered about 1.5 million rules."

"Seal upon seal," Payne murmured, "system upon system. So did the Nolan attempt. Increasing complexity ends in disaster."

"If your definition of disaster is inexplicable software crashes," Ellen said grimly, "you couldn't be more right. And that's why I really have to get going." She rubbed her forehead. The pulses along her temples had just started throbbing, and she was getting the flashes of light that preceded a migraine. Who was the Nolan, and what was this nonsense about seal upon seal? She decided it was Payne's conversation that was giving her the migraine, and the best thing to do was to drive to her office at GIC where she could work on nice soothing *logical* problems.

"Allow me." Before she could stop him, Payne rested the tips of his long fingers on either side of her forehead. *Cool running water, shade under trees, birds singing . . .*

The headache was gone. But the subtle memory of bird song and running water stayed with Ellen

all through the long drive down Research Boulevard
to work.

Three blocks from the house on Avenue F was a
vacant lot where the tall dead grasses of last fall
whispered, pale golden stems shading and covering
the thrusting green of spring's new growth. Payne
stepped from the cracked sidewalk into the knee-
high rustle and sway of dry grass. The sun beat down
upon his uncovered head; in that light he shone
more golden than all the dead grasses that brushed
against his legs. The air stirred about him, a mist
condensing out of nowhere, the sweet humid spring
air taking shape and form. He sank into that misty
blur between one breath and the next, shaking off
the sharp clear lines and dazzling sun that blinded
him.

What was a shapeless fog to mortal sight was the
element in which he saw most clearly. No blinding
dazzle here, but a pure radiance without shadow
and a world that shifted to mirror his will. The language
of birds and music was spoken here; the physics of
dreams was the only law. Payne felt his own shape
sliding with the wind's will, transmuting, refined to
elemental forms of fire and air. The chains of mortal
time and law fell away without sound, dissolving
into the brilliant mist where everything changed
and all was eternally the same. He exulted.

Here was freedom, true light, silver music unending.
Home; the other sphere, unbound, ever-changing
and ever unchanged in its timeless perfection. The
landscape of mortal dreams shifted about him, crevasses
opening at his feet, winds on which he soared with
outspread wings, a winding maze of paths through

a wood where every tree was rooted in stone and caught the sky in its branches.

Ladyswood. The true wood at the center of the Faerie sphere, compared to which the green copse in Dorset was but a reflection without life. The wood where each tree was at once green with new life and burning with the little death of autumn; poised between the spinning stars, the still center he had never left.

His voice was one more chime in the continual silver ringing.

She does not know herself, or her true meaning. She is blind as any other woman. She will not come.

The dry leaves of autumn swept through the wood in ceaseless, ever-changing whirls. The silver answer accepted failure, unchange, the stuff of which their sphere was made.

Kit too has forgotten. He is our ghost, and we are theirs.

Payne was still too close to the mortal world of action and effect; he could not accept inaction. *Once he stirred, as though she called him back.*

He sleeps now. The bells rang down, down to an unearthly end. If Kit Arundel had once remembered the mortal world, that was past now; and what was past held no meaning here. The form of a man appeared among the trees; a young man, dark, in trunk-hose and velvet doublet unrotted by the years, here where no time passed. He moved without sound, with wide dark eyes that remembered nothing, and he was dim as a shadow among the sourceless lights of Ladyswood.

Payne could not remember when Kit had awakened last. *When* was a mortal word, like the meaningless divisions in which they delighted: a day, a night, an hour. Here one knew only *is*, not *was*, never *will be*. Here the dance of the dry leaves changed always and never; the new leaf and the dry were the same without the contradiction of mortal law, green and burning on the one tree.

But the sun of the other sphere had burned his head, burned into the mortal body he assumed; and Payne could still remember time and change, daylight and darkness, the chains of the other sphere. He tried to recall why they should matter. His freedom here was an illusion; he had come bound in urgency, half tied to time. *There is something of beauty in their sphere.* He felt a faint chiming of regret for what he had been sent to destroy, for sun and stone and candlelight and a girl walking in darkness with her memories unawakened.

What matter? Soon all will be one again. The promise on which they had fed so long, so often denied. The dance of the stars that brought the spheres together and apart; the windows between the worlds, open so briefly, soon to close again.

It was what they had all wished for; but the longer Paien walked in the mortal world, the less he loved the thought of seeing it dissolve into Faerie. He tried to convey what he had just learned of time and change, but the song was a discord in the sweet chimes of this sphere: he could not show the painful beauty he had grasped, like a nettle, in the mortal world.

Are you turned traitor? Corrupt, like a mortal? You who have sat at my left hand, will you leave us and die and be stinking meat?

The Lady's delicate amusement was like a whiplash

across his face. Paien bowed his head and returned
to the matter which had brought him here.

I need gold to bring Eleanor to the place appointed.

"Eleanor." The mortal voice was dull and heavy,
the sound of a sleepwalker called in the midst of
his dream. The young man in hose and doublet turned
wide blank eyes towards the coalescence of air and
darkness that was Payne. "Eleanor?"

When no answer came, he sank into dreaming
again, but ever drawing closer to Payne's perturbed
shape.

*She will come, she will sing, I have a plan, but I
must have gold.*

"I did sing once," the moving shadow murmured.
His fingers touched a branch, and the shadowy form
of a lute formed about the wood. A chorus of rippling
notes, like water running over stone, echoed Payne's
promise in mortal music.

The burning leaves clustered and rang and shone
with a dull gleam about Payne's place of air and
shadow, heavy shapes of mortal gold. He lifted them
and scattered the pile once again to the ceaseless
wind, dry parchment of tree-skin to flutter through
the air.

*It will not serve. They change, these mortals. They
change. It must be thus, and thus.* As he explained
the wood turned about him, becoming a golden house
of stone, a shining silver bird, a court where jesters
capered and singers tuned their lutes beneath the
spreading trees. Leaves of gold fell again in showers
around him, and this time he accepted them.

Sun called, and he turned to follow the golden
clue out of the maze. Labyrinth and dance, stone
and water, tree and leaf, he followed and the light

receded. Beside him walked a half-seen form in earthly shadow, untouched by Faerie's calm light; a ghost who lost himself in wandering through the ever-shifting land, though his song followed Payne through earth and air to the place where a May sun dazzled over a field of last year's dry grass.

Follow thy fair sun unhappy shadow,
Though thou be dark as night
And she made all of light
Yet follow thy fair sun unhappy shadow.
Follow still since so thy fate ordaineth:
The sun must have his shade
Till both at once do fade
The sun still priz'd, the shadow still
    disdained.

Fragments of long-forgotten melodies floated through Ellen's head as she settled into her cool white office at GIC. "Follow thy fair sun unhappy shadow . . ." No! She would *not* get back into that; the songs were not simply forgotten but buried, and they had better stay that way! Spacing out that morning had upset her more than it should. The cure for that was work, Ellen told herself firmly; good, hard, absorbing intellectual work, with nobody around to interrupt her train of thought with meetings and coffee-schmoozing and office gossip and office politics.

While her terminal hummed to life, Ellen stared at the white wall above the monitor and practiced letting her mind go blank, relaxing from toes to ankles to knees to . . .

KNEE. Okay, it *was* a silly acronym. But that Payne was wrong; the system wasn't as complex as all that. They knew better, now, than the AI workers of the '70s and '80s. They weren't trying to define the structure of the universe with their bare hands, having a programmer input a specific rule for everything from the law of gravity to the speed limit in Luckenbach. The complexity was in the analysis and design, not in the program itself; ideally, it should consist of no more than a handful of definitions and inferencing rules that could then "learn" the world the way an infant learns it, from first sensory input to complicated and wrong-headed adolescent reasoning.

There were still a lot of rules, though. Ellen brought up a status report on her screen. The number of "basic" statements had increased from 1.52 million to 1.56 million since she last looked.

Fortunately, she didn't have to deal with all that information in the module that her programming team was responsible for. They had the heart of the system, the temporo-spatial module, the basic topology and metrics and temporal relations of the universe. At a gross level, of course; KNEE wasn't trying to compete with the theoretical physicists, who never could make up their minds anyway. Basic Newtonian physics was more than enough to handle the kind of "common-sense" knowledge engine they were trying to build.

Unfortunately, this piece had to be working before most of the other modules could be tested. And last week had been full of software crash reports from the other teams, most of them blaming Ellen's group and their module. Two-thirds of those could be discounted; some programmer would wail, "But I only changed one line of code, that *couldn't* have made it bomb!" until suddenly he realized exactly

what dumb thing he had done and scurried off to
fix it.

It was the other one-third of the reports that worried
Ellen. If the temporo-spatial module was fully and
correctly programmed, and was still giving inconsistent
results . . . It *couldn't* be. The *universe* was consistent.
There was a bug somewhere, and she was going to
trace back through the levels of inferencing until
she found it.

The work was absorbing; she lost track of time,
tapping at the keys that brought up one web after
another of basic semantemes and their relations,
sending out inferential reasoning sequences that
displayed as darting green lines tracing through the
yellow web. It was all artificially slowed far below
the computer's real speed, of course; she needed
to watch the inferences as they happened, not to
be dazzled by seemingly instantaneous flashes from
yellow webs to green—

Aha! A green snarl, a tangle that spiraled in on
itself. Ellen fixed that one while mentally composing
a sarcastic E-mail to her staff. "Some little boy or
girl hasn't been reading the directions on the work
sheet. Can we all say, 'Second Law of Thermodynamics,'
now?"

There, that was better. She hummed under her
breath as she traced back through the series of
incorrect inferences generated and stored in the
system after the initial error. Everything made
sense, everything had to make sense; if it didn't,
you had made a mistake, that was all. "The sun
must have his shade," she hummed, "till both at
once do fade . . ."

"*No,*" she said aloud. "We're not doing entropy,

thank you very much. A simple common-sense real world model will do very well."

She saved the corrected data structure. She ought to run it a few more times, just to make sure that she'd caught the only basic error, but she felt tired of following the darting green inference lines. First she'd compose that E-mail to her programmers. Let's see; how about a pithy quote on the nature of time and space to start things off?

She exited the KNEE system and hit the random-quote generator. Having an on-line Bartlett's Quotations was one of the minor perks of working at GIC. "Time," she requested.

The screen blanked and came up with a text in Gothic print, neatly framed by a series of graphic moons and stars.

> "Time seizes and returns everything, for all is change; everything that doth exist, is either here or there, either nearby or remote, either present or future, either early or late."

The bar line under the quotation attributed it to one Giordano Bruno of Nola, also known as Nolanus or the Nolan.

The Nolan. Who had been talking about that? Ellen rubbed her temples; the headache was coming back.

It was an interesting idea, though, if you translated it into modern terms. Basically this old geek was saying that one of the basic axioms, temporal sequentiality, really didn't exist.

He had no way to test the consequences of his assertion, but Ellen had. Just for fun, she called up a copy of the temporo-spatial module, clicked on the menu bar to get to the axiom list, clicked again to delete the law of sequencing in time. Then she saved the amended module as "TEMPORAL.SCR" and ran it in slow-display mode, just to see what would happen. Probably it would crash almost at once; you couldn't delete something that basic and not run into trouble.

The yellow webs of data relations formed on the screen, and a green line of inferencing traced through them, looped around itself, deleted data relationships and added new yellow lines. Fascinated, Ellen watched while the shape of the world as semantic relations pulsed and decayed and built up again into an image of two interlocking spheres in a cycling dance, now together, now drawing apart until a single glowing line connected them, now semi-overlapping again. . . .

Christopher Arundel to Edward Guilford
May 1594
My most assured friend,

This day past have I been favoured with a most fortunate meeting, which offereth to us the fruition of those plans we spake of, that we may truly say with Virgil, *Magnus ab integro saeculorum nascitur ordo*.[1] Thus came it to pass:

Having visited the Tower to discover how my kinsman of Arundel[2] fared in his long imprisonment there, I did then in obedience to his desires wait upon his lady at Arundel House. Though Lady Anne (as you

1. "A great order of the ages is born anew."
2. Philip Howard, Earl of Arundel, had been confined in the Tower since April of 1585 on suspicion of being involved in one of the many Catholic conspiracies against the Queen.

know) mislikes my faith, which she would rather
call *unfaith*, yet she did press me to dine with her.
And so did we sit down but three to dinner in that
house which was wont to entertain the flower of all
the Court: the other guest being made known to
me as one Mr. G. Cavendish, an English gentleman
lately residing in Italy.

Mr. Cavendish is a man of middle years, stooped
with much study, with eyes that do seem to look
into some far place not visible to mortal sight. He
sat silent through the first part of the dinner, while
Lady Anne did chide me as is her wont for having,
as she would have it, deserted the true Catholic
faith in search of worldly advantage. I did humbly
pray her not to impute false motives to me, and
did say once again that I could not reconcile it with
my conscience to hold fast to a faith whose very
leader, that is the *Pope*, should incite Englishmen
to rebel against their lawful monarch.[3]

This defense of mine Lady Anne did let fly at
with so many wounding words as might have been
arrows at a target, until I feared me she might have
spoken outright treason; but G. Cavendish spake
on my behalf, saying that he knew to his own sorrow
how an honest man might be led into conflict with
the Church through no intention of his own. Such
had only recently been the unhappy fate of his good
friend and teacher Messer Bruno.

These words did mightily disquiet me. "Bruno
the Nolan?" I cried. "Are you a student of the great
Giordano Bruno, sir?" And I did earnestly entreat

---

3. The Papal bull *Regnans in Excelsis*, issued by Pope Pius V in
1570, declared Elizabeth I a heretic, excommunicated her supporters,
and commanded loyal Catholics not to obey her laws.

him that he might relate what disaster had come upon the great philosopher. It seems that Messer Bruno has made the grievous mistake of returning out of Germany to his native country; where, certain zealous priests misliking the philosophical enquiries he had pursued and published, he has been arrested by the Holy Office and is now under inquisition of heretical opinions; a questioning which Mr. Cavendish feareth can have but one end.[4] As a known student and associate of the Nolan, he thought it wise to remove him out of Italy before the same net flung after Messer Bruno should catch him also.

I did most earnestly desire Mr. Cavendish to tell me somewhat of Messer Bruno his most recent work, and we spake long into the night concerning the Nolan's theories of Unity, his search for the fountain of light in which the innumerable is made One. A cause of great concern to the Holy Office, as it was to our own dons of Oxford at the time of the Nolan his visit to England, is his insistence that as the soul is the center of man, so is the sun the center of the celestial cosmos. We discussed his proofs of this assertion, deriving from the mystical wisdom of Hermes Trismegistus, and did compare them with the merely mathematical and rational arguments put forward by Messer Copernicus, until I perceived that our discourse wearied our good hostess.

So great was my thirst for knowledge that I could not be satisfied with a single night's discourse; yet it could hardly be supposed that I should inflict my presence longer on Lady Anne, knowing her

---

4. Bruno's imprisonment ended as feared, but not for some years. He was finally burned alive on the Campo de' Fiori in Rome on February 17, 1600.

distaste for the principles of that reformed religion
to which God hath led me in despite of my family.
Therefore have I invited Cavendish to spend some
weeks at Greenholt, and the purpose of this letter,
my dear Edward, is to desire you and your good
lady to join us there. Among the three of us I have
some hope that we may put into practice what you
and I spake of once as but a theory—that union of
music, poetry, and philosophy by which the followers
of the Nolan may achieve the universal understanding
of the world to which all his writings aspire. As our
mortal world lies beneath the spheres of daemons
and angelic creatures, and they beneath the stars,
and the stars beneath God, so shall we begin by
employing music and masque to join our selves with
the angelic spheres, that their greater understanding
may be added to our own. Cavendish assures me
that the very stars favor this undertaking, being at
a conjunction of spheres such as shall not be witnessed
again this four hundred year.

So for our spiritual voyage, we be now at a point
to set forth for the great Unity of the world, and as
Drake did encompass the world in his ships, so may
we in our minds; as Princes reign over the temporal
world, so shall our little company of adventurers
gain equal power in the celestial spheres; and indeed
I am fully persuaded it will fall out the best voyage
that ever was made out of this realm, as far surpassing
the earthlie adventures of Drake or the Muscovy
Company as doth the sun surpass all lesser lights.
Are you resolv'd to be as deep an adventurer as
Cavendish and my self? If so, then you will not take
it amiss that with this letter I do send my man with
a purse to defray the costs of your journey into Dorset;

for it would be great pity to allow mere material want to hinder our venture at this passage.

Having been in London but these three days, and the Court almost empty of company, I have but little news to send you beyond this matter. Sir W. Ralegh is come well out of the inquisition into his atheistical talk, as nothing could be proven against him for want of witnesses to the worst statements; but this availeth him naught in the face of the Queen's anger over the matter of his hasty and secret marriage, and he is retired to Sherborne, being denied the Court. There is plague in the City as usual, and rumor saith the stars portend a hot summer and many deaths of it, wherefore is another reason that we should retire in peace and philosophy to Greenholt. Yours to command as ever,

Christopher Arundel

3

Through the hot second week of May Ellen was grateful to the pre-release frenzy that kept her debugging last-minute program changes for twelve to sixteen hours a day. She fell into bed for a few hours each night, dreamed in C instead of English, and did her best to ignore Bethany's growing involvement with the strange young man who'd followed her home from Hyde Park Bakery.

On Thursday she made the mistake of coming home before midnight. Bethany was waiting for her, eyes glowing with excitement, talking so fast Ellen could hardly take in what she said, and waving a flyer printed on pale green paper.

And behind Bethany, Payne waited with a smile that never reached his eyes.

"Ellen, look at this!" Bethany demanded before she had a chance to sit down. The printed flyer, pale and soft as the green of new leaves in a misty springtime, jiggled and danced before Ellen's tired eyes. She could barely follow Bethany's excited babbling.

"Contest . . . great musical discovery . . . *Arundel's Ayres* . . . free trip to England if we win!"

Ellen took the flyer from her hands and held it in the light. The top half announced in large Gothic capitals just about what she'd heard from Bethany: there was to be a singing contest at the Renaissance Faire next weekend. The group who best interpreted Arundel's *Ayres for Lute and Voyce* would be given a free trip to England to perform in the Midsummer Eve re-enactment of the recently discovered *Masque of Diana and Actaeon*.

Two columns of smaller type down below, evidently a reprint from some English newspaper, gave some background on the contest. It seemed that the manuscript of this masque had recently been discovered, along with a number of other papers, under the eaves of a small Tudor country house in Dorset. Apparently some wet and hasty Elizabethan had used the manuscript to stop a leak in the roof. The papers had been discovered when the Dorset Historic Trust, the present owners of Greenholt, hired a local firm to repair the roof. In the hope of increasing tourist interest in the county, the Trust had paid to have the words and music of the masque transcribed into modern notation. No, not the Trust. An anonymous benefactor had paid for it, with the proviso that the masque should be re-enacted at Greenholt on Midsummer's Eve, 1994, the four hundredth anniversary of its first and only performance.

"I don't understand," Ellen said after working her way through the two dense columns of text. "Why come to America for people to sing an English masque?"

"There were no . . . suitable . . . performers in England," Payne said. He was watching her as a nervous man might watch a cat on the table, waiting to see whether she would leap for the curtains or attack his ankles.

"That's hard to believe."

Payne shrugged. "There are rather specialized requirements for the two principal singers."

"For heaven's sake, Ellen," Bethany interrupted, "don't look a gift horse in the mouth! Wouldn't you rather spend June in England than sizzling away here in the middle of Texas? It can't hurt to try for the prize, can it?"

"*Can't* it?" Had Bethany forgotten why Ellen dropped out of the music department and lost her scholarship?

"It sounds like lots of fun to me. Payne's been telling me all the old legends about this masque. Supposedly it was written by Wicked Kit Arundel, and he was snatched away by the devil during the first performance of the masque, and they think that's why the book was put away and the masque was never performed again." Bethany clasped her hands together. "Ellen, this was *meant* for us. I can feel it. It's almost as if I had been there for the first masque. . . . I can see it all now, ladies in tall powdered wigs and gentlemen in red high-heeled shoes, with small-swords at their hips." She gazed out into space with a vague unfocused look.

"What you're remembering," said Ellen, handing back the flyer, "is the time you understudied Marcellina for the student production of *Figaro*. Wigs? Red shoes? Eighteenth century. This music is late sixteenth."

Bethany opened her eyes and glared at Ellen. "You always were a skeptic. I probably can't receive the message clearly with your hostile vibrations interfering."

"Fine," Ellen said, "I'll take myself and my hostile vibes back to work while you and Payne rehearse." Maybe she'd just sleep in her office, too. Better that than listening to Bethany and Payne sing the music that haunted her dreams.

"But Ellen, you don't understand," Bethany said. "We need a soprano. One who's been trained to sing early music." She paused. "The finest voice in the class of '88."

Quant voi renverdir. Par maintes foys. Veni Sancte Spiritus. Draw on sweet night . . . The hauntingly sweet melodies hummed around Ellen like bees, but the sting was in the last memories, the semester of Renaissance Vocal Music. *Harke al you ladies that doo sleepe . . . Dreames and imaginations . . . When Love on Time and Measure makes his ground . . .*

"No." The first time she spoke, the word came out as a shaky whisper. Ellen swallowed and tried again. "No. I can't do this."

"You sing with me. Sometimes you even sing for parties. What's the difference?"

Ellen glared at Payne, who was following the argument with a look of courteous interest, as if he were watching a—a cricket match or something. "Come into the kitchen for a minute," she said.

With the swinging door between her and the stranger, Ellen felt safer. She glared at Bethany. It was time to stop this nonsense once and for all. "You know perfectly well what the difference is. The music we sing for parties is safe. But I can't do this! I can't take the chance."

"How do you know?"

"Remember what happened?"

"That was six years ago. Maybe it's time for you to try again."

"*I'll* decide when I try again."

Bethany sighed. "Ellen, six years is long enough to be spooked about some minor emotional problems when you were an undergraduate. I know you're good at your work, I know you like computers, but it is *wrong* for you to cut music out of your life. And that's not all. Year after year I've watched you narrowing your life down, cutting out anything that could possibly remind you of that time. First no early music, then no walking past the Fine Arts complex, now you won't go on campus at all, you won't go to concerts, you're spending every spare minute at work—and don't try to tell me it's just for this software release, because there'll be another crisis after that, and if there isn't, you'll manufacture one. Do you want to spend the rest of your life sitting in a blank white cubicle, afraid of your own shadow?"

"I. Am. Not. Afraid," Ellen said between her teeth.

"Then sing this music with us. If you're not afraid to try, then what's your excuse for refusing to do your oldest and dearest friend a favor?"

"Bethany, *get off my case*." Bethany had neatly boxed her in. No junk about meditations and vibes, just the incisive logical reasoning her roommate usually concealed beneath a fluffy exterior. Ellen had to get out of this corner, distract Bethany somehow—"At least," she said, "I've got enough sense not to invite a total stranger into our house."

"What are you talking about?"

"This Payne. What do you really know about him?"

"*Payne?*" Bethany's eyes clouded over, opaque

as marbles or stones. She seemed to be looking
somewhere else; at the cabinets behind Ellen, or
at some scene of floating clouds and sunsets beyond
the cabinets and the kitchen walls. "You must be
joking. I've known him for . . . oh, it must be years
and years."

"Where did you meet him?"

"Ellen, you're just trying to change this subject.
Look, we have a perfectly wonderful opportunity
with this contest—"

"Payne," Ellen insisted. "If you've known this man
for years, how come I never saw him before he followed
me home last week? Where've you been keeping
him—in storage under your bed?"

"What do you have against Payne?"

Ellen threw up her hands. "I don't have anything
against him. But don't you think he seems—well—
strange?"

"Not to me," Bethany said.

"Well, he does to me. Kind of . . ." Ellen searched
for the right word to describe Payne's quick gliding
movements and elusive non-answers. "Squirrelly.
I'd like to know a little more about the man."

"Well," Bethany said in tones of sweet reason,
"you're *not* going to get to know him better by hiding
out in the kitchen, are you?" She pushed the swinging
door open with one shoulder. "I live here too, remember.
Don't I have a right to entertain my friends? Now
come sit down and let's discuss the contest like
reasonable people."

Ellen followed her back into the living room, but
at the sight of Payne's innocently inquiring glance
she felt a panic that wouldn't let her be reasonable.
She wanted to scream, to run away. All her safe

havens were dissolving into the mist. Her quiet office was full of frantic programmers, her home was invaded by strangers, even Bethany was bent on pushing her headlong into a confrontation with her past. She enjoyed a moment of feeling thoroughly sorry for herself, turned that sorrow into anger at Bethany. "Never mind! There's nothing to discuss. If you want me out of here, you don't have to do it this way. I'll move out tomorrow."

"Ellen, you don't mean it!" Bethany wailed.

"Maybe I do. I'm beginning to feel as though I could stand to spend some time in a real place, with real people who just want me to work and pay the rent and who aren't bent on excavating my psyche with a jackhammer. In public," she added with a glance at Payne.

Two large, glittering tears rolled out of Bethany's eyes. "I was only trying to help you."

Payne bent and brushed his lips across the top of her head. "Of course you were," he said in his soft voice. "We are all tired, and this heat makes it worse. Perhaps you could make us all a cup of tea?"

Bethany brightened, blinking away the tears as though she had quite forgotten her reason for being upset. "Of course. I'll make some of my special herbal blend." She patted Payne on the arm and disappeared back into the kitchen.

A cup of tea. That, Ellen thought, was supposed to be the classic English way of handling anything from a domestic quarrel to the Blitz. So Payne *was* English. Why did that only make her feel more dubious about him? She looked at him, seated now in the slipcovered chair they'd found at a neighborhood yard sale, long legs stretched out before him. It hadn't taken him long to make himself perfectly at ease in their home.

As if he could feel the weight of her gaze upon him, Payne turned his head slowly. His eyes met hers and his lips curved up in the faintest hint of a smile. Belatedly Ellen canceled her first impression. He wasn't at ease; every line of the long slender body was alert, sensitive to a breath of air or the shadow of a doubt in a stranger's eyes.

"You're not a travel agent, are you?"

Payne inclined his head gravely. "I never claimed to be. That was your idea entirely."

"And you don't have an English accent." She was reaching for some way to bring out what she felt to be false in him, but she was asking the wrong questions, she knew that; he would slide away from everything she said, somehow turning every incongruity into sweet reason, and at the end she'd still be no further to understanding him.

"I adapt quickly to—whatever place I happen to be in."

"How nice for you," Ellen said. Was that what she wanted—to understand him? If she had any sense she'd only want to be rid of him. He was changing everything around her; there were no safe places left, and it was all his doing.

The light under the ceiling fan played over his yellow hair; the crisp creases of his slacks cast long shadows down his legs. Just by sitting there he made the room shabby and dark around him, made himself the center of light. Ellen resented him fiercely and without excuse. This was her home, lovingly furnished by her and Bethany over the years. This morning it had all been beautiful to her—the lace tablecloths from Goodwill that hung over the curtain rods, the high narrow arched windows with their panes of beveled glass, the scatter of velvet pillows in jewel tones of ruby and emerald and sapphire that softened the stained oak floor. Now it seemed like a collection of shabby makeshifts, and Payne had brought the one thing she could not face to squat between her and Bethany like an ugly monstrous toad, a witch's familiar croaking out disaster. The skin along Ellen's arms and the back of her neck prickled.

"Oh, I wish you had never come here!" she cried out, and then, "I'm sorry, that was rude of me."

"The truth often has rough edges," said Payne. "Do not excuse yourself, Ellen Ainsley. But I think you may yet be glad of my coming."

"*Do* you?" Ellen could sit still no longer; she walked over to the east window, the wide flat one they kept draped over with a crocheted tablecloth, and twisted the corner of the lace between her fingers. "If I asked you to go away, would you?"

Behind her, Payne's head was a golden gleam half veiled by the reflection of the curtain. "No," he admitted, "but you are not asking the right questions."

"What should I ask, then?" Her own face looked back at her from the darkness outside the window, an oval framed by wispy tendrils of fine hair, the features softened through lace and shadows until it could have been any young woman's face, a blurred shadow of light against the darkness. "Should I ask who you are and what you're doing here?"

"I am looking for singers who might be able to interpret Kit Arundel's music as it was meant to be sung," Payne said. "It was told to me that you might be such a one."

His speech was slow, laden with archaic rhythms; Ellen felt as though her responses were part of a centuries-old ritual.

"Who sent you to me?"

"One you will be glad to know again."

The gleam of his golden hair in the reflections from the window was all Ellen could see of him; but for some reason she was reluctant to turn and face him directly. She leaned against the windowpane, pleating the soft worn lace between her fingers until the pattern of flowers and trailing vine was imprinted on her skin.

"Why have you come to America? Surely there must be more suitable singers closer to home. And they would not have American accents to overcome."

Payne's smile flashed, momentarily brighter than the yellow light overhead, glittering round the edges of the shabby furniture and lighting the dusty corners. "Do not concern yourself about accents; whoever sings for us, from whatever side of the sea, will have to learn the old manner of speech. It is most important that everything be done as it was in the first performance of the masque."

"You care that much about authenticity?"

"It is important," Payne repeated.

"There must be many who could do better than I," she insisted. "I washed out of the performing music program six years ago—and I wasn't all that good even then."

"Oh, yes, Ellen Ainsley," Payne breathed softly. "You were that good. I am quite sure of that. Pray believe me, no one else could sing this masque as you could."

"I find that a little hard to believe," Ellen said,

"considering that you haven't even heard me sing."

"Oh, but I—" Payne stopped as if changing his mind in midsentence.

Bethany swirled back into the room, balancing a tray with a Japanese teapot and three mismatched cups. She set the tray down on the bamboo end table with a flourish. "Here's my special hot-weather cooling herbal blend, Payne. Raspberry leaves, camomile, mint . . ."

Payne glanced up at her. For the first time Ellen saw him looking irritated. He murmured something under his breath and held out one hand towards Bethany, twisting his fingers into an impossibly contorted shape.

"Mint . . ." Bethany repeated. The vague unfocused look had come back to her eyes. "Mint and . . . I can't quite . . . remember . . ." She stretched and yawned. "So tired," she said in a small, apologetic voice, and sank down on the carpet. Her head and one outflung arm rested on a crimson velvet pillow.

"What are you doing?" Ellen started forward, but Payne stopped her where she stood with another twirling motion of his long fingers.

"Fear not," he said, and Ellen felt slightly ridiculous for having been so afraid. "She sleeps, nothing more, and shall wake all in good time."

Ellen looked down at Bethany's black hair where it spilled over the crimson cushion. Her face was relaxed under the fan of black curls, her mouth was slightly open, and she breathed slowly and regularly.

"She sleeps," Ellen agreed, and then a voice so bitter she hardly recognized it as her own added, "Would God I might so rest at peace!" She turned

away from Payne and leant her forehead against
the cool hard glass.

"No, you have slept long enough," said Payne,
"time to awaken now, Eleanor."

"My name is Ellen."

"*Is* it?"

Ellen blinked, uncertain. "Why—I—I should know
mine own name, should I not?"

"Know, then," Payne said softly.

Something moved in the mingled shadows and
reflections before her; she had a sense of small things
scurrying outside the house, shadowy forms that
grew more solid with the darkness, watching and
waiting. *From ghoulies and ghosties and things that
go bump in the night, Good Lord deliver us.* But it
was only Payne in the mirror of the dark glass, rising
from his chair and coming to stand behind her. The
long, cool fingers touched her neck. "You are afraid,"
he said. "I can remove the fear for you."

Ellen remembered how her headache had slipped
away between Payne's hands.

"And who will I be, if you do that?"

"Only yourself. Perhaps more yourself than you
ever were before. I should be glad to see that," said
Payne softly. "I wish to know what you were, that
love of you has kept Kit Arundel's mind fixed on
the mortal world all these four hundred years."

It was quite dark outside now; a car moved slowly
down the street, and the white glare of its headlights
brought dancing, leaping shadows to life all down
the rows of neat small houses and shady trees.

"I don't know anybody called Kit. And I do know
who I am," Ellen cried. The moving lights blinded
her, splintered brightness and shadows all through

the room and cast her words back like the mirrored shards of a lie. She turned away from the brilliant artificial light and paced through the moving shadows of the room. Bethany slept on, happily unconscious. "I do! And I don't want you to take my fear away from me. All I want is to be let alone. Why won't anybody understand that?"

"You are . . . stronger than I had believed," Payne said. It seemed to Ellen that he looked at her with a respect he had not shown before. "Do they not cause you pain, these shadows in your mind? Would you not be free of them?"

"I know who I am," Ellen repeated. "I can take care of myself. I'm not crazy. I don't need to be hypnotized or regressed or channeled or whatever you people call it these days." She crumpled the flyer into a ball and dropped it on the floor. It floated too slowly; Payne caught it in midair. "I wish you'd never shown this to Bethany!"

"Do not think of it as a threat," Payne advised. He smoothed out the crumpled ball of paper. "Think of it as . . . folding green stuff. What you wanted, no?" The paper slid and crackled between his hands. He folded it into the shape of an airplane. "Bethany showed me how to do this," he said happily. "It is a great marvel."

He launched the paper airplane over Ellen's head, to loop and glide in the draft of the ceiling fan until it drifted to the floor like a falling leaf. And as it fell, so did she, sinking into a sleep of forgetfulness.

In the morning she woke, stiff from sleeping on the floor. "What the heck did you put in that 'special herbal blend,' anyway?" she demanded of Bethany.

"I don't remember exactly," Bethany said uncertainly.

"Camomile, red clover maybe. Something to relax you. Anyway, it worked, didn't it? You've been really wiped out. I hope you get some rest this week."

"Why this week specially?"

Bethany widened her eyes. "Melville's party is on Saturday."

"I don't go to Music Department parties," Ellen said automatically.

"You *promised*."

"I did?" Something stirred, lazy and slow, uncoiling at the back of her mind; memories best not looked upon in daylight; fear without reason, and an overriding command that almost laid the fear to rest. "Maybe I did," she conceded, quickly, before Bethany could remind her of anything she didn't want to think of.

"You'll like it," Bethany assured her.

Ellen gritted her teeth. "Did I also promise to like it?"

"It's not all music people," Bethany said. "Melville's wife is a lawyer. They're inviting a bunch of people from her office."

That did make the prospect better, but Ellen wasn't about to admit it. She couldn't even remember why she'd agreed to go to the party, or how it had come up. And for some reason she was reluctant to examine her own memories too closely. She felt calm and peaceful this morning, if a little stiff from falling asleep on the floor.

She frowned. On the floor? Why would she have slept on the floor? She must be imagining things. . . .

By the time the coffee was ready, she had convinced herself that nothing untoward had happened the previous night; Bethany's friend Payne had dropped by and for some reason she'd agreed to go to a party with the two of them. That was all. Absolutely all.

By eight o'clock on Saturday evening, Melville Ridley knew that he could stop worrying about whether his wife's friends from law school and his friends from the music department would manage to have fun together. Whatever Alice had put in the punch, it was potent enough to dissolve inhibitions and loosen tongues. In one corner of the house a classical pianist was lecturing Alice's senior partner about the misdeeds of lawyers; in another, three law students were happily explaining jazz to a music professor. At least two fights had been broken up already, most of the guests were shouting to be heard over the music, and a lawyer was quietly throwing up over the back balcony. And there were still people arriving; he could hear the distinctive sound of a car grinding its way up the steep hill to the house. Melville smiled in pure bliss. It was going to be a *good* party.

His smile broadened when he recognized Ellen Ainsley's battered VW. So Bethany had borrowed her roommate's car, or—surely not? Melville blinked and grinned and took Ellen's hand in both of his. "Ellen! It's been too damn long. But I thought you couldn't come. When I called Bethany on Thursday—"

Ellen's smile was slow, but as warm as ever. "I've been working late. She probably thought it was never going to end. But I *think* all the bugs in the temporo-spatial module are fixed. The next level up is somebody else's problem."

"Bugs? Module?"

"Computers," Ellen explained.

"Oh, yes, I remember; you got a programming job, didn't you? Poor you. How boring."

"Not at all," Ellen said briskly. "KNEE happens to be *the* major artificial intelligence project of this decade. When completed, it will provide a platform for easy development of truly self-understanding, self-teaching expert systems drawing on a complete common-sense world-knowledge base. In the last year alone my team has been specifying the base set of specialized deduction processes for the Newtonian time-space model, with specific integrity verification system-based facilities for each one. Then, to make things easier for the general user, we wrote KNEEJERK, a language translator that accepts additional rules in the predicate calculus form that everybody knows, then translates them from the generic epistimological state to the internal form required by the inferencing engine."

Melville felt as though he'd just been hit over the head with several blunt instruments. And he'd deserved it. There *were* other interesting things in the world besides music, as Alice kept trying to tell him. "Ah—that sounds very impressive."

Ellen grinned. "Yes, doesn't it? There's just one little problem."

"What's that?"

"It doesn't work. But the parts that don't work," she said cheerfully, "are now all in other teams' modules. Not my problem." She smiled again and drifted past him towards the living room. For the first time Melville noticed that a third person had got out of the VW after Bethany and Ellen; a young man, slender and quiet in the shadows.

"This is Payne," Bethany said, drawing the boy

forward into the light at the porch. Melville caught
an unsettling glimpse of hair like spun gold, smooth
skin, and ageless eyes of no color at all. "He's a very
old friend of mine. From England. And since he's
visiting, I felt sure you wouldn't mind . . ."

"No, no, not at all, glad to meet you," Melville
said automatically.

"I'd better see how Ellen is doing," Bethany said.
She slipped past Melville, leaving him to face the
stranger with old eyes in a young, unmarked face.
Though why he should feel so panicky—

"There is no reason to fear me," said Payne in a
low, pleasant voice. His fingers moved restlessly by
his side; Melville found the twisting motion soothing,
almost hypnotic.

"Of course not," Melville answered, smiling again.
"No reason at all." He felt remarkably good all of a
sudden; maybe another of the secret ingredients
in Alice's punch had just kicked in. One of these
days he really would have to get that recipe from
her.

"Ellen was afraid to come here," Payne said, still
in that casual drawl as though he were just exchanging
social pleasantries. "Why?"

Melville felt a small knot of resistance within himself,
a place where the wonderful punch had not yet
smoothed out all worries. "If you're such an old
friend of theirs, I should think you'd know all about
that business."

"But I don't," said Payne. He drew something
from his pocket; a small ragged shape that glittered
in the porch light. "I have been over the sea for a
very long time," he said slowly, twirling the bright
knickknack between finger and thumb, "and Bethany

will say only that she was not there when it happened."

"When what happened?" Melville felt stupid and drowsy, unable to concentrate on anything more complicated than the flashes of golden light coming from the edges of Payne's toy.

"I do not know," Payne said. "She says . . . you were there. She says . . . you should tell me all about it."

"All about it . . ." Melville echoed. The uneven edges of the thing in Payne's hand flickered, gold and blue and then all colors mixed together and then no color at all, pure as moonlight. The cool pearl-white light helped him to focus his thoughts. It *had* been some time; six years, to be precise. But he could remember Ellen's eager face as though it were yesterday; and more than her face, the pure clarity of her singing voice.

"I think maybe it was because her parents couldn't be bothered to come up for the concerts," Melville said slowly. "Or maybe it was the pressure . . . She was only a sophomore and everybody was saying with her voice, she ought to drop out of the degree program and go professional. Opera. But she didn't like opera, she liked Renaissance music. And she had a scholarship, you know, and she said she'd have to teach or something after, her parents wouldn't help out, they didn't approve of her going to the university."

"What happened?"

The edges of Payne's spinning trinket flashed gold around a dark center: bright, dark, bright, dark, until they blended together into a soft luminescence in which nothing and everything moved.

"She started having headaches. I think it was the

stress; Haines insisted on having her in his Renaissance Vocal Music class, and it was supposed to be a graduate course. *I* had trouble keeping up," Melville remembered, "and I'd had five years of music history and theory. Ellen didn't have any theory, but she could sing like an angel. Only the headaches kept getting worse. One day she picked a fight with Haines about something she couldn't possibly know anything about—claimed all the embellishments to Campion's 'A day, a night, an hour of sweet content' were late Jacobean and the original had been a duet for two voices, tenor and soprano. And that somebody else had written it." Melville stared into the still center of the spinning trinket. "She could have been right, as far as that went, you know," he said absently. "A lot of these songs were passed around in manuscript for years before anybody ever published them. But she didn't have any *evidence*. And then—"

"And then?" Payne prompted softly.

"The next day she did it again. Only this day it was one of John Lilliatt's songs. Haines was explaining some details of the phrasing, and Ellen jumped up and said Lilliatt didn't write that song, somebody else I never heard of did, and Haines had the phrasing all wrong, and then she started to sing it the way she thought was right, and—halfway through her voice stopped. Just stopped. Like a power failure. Lights out. I took her arm," Melville said, remembering, "and she stared at me and asked who the devil I might be. After I'd helped her cram enough music theory to pass midterms! And then she fainted, and— we took her to the Student Health Center, and her parents came up from Baytown to collect her. I heard they put her in a private nursing home. No money for college, no help when she could have used it, but plenty of money to hide her when they thought she was crazy and might embarrass the family—I will *never* understand people like that," Melville said, glowering at the spinning light in Payne's hand.

"Ah. But she came back?"

"She came back," Melville agreed. "Six months later, so thin and pale I hardly recognized her the first time I ran into her on campus. She'd lost the scholarship, of course. She said she wasn't interested in music anymore. She obviously didn't want to talk to me or anybody else from the music department—except Bethany—they'd been roommates before the breakup, and afterwards I gather they rented some kind of house north of campus. I think Bethany was the one who found out where she was and talked her into coming back to school. But she never did have anything to do with us after that. I didn't even know until tonight that she'd gone into computers. Makes sense, though. A lot of musicians are good mathematicians—you probably wouldn't expect that."

"On the contrary," Payne said, "in my own land I have known a man who sought to bring together the arts of music and philosophy, and he was as well a stargazer and an indifferent skilled geometer."

Melville nodded. "I would expect Ellen to do well at whatever she concentrated on. But it's a damn shame about the music. I wish you could have heard her singing—like a bird. A star. A stream running over rocks . . . She did have the voice; and she had something more too, but I can't explain it. You'd have to hear her."

"I look forward to it," Payne said. "She has agreed

to sing tonight—a trifle of music from my country. Renaissance airs for lute and voice."

"She has? How the hell did you pull that off?"

"I put a spell on her," Payne said. He flipped his trinket up into the air until it seemed to float, spinning, above their heads; then it drifted down, slow and light as a dried leaf. And still the jagged edges shone like gold. Melville followed their spinning path of light while Payne asked idly, "By the way—what was the song?"

"Song?"

"That caused her to slip between the worlds."

"Oh. Strange way to put it." Melville frowned. "Something attributed to Lilliatt—I told you that— I don't recall exactly, it was never one of my favorites. Something about time and measure . . ."

"'When love on time and measure makes his ground,'" Payne quoted softly, almost under his breath, "'Time that must end, though love can never die . . .'"

"Yes! How did you know?"

"She was quite right, as it happens," Payne said. "That particular song is not by John Lilliatt. The poem was written and set to music by Christopher Arundel." Payne frowned. "I do not understand, though, why just singing it should make her faint. That worries me."

"It wasn't the music. It was the stress."

"I hope you're right. I do most heartily trust that you are right," Payne said. He was not looking down at Melville at all; his eyes were raised to the sky, where his spinning trinket still whirled lazily on a breath of evening air, flashing between starlight and sunset. "Down, down, an end, an end, an end," he murmured, and inclined his head to Melville. "If you will excuse me; I must tune my instrument."

Melville stared after him. "Now where the hell did he get that lute?" he murmured. "I could have sworn he wasn't carrying anything a minute ago. And that *thing* he was playing with . . ."

The breeze quickened into a tiny whirlwind, a gathering of air and sand and twigs funneling down to the steps, and in the middle hung something bright as gold. Melville snatched at it and felt something crumbling to nothing in his palm. He opened his hand and looked at the crumbled bits of a dry leaf, brown and gold and rust-red and burning with autumn fire in May.

The living room was two stories high, with walls as thin as the sides of a cereal box. Voices drifted up like coils of smoke, echoed through from kitchen and hallway. Ellen was drowning in a sea of half-heard words and questions and laughter, music department gossip and dead lawyer jokes— Melville had married a lawyer, it seemed, but she had a sense of humor about her profession's image. She must have money, too; Melville's salary from the Austin Symphony wouldn't pay for this shiny new house.

Half the guests were lawyers, friend's of Melville's wife; the other half were students and orchestra players. The musicians congregated in the kitchen, where the snacks and drinks were. Music department gossip, old and new, arguments about sonority and atonality swirled about Ellen until she retreated into the high-ceilinged white living room with the young professionals in suits. Somebody pushed a glass of white wine into her hand; she sipped and smiled and let the noises blur around her. Perhaps Bethany had been right. . . . Or was it Payne? Ellen frowned slightly, trying to remember the conversation, then gave it up with a shrug. What did it matter? The important thing was that she was no longer afraid. And certainly she had nothing to fear here; she'd encountered several acquaintances from the Music Department, and nobody had so much as mentioned her breakdown. Perhaps Bethany had warned them to be tactful.

Or perhaps not. The crack that had split her life in two might not be terribly important to anybody else. Ellen drained her plastic glass of very dry white wine and held it out for a refill. The young man in the blue pinstripe suit who was talking to her poured deftly without missing a beat in the joke he was telling.

"Because there are brake marks in front of the armadillo!"

Ellen managed to laugh while wondering vaguely what the first part of the joke had been.

After the second glass of wine she found that she could laugh whenever there was an expectant pause, without even listening for the punch lines. All she really heard were the snatches of conversation and song from the kitchen. The world she had lost. Ellen drank a third glass of something that turned out to be punch, not white wine. A pleasant haze enveloped her, pierced here and there by memories like shards of ice in her heart. Maybe another glass of this punch would melt the ice. Maybe she'd be normal then: just a girl at a party, backed into the corner by an earnest young man who was trying terribly hard to amuse her.

"'Scuse me," Ellen said, slipping past the lawyer to find her own way to the punch bowl.

"Oh, no, you don't." Bethany was suddenly there. "You don't need any more to drink, Ellen. So how's the party?"

Ellen had to think a moment before replying. She felt pleasantly relaxed, but it was hard to remember how to make conversation; she hadn't been expected to do anything but listen and drink since she drifted into the living room.

"Lawyers," she said finally, "know more dead lawyer jokes than anyone else in the world."

She picked up a clean paper cup from the stack on the table by the punch bowl, but Bethany got in her way. "Come on, Ellen. Don't drink any more or you won't be able to sing. Everybody sings at Melville's parties."

"You didn't tell me that." Ellen looked at the young professionals clustered around the empty fireplace. "Even the lawyers?"

"Everybody," Bethany said firmly. "Don't worry, we're not performing. Just joining in." Melville shepherded them all to seats; a circle of chairs supplemented by cushions made places for everybody.

No. The word wouldn't come out; absolutely nothing would come out of her throat. It was one thing to sing with Bethany at home, or at parties for her programmer colleagues from GIC. But to sing real music, in front of people who knew about her breakdown? She couldn't do it. Ellen clenched her hands in her lap while the lead violinist from the orchestra sang something from Mahler's *Songs of a Wayfarer* in a voice like dark molten copper. *The world she had lost . . .*

Payne squeezed in between her and Bethany. "No fear, no fear," he murmured, and Ellen felt herself relaxing under the soothing purr of his voice. Besides, after the Mahler there wasn't much real music to speak of. The second violinist had no kind of a voice at all. Two lawyers in a row abstained and the third one sang a Gilbert and Sullivan patter-song from *Trial by Jury*, with names of his colleagues deftly inserted at appropriate points. The listeners cracked up and drowned out half his words. The laughter was contagious; Ellen found herself giggling, even though she didn't know the people he was satirizing. Watching their faces was enough. Then Payne handed her some sheets of music with something stamped on the top margin. . . . *Transcriptions from the Masque of Diana and Actaeon, by Christopher Arundel* . . .

Ellen stiffened. "You didn't warn me!" she whispered at Bethany.

"What's the matter?" Bethany whispered back. Her eyes were wide and innocent. "Forgotten how to sight-read?"

For a moment Ellen felt really angry with Bethany for putting her on the spot like this. She couldn't even get up now without drawing too much attention; there wasn't room to slip quietly out of the circle. Damn Bethany! If people would just *let her alone*, she could be—

What? Safe? Alone in her white-walled cell? Dead?

"Forgive Bethany," Payne whispered, "the fault was mine. And there's nothing to fear, is there, Ellen? It's only music." *Only music.* And she wasn't afraid. But it still hurt too much, remembering all she'd once had, all she had turned her back on. Payne had done nothing to take away that sorrow, or the older, darker grief beneath it, the mourning for something lost she'd never had.

It was their turn. Ellen shook her head and gestured vaguely towards her throat, trying to look like somebody who would just love to sing if only she didn't have a sore throat. Bethany glared at her and started to play the introduction on her lute.

There was something wrong with the music. Against her will, Ellen glanced down at the transcription. Yes, Bethany was playing the notes as they were written, but it still sounded wrong. "Up half a tone," she whispered, "and a little faster."

Bethany nodded and smoothly changed keys in midstream, picking up the tempo. There—now it sounded right.

But Ellen still wasn't about to sing. The music was transcribed as a part-song for soprano and contralto. Tough. Bethany started this, let her figure out how to finish it. It was bad enough that Ellen would have to sit and listen.

She was *not* going to cry in public for everything she'd lost when she dropped out of the music program. No matter how much it hurt to hear this music, this strange, newly discovered song that sounded like something she'd known and loved forever.

Bethany gave Ellen one last pleading look and launched into the song, doing her best to carry both parts.

> *Circe bids you come away,*
> *Come away, come away . . .*

Bethany's contralto should have been blending with the soprano line, not trying to carry the entire burden of the music. Ellen could almost hear how it should sound. . . .

"Eleanor and Jane will give us a song to accompany the virginals." A tall man, greying early, dressed with simplicity and near-Puritan severity all in black velvet; his hand hard on her arm as she would draw back. Edward.

"Prithee, Edward, not now. I am——" Searching for an excuse that would not offend; afraid to meet the eyes of that other one who stood now in shadow, all a dark blaze of black hair and eyes. Wicked Kit Arundel, a bye-word at Court, the Wizard of Dorset. She had not imagined he would be so young. Or so well-favored. Not that it should make any difference; she'd promised Lady Margery not to take part in any of the atheistical talk and dangerous devil-raisings that rumor credited the master of Greenholt with, and she meant to keep that promise for her soul's sake. "The dust of the road fills my throat still. Perhaps tomorrow——"

The notes of the lute song resounded through the white-walled room, filling Ellen's ears with a roaring like the sea. Anger rose in her like a salt tide. Why should she not sing? Who dared take that away from her? She had lost so much more than a music scholarship—so much more— She couldn't quite remember what she had lost; but it would all come back if only she sang.

From the rivers, from the sea . . .

Ellen's clear soprano lifted the melody and carried it, soaring with the music.

From the sea, from the sea,

the echo cried.

Voices— *Who was talking?* and music ran together
in her ears so that the melody had no clarity anymore.
But it was still there, even blurred and running together
as raindrops will streak a windowpane until the world
is all hazy without, and the call of the song was leading
her through the rainwet glass as a ghost will pass
unhindered by locks and doors.

From the green woods every one,

she sang, and Jane's—no, *Bethany's*—lower, softer
voice carried her up with the echo:

Every one, every one.

The rough white walls of the new house seemed
to be wavering now, greening, springing to life; and
there was no crowd around her, only a troubling of
the air that stirred those other shapes and trembled
all the hanging candle flames.

Of her maids be missing none,
Missing none, missing none.

"A cup of sack for my sister!" Servants moving in
the darkness beyond the ring of trembling light; a
cup of worked silver, heavy enough to hold with
two hands, and the sweetness of hot strong wine
flavored with sugar and spices, driving out the chill
of the misty day. Her head swam with the fumes of
heated wine, and the drink burned warm within
her. Very well—she would sing. Not for Wicked Kit,
but for herself. No harm in singing, no danger in
music; music had been all the joy and all the sweetness
of her life, and she would not let this devil-raiser
spoil it for her.

It was only a song.

How had the room grown so dark and close, and so cold? Ellen could not think. The music was drawing her through the glass. *It was like this before—*

It was all wrong. Who were these people? She was a modest maid, no court damsel to flaunt herself before a crowd of strangers. Where was her brother? How could she sing in this strange place?

How could she not sing? The music was a cord drawing her heart with it.

> *No longer stay except it be to bring*
> *A med'cine for love's sting;*
> *That would excuse you and be held more*
> *   dear*
> *Than wit or music, for both they are here.*

The two worlds swirled and ran together, two rivulets of rain joining in a trickle that became a flood through her, foaming and raging. No light here, no sun or moon or even candlelight, but the sea roaring in her ears and the world a wind-tossed wood about her and a voice completing the words that should never have been sung in this life.

> *They are here, they are here.*

And they were all about her.

4

The cool misty light of a West Country spring afternoon spilled through the opened casements of the dining parlor, carrying with it the scents of rain and damp earth and grass and sheep. Where it lingered on the Venetian glass goblets at the table, the grey light was transmuted: air becoming light becoming jewels, ruby and emerald and sapphire, an alchemy of illusion. The lively hues died on the dark wood of the table; the grey daylight flowed on, casting pale gleaming highlights on the great carved chimney-piece.

Here Actaeon stood at one side of the fireplace, gazing on the bathing Diana, her nymphs caught in grain and swell of carven wood and unable to hasten to her, his pack of hounds swirling with open panting jaws about the hunter and the Huntress. And on the far side of the chimney-piece the same hounds rent a strange figure, half man, half stag, while the chaste Diana looked on with a secret smile like a crescent moon set askew in the night sky of her face.

Eleanor clasped her hands together and looked at Diana triumphant in polished oak, refusing to meet her brother's eyes. If only she could master the secret of that closed smile, if she could make herself cool and remote as Diana, then she would sing with a right good will. *Think not on heathen goddesses, but on the Heavenly God.* But she could remember no prayers. Was Wicked Kit's magic already working on her soul?

"There is time and enough for music," said Christopher Arundel, unexpectedly, from the dark far side of the dining parlor where he stood in shadow. His voice sounded confident enough. Was he so sure, then, that she would dance—or sing—to his bidding?

Of course he was. Arundel was rich; he was Edward's patron. He might take a fancy to receive them as equals, but the hard realities stood between them: the pinched narrow existence of Edward's household, the broad acres and wool rights and exemptions that made Arundel's fortune. Grants won from an aging, susceptible queen, men whispered at Court; grants won by who knew what dark deviltry working on the queen's mind with tales of mirrors and stars and visions? Arundel had studied with Dr. John Dee, the Mortlake wizard who was the Queen's astrologer.

Eleanor willed her fast-beating heart to calm itself. All that did not matter now. The hard fact was that Wicked Kit Arundel was her brother's patron, that Edward lived on his bounty and depended on Arundel to have his poems circulated at Court where they might earn the family some favor in the Queen's eyes.

Edward would write whatever songs Master Arundel

required. Edward would be delighted to do anything Master Arundel desired of him. Edward would— Eleanor set down her cup of sack, slowly and carefully, upon the heavy carved sideboard. Edward would pander his own sister for Master Arundel's delight, if he thought that was what his patron wanted.

"We can play and sing at our leisure to beguile the rainy days," Kit said now. "Pray pardon me for making an unwelcome suggestion to your sister, Edward. You did say that she had an excellent clear singing voice, and I had thought that in your household she would have been brought up to read music from the book and to sing and play like any fine lady. If I had known she had no skill for music, I had never embarrassed a simple maid who would rather sit in the corner and ply her needle."

All the words were grave and polite, but his eyes were upon her, dancing, mocking, daring her to fly into a temper and refute him. He must know she was no ignorant country girl. She had served Jane's lady aunt at court these three seasons; he knew perfectly well—if he'd ever troubled to distinguish her from all the other gently-born girls who carried dogs and brought tambour frames and did other small services for the great ladies—he must know that she was as well able to play at the virginals or on the lute, to sing a part-song or madrigal or round, as any educated lady should be.

What Master Arundel wanted, it seemed, was to tease her into complying with his will—into playing his games that led from heresy to hellfire.

The damp air that sighed in at the window smelt of leaf-mould and bark and green twining vines. The wood they called the Ladyswood covered the

slope from the high Downs right down to the very
threshold of Greenholt; instead of a proper park
with green turf and pleasant rides and marble statuary,
Wicked Kit Arundel had this wilderness at his door.
Eleanor felt it as a pressure all around her, a subtle
flowing and shifting of the air as though it were
already inhabited by those invisible spirits Arundel
was said to call up at will. She had to get away from
this sinister room with its many winking mirrors
and panes of glass and polished panels, where the
light bent in strange ways and these men would bend
her to their will. It was worth risking Edward's anger
to escape this place, even if she was only putting
off the confrontation.

"Pray you forgive my attendance," Eleanor said,
letting go the handle of her tankard with fingers
that ached from gripping so tight. "I find I am more
fatigued from our journey hither than I had thought."

She made as deep a courtesy to Master Arundel
as she would have made to the Queen herself, sinking
almost to the floor and rising straight-backed with
a rustling of skirts and petticoats about her before
she swept from the room. Oh, she'd been at court
long enough to see how the great ladies carried
themselves; he'd find no excuse here to gibe at her
for a simple country lass.

Greenholt Manor was built on a generous scale
in the golden stone of the region. It was no great
lord's house with wings enough stretching out from
the main building to form the shape of an E for the
Queen's name, but it had hall and gallery and parlor,
with rows of bedchambers above for housing master
and servants and guests. Eleanor had been given a
chamber of her very own, even though she did have

to pass through Edward and Jane's room to reach it; and a fine room it was, too, all new-furnished and painted with a ceiling of heavenly stars against a deep blue ground. But she had scant privacy to enjoy it. Edward's feet were heavy on the stairs behind her, and before she had passed the tester bed where he and Jane would lie, he had caught up with her, grasped her wrist, and turned her to face him.

"What foolish manners are these, girl?" he demanded.

Behind him, Jane entered on soft slippered feet and closed the door, quiet and economical as she was in all her movements. She opened the chest at the foot of the bed and took out a piece of fine linen partially embroidered with black work. "Mr. Guilford, would you be so kind as to set a branch of candles on the chest?" she asked as though she had not quite grasped what was going on. "The clouds have dimm'd the sunlight so that I can scarce see to finish this cap." Her eyes were lowered, her hair neatly concealed beneath her headdress. But somehow it was impossible to quarrel in Jane's calm presence.

Edward let go of Eleanor's wrist and brought a branch of candles to Jane's side. Eleanor lowered her arm, feeling the ache in the small bones where Edward had held her. She would have a bruise there the next day, but she would not give him the satisfaction of rubbing her arm while he watched. Not for the first time, she blessed the chance that had given her hot-tempered brother such a calm, kind, cheerful wife. Dear Jane; no one could stay angry when she was being so pleasant and sensible.

"Thank you, husband." Jane looked up and smiled sweetly, charming away the last of Edward's black frown. "We ladies are not so strong as you; in truth, I do not think I could trust my poor fingers to keep time so soon after the rattling of the journey. It was good of Eleanor to spare me the effort."

But she went too far there, trying to take all the blame upon herself. "My young sister is a fool, wife," Edward grunted, "and you are a worse fool for aiding her in her folly. Why, here's such a chance as may not come twice in a lifetime, and she'd throw it away to play the shamefast maid! She may at one and the same time aid me in this our great endeavour, and bring herself well into Arundel's notice."

"Small chance of escaping it," Eleanor said, "an he invites no more guests than ourselves and that astrologer to share this great house."

Edward's black-featured face softened and he stroked Eleanor's unbound hair. "Aye, he must see how fair a maid you are. But I'd have him hear you sing, too. Our Kit does love music, and if he hears your sweet voice singing his own airs—not in a crowd as at court, but just yourself and Jane—I'll wager he'll not forget you again. See you, our Eleanor, here's your chance to make a match will set up our family again."

"With *Christopher Arundel*?" gasped Eleanor. She made a dart for the doorway to her own chamber; she felt safer standing there, where she could have a closed door between herself and Edward, should he lose his temper again. "Are you mad? I'd as soon wed with the Devil himself—and small difference, to judge from what's said of him at Court."

"Y'are a prating fool, Eleanor. Were there aught sinful in Arundel's philosophical experiments, d'you think I'd wish the match for you?"

She did think so. Edward was blinded by Kit's
wealth and brilliance, else he'd never have come
to this secretive house deep in the country to play
at devil-raising with his patron. But to say so would
earn her nothing but a beating. Fortunately another
avenue of escape opened before her. "Call that a
match? He'd as soon wed his serving-wench as me.
Why, he could have had his pick of many a lady at
Court, with fortune to match his—or Sir John Banister's
only daughter, who'll have broad acres to march
with this land of his—why would he look twice at
me?"

"He is main fond of me," Edward pointed out.

"Aye, that's another mystery," Eleanor said, then
cried out involuntarily as Edward lunged forward
and slapped her across the face.

"Dear, dear," Jane said calmly, setting another
stitch into her blackwork by the light of the wax
tapers, "brawling like children in the nursery! For
all you are so black and your sister so fair, Mr. Guilford,
it's easy to tell you are sibs. Such tempers as the
two of you have!"

Edward drew back again, shamefaced by Jane's
calm manner, while Eleanor marveled. She might
make pert replies to Edward because she could not
remember to hold her tongue, but she would never
have dared speak to him as Jane did. But no one
ever took offense at Jane's words.

"Now let your sister rest, husband, and I shall
speak to her while you go downstairs and talk with
the other gentlemen, for 'tis not fit you should trouble
yourself with women's matters," Jane advised. And
for a wonder, Edward took her advice, withdrawing
from the bedchambers with a muttered warning that

by tonight Eleanor had best learn to see sense if she did not wish to spend the remainder of her visit to Greenholt locked in the inner chamber.

"There, now may we be comfortable," Jane said when the door closed behind him. She sighed and put her feet up on a small stool. "Shall I call a servant to have a tisane made up for you, Eleanor?"

"I think you need it more than I." Eleanor knelt by the chair and laid her head against Jane's worn green gown for a moment. "You have the head-ache again, have you not?"

"Yes, but do not speak of it to Mr. Guilford. You know how it wearies him to hear females always complaining of their little aches and pains." Jane set her needlework down carefully upon the chest and blew out the candles. "There, that's better; the brightness did hurt my eyes so."

"You only asked for the candles to distract him."

Jane's laugh was soft and calming, like all else about her. "Y'are slow for such a great girl, Eleanor. Sometimes it wonders me how you did survive these three years past at Court, where all is intrigue and double meaning."

"Serving Lady Margery," Eleanor said drily, "and keeping out of the way of men like Wicked Kit Arundel." She raised her eyes to Jane's. "I cannot play the part Edward would have me do, Jane—I *cannot*. For my soul's sake, Jane, persuade him to let me be!"

"You seem certain he will endanger your soul," Jane observed.

"I'm sure enough it would come to naught else!"

"I see." And Eleanor felt uneasily that her brother's wife saw more than was safe for her. "Well, then, it

can't be helped; I shall tell Mr. Guilford that you
are already in the throes of such a mad passionate
desire for Mr. Arundel that your virtue is not safe
in his presence, and that we'd best make some excuse
to send you away before you shame the family by
tearing off your clothes and begging him to have
you as his leman, and—"

Eleanor pressed her lips together, but an unladylike
splutter escaped. "Give over, Jane, do! 'Tis no such
thing. I'd not be drawn into his devilish work, 'tis
all. If Edward means to join him in raising demons,
I cannot stop him, but I'd not be made a part of
their rituals."

"If Mr. Guilford sees no harm in't, there can be
none," said Jane, and went on calmly stitching at
the cap as though she had no more problems in
the world than to set her small stitches in a neat
white line. "Remember that we owe obedience to
those set in authority over us. As his wife and sister,
we should obey Mr. Guilford and trust his judgement,
just as he serves Mr. Arundel, and Mr. Arundel the
Queen, and the Queen herself serves God."

"God should come *first*, not *last*," Eleanor protested.

"In your heart, I'm sure, love. But in this world
we must obey the degrees to which God has assigned
us. Else what monstrous anarchy 'twould be, to see
the child set against the father, the father against
the Queen, and all against God while calling His
Holy Name to bless their strife!"

Eleanor smiled. "You should have been a man
and a preacher, Jane. A little more, and you would
persuade me that God's will is for me to accompany
Wicked Kit Arundel on his path to damnation."

"There can be no damnation in a few songs," said

Jane, eyes on her fine stitchery. "What harm can it do to bend a little to your brother's wishes? We need only be civil, and sing and talk and enjoy ourselves in the country; there is no more to it than that."

"*You* may know it," said Eleanor gloomily, "but what of Edward? If he will have this come to matchmaking—"

Jane rose, shaking out her skirts, and went to the window where tiny diamond-shaped panes of glass captured and diffused the cloudy afternoon light. "Do you leave me to manage Mr. Guilford," she said looking down into the gardens of Greenholt from this high vantage point, "but in faith, I am sore fatigued and would rest now. Eleanor, dear, why do you not take a turn in the maze before dinner? The fresh air and exercise will be calming to your spirits."

The maze was a high hedge of trimmed box, entered through an arch and then turning into a labyrinth of little paths that went nowhere. Eleanor turned back from a blind alley, scuffed her toe along the path of low sweet herbs before her, and muttered, "Calming, indeed! Who was ever calmed by being set a puzzle to solve?" But it would have been churlish to refuse Jane's suggestion, when clearly her sister-in-law wanted only to be alone for a little while; and at least here she was safe from the embarrassment of having Edward throw her at Kit Arundel's head.

And the puzzle could not be so very hard to solve. Eleanor applied herself to the problem, counting blind turnings and paths that doubled back upon themselves, and scarcely noticed that the clouds had parted to flood the garden with warming sunshine.

The sweet smell of crushed herbs underfoot rose all about her, mint and creeping thyme and burnet, and her lips moved silently as she counted the turns. She was almost sure, this time, that she had gotten the trick of it: first turn to the left, second to the right, third to the left, fifth to the right. Seven false branches, now, and the eighth to her left, and now a long count . . . At the thirteenth branch to the right Eleanor turned, sure of success, and ran forward into the center of the maze.

Here low shrubs of silver lavender and green box twined in a series of interlacing knots that led to the willow tree at the heart of the maze. Eleanor stopped where she stood. Around the willow tree was a low wall, a stone circle holding green turf to make a garden seat. And on the seat, watching her with cool amusement, was the one man she most desired to avoid. A lute leant against the tree beside him; his hands were linked around his knees, and the rings winked at her in the afternoon sun, brief dancing dazzles of true emerald and diamond.

She made as if to step back behind the last screen of the mazy hedge, but it was too late; he'd seen her. Had been watching for her, waiting for her. In traitorous silence, the lute set aside. "I'd not have thought Edward's sister would be such a fearful maid," Arundel said as if to the whispering willow leaves that shaded his head. "Must ever run away, Eleanor?"

"I do not so," Eleanor said, and glared at him, daring him to challenge the lie. "I am come here in the desire to walk alone, and since that be denied me, I shall seek my solitude elsewhere. If it please you." Jane must have seen Arundel from the window. Eleanor had seen often enough how Edward underrated

Jane and found himself doing her will without really knowing how it had happened. She might have been clever enough to avoid the same trap herself.

"Well, before you run away," said Arundel with a lazy smile, "at least tell me how you came so quickly to the heart of the maze. Most of my guests do search for hours with less success. Had you the secret of your brother before he sent you out?"

"He did not— I would not— You," Eleanor said when she controlled her stuttering, "are abominable. Sooner would I seek out the company of your swineherd!"

"Ah. But you have not found the swine. Rather are you come direct to the heart of the maze. Shall I take that to be the purest chance?"

"A most unchancy chance, since 'twas you I chanced to meet here," Eleanor said. "You make much of a simple matter. Anyone with wits to count could discover the pattern of the maze after the first few turnings— although," she added, "I fear me all too few of your guests can claim even so much wit."

Arundel threw back his head and laughed, long enough for Eleanor to hear her own words. How appallingly rude she had been! "I repent me of my hasty words," she said.

Arundel had recovered from his brief fit of laughter. "No. Do not. You have the right of it, mistress; none but you and Mr. Giles Cavendish have found the center unaided. How he found the secret I can guess, for we studied in the same school of philosophy; but the plague take me if I can tell how a woman came to know the secret of Fibonacci. Will you be seated and tell me, or shall I go on in the belief that Edward gave you the key?"

She *was* growing tired of standing in the sun. And she'd not have this arrogant young gallant saying she'd run away from him, or—worse yet—that her brother had sent her as some kind of offering. Which Edward probably would have done, Eleanor admitted to herself, had the thought occurred to him. Hadn't Jane done almost the same thing, albeit without her knowledge and consent? She moved stiffly forward, skirts brushing across the stems and flowers of sweet herbs, and sat on the green-turfed garden seat. Arundel's discarded lute leaned against the tree between them like a silent chaperone. Here amidst sun and flowers, with the warmth releasing the sweet scent of herbs, she could not believe this young man posed any danger to her soul. Whatever fooleries he and Edward engaged in by night, with their scrying glasses and visions and secret alphabets, here under the sun all things were blessedly commonplace. And the secret of the maze was no more than a game of numbers.

"It is plain to the meanest mind," she said. "Left alternates strictly with right, and then 'tis only a matter of counting the turns."

"So much Edward might have taught you," Arundel pointed out. "Did he also tell you the rule that governeth the number of turns?"

"He had no need to," Eleanor said shortly. "I've enough wit to see a pattern laid plain before me, believe it or not as you will. The number of turns before you take a path is the sum of the last two numbers of turns. First left, second right, third left, fifth right, eighth left, thirteenth right. And I made certain this was the end of the sequence because you have not space enough in this garden to limn out another twenty-one paths."

"The Fibonacci sequence, by my faith! How many times have I not explained it so to Edward, yet must he ever bear the written key when he passes through the maze. He must have comprehended more than I did guess, so to teach it to you."

"Edward has taught me *nothing*," Eleanor cried. "What little I understand, I have contrived of mine own self." And how little that was, in comparison with the riches of books and learning and discourse available to such men as Arundel!

He was looking at her as if he'd just come across something amazing and interesting: a scientific rarity, a woman with a sense for numbers. *Men*, Eleanor thought crossly. How did they think a woman could buy the cloth for household liveries and check if the cook was cheating and provision a house for a winter's worth of guests, if she'd no sense for numbers? Did they believe a household could be managed by counting on one's fingers? More likely, she concluded, a fine gentleman like Arundel had never thought about the matter at all; the smooth running of a house was to him an act of God or nature, like the growing of grass or the running of water downhill to the sea.

"And I've never met Messer Fibonacci," she added.

"You could not," Arundel interrupted, "he is dead these hundred years."

"But this maze is only a pattern," she went on as though he hadn't spoken, "a pattern in numbers, as music is a pattern in sounds, or . . ." She looked sidewise at him. "Or magic a pattern in images."

"So it is, by God!" He did not seem offended.

"Pray do not take the Lord's name in vain, Mr. Arundel. And I do not mean to insult you, but by my troth, your guests must be dull indeed if they fail of so easy a test as this. Even Edward—" She swallowed the disloyal words. Edward drove her mad with his laborious progressions through the obvious. But he was a man, and learned in Latin, and had even a few words of Greek, and had studied mathematics with the same tutor as Arundel. He must be cleverer than she could understand. And he would certainly be angry to hear her bandying mathematics and philosophy in such an unmaidenly fashion. "If I have satisfied your curiosity, I beg your leave to be on my way."

"No. Do not go yet." Arundel's dark face was alive with excitement; he reached to take up the lute that lay between them, and Eleanor tensed. "O marvel of marvels! You have been sent here—"

"Nay, have I not told you often enough I found the way myself?"

"Sent," Arundel continued blithely, "by a power for good."

"Of which you stand in grave need, I doubt me!"

"I do," he said without heeding the sarcasm. "The music of the masque cannot be complete without the voices of women; but I never hoped for one who could understand."

"And what would you have us comprehend?" She would wager her understanding against his or any man's, though Edward should beat her again and say 'twas not seemly for a maid to shew her quick wits.

"Comprehend? Why—everything I mean to do!" Arundel gestured with both hands; the lute fell forward and Eleanor caught it in her skirt, automatically, before the full round belly of the instrument could be scratched or marred in the fall.

She stood and handed the lute back to him. "I've no wish to understand or to meddle with what wasn't meant for us to know, Mr. Arundel. You and my brother had best look elsewhere for the soprano of your masque."

"And how," Arundel inquired most earnestly, "do you recognize what we are not meant to know?"

"It was made law in my father's father's time that those who unlawfully practice invocations and conjurations of spirits are practicing witchcraft," Eleanor said, "and my lord Cardinal Wolsey's sad end showeth us what doth come of such matters."

"I had thought it showed rather the danger of giving offense to princes," said Arundel.

"Nay, he had a magic ring that whatsoever he asked of the King's Grace, that he might have of him," Eleanor explained. "Did you never hear the tale?"

"If he had such a ring, it served him an ill trick in the end."

"Precisely!" Eleanor shook out her skirts, amazed at the willow leaves and sprigs of herbs that had gathered there without her knowing. "So will all evil spells and incantations do at the last. And so I give you good-day, Mr. Arundel."

"No—wait! Eleanor," Arundel added, "are you truly such a foolish maid as to believe these old wives' tales? I do promise you, mine intent is naught such as Wolsey's might have been. It is not power for myself I seek, but heavenly enlightenment."

"It seems to me," said Eleanor, "that Heaven has

very little to do with it." But Arundel was speaking
to her intelligence and not to some imagined meek
maid. The temptation was too great to flee at once.
Lead us not into temptation, she prayed, and sat
down again.

"If you think so," said Arundel, "you are not *listening*.
There is no more of evil or witchcraft in what I
would do than there was in Messer Fibonacci's
numbers." He took her hand and traced out lines
on the palm as he spoke; Eleanor stared at the invisible
maze of lines and saw nothing at all. "You must
understand," he explained, "as you did say, 'tis all
patterns; everything is a pattern. That is the secret
of the order of the universe, the great linked chain
of creation."

Eleanor frowned. "Of course we must have order
in the world, and every man to his place; but I cannot
see what that has to do with numbers." It had, on
the other hand, a great deal to do with why she
should not be sitting here chatting alone with a man
like Christopher Arundel; a man who was not of
her world, as she was not of his.

"Oh, *think*, Eleanor." She should reprove his
familiarity; she should reclaim her hand. She did
neither. A virtuous maid would have fled earlier. A
virtuous maid would be sitting within doors, working
at a tambour frame and bored to distraction. "Does
not every class of created things stand in its proper
place, nourished by those below, serving those above?
As plants take their sustenance from the elements
of air and earth and water, so do animals feed on
plants, men on the flesh of animals, and our prayers
and songs are that heavenly food on which the angels
subsist."

Eleanor nodded. "What about fire, though?"

Arundel frowned.

"I have always wondered," she explained, "how it is that three elements nourish plants, but the fourth takes no part in it."

"Women," Arundel said, "are too bound to the concrete. You wouldn't understand if I explained it to you." But he looked unhappy. After a moment's silence his face cleared. "Sunlight!" he exclaimed. "What is the sun, but essence of fire? And its generative heat is necessary to the growth of plants; thus you may see, Eleanor, that the chain is perfect indeed. Fire, earth, water, air, all do go to nourish the plants."

He counted off the list of elements on her fingers. Eleanor was not inclined to argue with his reasoning, or even to speak at all, for fear he might recollect he was speaking to a woman—worse, a green girl with little learning, who could hardly be expected to delight in such discourse. She drank in the words like water she had always thirsted for, rejoicing in the quick leaps of his mind and seeing whole worlds within worlds illumined by his thought. If only she could read Latin, she might have learned as much for herself—but Edward would not have maids schooled beyond their destinies, and she had no lantern of learning to light her way out of ignorance. An opportunity like this was not to be squandered.

Fortunately speech did not seem to be a quality Arundel often required in his interlocutors. He went on with undiminished enthusiasm, explaining how every class in the chain of creation excelled in some quality: plants in assimilating food, beasts in physical energy and desires, man in the power of learning. "The angels who are above us, through their gift of

adoration, have already all knowledge in their grasp.
Only we poor men, being imperfect, must needs
always strive towards that state of perfect knowledge,
and so must perpetually increase our powers of learning
and memory. Only consider the great systems of
memory which Messer Giordano Bruno created in
his time: the ranks of seals and images, the great
theatre of the world in which a man's mind might
hold in its proper place all knowledge of the created
world, and so doing, might encompass the uncreated
world of God and his angels. For if the world be
held in the mind of God, and a man could learn
the secret to hold it in his mind, he might be—"

"God?" Eleanor caught her breath. "You blaspheme!"
And in the next breath she regretted her interruption.
It was such *interesting* blasphemy.

"Not God, nor yet His angels," said Arundel slowly,
"but—something more than man, perhaps. But Messer
Bruno was wrong."

Eleanor felt, for the first time, great relief at hearing
that a philosopher's theories were incorrect. While
Arundel spoke with such passion, the little garden
where they sat had seemed to grow and shine with
an unearthly light; as her hand trembled in his grasp,
so the tree and the flowering herbs at her feet trembled
in the light of such perfect knowledge as was not
meant for man in this life.

"Such mechanical piling up of system upon system,
seal upon seal, can never by itself achieve the desired
end. Messer Bruno relied entirely upon man's faculty
of learning. The systems of memory he designed
may do very well as a starting point, to which end
have I desired Giles Cavendish to teach me what
he can remember of Bruno's philosophy. But some

higher power must be called upon to bring us to a higher state."

"Prayer, and God's grace," hazarded Eleanor with a curious sense of safety and disappointment mingled.

He grinned at her; the conspiratorial smile of a schoolboy to his comrade. "No, God is too far above us; think on the quires of angels and cherubim between us, not to mention the blessed saints!"

"Papistry?"

Arundel spread his hands. "Very well. I grant you the saints; I do not believe in them either, but I was brought up in the old religion, and it is hard to forget childhood devotions. But the best Protestant living would not argue with me that God has not His orders of angels, one superior to the other as on earth one order of being is placed above the next. No, I would but reach one link above me in the chain."

"How?"

"Music," Arundel said. "That is what Messer Bruno forgot, for all his wisdom. He should have listened, when he was in England, to our own scholars. Philip Sidney would have told him that music is what brings man closer to the divine; that music is the natural companion and aid of the art of memory, bringing the soul to the aid of reason. As Actaeon was torn to pieces by his own hounds at Diana's command, so will the questing soul that relies on reason alone be lost by reason of those same reasons. And that, you see, is the theme of my masque: Actaeon as the soul of man, searching for that higher understanding which is the light of mortal learning; Diana, the queen of air, the lady of the moon, shedding that light upon him."

"A sad prize that Actaeon did win," Eleanor observed. She knew the story well enough; Edward had told her the classical myths, though he would not teach her enough Latin to read them for herself. For daring to glimpse Diana bathing, Actaeon had been turned into a stag and hunted to death by his own hounds.

"The tale of the ancients did end ill," Arundel admitted. "I mean to change the tale. In the version which your brother shall write for me, Diana pardons Actaeon and consents to share the heavenly light of understanding with him. And as it is writ, so may it be—by the power of music. Do you know Ficino's theory of how music may be used to set knowledge in the memory and to invoke daemons?"

Eleanor shook her head slightly. She was disturbed by a word which sounded so close to "demons," but she had no inclination to halt the eager flood of Arundel's discourse.

"Well, then." He sounded relieved to have discovered something she did not already know about. "I'll not bore you with the details. It suffices to say that by the union of poetry with music rightly composed, man can reach above his rational self and call down the aid of celestial beings. Think how your very soul may be transported by great music, Eleanor, and then tell me you do not believe this possible! I have studied Ficino's laws of music, and the writings of that Egyptian sage Hermes Trismegistus who wrote of wisdom that was ancient before Moses that wise man, and I do tell you that by our work in this masque, by uniting poetry to myth and both to music, we must surely call the spirits to our aid. And now that I have you to help me, a woman's voice to join with mine, and a woman who can understand the patterns and order in all things on which the music is based, how can I fail?"

Somehow he had taken both her hands in his by now; and Eleanor could not conceive that he would fail of anything on which he had set his heart.

"Will you venture with us, Eleanor?"

"I have no learning," she said slowly and stiffly. "How can I help you?"

"I will teach you."

"Nay, but—" *You ask too much, Eleanor*, her brother's remembered voice chid her. Still she could not forbear to say it. "I would read these philosophers for myself, that I might truly understand their words."

"And so you shall."

"I have no Latin."

"I'll teach you."

"You would do that?" How had she thought this day cloudy? It glowed with light; the grass and small flowers were blazing jewels, the high hedges danced with joy.

"After the masque," Arundel said, and then, as the joy dimmed, "Nay, nay, 'tis no manner of price! Sing or not as you will; I'd not deny learning to one so hungry for it."

"After the masque," Eleanor said, "Edward may wish to return to the city."

"Why, then," said Arundel, "we shall contrive some means to keep you behind. Shalt study with Cavendish and myself, and we three shall discover the secrets of the stars."

"I should love that above all things," said Eleanor, "and I shall be honored to sing in this masque."

At her agreement, his dark narrow face leapt with light—no, it was only the sinking sun, sending its rays to dance among the trailing willow leaves. Still she had the sense of having participated in some ceremony more binding than betrothal, more magical than marriage.

"Then let us make music together after the evening meal," he suggested. His hand strayed to caress the lute still caught in her skirts; he lifted the instrument and ran his fingers across the strings as a man touches his beloved mistress.

The dining parlor was brilliant with candles for the evening meal—and wax ones, too, scented with the essence of roses and violets, instead of the sputtering, stinking tallow candles that most people used for economy. With all the tallow that must come from the sheep on Arundel's lands, it was sheer waste to expend good wax so generously. Edward used the example of the wax to point out Arundel's wealth to his womenfolk; Eleanor thought that his steward was probably selling the tallow, and that if she were mistress of Greenholt she'd order matters with somewhat more sense and economy.

It was something to think about until Arundel appeared; moving out of the shadows as usual, dark brows and ready smile and white ruff all exaggerated in the candlelight. He did something with his hands to a silver tankard in the shape of a galleon in full sail, down at the far end of the table where few candles lit his work. A moment later the galleon made a whirring noise and crept down the length of the table, somewhat drunkenly and crab-wise, to offer its burden of Rhenish wine to Edward.

"Magic!" he cried, stepping back. Eleanor caught the galley at the edge of the table. Small metallic parts chittered and moved in her palm when she scooped the thing up; it was like holding a great insect of some unknown kind.

"One of Dr. Dee's contrivances from abroad?" she inquired of Arundel with a raised eyebrow.

"One of mine own, an it please you," he said with an injured look. "A small device, made more impressive by the shadows. But this dim light, though it aids these petty tricks, is all too poor for us to read music."

"Music?" Edward repeated with a suspicious glance.

Eleanor made a small reverence to her brother, a mere bend of the knee compared with the stately courtesy she had shown to Arundel earlier. "I have thought me of your wise counsel, brother dear, and I do most heartily apologize if I have given offense," she said, meek as could be, with her head bowed. "I shall be delighted to lend my poor talents, such as they be, to whatever music shall please our host."

She raised her head and met, not Edward's eyes, but Arundel's, glimmering with a dark amusement that made her humble words to Edward no humiliation; only part of a glorious joke which they two shared.

"Lights for the music!" Arundel cried now, and a serving man appeared with a taper which he seemed to wave before him in midair. A circle of flames sprang up in the very air, surrounding the virginals where the music Arundel had prepared lay writ out in a fine Italian hand.

"Wires?" Eleanor inquired.

Arundel laughed. "Y' have no sense of mystery. Yes, wires in the candle wicks make my lights to dance upon the air. But is't not a pretty show?"

As she came forward to read the words to the

song, he moved to stand beside her, and murmured, "And when we have done our work, then shall I stand in such light as needs no wires nor wicks nor dripping wax."

"Is *this* part of the work?" Eleanor could read the words clearly enough now. "I never heard that Circe the enchantress made part of the tale of Diana and Actaeon."

"All tales are but part of the One great story." Arundel dismissed her objections with an airy wave of his hand that put the floating candles at some risk. "As you say, Circe was an enchantress, with the power to turn men into beasts, and to raise those beasts again to men. It seemed as well to call on her power. 'Tis a song for two voices," he went on, "or rather, for a soprano and chorus. If Jane will be good enough to play the virginals and sing for the chorus, we may have some idea of how it will sound in the masque."

Jane always did what was asked of her. She took her seat; Eleanor stood on one side of her to read the words, and Arundel stood beside her, not quite touching, as if ready to mark time or correct a mistake. His presence steadied her; she felt as if the Rhenish wine sent to Edward were flowing through her veins, as if she could float like the candles suspended in midair by invisible wires. And the music was deceptively simple: clear and pure, no embellishments to distract her, nothing but the perfect notes to match the words and meaning of the song.

Circe bids you come away, she sang, and Jane echoed after her: *Come away, come away*. The candles faded to glowing stars in the darkness and the sky was all about her, and then only night and Chaos absolute.

Sunday, May 15, 1994

The morning after the party Ellen awoke with a headache and a sense that something had gone disastrously wrong. The garden of her dreams was as real to her as the asphalt parking lot outdoors; she could not separate the dream and the reality, the English mists from the Texas sun.

"I was wrong to ask you to sing," Bethany said when she found Ellen moodily swirling black coffee into a whirlpool in a cup, staring into the glossy depths as if a little more attention would show her the story that had been broken off when she woke up. "I can't think what came over me."

"Can't you?" *I can take away your fear*, Payne had said, and he'd kept his promise. Ellen felt perfectly calm, and at the same time she knew that somewhere deep inside her the fear was waiting to be released. She dreamed still; Bethany had awakened. Ellen looked from her deep stillness at Bethany's agitated face and chose not to awaken. As long as she could stay within this cool misty place, where Ellen's memories and Eleanor's mingled like shreds of dreams, she need not feel whatever it was that plagued Bethany.

Only, she remembered green lanes, and weeping that came from the heart, and something lost that could never be found again. . . . Ellen frowned, trying to capture the fleeting images, but they danced and disappeared like light reflected from shaken water. "It was good to sing," she reassured Bethany. "I want to sing again. When did you say this contest was?" Perhaps in music she could remember it all.

"Next weekend. At the Renaissance Faire."

"Oh! That soon?" Ellen wandered to the window and stood absently twisting the lace curtain between her fingers. The brilliant, merciless spring sunlight illuminated every detail of the outside world, from the tangle of vines growing up along the window to the cracks and subtle lines and shadows of the unevenly paved parking lot next door. In that sun there could be no creeping shadows, no menace unseen and unheard. But the longer Ellen stared into the day, the more the heat and light themselves troubled her vision. The parking lot absorbed sunlight and sent back quivering waves of heat that acted like pools or mirrors, trapping the shimmering ghosts of images. When she turned back to the shadowed room, the sun's glare left afterimages on her vision; Bethany was a shadow amid green brightness, the soft furnishings of the room were as formless and unanchored as clouds across the sun. She found it hard to concentrate on what Bethany was saying. Her words seemed immaterial compared with what Ellen could almost see in the green lines and dazzle of the sun's afterimage.

"Ellen, I don't think this music is what you're meant to be doing now. If it were the right time for you to face this, it wouldn't be hurting you so much."

"Who told you that the right thing never hurts?" Ellen smiled. She felt hundreds of years older than Bethany. "And anyway, I'm perfectly all right."

Bethany snorted. "Call this *all right*? Fainting at Melville's, sleeping fourteen hours, and now you're acting as if you can barely see anything around you."

"You did warn me about the punch," Ellen said. "What was it spiked with, anyway?"

Bethany shrugged. "I didn't taste it; you know I don't drink alcohol. But I could smell the gin. There were a couple of empty vodka bottles around. And I wouldn't put it past Melville to have added a few recreational pharmaceuticals; he'd think it funny to get his wife's lawyer friends stoned out of their minds."

"Good God," said Ellen, "how dare you accuse me of anything worse than bad judgement? After four cups of that punch, it's a tribute to clean living and a healthy body that I can even walk and talk the next day. You mustn't expect me to make sense for a couple of days."

"*Four* cups?"

"At least," Ellen said without blushing. She couldn't remember having had more than one, but that wasn't important. If she had drunk three more cups of that lethal mixture, she probably wouldn't remember it. And the important thing right now was to reassure Bethany so that she wouldn't give up on the contest.

"Well . . ." Bethany said grudgingly. "If you're sure that's all it was . . ."

"You don't think I'd make up something so embarrassing as that!" Ellen protested. "Swilling down four cups of the poison punch and passing out in public?" Not unless the truth were something even more embarrassing, like having visions so real that you were desperate to find out what came next.

She'd had a brief taste of that six years past, and it had terrified her into silence and retreat. But that had been different; less than this, and more frightening, the constant wavering of images between one world and another, until she could not any longer be sure

what was real and what was not, until mute immobility
had been her only refuge.

This was different. She'd seen and heard more;
it was like reading the first chapter of a story so
compelling she knew she must read the rest, even
though she knew it must end badly.

Ellen felt cold. This argument with Bethany was
waking her out of her pleasant dreamy state; she
wished Bethany would be quiet. *How* did she know
it would end ill? Because of the old dream? The
dark man—Kit—vanishing in a dark flame, while
Eleanor stood mute and unable to move. The mists
through which she ran, seeking what was lost and
could not be found.

If only she could know the rest of the story, what
lay between that meeting in the maze-garden and
the tragic end, perhaps she would be free of the
dream and the questioning and the longing that had
tormented her all the days of the last six years.

She felt an absolute, irrational conviction that
what she had seen, the dream that felt so much
like a memory, was—had been—real; like looking
through a window in time, living somebody else's
life of four hundred years ago.

Not somebody else's. Ours.

The correction was in her own head, but not in
her own voice; it was the voice and accent of the
headstrong Eleanor Guilford. Ellen grasped a chair
for support. The room whirled round her for a moment.
Had she gone as white as she felt? It didn't matter;
Bethany wasn't watching. She was fiddling with some
papers. Music. Sheet music.

"Give me those." Ellen was surprised at the
steadiness in her voice, in her outstretched hand.

"I'm still not sure this is a good idea," Bethany muttered.

"What would it take to make you sure?" Ellen meant to have that music, one way or another. If Bethany wouldn't give her these transcriptions, she'd find Payne and—

She frowned. Exactly how *would* she find Payne?

"Tell you what," Bethany said. "Let me hear you sing one song from Arundel's Ayres, all the way through, without passing out or turning into a stranger or throwing up, and we'll go on with the contest."

"You're on," Ellen said promptly, and then, as soon as she had her hands on the music, "but not right now."

"Why not?"

What excuse had she been using a moment ago for all her strange behavior? Oh, yes. Melville and the Mystery Punch. "Because," said Ellen, making for the front door, "I've got the kind of hangover you'd expect after last night. I'll just take my copies of the music in to the office and look them over in my copious spare time, and then we can run through the songs later this week—when I'm feeling more myself." Whoever that might prove to be.

Ellen felt a twinge of guilt at her evasions, but it did just occur to her that it might be wiser to put off rehearsing until they were actually at the Renaissance Faire, preparing for the contest. It would be too late for Bethany to back out then; and Payne would surely be there, to calm her fears and Bethany's alike with his subtle magic.

Magic? she questioned herself.

Magic and raising of demons, said a younger and

surer voice within her. *I knew it would come to this in the end.*

On Saturday they drove east through a cooling rain to Magnolia, Texas and the spring Renaissance Faire. The plan was to rehearse in costume just once, that night, before their scheduled time in the contest the next day; an insane way to go after a prize worth hundreds of dollars, but the only one open to them in the time. Ellen had flatly refused to take time off during that last stressful week for rehearsals. A plane ticket to England and two weeks' lodging in Dorset were all very well, but hardly replaced the job she'd lose if she disappeared without notice during the last desperate days before a new software release.

"You *will* take a vacation in June if we win?" Bethany demanded.

"If we win . . . and if I can get away." The new release was probably buggy, they never got everything worked out ahead of time. Customers would be calling, there'd be emergency meetings to patch the problems . . . The thought made Ellen feel secure, not hassled. This was her world, the cool reasonable world that she could handle, where things worked in predictable ways and if they didn't, there was always a reason for it. "I might not be able to get the time off."

"You will," said Payne. "And we shall bear away the prize tomorrow."

Ellen wished she could share his confidence. This night's rehearsal would be the first time since Melville's party that she had dared to sing that strange, disturbing music, though she had read the songs over daily.

"I hope I don't let you down," she said while she and Bethany were dressing.

"You won't," Bethany assured her. "You couldn't." They had driven all that way with Payne humming to himself in the back of the car; Bethany was moving slowly as a dreamer now, wrapped in the spell of the music. "Raise your arms, this dress has to go on over your head."

Ellen raised her bare arms to the attic roof and stood passive while the folds of dark green velvet sank about her, soft as wood moss, heavy as sleep. A satin bodice, boned and wired, clasped her upper body and held her straight within the flow of velvet. Bethany straightened the gown, tugged one long sleeve down, and stepped back to admire her work. "I knew this one would be right for you."

"It's beautiful," Ellen said truthfully. The stained, bubbled mirror on the back of the door reflected her as though from under water, or from a great distance: pale face, pale hair, white skin all framed by the soft green of the gown. "You should be wearing it, though. It's the richest costume you have."

"Yes, but it was always tight on me," Bethany said cheerfully. "I was in my super-authentic phase when I made that outfit. I kind of, you know, spill over the top of the bodice."

"Well, that's authentic enough," Ellen said absently, "if you desire to look like a court trollop."

Bethany opened her mouth, looked as if she were about to ask something, then visibly changed her mind. "Besides," she went on, "the sleeves get in the way when I'm playing. You should keep it. You could wear it to the Faire every year." She shook her head, smiling slightly. "Just listen to me. Five years I've been trying to talk you into coming and enjoying yourself with me, and the first time you give in a little I start acting as though it's all settled. Why don't you ever tell me to back off?"

"I did at first, didn't I?" Hard to remember now, the panic when Bethany and Payne first closed in on her with their demands and their music. But then, why remember such disturbing things? She was happy now, and perfectly calm. She was glad to be here. The green dress was far too hot for a Central Texas spring evening, but it felt right. So did the memory of music in her head, and the images of the green wood and the valley and the manor of golden stone. "Let's rehearse, shall we?"

It was too hot to rehearse in the farmhouse attic they'd rented, a few miles from the Faire site. The downstairs rooms would have been better, but they were already taken by three other groups of musicians. Ellen lifted the skirt of her gown in two fingers and went down the narrow, sloping stairs. Some of their fellow tenants were ensconced on the shady side of the porch, looking over pale green sheets of music just like those Payne had brought to Bethany. The two women whispered and giggled as Ellen passed in her trailing skirts, and the man scowled under heavy dark brows. Ellen felt a prickling discomfort that had nothing to do with the weight of her gown. Why had she thought it was only a matter of appearing and singing their piece? A prize like a trip to England would bring every early music group in the state to compete this weekend.

"What's wrong?" asked Bethany.

"I like it not," Ellen said, "to see these ill looks

from other singers. What shall our music be, without harmony in all things?"

Bethany could not answer that; they went across the yard to find Payne in the warm, dark evening under the trees.

"How do you like Ellen in costume?" Bethany demanded. "That dress could have been made for her."

"She looks well enough," Payne said.

Back straight, Ellen bent her knee and head in a formal curtsey that left her soft velvet skirts swirling about her on the grass. "Y'are too kind."

"And so do you," Payne told Bethany before she could demand a comment. "That dark red is like the petals of a rose about your face, which is itself fairer than any flower. I shall be proud to escort two such beautiful ladies tomorrow."

"We shall be outshone by our tenor," Ellen said with a smile, looking Payne up and down. In the soft sunset glow he seemed to capture all the light and take it to himself. Pearls looped over his black doublet in fantastical flourishes, returning the sunset rays with their own soft white luminescence; a single large pearl in his ear caught and echoed that moonlight shimmer. His cape of sooty black velvet was sewn with little jewels that winked and glittered in patterns that were old when time was new: the Plough, Andromeda, the Cross. When he moved, the stars on his cape seemed to dance in dizzying swirls, until Ellen had to look up at the bright unchanging stars overhead to steady herself.

"You find the night sky more to your taste than *me*?" Payne demanded in injured tones.

Ellen laughed and pointed up at the pattern of

branches and leaves above them, and the stars so far overhead. "Isn't it beautiful?"

"I find it . . . rather dull," said Payne.

Ellen blinked. "Dull?"

"Monotonous," he amended. "These stars never change, never move."

"They are moving," Ellen said. "There, that's Venus; she moves around the sun as we do, and so do all the other planets. And beyond that, the whole universe is expanding; those stars are rushing away from us. . . ." She felt queasy for a moment, sharply aware of the turning ball beneath her feet, the cold emptiness of space, and the distances between those little lights in the sky.

Payne stared upwards. "The dance of your sphere," he murmured, "law upon law, all governed, ordained, and unalterable . . . and yet . . . there is beauty in it." He sounded surprised by the discovery.

"Remind me to take you through the Houston freeways at night some time," Ellen said absently, "you'd get enough of lights rushing about and moving by no law save their own whim."

Payne moved abruptly; the glittering star jewels on his cape came together like sparks running into fire, and then spiraled free again. Ellen looked at his profile, white in the moonlight. "You are angry."

"I am . . . confused. But I must complete that which I came to do." His voice sounded strained.

"What's the matter?"

Payne gestured abruptly, and the patterns of twinkling stones dissolved into fountains of light swirling around his cape. "Nothing. Everything. I don't *know*."

"My goodness," Ellen said, "you sound almost like a human being."

"That," said Payne, "is half the trouble. I have been here too long."

"We just got here," Bethany said, "and it wouldn't seem half so long if you two would stop talking philosophy."

Ellen laughed. "You have a point there. I'm sorry if I offended you. Indeed you are a pretty gentleman tonight, Payne, dressed as finely as even Sir Walter might envy."

"Who?" Bethany demanded.

The image that flashed across Ellen's mind was of a tall, pale gentleman with glittering eyes and curling black beard, dressed in a satin doublet and a cape that dripped with seed-pearls like the dew on the morning grass. "Raleigh," she said slowly.

Payne handed Bethany a lute. "Start tuning."

Ellen sat down against a tree and watched the stars. She felt peaceful, wrapped in night and velvet and the tentative notes from the two lutes; but within that peace her mind was skittering nervously from one bright impenetrable idea to another. The music. Sir Walter Raleigh; what had made her think of him just now? The stars. *The stars be hid that brought me to this pain.* That was Wyatt, though, a poet of an earlier reign; nothing from the songs they were to sing tomorrow. Pain? Payne? Suddenly she knew that wasn't right; she and Bethany had missed something.

"Payne," she said without thinking. "How do you spell your name?"

"P-a-i-e-n," he spelled out the letters for her. "Paien," and this time she could hear the faint hint of two syllables, the little break between the vowels.

"Pagan," Ellen said.

"Well, yes." He sounded amused, as though she

had guessed the answer to a question long since settled.

"That doesn't sound very nice," Bethany said.

"It is no insult." The lazy amusement was still in Paien's voice. "Only a true description."

"Are we ready yet?" Ellen asked.

"Right, then," said Bethany, shifting into her role as stage manager. "Now, here's what I've planned . . ."

Ellen felt somewhat ashamed of herself as Bethany went through the instructions. While she'd been avoiding rehearsals, Bethany must have been working hard to learn the lute music and think up the stage arrangements. She'd reordered the songs from the masque so that they began with the pieces for three voices, then moved to the duets between Ellen and Paien, and finished with Ellen's solos. They would begin all standing together on the ground before the stage; for the duets, Ellen and Paien would move up to the first step; for her solos, Ellen would move up to the stage itself, poised above Paien and Bethany while they accompanied her with both lutes. It was all very formal, and would probably be very impressive, and Ellen felt fiercely uncomfortable with it. And she couldn't possibly say so after Bethany had worked so hard on the arrangements and lent her a costume and done everything else to make their contest entry a success. She would just have to survive being the center of attention for a few minutes.

But that wasn't what was bothering her.

Something about all this formal staging felt all wrong. Ellen shook her head. The lute music was humming in her ears; she couldn't think. Besides, it was time to sing.

Come away, away, away,
See the dawning of the day,
Risen from the murmuring streams . . .

Ellen sang with Bethany and Paien, almost automatically. For a moment the sky and the earth were bright about her; their music seemed to call forth another dawn, the grey soft light of morning in a rainy country. Then the notes died away and she shook her head and the velvety blackness of a Texas night surrounded her again, soft warm air scented by the waxy white flowers that bloomed around the farmhouse.

Something felt very wrong. They were starting at the end of the masque; this should have been the closing song. But what did it matter? The folk who heard them would have no sense of the original. *What did it matter?* At least she'd made it through that song without confusion. Ellen raked fingers through her hair and wondered how these authentically heavy Elizabethan costumes would feel in tomorrow's sunlight. Oh, well, it could be worse; at least Bethany hadn't felt authentic enough to recreate the layers of padded petticoats and the heavy bum-roll that she remembered.

Had read about.

Remembered, insisted her nervous skittering mind, and she was into a duet with Paien:

A day, a night, an hour of sweet content
Is worth a world consum'd in fretful care.

At the end of the duet Paien stood and offered Ellen his hand to help her mount onto the fruit crate he'd been sitting on. His fingers were cool and dry under hers, and so steady that she might have been holding

the branch of a tree for balance; she had no sense
of the quick pulsing of life beneath the skin.

It was quite dark. She was imagining things. And
it was time for her first solo; time to show Bethany
that she could do this without fainting or going mad
or having strange visions.

Shake off your heavy trance,
And leap into a dance
Such as no mortals use to tread,

sang Ellen. She was Diana, Astraea, the crescent
moon, and the grass and the trees and the old battered
farmhouse drew on her light and gave it back, all
brilliant and edged with silver and quivering with
life. The stars on Paien's cloak merged with the
constellations in the midnight sky; they wheeled
around her, formed and reformed in the stately dance
as if keeping time to Kit's music. She was here and
in another time and in all times at once; she was no
more Ellen, nor Eleanor, but only music calling the
stars to earth, bidding the spheres join again that
had been apart too long.

5

DIARY OF JANE GUILFORD
(B.M. MS LEICESTER 2517)
May 1594, 18 Saterday
After private prayer in the morning I walked in the
knot-garden with Mr. Guilford. He was still much
wroth with Eleanor for good cause of her undutiful
ansers, even though she did submit to his desires
and sing in the evening. I did attempt to turn aside
his anger by shewing him how in this matter Eleanor's
will may work well to the desired end. If shee did
turn a smyling face to Mr. Arundel and endeavour
to engage his fancy by divers arts, how would shee
seeme different from anie young ladie about the
Court? But if shee remaine resolute agaynst him,
may he not be Curious to discover, why his winning
face and ayres win her not over as he have won so
manie fayre ladies?

Mr. Guilford shewed littel fayth in my Reasoning,
but did say with lowring face that he hoped indeed
the affayr might turn out so well as that. Soone after
we went to dinner, where the talk was al of this

Masque that Mr. Arundel will make, though what can be the reason of going to such Expence for costumes and scenes, for a meer Country Entertainment, I cannot for my lyfe understand. Mr. Guilford did annoy Mr. Arundel heartily with his suggestions that wee shou'd make up a party to Ride Abroad, or to visit Sherborne Castle, or some such nonsense, for it was cleer all his thought was to bring Mr. Arundel into more closer company with our Eleanor. Mr. Arundel desir'd him to remember the great aim of the masque, and that the signs of the stars did shew the great tyme of the joyning of the spheres to approach soon, beeing now littel more than a month away. Of this the Astrologer, one Mr. Giles Cavendish, did say but littel, as is his wont, but to agree with Mr. Arundel.

Mr. Cavendish is not an ill-favored man, though something older than Mr. Arundel, and cou'd I but discover something of his Family and Condition, who knows but he too might be a suitable match for our Eleanor? But he seemes to have no Interest in the company of Ladies; he spends his evenings shut up in his chamber, wryting by candle-light, or else occupying the other gentlemen in straunge Philosophical speculashuns of which I understand not a word.

Teusday 21 May

The gentlemen beeing all absorbed with talk of this Masque, and Eleanor describing to me her part in it as they have planned, I saw that as devysed the Masque would afford littel opportunity for bringing of our young people together. Wherefore I did desire Mr. Guilford to consider if *Diana* ought not to have as much to say or sing as *Actaeon*.

"What has that to do with you, woman?" he demanded. "Do you think it is but a shew for idle ladies that we make here? Woman, you know not what Powrs we draw down from the Heavens with this great worke."

"I know naught of Powrs beyond those of Our Maker, nor do wish to," I ansered him, "but this I do know: that a Masque is always an excuse for hiding and flirting in corners, and prinking in Costumes that shew a young ladie's limbs, and singing of love-songs that turn young people's flighty harts to that they sing of. And if you wou'd make the Match wee spake of, yow shou'd see to it that our Eleanor has much business and some Songes with Mr. Arundel in the course of this Masque. At present *Diana* hath but one Songe at the beginning of the Shew, and one at the End, and how will Mr. Arundel fall in love with her if they have naught to do one with the other during this Masque which doth take up all his attention?"

So Mr. Guilford hath promised me faithfully to look out what songs the *Ancients* sung in *Diana's* prayse, as well as to mak or borrow such poems as fit well with the temper of the masque; and this, if it serve not the end of bringing the young people together, will at least keep him well busy in the library, and I think I may trust young Mr. Arundel to find his own means of coorting our Eleanor if Mr. Guilford will but leeve them to them Selves.

Tuesday 4 June 1594

Plans for the Masque are well afoot now. Mr. Arundel having desyred me to see to the Costumes as should be fitting, and to spare no expence, I have sent to London for some Greene Taffety at four nobles a yard, for *Diana*, and Scarlett at the same pryce for *Actaeon*. This evening after supper did Mr. Arundell and Eleanor take themselves to the great hall to practise theyr songs which they doo sing together, or so they sayde. But I did just peepe into the hall on my way to the buttery, and there sat our Eleanor all in the shadowes, leaning a littel way apart from Mr. Arundel, while he with Lute in hand did sing a Poem of his own composing, which hath no part in the Masque:

> When love on time and measure makes
>   his ground,
> Time that must end though love can never
>   die,
> 'Tis love betwixt a shadow and a sound,
> A love not in the heart but in the eye.
> A love that ebbs and flows, now up, now
>   down,
> A mornings favor and an evenings frown.

Al this *philosophy* in *Poetrie* seemeth to mee a verie straunge manner of Wooing, but it did appear that Eleanor lyked it passing well; and so I went to praier, and now to bed, and verie well satisfy'd with the progress of this private *Play* within the play.

Saterday 8 June

All the household in an uproar today over the arrival of Sir W. Ralegh with his younge wyfe *Bess*, and theyre friends from Sherborne to the number of six or eight in all, beeing more gentry than this littel country place hath seen this twelvemonth. Mr. Arundel did seeme as surprised as anie at this incursion, and his chamberlain did praie mee that I would advise him how to supply the table, there beeing not wine to serve so manie guests a fortnight, nor above six quarntern of malt in the bailiff's hands. I fayned weariness and the head-ach and did advise him to consult *Eleanor*, then did call her to me privily and warn her how to order all things as they ought to be, and not to miss this opportunity of showing Mr. Arundel how well she hath been taught to keep household. For indeed Greenholt needeth a *Lady* to see to such things, and the sad lack apparent in the household can not but be seen when so many noble guests descend upon us. Was ever turne so luckie! I must give thanks in my praiers for the plague at Sherborne which inspyred this visit of Sir W. Ralegh's.

Sunday, May 23, 1994

Some time between night and morning Ellen lost the clear knowledge of the spheres that music had joined. She sank back into the restless body that lay with open eyes, watching the invisible dance of shadows against the night. Here she knew nothing clearly, not even who she was; Ellen and Eleanor mingled rags and snippets of memory into a crazy-quilt of plain denim and rich gold brocade and star-sprinkled black satin.

"Are you sick?" Bethany fussed over Ellen in the morning. "I had a hell of a time waking you up. You're pale. How do you feel?" While she talked, her deft fingers plaited her hair and piled it in a high mass of tumbling dark braids.

"Well enough to sing. Y'are too apprehensive, love." Ellen smiled into the mirror at Bethany's worried eyes. She had not slept until nearly dawn, and then only to fall into a confused dream of lost loves and sudden executions and long corridors where treasons might be whispered behind the tapestry. Now she felt the tranquility of extreme fatigue; floating in the hazy state brought on by sleep deprivation and the shadows of nightmares, she could not feel that anything in the world was quite real or quite imaginary. Ellen Ainsley, onetime singer, now a computer programmer, was neither more nor less real than Eleanor Guilford; no more rode on her performance today than had ridden on the midsummer's eve singing of the original masque. "'Tis a small matter to sing an hour for strangers, Bethany," she said now, standing and shaking out the folds of her green velvet gown. "Surely y'are not affrighted at the prospect?"

"I'm afraid for *you*," Bethany said sharply. "You've been acting strange, Ellen."

"These are passing strange times we have been born in," Ellen said. "Now I tell you plainly that I am resolved to sing the masque this day. Will you venture with me or no?" She turned on the last word and swept down the stairs without giving Bethany a chance to refuse.

Behind her she heard a disgruntled, disjointed mutter. "*Ayres*, not a masque. And I'd feel easier about it if you'd talk like yourself."

Ellen shook her head. What was the matter with Bethany? Kit had written a masque and desired her to sing in it. And she had never felt more like herself than at this very moment, slender and upright in the tight enclosing bodice, trailing full skirts of green velvet, ready to sing for her heart's love.

The heat and sun outside made her head ring as if she were standing in the church belfry. All but mindless in the sun's glare, she followed her companion until they fell in with a throng of commoners who passed through doors in a great wooden wall, painted and bedizened to give the similitude of a castle—a strange conceit indeed, and of no utility at all that she could see, since the wall was slight and easily broken through.

On the other side of the "castle" was an open space shaded with great trees and set about with small cottages of fantastic style. They seemed to be tradesmen's stalls, but she saw nothing of any use to anybody displayed in the stalls they passed: there were ribbons and bright flimsy shirts and all manner of cheap gauds and trinkets, but no bolts of good woolen cloth, no spices, no needles. A strange fair, she thought, and the folk about them most outlandishly dressed. One passed by wearing only some strips of leather wound about his body; his companion sweltered in a black fuzzy cape made after the fashion of furs, but not like any animal's fur she had ever seen. "'A mercy, what is this place?" she demanded.

The dark girl who was not Jane Guilford looked long at her. "The Renaissance Faire, Ellen. You do remember? We're here to sing for the contest? Paien's bringing the lutes."

"Oh. Yes." Ellen blinked in the sunlight. How could she have forgotten so quickly? She had seen the Faire as something altogether foreign and outlandish. Could still see it that way, with a strange double vision. If she looked straight before her, she saw only a perfectly ordinary scattering of people in shorts and T-shirts, Renaissance costumes, and fantasy outfits. But in her peripheral vision she was seeing half-naked peasants, gentlefolk whose fine clothes had somehow been replaced by makeshift gauds, and— "Players," the part of her that saw only out of the corners of her eyes said. "Only players would make such a shew of themselves," and that, apparently, made the scene more or less acceptable.

Paien was waiting by a small round stage in the center of the grassy space, holding his lute and Bethany's. Ellen frowned, confused. How had he come there ahead of them? She would have noticed— But then, he hadn't slept in the farmhouse last night; Bethany might think he'd come in late and left early, but Ellen knew that while she tossed in her bed until dawn there'd been no light footsteps on the stairs.

She felt dizzy and confused, unable to hold on to any single thought long enough to follow it through the maze of her mind. Why should she care how or where Paien had spent the night? He was here now, and they would be singing soon; that was all that mattered. She fixed her mind and heart and soul upon the silver sound of the music remembered, and in the melody felt herself one again. It was not exactly that she stopped seeing the Renaissance Faire as something foreign and altogether strange; rather, she accepted that double vision as part of herself, and herself as only part of the music.

If they could have gone at once to sing, it would have been easy. But there were two other groups ahead of them. Bethany and Paien retreated to a bench out of earshot to tune their lutes yet again. Ellen leaned against a tree and tried not to wince as the Gentle Gypsy Gallants gave a folk-rock interpretation of Arundel's *Ayres for Lute and Voyce*.

Well, they'd be no competition for the prize. What with the tambourine and the cimbalom and the Gypsy shrieks and the rhythmic beat of a Hungarian dance tune, what they were playing didn't even rouse the painful echoes of memory within her heart; it was just barely recognizable as coming from the same original music. But she wondered how many times people could stand to hear various renditions of the same set of songs, no matter how creatively arranged; and whether the judges would be tired of listening before their turn came; and whether anyone would even notice their simple, unadorned music after the frills and flourishes added by more experienced performers. Oh, well, Bethany's artful staging should at least make their performance more interesting.

Ellen glanced around the green lawn where people strolled and ate and shopped and listened halfheartedly to the Gypsy band. Which of these onlookers were the contest judges? She amused herself for a few minutes by trying to pick them out. Surely not the red-faced man in a baseball cap, or the harassed young mother pulling a red wagon with two toddlers inside. She discounted several adolescent girls with wreaths of flowers confining their streaming hair, paused for a moment to watch a tall dark-haired woman in a tailored suit who didn't look as if she belonged at the Faire. She did look vaguely familiar; one of the music faculty, perhaps? But she wasn't taking notes or paying much attention to the group on the stage. . . . Finally Ellen decided that the contest judges must be comfortably seated in one of the booths that lined both sides of the open space. Unless—

"Paien." She put a hand on his arm as he came up to her, elegant and cool-looking in his bejeweled doublet and cape. "Is this the right date for the contest? I see no judges here." And now she thought of it, she wouldn't put it past Paien and Bethany to tell her the wrong date for the contest, just to get her down here a week early and make sure she didn't faint or lose herself during a trial run-through.

"It is the appointed day," Paien said with a faint smile. "And we will be heard. So much, at least, I dare warrant you." He looked towards the stage and gave a faint exclamation of annoyance. The Gypsies were leaving and another group was taking their place; a group composed, as theirs was, of a man and two women.

"Pigs," Bethany said in a passionate undertone as the new players arranged themselves on the stage in a vaguely familiar configuration. "Look, Paien! They're going to rip off our arrangement."

"How can you be sure yet?"

"Look at them! Exactly how we planned to open. And they're staying at the same house we were. Remember? They were on the steps listening last night. I saw that guy taking notes when we finished rehearsing."

Ellen could not remember anything at all about the end of the rehearsal.

"And now look at them," Bethany muttered as they launched into their opening song.

Come away, away, away,
See the dawning of the day . . .

It was the same one Bethany had picked to open with. Ellen leaned back against the tree and listened with growing disquiet as the singers moved through the exact sequence of songs Bethany had chosen, each time shifting position a little to make their soprano more prominent in the group. They were cool and quite professional, and their rendering of the songs was at least competent. As they sang, Ellen felt herself coming out of the haze of fatigue that had blurred everything around her. She felt strong and sure of herself. The stage was sharp and clear in the late spring sunlight; every detail before her, from the scalloped lace on the competing soprano's sleeves to the brown carpet of pine needles beneath her feet, stood out with its own shape and form and beauty. A bluejay's feather glowed blue against the brown pine needles; Ellen stooped automatically and picked it up. "Here, Paien," she said, "wear my favor." She placed the jay's feather in his cool palm.

Paien stared at the feather as though he'd never seen anything like it before. "What . . . is this?"

"A feather," Ellen said patiently. Sometimes talking to Paien made her feel like a kindergarten teacher. "A sign of good fortune. There's no color lovelier than the blue of a jay's wing, shading into black and white and grey."

Paien held the feather up to the light. "A pretty thing," he said, and then, dismissively, "but fleeting. 'Twill decay and perish with time."

Ellen laughed at him. She felt light and carefree, a bubble floating on the music that filled the air. "And last night you were complaining of the stars, that their dance was too grave and orderly. I suppose in your country the stars spin like whirling dervishes and feathers are made of stone."

A shadow passed over Paien's face; for a moment he seemed still and remote as the stone feather her words had conjured up, unutterably alien; the bluejay's feather lost its color and the world its sunlight.

Bethany broke the stillness between them, a silence that had grown teeth and claws. "How can you talk about *feathers* at a time like this?" she demanded.

Paien moved, and the spell was broken. Of course he was an alien, Ellen thought. All men were aliens— and they couldn't take being laughed at. It was nothing more than that. "Why, lady, what would you have me do?" Paien answered Bethany. "Shall we sit weeping, like Peter on his marble stone, because we are not the first to sing?"

"It's worse than that," Bethany insisted.

Ellen shook her head. She felt almost relieved that the competing singers had stolen Bethany's arrangements and staging; now they would be free to present the music as it wanted to be sung, in the proper sequence. She could feel the music fighting this arrangement, wanting to be sung as it was when first Kit Arundel pinned the living notes to dry paper. "Never fret," she assured them, "we shall do well enough."

"How?" Bethany almost wailed. "There's not time to work out a new staging and sequence—we'll look as if we were imitating them. And it's not *fair*," she added, close to tears, "you're so much better than their soprano."

Ellen grinned. "I must confess, I'd not have chosen to ornament the music with such airs and graces if my upper register were as uncertain as hers," she said. "But we'll not lose by the comparison, will we now? Look you, Bethany, since they've taken our staging, let us go on without any. Can you play the songs in a new sequence?"

"I can play any lute music in any sequence you suggest," Bethany snapped, "but I don't want us to look like a bunch of amateurs."

"Why, so we are," said Ellen, "and these songs were written by another amateur, a gentleman who'd have thought shame to be grouped with such poor creatures as these strolling players."

"How do you know that?"

Ellen blinked. How did she know it? "Class . . ." she said vaguely.

"Indeed." Bethany seemed to relax suddenly. "I didn't know you remembered anything from that Renaissance Vocals class. I guess you are getting better. But that doesn't solve the staging—"

And there was no time to argue; the competing soprano was ending Diana's song with a wealth of improbable flourishes on the word "sphere." Her strained voice seemed to hang in the air about them forever, drawing out the last "spheeeeeere," into an embellishment on the original melody that made words and music together all but meaningless.

"Now is it our sphere to play, and theirs to listen," said Ellen as the music died away. "Do you but take your measure from my words, love, and all shall yet be well."

"I don't know what you mean," complained Bethany as Ellen shuffled the pages of music and handed them back to her in a new order.

"I do," said Paien unexpectedly. He bowed to Ellen with a flourish of his star-sprinkled cape. The bluejay's feather was pinned to his cap by a gold brooch in the shape of an oak leaf.

Ellen set one foot on the step leading up to the stage and turned to take Bethany by the hand. She raised her voice so that the crowd could hear. "Sister, I am dull today. What say you, shall we sing and play a while for our own pleasure?"

"If it please you ladies," said Paien with another flourish, "I have here some excellent new airs for our entertainment, lately set down in writing by my good friend Kit Arundel."

Ellen smiled and inclined her head. Paien handed Bethany up the single stair as if he were helping a court lady into her chair, and she sat on the floor with her full bloodred skirts puddling about her knees. Paien took the step for his seat, and Ellen stood behind Bethany, leaning lightly against one of the posts that held the small peaked roof over the stage.

"Can you see the music from there?" Bethany whispered.

"These airs are indifferent familiar to me," Ellen replied in the same clear, carrying voice. "Do you play, sister, and I will undertake to follow wheresoe'er you may lead."

Paien glanced up with a wicked grin. "Could I but obtain the same pledge!" He pretended to languish at Ellen's feet.

"Go to, go to, y'are a careless knave," Ellen cried. There was a murmur of approbation from the passers-by; more and more of them had stopped to watch this little play before the music. This would be the time to start the singing, while their audience was caught up in the fantasy that they were watching three Elizabethan gentles playing and flirting for their own pleasure; the lazy, laughing

atmosphere that had surrounded the original songs.
How did she know that? No time to think or worry
now; the audience was impatient. Ellen took a
deep breath of air that seemed too cool and rose-
scented to belong to this hot place. Paien's fingers
picked out the melody of the first song in the
new sequence; Bethany followed him, and after
they had strummed through one repeat Ellen began
singing in such a low quiet voice that the growing
crowd hushed to hear her better.

> *Praised be Diana's fair and harmless light,*
> *Praised be the dews wherewith she moists*
> *the ground,*

she sang, and Bethany's and Paien's voices joined
under hers to drop down and down again on the
last word, painting "ground" in music.

The sound was true, but too thin, Ellen thought.
There should have been a full chorus of Nymphs,
and another of Hounds, instead of the three voices
here. Kit had put this poem into the masque to flatter
Raleigh, but he had written the music himself. . . .

Ellen's voice quavered in midnote; she recovered
herself and caught the next note true and pure.
Sing. The music is what matters. She was imagining
herself into the part she played. No. These were
true memories; but not her memories. They belonged
to that presence who looked through her eyes and
saw the Faire as a strange and alien place, the voice
that spoke with her throat and gave orders and
reordered a performance.

But while she sang, there was only one voice.
She would listen to these memories later. They had
a contest to win. And the next song was beginning.

Shake off your heavy trance,
and leap into a dance
such as no mortals use to tread;
Fit only for Apollo
to play to, for the moon to lead,
and all the stars to follow.

Now she could catch her breath and her wits while
Paien sang Actaeon's lament. His voice was too light
and high; Kit Arundel would have made better work
of his own song. Pain uncalled, unanticipated, stabbed
through Ellen's breast. What had become of Kit?

Dead four hundred years, her rational mind replied.
Have you forgotten what century we are in?

Not so, not so! cried the other voice within her.
Find him for me. . . .

Paien brought his song to an end.

Stars hold their fatal course, my joyes
    preventing:
the earth, the sea, the air, the fire, the
    heav'ns vow my tormenting.

There was a spattering of applause from the crowd.
A girl stepped up to the stage beside her. Jane? No,
someone else, someone Ellen should know: black
curls, very low-cut red bodice, a sense of concern.

"*Curtsey,*" the girl who was not Jane whispered
urgently. Bethany. The name came back from nowhere;
Ellen all but staggered with relief, and managed to
convert the stagger into a wobbly curtsey.

Bethany smiled and caught the wreath of flowers
someone threw from the fringes of the crowd, curtseyed
again, and reached up to place the circlet on Ellen's
head. "Are you all right?" she whispered under the
sound of applause. "You look . . . I don't know."

"I can sing." Her head was all full of music; her tongue tripped over the songs that clamored for a voice. *My dalie note shall be therefore, Heigh ho heigh ho I'll love no more . . . Long, long to sing by rote, fancying that that harmed me . . . but such a song, song never was, nor ne'er will be againe.*

Paien was already playing the introduction to something as familiar to Ellen as sleep, or breathing. She lifted up her voice and felt herself flying with it, free of time and space, heat of the sun and weight of earth.

A day, a night, an hour of sweet content
Is worth a world consumed in fretful
care.

"Sweet content." Paien's tenor was like a firm arm holding her up.

"Sweet content." Bethany came in, strong and sure on the contralto.

Together they sang, "Is worth a world consum'd in fretful care," and the world around them was consumed with the sun of noon. Heat quivered in the air and distorted shapes and faces; the trees around them seemed to move in stately measures to the music, and the listening crowd was still as any trees. Only on the farthest fringe of the crowd was there some disturbance.

Unequal Gods, in your Arbitrement
To sort us days whose sorrows endless
are!

Pushing through the crowd was a young man with a dark thin face as familiar to Ellen as her own. She had never seen him before in this life.

It was a face out of her dreams. He belonged in an Elizabethan maze-garden, not in the trampled fair grounds; he should have been lighting floating candles or sending a ship of silver down a long table.

He was shouting and thrusting people out of his way and his eyes were fixed on her every second, holding her pinned to the stage by the intensity of his look and his need.

Everything else was *real*; only that face out of dreams and visions, only the painful calling of her heart to him, held Ellen poised between the worlds. She went on singing, automatically, and with every note he came closer and his face was more vividly real and part of the hot bright world around them.

> *So bitter pain that none shall ever find,*
> *What plague is greater than the grief of*
> *mind,*

Ellen sang, with no idea how she had come almost to the end of the song.

"Grief of mind," Paien's tenor echoed, and beneath the light plucking of the strings Ellen could almost hear another voice taking up and repeating the words:

> *"What plague is greater than the grief of*
> *mind?"*

For the world to shift around him was nothing new; he had inhabited the landscape of dreams for longer than mortal mind could imagine. Or so it seemed. It might be that no time at all had passed beneath the sun; he could not know, for the count of days and years meant nothing here. Those who had taken him kept no measures of dance or time or roundelay, knew not the heat of the sun nor the

daily passage into darkness nor the everlasting night
at the end. No mortal mind could inhabit their world,
ever changing, ever constant, and still keep its knowledge
of mortal passing days, nor yet its sanity.

From madness he had passed by stages to raging
at his fate, to vain attempts at reaching the true
honest world he had lost, to dreams and imaginations
and a long withdrawal. Beyond the pale shadows
of the Faerie sphere, nations might rise and fall
again, the world might be torn with wars and the
seas run with blood; what was all that to him, or he
to the world? He had become a shade among shadows.

Visions of Eleanor called him from his sleep, pricked
him with mortal thorns of love and grief and longing.
He felt as though she were always there, at the periphery
of his vision, calling to him, offering him a path out
of the dreaming maze where he had lost himself.
But he would not be tricked into turning his head
for her. He had made sport enough for these cold
inhuman beings when he first entered their sphere
and found himself caught therein; he would not amuse
them now by following a shape of mist and glamorie,
an Eleanor-phantom that would dissolve before he
had caught her in his two arms and felt the sweet
living flesh of her.

Yet the songs he had made in the mortal world
teased at his mind, and there were times when he
could hear his own music calling him back, suffusing
him with the warmth and light and life he had lost
when he made his bargain in this sphere. "Those
are times when they play and sing your music in
their own sphere," Paien told him once. "The singing
binds you to that sphere. Do you not wish to return?"

"You know I do. I cannot find the path." When

he followed the ghostly whisper of music, it turned into running water and bird song, and the ways he walked became a twisting labyrinth where no two turns were ever the same. He wandered blind in mist then until the Lady took pity on him and led him back into the sphere of Faerie; sometimes it seemed to go on forever, that aimless wandering. "Damn you," he cursed, and Paien's laughter was a silver ringing about him.

"We cannot be damned who have no souls to save. You had a soul once, Christopher Arundel: will you find it again?"

"I would an if I could. And damn you anyway. I would you had a soul, that I might see it burn in fire eternal."

There had been no music for a very long time now; either the cold ones had given up tormenting him with it, or—if Paien had spoken truth—no one in the sphere of mortal men now played and remembered his songs.

Now it was back, and all around him, changed and stretched and embellished out of all recognition; the air was thick with voices and instruments jangling at distorted versions of his own songs. The very words of the masque came back to him and echoed from all sides: *Shake off your heavy trance*, strange voices commanded him, *and leap into a dance*. The words turned and changed and joined in new patterns, teasing him with the remnants of sense in a sphere where no sense was the same: *Circe bids you come away— fear not to follow— stars hold their fatal course— a day, a night, hour of sweet content . . .*

Eleanor's clear, pure voice was a shining thread through the maze. He was without will to resist it; he would not remember the times of his folly when the music had ceased and left him wandering in the wilderness. He followed the thread of light and it grew stronger and broader, a twisted rope, a space of true sunlight burning away the mist, until he felt green growing grass beneath his feet and bruised his forehead on a tree that stood still instead of writhing away in coils of mist when he drew near it.

"Hey, man, watch it there!"

A friendly hand steadied him. The true sun burned fierce and hot around him; his skin drank in the golden light. A trickle of dampness cooled his forehead. He put up a finger to touch the throbbing pain at the center of the dampness; it came away wet and red. He licked it without thinking and tasted the warm saltiness of his own blood.

"You all right?"

The words were drawled out until they were very nearly incomprehensible, but the young face looking into his was human and earnest; a boy with a straggle of silky beard, playing the gallant in a suit of brown velvet with curious gilt bands. Some foreigner, perchance. At the moment Kit neither knew nor cared what made the boy talk so strangely; he was full to brimming with sunlight, dizzy with the movement of the spinning earth.

"I've cut myself," he said. "I walked into the tree and cut my forehead!" And he laughed aloud, exulting in the solid reality of the moment.

The boy drew back a little; Kit sensed that he thought him mad. "Dunno," he murmured to the girl who had come up to lean on his arm. "Guy came out of nowhere, walked into the tree like he expected it to make way for him, started laughing like crazy."

And what would you think, young sir, if I told you where I really came from? Kit laughed again. In the pure joy of the moment he could not even take offense at the way the girl shrank from him and murmured something about people who couldn't hold their liquor. He was newborn, a child, an innocent, clean of sin and guilt. The girl must be a whore; no ladies except those of the Court painted their faces so gaudily, and she was too brown, and her dress too shoddy, for a fine lady. No matter. Whores might have their sport of him, and welcome; what did it matter to him who'd lost and gained a world?

"Fear not, sweeting," he said, pinching her chin, "Today's a blessed day if ever was one. I mean you no harm; here's a coin for Saint Christopher's day." He fumbled in his purse, tossed a gold angel sparkling through the air. She caught it one-handed, staring at him and not at the coin. "Or do I mean Saint Lazarus?" he mused. "No matter. Canst set me on the road to Greenholt?"

"Never heard of the place," shrilled the young bawd. She tugged at her gallant's arm. "Come on, Hank! Cain't you see he's drunk out of his mind? Cain't even talk right. Here, I don't want your toy money." She thrust the coin back at him and dragged the boy away.

Kit stood a moment staring after them, then relaxed and took a deep breath. The air was hot and still, smelling of sweet cakes and ale and roast meats. He exhaled slowly, shaking himself all over like a cat roused from sleep. It was real, then. *He* was real. Not one of his dreams had included such outlandish elements as a foreign whore who didn't take good coin. Nor had his dreams been so full of the busy details of the senses.

He seemed to have come into some fair or show of mountebanks; he stood under a spreading tree on a fair green lawn, and to either side were merchants' houses open for trade, and thronging the open space were peddlers and players in tawdry costumes and—He stopped for a moment, jaw agape like any country Jack, as a girl strolled by wearing nothing but an extremely inadequate pair of trunk-hosen without any stockings and a sort of abbreviated corset with all the boning removed. Kit felt his eyes running riot in his head at the sight of all that smooth golden flesh so opulently displayed. When the girl had passed, he swallowed twice and saw that she was not much more extravagantly dressed—or undressed—than most of the other females in the vicinity. Most of them wore some kind of tight hosen of blue fabric that clung to their feminine curves; the few who'd managed to find gowns didn't know how to lace them properly, or had no under-shifts to cover themselves.

"Marry, *all* the females here be bawds—or players, which comes to much the same thing." And the dryness of his mouth reminded him that it had been much too long since he'd satisfied any of his mortal appetites.

Directly across the green was an establishment that called itself a tavern, though it looked like no tavern Kit had ever seen. He smiled sweetly at the buxom lass behind the counter and requested a cup of ale.

"That'll be two pounds," she told him.

Kit laughed his appreciation of the jest. Ah, well,

the other girl hadn't wanted his gold angel; he'd give it to the barmaid as a thank-offering for his good luck in being back in the world of trees and grass and pretty girls and sunshine, the blessed sunlight. "Here, my lass—and cheap at the price, for the thirst I've on me!" He tossed the coin at her, took the mug of sparkling pale stuff, and drained half of it at a gulp before the shock of it hit him. What kind of fair let folk sell such thin, sour stuff as good ale?

The girl was shouting at him, waving his coin and crying that he'd not cheat her so; she wanted real money.

Kit spat out the bitter ale that remained in his mouth, politely turning aside to hit the grass rather than the front of the stall. "The gold's true, sweeting," he said. "Would I could say as much for the drink. Take care lest the fairwardens put you in stocks for selling of bad ale."

The girl giggled as though he'd said something extremely witty. "Oh, why didn't you tell me you worked here? Okay, one drink on the house for a fellow oppressed worker, but you'll have to put on the act elsewhere to get another."

"Another? Beshrew me if ever I drink that devil's brew again!" But the girl was too pretty to have her face marred in the stocks; he'd not complain of her if he did catch sight of the fairwardens, only ask them to point him to an honest brewer's stall. "Gi's a kiss to take the sour taste away, and call it quits, sweet," Kit suggested.

Her lips were too soft and too moist and she smelled of strange flower essences and something else, a sharp chemical stink like a 'pothecary's shop; but she was the first living woman he'd kissed in who knew how long, and the touch of her soft face reminded him of what had called him into this world.

"Eleanor," he said, letting her go. "Eleanor?"

There was music somewhere beyond all the shouts of the hawkers and the babble of the crowd; he plunged towards it, sweating. Some sort of procession barred his way; he dodged between two half-dressed bawds and rolled under the feet of a troop of marching men in skirts. Wild Irishmen, he guessed, hearing the hellish squeal of their pipes, every bit as bad as described by the men who'd served in Ireland. But they seemed a scrawny bunch, too thin-shanked and soft to make good fighters. Hostages, no doubt. And nothing to do with him—nor was the rest of the procession, though he laughed under his breath at sight of the painted strumpet who styled herself the Queen. This fair of rogues and bawds would soon be cleared out if the true Queen were to hear of such claims.

A thought struck him then, and he stopped where he stood.

"Hey, man, you're in the way!" cried a man with a wooden foil in his hand, skipping around Kit. He waved the foil up and down like a child playing at swordfighting, and his opponent matched the wobbly strokes. Both were breathing hard.

"*Git* outa the *way*, asshole!" The second playactor broke off the pretense of swordfighting long enough to waggle his foil at Kit. "Cain't y'see we're giving a demonstration of swordfighting style here?"

He made as if to poke Kit with the wooden sword. Years of training took over; Kit dropped to one knee and came up under the roaring boy's arm, twisted his wrist, and took the foil all in one smooth motion.

"Demonstration of players' mumming, you mean," he said pleasantly. "Look at you, you're open here—and here. Now should one go aside with the right leg," he said as the other man lunged at him with the foil, "following towards your left hand, so can this stoccata of yours be broken with the left hand, and at the same time I aim the imbroccata at the face. No, no!" he expostulated as his opponent ducked clumsily. "See you, part now with your right foot circularly and you might beat the thrust outward. . . . No, not like that! An I thrust a stoccata to your belly, would you be dead now; you should have parted with a counter-time towards my left hand, as laid down in Saviolo his excellent treatise." Kit parried a clumsy blow backhanded and explained in even tones the disadvantage of the edge compared to the point. His opponent was puffing and blowing like a great fish; time to end this play. "Now shall I, as the maister, answer with a punta riversa to the head, beating aside thy foyne—" he struck the other man's foil from his hand with a backhanded stroke—"and ending with a stoccata—*thus*!"

He stopped his lunge with the point of the wooden foil just resting on his opponent's breast. There was a roar of applause around them.

"Now that," Kit said, "is a demonstration of the Italian style of fence, albeit none so elegant and precise as might be given by Messer Saviolo himself. Your pardon, gentles; it has been too long since I practiced." It would be discourteous to mention that one couldn't really display fine swordsmanship against such careless novices; if Kit had not restrained himself, he'd have disarmed both men and had the foil at their throats before they'd known of his presence.

Clearly they were not accustomed to defending themselves in road or tavern, or to answering the demands of honor at the court.

"Who hired *you*?" demanded the fat man he'd disarmed first.

Nor had they the courtesy of one gentleman to another. "What," Kit demanded, "do you think me some hireling knave?"

"Never mind," said the other one, retrieving his foil from the bystander who'd caught it in midair. "He talks as good as he fights. What's your household, stranger? I hight Lord Parthalan ap Gryffyd, of the Barony of Iarfhlaith," he added courteously.

A gentle speech demanded an equally courteous reply, no matter how strange his new acquaintance's ragged dress and medley of peculiar armor appeared. "Christopher Arundel, of Greenholt," Kit replied with a bow, "with no title but that of honest English gentleman." And that should be worth ten of such high-sounding bastard Welsh genealogies and Irish titles, though 'twould be discourteous to say so.

"Well, Chris, you're one hell of a fighter," said Lord Parthalan, mopping his brow. "Want to stay and do another demonstration round with us, or are you just passing through?"

"Just—er—passing through," said Kit. Was that singing he heard, coming from the miniature round stage ahead? He could not see over the heads of the churls who crowded about the stage. But even while the music drew him, the question that would not be denied burst out.

"I would fain know one thing, though the question itself may seem passing strange to you," he said apologetically. "Doth Elizabeth still reign?"

"Who?" The Welsh swordsman looked blank, and for a moment Kit felt the good solid earth spinning away beneath his feet, and darkness opening for him.

"The Queen, man," he prompted impatiently.

"Oh—the queen of *England*! Yeah, sure, man, far as I know."

"My thanks to you," Kit said. How like a Welshman, to pretend he owed no reverence nor even any thought to an English monarch! If he had time, and if the fellow hadn't spoken him fair already, he'd have stuffed one of his own Welsh leeks down his throat for speaking so casually of the queen. But the music was a thread that drew his heart towards the stage, and he could not tarry to teach some strange Welshman manners. "Give you good day," he called over his shoulder. He glimpsed Lord Parthalan and his stout partner beginning again with the strange ritualized dance that they called swordplay; then he was between the two circles, and fighting his way to get within shouting distance of the stage where Eleanor's voice was twining round his soul. He pushed between two buxom dames most immodestly attired in scraps of bright cloth, trod on a mountebank all covered with fur, apologized, looked up, and saw her.

The earthly sun passed behind a cloud; the air about him quivered with the strange intensity that presaged a dream-shift in the other sphere.

No. He raged against the insistent drawing of the other world, clung for his life to this little scrap of the true mortal world. Bitter ale in his mouth, hot sun burning him, sweet music in his ears: the muted sphere of Faerie was never so hot and strong and bitter and sweet. All the living senses of him cried out to stay here. Better to be buried in the ground whereon he stood than to be drawn back to the sphere of the Dark Lady.

"Eleanor!"

His voice was faint and pale, as near extinction as a candle in the wind. He summoned up all his love of this rude mortal world, all that Eleanor had been to him and all that she might be: the simple goodness of new bread, the sun rising on a new day, dew on the grass. Love and desire ripped through him and left his throat raw with effort; but the mists of Faerie were descending between them. His voice was a whisper on the wind, drifting inaudible over the heads of all the gypsies and mountebanks and players and sturdy rogues gethered in this strange mockery of a fair.

She heard him; her eyes were fixed on his face, and the shock she felt was written on her own face for all to read. Her voice quavered; the song came to a halting end, and in the silence he felt the hold of Faerie upon him, drawing him inexorably back to the changeless sphere that claimed him body and soul, and now there was no more music to lead him home to the sunlight.

"Time stands still . . ." he whispered on a thread of half-remembered song, before the shifting, timeless sphere of Faerie claimed him again, and all love and delight became no more than the dream of a ghost.

> *Time stands still with gazing on her face,*
> *Stand still and gaze, for minutes, hours*
>   *and years to her give place,*

Paien sang, looking up and past Ellen. She followed the direction of his gaze and saw the woman she'd noticed earlier, cold and perfect in her beauty, watching the group with no expression at all. And when she looked back into the audience, the dark familiar face out of her dreams was no longer there, and she could not explain why tears streaked her face.

All other things shall change, but she
  remains the same
Till heavens changed have their course,
  and Time hath lost his name.

It seemed to Ellen that the woman Paien watched was more real than anything else; the audience had become shadows around a stage of dreams, and the trees that whispered around them were as like to dance as any of the people there. The sun's light dimmed while the sweet music went on and on, and around Paien and the strange woman a cold unearthly light glowed.

Something stung Ellen's ankle: she looked down and saw that Bethany was pinching her with one hand while she sang over the last words of Paien's song in an unrehearsed chorus. "And Fortune, captive at her feet—wake up, Ellen, it's your last solo—condemned and conquered lies."

Ellen caught her breath and launched into the final song while Bethany swore under her breath and scrambled to catch up on the lute. She had been dreaming again, imagining things, and the man she thought she'd seen had only been part of her dream.

The sun came out from behind its clouds and beat down on the circle of grass around them; the pale woman withdrew, frowning, to the shade of the trees; Ellen sang with a breaking heart for a dream dissolved.

Come away, away, away;
see the dawning of the day . . .

There was silence when she finished, broken only by the last notes plucked from Paien's lute: the quiet dropping of water into a still pool, the ripple of a secret spring. For a moment Ellen felt a despair too great to have anything to do with the day's contest. She had failed unimaginably at a task she could not even define: all was emptiness about her.

Then a sigh passed like a breath of cool air through the crowd. One person began to applaud, then another, and then Ellen swayed under the bruising noise of so many hands beating one against another. Even the cool remote lady to whom Paien had addressed his songs was smiling: a curve of perfect lips, a cold passionless smile that showed her little pointed white teeth. The crowd surged about them, rocking the little stage.

Bethany laughed aloud with delight, jumped up and hugged Ellen. "I think we did it! You sang like— like an angel, Ellen! If we win, it's all your doing. I knew you could do it," she said, blithely ignoring her own premonitions of disaster. "You see, everything's going to be all right now."

"The man shall have his mare again, and all shall be well," murmured Paien, his words almost lost in the noise about them. "I wonder . . ." He looked directly at Ellen, and she felt her usual shock at seeing so much beauty in a man's face, so much intensity in the gaze directed briefly at her. But this time the shock, like all else, was muted in comparison to what had just happened.

Which was, she told herself, precisely nothing. Someone whose face was familiar to her had come up towards the stage, then had gone away again while she was looking elsewhere. Nothing in that to upset her; certainly nothing to make her feel that her whole world had been swept out from beneath her feet and that nothing was as she'd believed it. Yet the despair stayed with her, making all that followed seem empty and unreal. The spring sunshine that fell slanting through trees and green leaves to dazzle her, the remote face of the woman who might have been Paien's dark sister and who turned out to be in fact the sole judge of the contest, the softness of the grass under her feet as she curtseyed in fine court style while the prize was announced: none of these things meant anything to her at all. Her head had begun to ache furiously, and she longed to find some quiet shady place where she could rest and think about nothing at all until the sharpness of intolerable loss eased within her.

"Take her back," said Paien to Bethany. "She is tired."

Ellen stood wide-eyed and blind with sun between them.

"To the house?"

Paien said something under his breath, an explosion of foreign sounds. "To *Austin*. You leave for England on—" He looked at the papers the dark lady had given them. "June seventh. Three weeks. Can you be ready by then?"

"I don't understand. Aren't you coming with us?"

"I will undertake to meet you there," Paien said.

"In Austin? But how will you get back?"

"In England."

"I don't *understand*," cried Bethany.

A smile briefly transformed Paien's severe golden beauty. "Sweetheart, my time here is accomplished. I shall be with you when the season of turning comes, never fear."

He bowed over her hand. The dark lady looked at them, only a glance from shuttered eyes, and Paien shivered and was all business again. "Do not fail us."

"I wouldn't," Bethany said, tucking away papers and forms and airline tickets. "I wouldn't miss it for the world."

A glimmer of amusement lit Paien's eyes. "For the world," he repeated. "My sentiments exactly."

When Bethany and Ellen had left, Paien offered his arm to the dark lady. She rested long white fingers on his sleeve, and they strolled away through the chattering fairgoers. Somehow people moved aside to make a path for them; somehow no one looked at them directly. The belly dancer in front of the chain mail shop blinked as a ray of sunlight shattered into rainbow on the jewels in Paien's cloak; for a moment she could see nothing, and then there was nothing to see. Light poured golden and thick as wine through the trees; the trees swayed in a breeze out of nowhere, and shadows danced among the trees, were movement, were a troubling of the air, were a memory in the mortal world.

Where the trees thickened into a dark wood, eternally storm-tossed, eternally still, the shadows moved and spoke, but not with any mortal tongues.

A young man ran through the wood, pushing aside branches that writhed and hissed or burst into cold flames under his hands.

And is this all your plan? The question chimed with echoes of a delicate scorn.

No. This was too soon. She could not hold him so far from the right time and place.

A wind rose in the wood; the spinning stars held the green and burning trees in place while all their branches strained towards the bright moon in the heart of the wood. *Time. Place. Mortal conceits.*

If you would master the mortal world, Lady, you must know mortal conceits.

And must I also wear mortal favors? The wind plucked the bluejay's feather from Paien's cap; the leaf-shaped brooch whirled away with it and blended with all the other leaves of the Ladyswood. *I begin to wonder which sphere you would choose, Paien.*

That was not a question he could answer; it should never have been asked; she should never have needed to ask it. He would not lower himself to reply. *Lady, we must know time and place as mortals do if we would act upon their world. If I have changed, it has been in your service.* So much was true, at least; he had entered the mortal sphere at the Lady's command. And did he not still serve her? She had no right to charge him with treachery. He was only a little confused with this continual passing between the spheres. *The time and place of the joining is come near again; else could we not act upon mortal minds as now we do, nor walk their world by day.*

The falling leaves, rust and brown, brightened to green again, became green flowers, white birds, sang in their endless flight. *See that you fail not, then, when the time of which you speak be come.*

I will not. It bodes well that she had the strength to call him, even all unknowing as she bides now.

When the spheres draw closer together, he shall come to her again, and then shall all be joined as it was in the beginning. No more dance of the stars that were ruled by eternal law; no more blue feathers.

"Damn you," cried the mortal man who ran unchanging through the wood that changed about him with each step. "Damn you, damn you, that would torture me with a glimpse of Paradise and then snatch me back to this accursed place."

Mist swallowed up his shape; the discordant songs of a world without time and measure drowned out the voice that cried curses on all the moving shadows.

6

Anno 1594: A declaration of great troubles pretended against the realm by a number of seminary priests and Jesuits, sent, and very secretly dispersed into the same, to work great treasons under a false pretence of religion. With a provision very necessary for the remedy thereof. Published by her majesty's proclamation.

Although we have had probable cause to hope, that now towards the end of 36 years wherein Almighty God hath continually preserved us in a peaceable possession of our kingdoms, the former malice of our enemies (especially of the king of Spain) would have waxed faint in him; yet to the contrary we find it by his present mighty actions, such as, to levy forces in Italy, to begin a most unjust war against the French king, and the preparation of other great forces for his seas, the with to make another attempt against our crown and dominions.[1] Furthermore,

---

1. The Spanish Armada of 1588 did not by any means end the fear of another such invasion; rumors of the rebuilding of the fleet were continually alarming England for the next ten years.

he hath gathered together a multitude of Jesuits and seminary priests which secretly and by stealth be conveyed into our dominions, with ample authority from Rome to move, stir up, and persuade as many of our subjects as they dare deal withal, to renounce their natural allegiance due to us and our crown, and upon hope, by a Spanish invasion, to be enriched and endued with the possessions and dignities of our other good subjects.

Therefore we have determined to have speedily certain commissioners to be appointed in every shire, city, and port-town within our realms, to inquire what persons, by their behavior or otherwise worthy to be suspected to be any such persons, that have been sent to move any to relinquish their allegiance to us, or to acknowledge any kind of obedience to the pope or to the king of Spain.

And furthermore, it is known by common experience that the said traitorous persons do come into the realm by secret creeks and landing-places, disguised both in names and persons; some in apparel as soldiers, mariners, or merchants; some as gentlemen, in comely apparel, as though they had traveled into foreign countries for knowledge. Wherefore we strictly charge and command all persons that have any intelligence with any such so sent, to detect them to the commissioners, upon pain that the offenders herein shall be punished as abettors and maintainers of traitors. Wherein we are resolutely determined to suffer no favour to be used for any respect of any persons, qualities, or degrees; nor shall allow, nor suffer to be allowed, any excuse of negligence for not detection; devised for the

good order of all manner of subjects to answer
for their behaviour towards the dignity of our crown
and the common peace of our realm. Given at our
manor of Richmond, the 15th of April, 1594, in
the 36th year of our reign.

7

DAY-BOOK OF CHRISTOPHER ARUNDEL
(HARLEIAN MS. 285, FOL. 31)
Monday 10 June 1594—I do fear me that this evenings idle talk may have done ill work indeed. The parson of St. Marys at Emminster, a worthy but dull soul, did visit us and I did invite him to dine here tonight; he doth ever hint after such invitations, and I thought at least that our expanded company might dilute his watery dullness with the wine of lively discourse. In this I foretold truly, but at what cost remaineth to be seen.

Sir Walter, being much exalted over rumors that the Queen might make an unannounced progress into the West Country (where he might perchance gain speech with her and become restored to favor at Court) did drink more than his wont at supper and did sit long at table after the ladies had gone their ways. He did incline him to philosophical speculation, in which at first I saw no harm, he and G. Cavendish debating with coolness on the nature of angels and other topics in which Cavendish shewed himself as well read as any Oxford divine. But as the argument turned to the nature of the soul Sir Walter, being then in his cups, did begin to utter words which any might consider rank heresy and fit to be taken up before the Privy Council.

"I have been," said he, "a scholar some time in Oxford, I have answered under a bachelor of art, and had talk with divines, yet hitherunto in this point (to wit, what the reasonable soul of man is) have I not by any been resolved."

To this replied our good parson Hensley, "It is determined by divine scholars that the soul is a spiritual and immortal substance breathed into man by God."

"Yea, but what is that spiritual and immortal substance?" spake Sir Walter.

"The soul."

At this Sir W. laughed, and drawing with his fingertip a circle from the wine spilt at supper, he said that all this disputation was no more than that, an argument without beginning or end.

"God is the *primum mobile*, the beginning and end of all things," said Cavendish.

"Marry, these two, God and the soul, be then alike, for neither could I learn what God is," said Sir W. "All these arguments be but circles, and the tales on which they be based no better: Moses whom we are taught to revere was but a juggler, and any man who knoweth the natural sciences can better his acts. Your galleon that saileth upon the table and Dr. Dee his hooting silver owl be as great miracles as the plague of frogs, Kit."

Thinking to turn the conversation from these rash ways, I did remind Sir W. of the mystical power of the circle, that he should not treat it so lightly. "Did not the Nolan affirm that the eye being placed in any part of the Universe the appearance would still be all one as unto us here?"

"If he did, then he spake jugglery," said Sir W.

"And what of Hermes Trismegistus, who said that God is a sphere of which the centre is everywhere and the circumference nowhere?"

Parson Hensley was speechless with shock by this time, but my friend and astrologer Giles Cavendish did take up the argument. "Master Arundel hath the right of it," said Mr. Cavendish then. "Your appeals to the divines can never answer these questions, Sir Walter, for they are the keys which imprison you in a black dungeon. Once released, you shall with us see the one heaven and the infinite cause of the infinite effect; you shall understand that God is not far distant but within us, for His centre is everywhere. Hence we should not follow other authorities, but the regulated sense of our own understanding."

Sir W. laughed at this, overlong and loud, as in a man of lesser standing might have been thought unseemly. "Well, Mr. Cavendish, I can see you are no priest, as my good friend Richard Topcliffe did suspect, for surely you would have been burned by now for such thoughts."

"I have suffered for my philosophy," said Cavendish. His brow was paler than its wont, and droplets of sweat did sparkle upon his whitened countenance.

"So may you again. England is not yet so free a state that men may speak rank heresy without being taken up on it, as I can prove out of mine own experience. Thank God we be all good fellows at this table and

can trust what we say shall not be spread abroad!"
And Sir W. did fix us each in turn with his piercing
look, then left abruptly.

"Let us say Grace and leave also," said Edw. Guilford,
"for that is better than this disputation."

Later did Edward seek me out in Mr. Cavendish
his chamber, where we two did observe the stars
while he did attempt to show me by what signs he
could predict the arrival of a Queen in this our little
sphere of Greenholt. He did earnestly intreat us
both to guard our tongues in the presence of Sir
Walter, saying that he had good reason to think the
man unscrupulous in putting down any who might
pose a danger to him.

"Why, man, what danger in idle table-talk and
speculation?" said I. "And for that matter, it was
Sir Walter, not we, who spake the most."

"Should this matter come before the Privy Council,
it will be we and not Sir Walter who will suffer for
it," said Edward. "Remember what fate befell poor
Marlowe, but last spring."

"Stabbed in a drunken tavern fight, as I recall,"
I said. "What has that to do with us?"

"This only, and think well upon it," said Edward.
"Marlowe was my friend. Last spring he did wait
upon Sir Walter at Durham House, hoping to find
in him a patron for his new play of Doctor Faustus
the German divine that did sell his soul to the Devil
for knowledge. He told me after that Sir Walter
spake to him in just such terms of the soul, doubting
whether or not such a thing existed in truth, and
jesting that God and the Devil were but tales to
frighten naughty children."

"So Sir Walter is in the habit of loose speech in

his cups. That seemeth me to be Sir Walters trouble and not ours."

"Think then on this," said Edward, "that rumors of Marlowes doings with Sir Walter coming to the ears of the Privy Council, they did issue a warrant for his arrest and questioning."

"What, Sir Walter?"

"Nay, you fool, my friend Christopher Marlowe! And but two days after, before his arrest, there came about this so-called 'brawl' between Marlowe and three men, two of them servants to Sir Walter, one of them in the pay of the informer Topcliffe. Wherefore is a poor scribbling poet dead in a tavern, and there was none bear witness against Sir Walter for his heretical speech, and he came away from the inquiries withouten scathe, as you yourself did write to me from London. Now think on, and ask yourself whether you will listen to the man another time, or say Grace and quit the table before he can speak such wild fancies as he may regret later."

"This is a grave charge that you make against a man of high repute," I said.

"And nothing can be proved. I know," said Edward, "that is ever the way of it with Sir Walter, that those who might do him harm be found dead of a sudden, and always by accident. Only once in his life has he let love keep him from destroying one who came between him and the Queen—and I tell you plainly, had Bess Throckmorton not been so fair, and Sir Walter so mad with love for her, the child that he got upon her had been her death rather than her marriage warrant."

"Hush, man!" I cried. "Would you have him hear you speak such things?"

"I would he were gone from this place," said Edward, "and if you two star-gazers had a pennys worth of wisdom between you, you too would wish it. You, Kit, did speak rank heresy with him this night; and you, Cavendish, until you spake against the authority of divines, did quote opinions more suited to a Catholick priest than to an English gentleman. I trust Parson Hensley will not spread talk of this night abroad."

Cavendish did smile, but in such sad sort that it seemed he was more like to weep. "I was seven years in the seminary at Rome," he said, "before I went into Germany to study with Messer Bruno at Wittenberg. But now I am forbidden to say Mass until the Holy Office shall inquire into my heresies—and that they may not do, I being 'scaped to England—so may I no longer call myself a priest."

Edward went white. "You fool, you have put us all in danger of our lives!" he cried. "Know you not that to be a seminary priest in England is treason, and to harbor one is death? And here in the house have we one who would betray his friend to gain the Queen her favor and prove him loyal; how better than by informing on you?"

"But I am no more a priest," argued Cavendish.

Edward spake passionately of the troubles brought on those who had harbored Jesuits and seminary priests, until Cavendish being brought to see that his bad standing with the See of Rome meant no good standing with the Church of England, did announce his intention of leaving the house at once, saying that he had been a foolish scholar who thought England open to new ideas and had no intent of bringing his friends into danger.

I did command him to remain with us, saying

that I was none so poor a host as to throw my guests to the dogs of informers and priest-hunters. "I hold not to the Catholic faith myself, but most of my family do so, and we Arundels know well enough how to hide a man from informers, and how to slip him safely out of the country," I told him. "A precipitate departure would but call attention upon us." Besides, the damage had already been done, for if he were taken up for a priest I should still be attainted of treason for having sheltered him, whether or no he were in my house at the time of taking. But this it disliked me to say unto him, as it would but trouble his conscience with what could not now be mended. "Bide quietly here a while, be careful of your speech, and I shall arange all so that there may no suspicion fall on you or any of us."

Christopher Arundel to Arthur Arundel
(Bodleian Library, Arundel Papers)
My very good friend and respected kinsman—

A certain parcel from Greenholt is prepar'd for delivery, and I shall be eternally obliged to you and yours if you may [indecipherable] to France as arranged, by whatsoever fishing smack or other boat as you may find convenient for such work, upon the midnight high tide tomorrow night, in the small landing-place you know of. The matter is [illegible] and of great urgency, and rather of concern to your faith than mine.

Pray destroy this message.[1]
From Greenholt, 18 April [1594]
Kit[2]

---

1. Arthur Arundel would have been wiser to do as his cousin asked, but he evidently waited too long, as the subsequent letters will show.
2. The handwriting of this brief note is abominable, and the signature is scrawled in slashing black letters that take up half the page, as though the writer were suffering both from great stress and from shortage of time.

R. Hensley, vicar of Emminster, to Sir Robert Cecil:

Right honorable good Lord,

Since the sending of my letter to your Lordship last month I have, according to yr instructions, made excuse to dine at Greenhold Manor that I might the more closely observe the astrologer Cavendish and question him as to the time and manner of his coming into the country. It fell out so, that I might not question the man direct, being forc'd to withdraw early from the table by reason of such blasphemous and heretical talk as it doth sadden me to hear from any of this parish; and this talk led by none less than Sir W. Raleigh, who hath brought himself and his wife hither by reason of the plague being broken out upon his estates of Sherborne. He did question the working of God and the writings of the Bible as hardily as any atheist. For my part I cannot believe that this G. Cavendish could be a seminary priest (although he hath a dark and sardonic look such as well would befit such a bird of ill omen) for he did listen and participate in the heresies being spoken. If your Lordship should wish to hear the tale of this nights work from other mouths, it were well done to set out a warrant for the questioning of Mr. Arundel on suspicion of harboring a Jesuit priest, and Mr. Cavendish on suspicion of being such a priest. Thus might the matter be accomplished without publicly accusing Sir W. Raleigh until his heresy be affirmed for all to know.

Richard Hensley, at Emminster, this 11 day of June *anno* 1594.

Thursday, June 2, 1994

They flew east at the beginning of June, from sunshine to mist, from a stifling Texas afternoon to an English morning where nothing was as it seemed. They were tired and confused and the vibration of the jets shuddered through them, but it was *England*, and the excitement of that woke them up.

Paien was not waiting for them at Gatwick.

"Not that I really expected it," said Bethany. "If he'd meant to be here, he wouldn't have sent us such detailed instructions." She squinted blearily at the fat letter that had arrived in Austin the previous week. "Take the Exeter train, but we get off before Exeter. Where? I don't see Emminster on the timetable."

Ellen rubbed her eyes and tried to concentrate on the small blurred red letters of the railway timetable. They danced in dizzy circles; the long columns of times and places advanced all in a row, receded, spiraled down to a red center. Exeter St. David's, Whimple, Crewkerne— "Sherborne," she said. "That's close." *Too close by half*, laughed a voice she'd heard only in dreams. *Sir Walter might settle farther away with my good will!* "Sherborne," she repeated. "Is that where we get off?"

"No. Wait a minute." Bethany riffled through the pages of Paien's letter. "Crewkerne, that's it. Is there anything like that on the timetable?"

"I think so." Ellen was too tired to squint over the fine print again. She felt lost, floating somewhere outside the world, seeing everything with that queer double vision that had troubled her ever since the singing at the Renaissance Faire. With her eyes she saw long polished corridors, tired people trudging along with too many suitcases, tiles and carpets and walls of windows. Some other sense insisted that there should be nothing but green fields and sheep here, and maybe a hint of London Town on the horizon. Not a sense, exactly; more like a memory so strong that it displaced what was before her eyes.

They had to change trains twice before they got to Crewkerne, once at Clapham Junction and again at Basingstoke. Bethany grumbled mildly as they hauled their luggage down the high narrow steps of the railway stations and back up to another platform to wait for another train. "This is supposed to be a *vacation.* How come you had to drag along six manuals and a notebook computer?"

"To convince my boss at GIC that I'm going to keep diddling with the temporo-spatial module and upload any fixes I make to the mainframes in Austin. The top levels of KNEE are still buggy and he's convinced there's something wrong with our module."

Bethany tucked two GIC manuals under her arm, slung her duffle bag over one shoulder, and bent her knees to pick up her lute case. "Is there something wrong with the module?"

"I don't think so. But it won't hurt to take a look."

"You mean you're really going to work at programming? *Now?* Wasting this gorgeous vacation?"

"I don't intend," Ellen said, "to waste all of it. Just enough to make it look as if I'm trying." She grinned. "He doesn't know how fast I can work when I really want to. Don't worry; I can fiddle with the module, rehearse, and have plenty of time to appreciate England."

Bethany sighed. "Well, once we get to Greenholt, it's your problem. Until then, I wish GIC didn't print such *thick* manuals. Too bad Paien isn't here; he could carry my lute case. Watch out, don't bump it!"

"If Paien were here," Ellen said, "he'd have his own lute case to carry, and all his own luggage. Wouldn't he?"

She had to listen for the names of the stations, but in between times she dozed on the high padded seats with headrests, woke and slept fitfully, while around them the landscape slowly changed from sooty brick walls and rows of houses to something that almost matched the shadowy memories in Ellen's dreams. At Salisbury Bethany sighed happily and said, "Now, *this* is England!"

Ellen agreed, silently, looking out at the rolling green hills and oddly shaped fields bounded by hedgerows. Green and darker green and pale gold made a patchwork landscape, dotted at intervals by flocks of sheep. The train roared past a field full of black and white cattle that never missed a beat of their placid munching, swishing their tails and staring without interest at the noisy hurrying monster. The hedges rose on both sides of them, carrying them down into a tunnel of green; then the land fell away again into its pattern of green and golden hills. In the distance Ellen could see a square church with Gothic spires; beyond that, rainclouds blue in the distance.

Standing on the dark concrete porch outside Crewkerne station was Paien, golden and gleaming as ever, making the dingy little station seem even shabbier and darker than men and neglect had made it. Ellen stumbled down the high steps of the train, yawned in Paien's face when he offered her a greeting kiss, fell asleep on her feet while they walked to the car he'd borrowed, woke to hear Bethany swearing at unfamiliar controls while Paien laughed soundlessly.

"Make some allowances, can't you!" Bethany snapped. "We're ignorant Americans, remember? Liable to forget which side of the road you Limeys drive on. You know the way, you drive." She dropped the keys in Paien's lap.

"Not if I can help it," he said. "I do not understand these beasts. *Here*." He flung the keys over his shoulder, a glittering rainbow of metal bits that came to rest with a jingle and a soft thump in Ellen's outstretched hand.

Paien's directions were belated and confusing and mixed with references to places that were no longer there: turn where Carew's barn burned down, then go by Fern Way—which turned out to be a bridle path.

"'S okay," Bethany said from the backseat, "there's a map tucked between the seats here. I think I've found us."

Ellen followed Bethany's instructions to a narrow road with a white stripe optimistically painted down the middle as though the act of painting could make the road wide enough for two lanes of traffic. Trucks and road-menders and honking vacationers all accepted the fiction of two lanes, whizzing past Ellen while she hung on to the wheel with both hands and prayed and sweated. Bethany rustled the map and exclaimed with delight over English village names. "Ilminster Parva! Hockney Puddington!"

"Roundabout Rumble," Ellen said between her teeth as a hooting truck chased them three times around one of the large round obstructions the British liked to place at crossroads. She saw a chance to escape and peeled off to a narrow westbound road, a strip of grey bordered by misty greenness.

"*Left* side of the road!" Bethany squealed, and Ellen switched lanes just in time to avoid an oncoming wagon. A moment later the distinction between left and right sides became academic; she crept down something narrower than an American driveway, walled in on both sides by high green hedges where white flowers bloomed.

"Oh, how beautiful!" Ellen exclaimed.

"What?" Paien asked, and Bethany said, "There are rather a lot of cars behind us."

"And flowers and meadows on either side," Ellen said happily, "'England's green and pleasant land.' Paien, I am so glad that you brought us here! Just look at that!"

A thorny branch of white flowers and green leaves thrust in at the open window; behind a gate, sheep munched the grass short and rolled nervous eyes at the line of cars. Rolling hills stretched blue into the distance, blending at the sky's edge into misty colors like the gentle haze at the horizon. Ellen sighed with pleasure and went even slower while Paien drummed his fingers on his knee. "You love things that will fade in a day."

"Nothing lasts forever."

"*We're* going to fade in a day," Bethany said, "if you don't speed up or find a place to pull off and let some of these crazy Limey drivers by."

The road widened for a village and the train of cars behind them flashed by, using the village square as a passing lane. Ellen glimpsed a stately old building on her left: the Admiral Hood Inn, with a picture of a man in ruffles and periwig hanging over the door.

"Gooseacre Lane," Bethany read a signpost. "Is that for real?"

"Well, I don't suppose they put the sign there just to amuse American tourists."

A brickwork arch, a narrow tunnel under the railway embankment, a flash of walls and flower baskets and women in flowered dresses, and they were into and out of Emminster market square.

"Do not stop here," Paien said. "Take the next—yes, yes, even so." Ellen was already maneuvering up the uneven street that led out of the village proper, past a gentle mildewed church and across a stream. The narrow road led gently upwards towards a cluster of trees; a wall of golden stone showed in bright flashing glimpses between the green trees.

"How did you know?" Paien asked.

Ellen couldn't risk taking her eyes off the road to glance at him. "Know what? This is the way to Greenholt, isn't it?" The paved road felt wrong, too smooth, too wide; but the direction felt right.

Felt like coming home.

"How did you know we were staying at Greenholt?"

Ellen considered briefly. Greenholt, Crewkerne, Gatwick, JFK, Dallas . . . she had been following this chain too long, she was too sleepy to know or care where any particular link had come from. "You wrote to us. . . ."

"Not about that."

"Must have." And here was the house: a small paved yard, a Tudor display of small glass panes set in the golden stone, a builder's van parked to one side, chickens pecking industriously at the grit and sand in the front, flowers spilling out of window baskets and perfuming the air. Ellen found the hand brake, set it, leaned back against the seat. She was limp with fatigue.

Bethany was out of the car before Ellen, admiring the stonework and the flowers and the garden she could just glimpse beyond the high stone walls. "This," she said, "is going to be wonderful. Imagine getting to stay in an authentic Tudor house!"

"Let's hope," Ellen said as she opened the trunk of the car, "that it doesn't have authentic Tudor plumbing."

Later, when all the suitcases had been carried into the chintz-flowered bedrooms on the second floor, she left Bethany and Paien tuning their lutes and made one last trip to the car. It didn't really matter, of course; but somehow Ellen felt that she would be easier in her mind if she could find Paien's letter of instructions and show him that he had told them how to reach Greenholt Manor. Because he must have done so; she could hardly have remembered directions she'd never been given, could she?

But the letter was nowhere to be found. The backseat where Bethany had juggled letters and maps and tourist brochures was quite clean and empty; only a few dried leaves, and one green one, rustled over the upholstery when Ellen opened the door.

The groans and whines of an overstressed car engine distracted her from the search. Ellen looked up and saw a very small car, dented and battered like an ancient and beloved fishing hat, pulling into the semicircular drive. The car stopped with a wheeze and an ominous popping sound. Before it had quite finished shuddering, people began getting out; more than she could count, fair heads and brown, men and women, all chattering away like birds twittering in the trees. Strange faces and voices and names swirled round Ellen in a babble of banter and introductions. Bethany came out in the middle of the introductions, and they had to start all over again. Finally Ellen thought she'd gotten it straight. The new arrivals were coming to help with the masque—in fact, they were the ones who'd first thought of putting it on. And despite her first impression of an uncountable crowd, there were actually only four of them. Roger, tall and sleek and brown-haired, introduced himself succinctly as "tenor, leading Hounds." The short blonde girl beside him was called Penelope and had the leading soprano for the chorus of Nymphs. "And this is Geoffrey," Roger said, waving at the chunky fair-haired boy, "baritone, Hounds. M'sister Fenella—" he nodded at a girl almost as tall as he was "—is just along for the ride, but she can always do another Nymph if we need one."

"You won't," said Penny. "The entire church choir wants to sing in this thing."

"We need *some* strong singers," Roger protested. It sounded like an old argument.

"You have them now, I think." Penny turned to Ellen with a graceful inclination of her head that made Ellen feel very crude and gauche and American. "You must be one of the American professionals?"

"Well, I wouldn't say—" Ellen began, but Roger interrupted her.

"No, it's quite all right," he said quickly. "We want the masque to be a success—that's the main thing, isn't it?" He glanced around the group and went on without waiting for agreement. "Good publicity, having you lot flown over from the States, and none of us have the voice to handle the material. Oh, in a pinch I suppose I could sing Actaeon to Fenella's Diana, but we're better off not having to try—right, Fen? Right. I can't think," Roger went on with scarcely a pause for breath, "how we missed you at Crewkerne. Good show, finding the way on your own. Hired Donovan's car, did you?"

"Paien gave us directions," Bethany said.

"Such as they were," added Ellen with a remembered shudder at the time she'd tried to turn right, following Paien's directions, into a green unpaved bridle path.

"But he's wandered off now," Bethany added. "Ellen, have you seen Paien?"

"Who's Paien?" Roger asked.

"He's singing Actaeon."

"Oh, right. There were to be three of you. But he's not staying here—we were only told to fix up two bedrooms— er, that is—" Roger's spate of words temporarily dried up as he thought over the implications of what he'd just said.

"*Are* we staying here?" Ellen asked.

Roger gratefully seized the lifeline she'd handed him. "You see, it's not so easy to get a lodging in Emminster, this time of year. Most of the places that let rooms are full up with tourists from the north. They come here for a nice holiday in the sunshine, you see."

Ellen was not altogether sure she did see. A gentle mist was slowly becoming a halfhearted drizzle around them, and she had not packed enough sweaters for this climate. She didn't *own* enough sweaters for this climate.

Roger was back in full flood, explaining half a dozen things at once and so succinctly that Ellen despaired of ever understanding even one of the explanations. The masque had begun as an amateur amusement— "One of Penny's bright ideas," Roger said, "and a jolly good one too, there's not much to do around here. Nobody knows where the money came from—"

"Anonymous benefactors," Penny said solemnly.

"And there were plenty of better uses for it than flying singers over from the States," Fenella grumbled. "I suppose we'll have to teach you lot proper English in the rehearsals."

Ellen could not think how to reply to this statement. She had to agree that flying singers over from America seemed like wanton extravagance for a village masque— but it hadn't, after all, been her idea. And was Fenella always so appallingly rude?

Fortunately, Roger kept talking and spared her the need to respond. "Condition of the donation,

Fen, as you know perfectly well. Now stop insulting our Colonial visitors and come inside so I can show them around."

The tour of the house got no farther than the Long Gallery, where Roger pointed out the marks of previous rains and the new wood replacing rotted roof timbers and a young man in paint-stained slacks.

"Sam's dad did the roofwork," Roger explained with a wave of his hand, "and he's donated Sam to the masque to make scene flats and paint 'em. The professional touch."

"Do you sing too?" Ellen asked Sam.

Sam said something like "Arrrgh," and retreated to squat over his paint pots in a distant corner of the gallery.

"Local dialect," Roger said, "you'll pick it up soon enough. Want to see where the manuscripts were discovered? There's a stair to the roof somewhere around here. . . ."

Fenella interrupted and reminded Roger that they were overdue for lunch at someone's house. Roger looked at his watch, paled, and whisked his friends downstairs, now talking about their anonymous donation. "Penny wants it to've been old Mr. Harbison—the previous owner. Legacy. Which would make sense, seeing he left the house to the county, *except* the manuscripts weren't discovered until Sam's dad got the contract to fix the roof, *after* probate, and I can't quite see Harbison returning to add a ghostly codicil to the will, can you?"

"Maybe he knew they were there all along," Penny said. "Maybe leaving the house to the council was his way of making sure they were found."

"And, of course, he was prescient enough to know

that once the music had been found, you'd have the mad idea of re-enacting the whole masque."

"He might have sensed something," Bethany put in. "He might have been Guided." Ellen stared at the ceiling mouldings and gritted her teeth. Bethany was going to go into her fluffy-headed New Age act again, she could feel it coming on. She wondered for the millionth time whether Bethany really believed this stuff or just found it a convenient way to camouflage her intelligence around beautiful young men.

She certainly sounded sincere now. She clasped her hands under her breasts and looked around the yellow-papered drawing room with an ecstatic shiver. "Such an old house, full of the memories and lives of all those people. I can feel the vibrations. Maybe I lived here once myself, in another life. The first time I saw the music I felt it calling to me."

"Roger," Fenella wailed, "we're going to be quite *desperately* late!"

"Well—check with Sam if you need anything," Roger said in parting, "and we'll be back to rehearse tomorrow."

Bethany drew a deep breath when Roger's ancient car had wheezed its way down the hill again. "Peace at last. I think I'll meditate right here. I can sense unquiet spirits with a need to tell us something." She sank down cross-legged on the drawing-room carpet and closed her eyes.

"Roger's gone," Ellen pointed out, "you don't have to put on that fluffhead act. Me, I can sense a need for coffee. Not to mention lunch."

Bethany looked up reproachfully. "Ellen, *must* you be so mundane? It's not all an act; there *is* something special about this place. Although now that you mention it, I'm hungry too. Where *do* you suppose Paien has got to?"

"Wherever it is," said Ellen, looking out the window at the empty driveway, "he's taken Donovan's car with him. I think we're on our own. Want to try translating Sam-speak?"

In the absence of Roger and the others, Sam turned out to be more articulate than they'd hoped, if no more knowledgeable. Bethany immediately started interrogating him about the history of the house, forgetting all about Ellen and coffee, but Sam knew no more than they'd already been told.

"Gone to the council, then, hasn't it? They're paying for the remodeling, aren't they? Dunno who's paying for the masque, do I, though?"

"*I* don't know what you know," said Bethany, fascinated, "why are you asking me?"

"Ah. Just a manner of speaking, innit?"

Ellen interrupted and established that they could buy food in Emminster village. There was a greengrocer's, a butcher's, and a grocer's, but they'd all be closed this time of day; never mind, they could get milk and coffee "down the Spar."

"Huh?"

"The *Spar*," Sam repeated impatiently. "Open till all hours—as late as seven or eight, most nights."

Ellen thought about American all-night supermarkets while Sam went on instructing the ignorant foreigners. They'd want a basket to carry their purchases home in, wouldn't they? Wait a bit, and he could run them down to the village in the builder's van, couldn't he?

"That's all right," said Ellen, "we'll walk."

Sam looked her over with dawning approval. "Always

heard Americans didn't walk. You sure you can stand
the heat, then? Something fierce for this early in
the summer, innit?"

It was at least seventy degrees outside, and the
soft grey clouds overhead parted every few minutes
to reveal pale beams of watery sunshine in between
the intermittent drizzle and mist. Ellen assured Sam
that they would be able to survive a walk to the
village without succumbing to exhaustion or sunstroke.

The road they'd driven up was easy enough to
follow back, a grey ribbon that started downhill and
then curved to the left between high green hedges.
Ellen stopped where a red-painted gate interrupted
the solid green line of the hedge. Her vision blurred
for a moment and she could hardly see the road
for the clear image of a rutted, unpaved track with
flowers covering the low sprawling hedges on either
side. This road ran through the field, through the
wavering image of red bars. . . . She rubbed her eyes
and the gate was there as it had been, and the track
was gone—or was it? A faint line in the pasture
showed where feet had worn a shorter way through
years of walking. She pushed the gate open.

"What?"

"There's a footpath," Ellen said reasonably, pointing
out the track in the grass. "Shortcut to the village."

"How do you know?"

Words and thoughts and a cry of panic chased
round and round in her mind briefly, like a squirrel
after nuts, like a leaf in the wind. Then her head
cleared and the answer presented itself, bright,
reasonable, impenetrable. "The village is down at
the bottom of the hill, remember? This path goes
straight downhill. The road doesn't."

The gate swung shut behind them with a hollow clang. Bethany picked her way behind Ellen, muttering about cow-flops and hostile chickens and other hazards of country life, until they came to a second gate. Beyond this boundary the path was clearly defined as a swathe cut out of long wild grasses. Farther down the hill was a cluster of houses, and rising among the huddled roofs, the tall square tower of the church, topped by a weather vane that flashed gold at them, dazzling Ellen's eyes. She walked faster, driven by a sudden urgency to reach the church and find out—find out—

The driving force behind her conscious thoughts shattered on a flock of birds that wheeled and scattered in the sky. More birds cooed and chattered in the eaves of the first houses before them, and Ellen's pace slackened; what had she been in such a hurry for? What did she need to know of Emminster, except where to buy coffee?

"Doves!" Bethany exclaimed with delight. "The moan of doves in immemorial elms . . ."

"Look like pigeons to me," Ellen said.

Bethany turned a wounded look upon her. "You," she said, "have no sense of romance and adventure. Anyway, aren't pigeons and doves the same thing?"

The Spar was on the high road through Emminster; Ellen could vaguely remember seeing its red and white doors flashing by as they drove to Greenholt. She filled a straw basket with instant coffee and milk and cans of soup, which the grocer called tins, and cookies, which the grocer insisted on calling biscuits. Bethany paid for the basket and its contents by holding out a handful of unfamiliar heavy change and letting the grocer pick out pound coins and shillings and fifty-pence pieces until the total satisfied him.

While the grocer counted out change and advised them on the notable sights of Emminster, Ellen stood in the doorway and admired the eighteenth-century house fronts with their curved and angled bay windows of many panes.

"Want to have a look at that church he was talking about?" Bethany asked.

A faint, premonitory unease fluttered in Ellen's mind like the wings of birds startled from their nest. "Is it worth seeing?"

"The west face is sixteenth century," the grocer offered helpfully.

Church Lane was a sloping cobblestoned street leading downhill from the square, lined with baskets of flowers at doorsteps and windows, ending in the high wall of the churchyard. Bethany set down her basket and prowled about the graveyard, trying to decipher the eighteenth-century stones with their timeworn inscriptions, while Ellen entered the silent cool shade of the church, out of breath and looking for something she could not name or even describe.

Sounds murmured through the dim interior of the church, a breathy whispering that became the echo of singing voices. Ellen looked around her at the empty pews, then up at the organ. Nothing moved. The singing was all around her; not the songs of the masque, but something measured and solemn. Something you'd expect to hear in a church; but the skin on her neck and arms prickled, and when something scraped on the stones behind her she jumped and let out a gasp that was not quite a shriek.

"Did you see him, dear?"

The wrinkled old woman who addressed her was surely no ghost; not in those sensible and extremely ugly green rubber shoes.

"I didn't see anybody," Ellen said. "Were you looking for something?"

The old woman settled herself comfortably in a pew. "Not to say *looking*, no, I wouldn't say that!" She laughed gustily, without sound, in a long moment of private amusement. "Some can hear them singing psalms, and some of those see him, or so they say. Mind you, *I've* never seen aught as shouldn't be here, but they do say he comes back from time to time; looking for his school-fellows, no doubt. They never found the body, you know."

Bethany had given up on the gravestones and come inside to find Ellen while the old woman was talking. "No, we don't know," she said, "but won't you tell us?"

"Poor little John Daniel. They thought he drowned in the creek, but no one ever found the body, and the water's scarcely strong enough to carry away a big boy of eleven. But his mother would grieve, so parson said the words over an empty coffin, to put his spirit to rest. It didn't work, though. He comes back—he comes back, every so often." The woman pointed to an engraved stone set in the wall at eye level, just beside Ellen.

"In memory of John Daniel, *aetat* eleven years, *anno* feventeen— I mean, seventeen," Ellen corrected herself, "seventeen hundred and twenty-eight." But that wasn't what she had come to find. "Where be the Arundels buried?" she heard a voice ask. It seemed to come from her own throat.

The old woman looked startled. "No Arundels here, dear. They're down Chideock way."

"I know," said the voice impatiently, "but what of Christopher Arundel of Greenholt?"

"Oh, they couldn't bury him, could they now, and no body to be found? Nor would parson say the words over such a wicked man." The old woman stood up, bringing her mouth close to Ellen's ear, and whispered, *"He raised devils, you know, and they carried him off in the end."*

It should have been laughable. Ellen tried to tell herself that the only reason she wasn't laughing was that it would have been rude. But her knees felt loose and liquid, and she had to sit down while the pews and the carved walls and the altar swung about her in sickening circles. When the church stopped shaking, the old woman was gone, and Bethany looked worried.

"I'm all right," Ellen said.

"I wasn't worried about you," Bethany claimed, "only wondering how we're going to drag all this heavy canned stuff back up the hill to Greenholt."

Sam was circling the market square in his van when Bethany and Ellen dragged their basket of groceries up Church Lane again. "Thought you'd want a ride back," he said. "Easier going downhill than up, innit?"

"It's just that we've bought rather a lot of stuff," Bethany said coldly. "I rather like climbing hills, myself."

"Go ahn," said Sam with admiration, "I seen the films, y'know. All flat where you live, innit?"

Bethany and Ellen wasted some energy in trying to convince Sam that Austin, even if it was in Texas, was neither flat nor periodically menaced by hordes of Comanche Indians. He merely smiled provokingly and waved one hand at the steep rise of the road past Greenholt Manor. "Nice up top, on Hackthorn Down," he said. "See almost to Bridport on a clear day, can't you? Want a ride up there come Sunday? New road—th'one they put in after the War—goes round about Horn Hill. Can't take a car up the straight way, can you then?" His voice lowered on the last words, suggesting dark old secrets, and Bethany took the lure.

"Why ever not? The track doesn't look that bad."

"Have to go through Ladyswood, don't you? Or where it used to be. Nobbut young trees there now, but they do say . . ."

Ladyswood. Ellen heard the word echoing and repeating on and on, endlessly, like circles spreading from a pebble dropped into a black and infinite pool. Ladyswood—swood—wood—

Dizzy, she leaned against the door while Sam tantalized Bethany with dark hints and almost-ghost stories of horses spooked, farmers unable to keep fences up, and car engines dying on the long steep haul up to the Downs. The only strange thing about Sam's tales was the timing. Most ghost stories, like that of John Daniel, were safely set in the distant past. By contrast, Sam claimed the mysterious occurrences around Ladyswood had grown much more frequent in recent years. In his great-grandfather's time there'd been a good earth road for wagons going up to the high Downs from Greenholt; his grandfather, though, had preferred to take the long way round. In his father's day there'd been an attempt to use the steep track as part of the route for sports car rallies, but the car engines always gave out somewhere between Greenholt and the Downs, and the disgusted drivers had to hire farm horses to pull their vehicles over the top.

The path was visible from the steps of Greenholt. "It doesn't look all *that* steep," said Bethany, glancing doubtfully up the shadowy green tunnel.

"Hadn't ought to be too much for a car," Sam agreed, "but it was. And it's worse now. Horses won't go up there now either. Nor people."

"And I thought you English were all such great walkers," Bethany teased. "*I* could walk up to the Downs from here. I think I'll go up now and watch the sunset."

"Here, now, don't you go up there by night," Sam said. He sounded genuinely alarmed. After a few minutes' teasing conversation Bethany agreed that maybe it wouldn't be a good idea to go climbing up an unused hill track, in the dark, her first night in England. She would wait until morning.

"You'll wait till I can take you up," Sam said sternly before he drove back down the hill to his home in Emminster.

"Ladyswood," Ellen murmured. The green shadows seemed to be whispering, calling to her.

"You're half asleep," Bethany told her. "I was only teasing Sam. We can explore in the morning. I don't really want to scramble up in the dark; we wouldn't be able to see anything, and if sheep use that track I do want to see where I'm stepping."

"Nettles," said Ellen, and then, "I don't want to explore. I was just thinking. . . ."

"What?"

"*Nothing.* I don't know." But she shivered in the imagined dark, almost feeling the shadows of the trees closing in around her; almost as though she stood there now—no, not now; in some other time. As some other person.

10

he country folk do call this place the Ladyswood," Arundel told Eleanor when they had walked up the steep hill.

She shivered in the gloom of the dark entangling branches. "By my faith, 'twas a strange place to consecrate to Our Lady!"

"There is a spring somewhere," he said. Eleanor could hear the quiet gurgle of water flowing over stones, somewhere behind the green banks of hawthorn and the clusters of nettles that lined the path through the wood. "The simple folk of times past would think every spring a holy well blessed by some saint or other; and since the church of Emminster is dedicated to Mary, they must take her blue cloak for mantle over this wood as well. So my father did explain it, when he did warn me not to put axe to these trees."

They were at the top of the hill now; were it not for the tree trunks clustering together so thick, Eleanor thought, they would be able to see Emminster town from here. "A clearance would make pasture for sheep, and provide a goodly view of the town and the hills," she said, too loudly for such a quiet place. A small breeze ruffled the new leaves of the nearest oak; Eleanor fell silent, and in the pause they both could hear the musical trickle of water falling downhill over rounded stones.

"And 'twould dispel any suspicion the Queen might hold, that I do secretly keep to the Old Religion," Arundel agreed.

"She is more like to charge you with black wizardry and heresy than with being overzealous in any religion," Eleanor told him. The breeze was stronger now, tugging at her hair and flipping up the hem of her gown. She felt something wild and free in the air, something that made her want to tease this serious young man.

"That may change," Arundel said, and then, as though he were continuing the same subject, "Giles Cavendish is departed."

"That was sudden."

"You are not grieved? He was to lesson you in philosophy and astronomy."

"That was your plan, and none of Mr. Cavendish's," Eleanor told him. "He was not well pleased. I think he believed no woman could understand his high reasoning."

"You would have shown him differently."

"Would I? I do not know." Eleanor broke off a twig from the hedge beside her. She twirled the leafy twig and a thorn unsuspected bit her thumb. "Oh!" A drop of blood welled out. She put her thumb to her mouth and sucked the blood away. "No one believes that I can learn aught, save you," she said. "No one else—" She bit her own thumb. It would be all too easy to reproach Arundel, who had casually

promised to teach her Latin and philosophy, then
as casually handed her over to his guest for tutoring
while he sat up carousing with his friend Raleigh.

"Think you I had forgotten?"

It was her very thought.

"I must needs spend some hours with Sir Walter,
while he bides here," Arundel explained.

"You owe me no explanations."

Arundel scowled at the innocent branches
surrounding them. "All our plans for the masque
may be destroyed by that popinjay of court. He
hath persuaded himself the Queen may make
progress into the West Country this summer;
and his own estate of Sherborne is full of the
plague. Hence would he impose not only himself
and Bess and his gentlemen upon me; he would
make Greenholt a lodging for the Queen, and
our masque is to become a shew of Raleigh his
offense against the Queen and his plea for her
mercy."

He had said, "our plans," and "our masque."

"Can the masque not be more than one thing?"
Eleanor ventured.

"It is not as I would have had it."

"He hath added songs," she conceded. "But consider
this. When we join words and music, what do we
make?"

"We make a song," said Arundel moodily, "and
what are you making now? Riddles for children?"

"And the song is more than either words or music
alone?"

"Aye."

"Even so may we join Sir Walter's ends and our
own. He will sue an earthly Queen for favor, we a

heavenly and incorporeal one. He hopes to win back his place at the court in White Hall; we hope to gain the aid of a higher Court. He wishes for worldly wealth; we for that which is beyond all wealth—that understanding of the universe entire in memory which, once granted, will allow us to see the true unity now hidden behind its multiple appearances."

"You mean that the little masque I wrote, and the great one which Sir Walter would make of it, with all its choruses of Nymphs and Hounds added to the original, are but two appearances of the same thing?"

"If these two cannot be One," Eleanor argued, "then what is our work? This court-dance of favor and lack of favor is but another part of the great dance of the stars. All Edward's words, all your music, are there as before; there are but some few more voices joined to ours. The essentials remain unchanged."

"I would I could know that are these essentials! What magic can be worked by a troup of giggling girls pretending to be Diana her nymphs?"

"The same as before," Eleanor insisted. "Look you, Kit Arundel: either you can or you cannot compose Music which shall allow you to carry the divine organization of the universe within your mind. If you cannot do this, then is our endeavour failed in any case."

Arundel was staring oddly at her. She faltered and heard her own voice as Edward would have heard it: strident, argumentative, unmaidenly. "At least—so I do believe," she ended weakly.

"You have learned somewhat from Giles Cavendish," Arundel said after a long silence.

"And would I might learn more."

Arundel made a dismissing motion with his hand. "Cavendish is better away, and you are better knowing naught of it."

"Aye, so do men always say," Eleanor said. This time she could not keep the bitterness from her voice.

"If Cavendish comes safe away out of the country," Arundel said, and then stopped for so long that Eleanor grew impatient.

"What then?"

He started as one roused from a dream. "Why, then—I shall speak to Edward, an it pleases you."

"You do speak with him each day."

"Not," said Arundel gravely, "to beg the hand of his lady sister to wife."

Eleanor drew in her breath.

"Is it so sad a fate?" Arundel urged. "All maids must come to it."

"I had not thought of it," Eleanor said with perfect truth. In the days past Edward had been too wrapped up in the masque to repeat his mad notion that she should charm Arundel into marrying her. Now she looked at him as if for the first time and saw neither the devil-raiser of her early fears nor the grave tutor she had tried to make him, but simply a man. Better favored than most men, not so very much older than she was, and with a quick mind and sympathetic intelligence that struck her own to fire.

A man she could live with. A man who would not shut her up when she argued with him—at least, not very often. A man who offered her access to the books she craved and the learning that would enable her to read those books.

A man whose rank and fortune were so far beyond hers that she had laughed outright when Edward first conceived his plan.

"Why," Eleanor said in honest bewilderment, "would an Arundel of Greenholt want to marry *me*?"

"For the same reason you would consent to wed with me," Arundel said. "Where else will you find a man with a mind to match your own?"

For a moment Eleanor could not answer, and in that moment she saw a trace of uncertainty on Arundel's face.

"Do you have any *idea*," he added, "how many times I've tried to explain the secret of the maze to Edward? The man has no understanding of numbers."

"You're not proposing to wed Edward."

"Exactly. Well?"

She could not have answered, save that he appeared uncertain of her answer.

"You may speak to Edward with my good will," she said at last, looking at the leaves behind his head and not at him.

"You did call me Kit once," said Arundel. "I would you might do so again."

"I did? When?"

"Even now. We were arguing about the masque," he added.

Eleanor laughed. "Then let us return to arguing, and perhaps I may grow bold again."

"I had rather make music than discord with you," said Arundel. "And we did come here to practice the duet. Could there be a better way to celebrate our accord?"

"Why, no," Eleanor agreed. Her whole body felt like a song; she was floating on a bubble of happiness.

There would be books in her future, and good learning
and better disputation; all the doors that Edward
had told her were forever closed to her, opening
now. How could she not love Arundel, who was giving
her this New World of the New Learning?

> *A day, a night, an hour of sweet content*
> *Is worth a world consum'd in fretful care,*

Arundel began. "Fretful care," Eleanor echoed, and
it seemed to her that the shadows of the wood were
something dark and thick for the hour. Was it not
still broad daylight outside this wood?

They went on, their two voices mingling exactly
as Arundel had said they should:

> *Unequal Gods, in your Arbitrement*
> *To sort us days whose sorrows endless*
>   *are!*
> *And yet what were it? as a fading flower;*
> *To swim in bliss a day, a night, an hour.*

An hour, a night, a life of sweet content, Eleanor
thought. But the movement of the wood disturbed
her. The breeze seemed to give life to the trees
that rustled around them; the rippling sound of the
hidden stream was a quiet counterpoint to Arundel's
music.

"A day, a night, an hour," she repeated with him.
There was a troubling of the air about them now; a
shining as if the daemons of trees and streams did
prepare to make themselves visible. Arundel turned
towards her with desire plain upon his face, and
something in that impersonal desire frightened her.
The air seemed to coil about them with immanent
life, and she felt very cold. She thought of those

demons that take the form of misty sprites, to confuse travelers that they may fall into a river or ditch.

"Sing," whispered the winds about her head.

"Music," chorused the running stream.

"Be one with us," rustled the leaves of the great oaks. But the song was over.

"Arundel—Kit," Eleanor corrected herself, "let us leave this place." Jane would be shocked to hear her speak so to him; Jane, who after ten years of marriage still called her husband "Mr. Guilford." But we shall not be like Jane and Edward, Eleanor promised herself, and felt the shock of incredulous joy again.

"Art tired?"

Eleanor shook her head. "Uneasy. I think there is something here that likes not good Christian men and women." And she fell into that category. She wondered about Arundel . . . *Kit*. No. He was as good a Christian as she herself; had she not dwelt at Greenholt long enough to see the truth behind those stories of devil-worship? A philosopher, a mathematician, a man who amused himself by tripping up the parson in theology and making mechanical devices to amaze his neighbors—Kit Arundel was all those things, but nothing worse. Eleanor told herself that she might not approve of all his activities, but there was nothing to fear in them.

And as they left the wood behind for the sunny slopes around Greenholt, she felt no more fear; only sunshine, warmth, and elation at the promise of the new world Kit was opening unto her. She stole a glance at him, slender and dark and dressed as richly as Sir Walter. "And he's none so ill-favored, either," she thought. "I shall be well content to have such a one to husband." Perhaps, she thought, a little too well content. She had been wise to insist on leaving the wood; for the first time Jane's warnings about walking alone with importunate young gentlemen seemed to make sense.

Kit had not importuned her. But her sense of danger had been true. I will not go again into the Ladyswood, thought Eleanor. It loves me not—and I do love it not.

And in the sunshine where they walked, turning aside into the maze-garden, there came presently a little shadow: the news that Sir Walter had departed in haste, after some quarrel with Parson Hensley, and saying he meant to ride south to Chideock. Kit paled at that news, and began to give orders to ride after him, then stopped, saying, "It is better he should not have his suspicions confirmed by my actions. And there has been time enough; he should . . . he must be safely away by now."

"What do you mean?" Eleanor demanded.

Kit's smile was forced. "Nought to trouble you, sweeting. Edward, I would have a word alone with you, if I may."

Friday, June 3, 1994

The dream left its usual grey filaments winding through Ellen's head, and here there was no blaze of Texas sun to burn away the fog. Morning brought only rain, pattering against the casements; a cold dull grey wind whispering in through warped frames and ruined roof; no chorus of masquers to sing Hounds and Nymphs to Ellen's Diana and Paien's Actaeon; for that matter, no Paien.

Ellen unpacked her notebook computer, made a

mental note to ask Sam where she could recharge
the batteries, and spent a desultory half hour running
routine tests on the temporo-spatial module. All
the yellow and green webs of data and reasoning
looked perfectly normal to her; she couldn't see what
the other teams were complaining about. Unless—

There'd been that extremely strange-looking version
of the model she'd created one Saturday at GIC.
Delete one basic assertion about the sequential nature
of time, and the whole module changed into an infinite
loop of interlocking webs that shifted in and out,
over and back . . . *No*. She *couldn't* have left that
in the system. Everything else would have failed
immediately. It was probably still sitting on the disk
as a scratch file, but it wasn't active in KNEE. It
couldn't be.

And until she found a way to recharge batteries,
she'd better not run them down while she stared
into space and invented imaginary problems she
couldn't do anything about anyway. Ellen shut off
the computer and went downstairs to find distraction.

Bethany's lute was out of tune in the damp and
the rain; she lounged on the straw-colored ruins of
what had once been an elegant gold-brocaded chaise
longue, fiddling with the lute and singing fragments
of old songs. The lights flickered on and off, on
and off. "I can't *stand* this," said Ellen on a rush of
angry breath. She rummaged in the ancient kitchen,
in cupboards filled with dirty rags and rusted tools
and burnt-out saucepans. A cupboard door stuck;
when she tugged it free, hundreds of old wine corks
burst light as rain over her head and pattered all
over the floor.

"Old Squoir wor a three-bottle-a-day mun, innit?"

grunted Bethany in an atrocious attempt to imitate Sam's country accent.

"I don't believe that story about the previous owner just dying recently. Nobody's lived here for *years*," Ellen said, "nobody *could* live in this. No Squire, no maiden aunts, no tenants pulling their forelocks."

"Well, somebody's been here," Bethany pointed out, "and whoever he was, he liked canned fish and he saved wine corks."

"*And* he had the same trouble we have with the electricity," said Ellen, triumphantly displaying a handful of dripped and smoky candle-ends. There were a dozen short squat ones no longer than her thumb and two fine tapers burnt only halfway down.

With the short candle-ends stuck onto cracked saucers and the two tapers burning lonely in a brass candelabrum that extruded from the sitting-room wall, the old room took on a gentle glow that tempered the gloomy day.

"*For the rain it raineth every day,*" Bethany sang to an untuned lute.

"Fire and fleet and candle-light," Ellen quoted absently, "and Christ receive thy saule." She lay on her stomach, ringed by fire like Brunhilde, peering myopically at the mouldering books of local history she'd unearthed in a dusty bookshelf. "Listen to this, Bethany—it's about John Daniel, you know, the ghost in the church?"

But the account in *Dorset Oddities* said little more than the old woman in the church had told them, and with less conviction. Ellen flipped over the pages, scowling at fly-specked paper and wavering type. "There was a Roman fort here once," she told Bethany.

"What, under Greenholt?"

"No—up on the edge of the Downs." Ellen sat up, cross-legged. "Where Sam didn't want us to go . . . It wasn't here long; there's something in Cassius Dio about it. This guy translates the passage. No, he doesn't, blast him, he only summarizes it; says the legion posted here had bad luck, the tribune went mad, and the surgeon drank too much—"

"The source of all those wine corks?" Bethany suggested.

"—and the men complained of ghosts."

"And their cars wouldn't start!"

"No doubt. Do you suppose all the English are like this, or are the people in Emminster just specially superstitious? Everyone we talk to is full of ghost stories and dire warnings. Even the *books* are like that!" Ellen thumped the offending volume with her fist and then sneezed violently as a cloud of dust and decaying paper particles surrounded her.

"They probably put it on to amuse the Yank tourists," suggested Bethany.

"Books too?"

"The English," Bethany said solemnly, "take a very *long* view. They've got history, you know. Not like us Johnny-come-lately Colonials."

Ellen grinned. "Too bad we can't stay to celebrate the Fourth of July."

"Maybe we can. Nobody's said how long we can camp out here, have they?"

"Nobody's said much of anything," Ellen agreed. "Bethany, there's something very odd about this setup, don't you think? If they're going to put on a masque, and if they care as much as Paien claims about authenticity, you'd think we'd be up to here in rehearsals. Only two weeks to go now! Are the English this casual about everything they do? If we hadn't won those airline tickets, I'd think—I'd think—well, I don't know what I'd think," Ellen concluded in defeat.

"But we did get the tickets," Bethany pointed out. "They worked. I mean, they're not—"

"Not fairy gold, that turns into leaves the next morning?"

"Not forgeries, I was going to say. Somebody paid real money for those tickets. And charmed as Paien is with you, you don't seriously think he'd spend that kind of money just to bring you and your roommate over to the Old Country for a vacation, do you?"

"Me! It's you he's interested in," Ellen said.

Bethany grinned. "Not for want of trying. Don't blame me; he's too beautiful to be true. But you're the one he looks at. I'll have to console myself with Sam. If he ever turns up again," she added, drooping slightly as she looked at the rain-streaked windowpanes. "A day like this makes you feel that nothing interesting is ever going to happen again— Oh, *listen* to me," she broke off in disgust, "a trip to England dropping in my lap like this, and here I am looking out the window and waiting for some man to make things happen. Let's explore the house."

Carrying dripping candle stubs on saucers, they investigated shrouded rooms with water-stained ceilings, dank nether regions where beetles scurried away from them, a winding narrow stair that twisted round and round until they emerged breathless onto the rainwet roof. The rain was no more than a fine drizzle misting their faces now, but the roof sagged and creaked and looked as though, given half an excuse, it would drop its remaining shingles into the garden.

"We can't walk on this," said Bethany, "let's go down."

Ellen lingered a moment, looking at the soft grey sky. It glowed with diffused light beyond the trees that grew dark and clustering all around Greenholt. The hill track was a ribbon of watery reflections twisting upwards until it disappeared in the shadow of the trees. Somewhere beyond the woods, a bird cried, and a cool damp breeze came from the clouds to brush across her face. From the top of the hill, Sam said, you could look out along the rolling downs to the north; or you could look south at the hills between Emminster and the sea.

"Come *on*," Bethany called, "I've found something!"

What she'd found was a long windowless hallway where her candle illumined a face on the wall, flickering light and dark oils combining to give an illusion of movement in the shadows. Ellen ran lightly down the stairs and stopped in front of the portrait. The face of a young man looked back at her, dark eyes dancing in the candlelight, the head seeming to float at some distance from the dark painted trunk.

Ellen let out a long shaky breath and tried to laugh at herself. "Isn't the light strange? For a moment I thought—it looked as though his head wasn't attached to his body."

"Maybe he was beheaded," Bethany suggested with macabre cheer.

Ellen shook her head. "No. It's a white ruff, see?"

"Elizabethan. Who d'you suppose he was?" Bethany brought her candle down to the lower edge of the gilt picture frame, looking for a name or a label, while Ellen looked into the face she remembered from dreams and nightmares and the Renaissance

Faire. Some memory older than any of these stirred in the back of her mind; she could almost put a name to the young man who stood before her, one hand on the hilt of his short sword, looking arrogantly across the centuries as though he had waited only for her to find him on this dark wet summer day.

"Christopher Arundel!" Bethany crowed in triumph. "Do you suppose this is the Wicked Earl himself?"

"Not an earl," Ellen said. She stepped down the last step to the landing. Kit Arundel's head was above her now, still looking out into the dark above the stairs, challenging eyes and smiling mouth and strong hands all caught and held for eternity in this empty place. "Not an earl," she repeated, "this was only a cadet branch of the family."

"You cheat," Bethany accused, "you've been reading up on Greenholt in those old books, and you never told me any of the good stuff, only about Roman forts and all that! Well, it's my turn now!" She darted ahead of Ellen, pushed open a door; cold daylight and a draft of damp air came through. Ellen's candle went out in the draft, and the dark oil painting of a man who'd been young four hundred years ago faded back into the general gloom. By the time she reached the sitting-room, Bethany had taken possession of *Dorset Oddities* and was flipping through the index.

"Affpuddle, Aggleston— I don't *believe* these names," she interjected, "Anglican customs, wonder what those are? Aragon, Catherine of, what's she got to do with Dorset? Arundel, Christopher. *Here* we are, page 326, listen to this!"

"Kit," Ellen said under her breath as Bethany read aloud, "Kit?"

"Greenholt Manor, near Emminster, was built by

Thomas Arundel and much improved by his son Christopher, whose mysterious disappearance is still a lively element of local tales. Christopher Arundel was among the daring souls of the later Elizabethan period who mixed demonology with philosophy, magic with mathematics. The historical record shows that in June of 1594 a warrant was issued for his arrest on charges of atheistical speech, but according to the tales still prevalent in Emminster, the real reason for the warrant was that Arundel had dabbled in witchcraft and held daily converse with demons. In any case, the warrant was never served; on the night when Sir Walter Raleigh, then Sheriff of the West Country, arrived at Greenholt, Christopher Arundel was performing a masque written by himself with the express purpose of raising the Devil. He staged a daring escape in the middle of the masque, apparently vanishing before dozens of onlookers. In a tragic epilogue to the story, Arundel's betrothed, Eleanor Guilford, went mad and persistently searched the woods above Greenholt for her lover. As a result of her barefoot nocturnal ramblings, she caught a chill and died not long after Arundel's disappearance.

"And what became of Arundel himself? He was never seen in England again. Popular opinion held that he had been spirited away by the Devil his master. Whether this was the case, or whether Arundel made his escape through some secret passage or priest-hole in the walls of Greenholt, cannot be resolved at this late date; but the curious visitor to Emminster may ramble through the dark woods surrounding Greenholt Manor, may listen to the shrieks of the black ravens inhabiting those woods and the howling of the wind through the trees, and may draw his own conclusions as to the life and ultimate fate of the ill-fated 'Wicked Kit.'"

Bethany clapped the book shut. "Well! Just like the old lady said—he raised devils, and they carried him off. Want to look for the secret passage, Ellen? Ellen! Where are you going?"

Ellen felt darkness filling her throat, choking her. She wanted to escape this damp close place and breathe the clean air outdoors. She walked slowly and carefully into the hall and pulled the heavy front door open. The drizzling rain had stopped, and pale sunlight shone through the tiny droplets of mist, reflecting off each one and diffusing the light so that it seemed to have no source, no ending, and no shadow.

"Out," she said. "I need air."

The green tunnel was still calling, waiting for her, and there was as much light as she could hope for this day. Ellen climbed as fast as she could, paying little attention to anything except the mud and slippery stones under her feet, until the path sloped so steeply upwards that she had to pause for a moment to catch her breath. She glanced back down at Greenholt. Sam's van was just pulling into the yard. Good; he would distract Bethany. Ellen wanted to be alone for a while. She was so angry that she could hardly breathe, and she didn't know why she should be so hurt by an old story in a book. "It's all a pack of lies," she said to herself. "Pack of lies! Pack of lies!"

Her voice raised on each statement; she plunged forward into the woods. A flock of birds rose shrieking from the hedge on the far side of the path; Ellen put her hands up to protect her eyes, and when the birds wheeled away, Paien was standing in front of her.

"And where have *you* been?" she snapped. "For that matter, where did you come from just now? I didn't hear you."

"You were making a fair noise yourself," Paien pointed out, "you and the birds between you. What's amiss?"

"Oh, nothing. Nothing at all. I just love being shipped across the world to walk in the rain and sing in a masque that . . ." Ellen shook her head. She was confused. Paien had done her no wrong and many great favors. She looked at his fingers, twining and flickering in the grey light, and almost forgot her distress.

When she looked away again, it struck her like a blow. Wicked Kit Arundel . . . *He raised devils, you know, and they carried him away in the end.* "It's wrong, all wrong, don't you see?" Ellen cried into the rising wind.

Paien looked down, ruefully, at the pattern of light twined into a net between his fingers. "It does not work," he said, "I can certainly see that. You are too strong-minded for a woman, Ellen—Eleanor."

She could not bear that he should call her by that name; it hurt worse than anything else. "Oh, just leave me alone!" she said, and started up the steep path again, knowing she was being rude and childish. Paien followed her.

"Something's amiss," he said reasonably, "or you'd not be trudging through mud in the rain. Come back down to Greenholt and have a cup of tea and tell me about it."

"I don't want tea. I want to go for a walk."

"In this?" Paien pointed skywards. Ellen looked through interlacing branches, a mosaic of dull green leaves against the duller grey of the gathering clouds.

"It's stopped raining." She trudged forward, welcoming the strain of pushing herself up the hill.

"Only for a moment. A great storm is gathering; you shall see." But Paien fell into step beside her.

"Where *have* you been?" Ellen challenged him.

"Here and there . . . Does it matter?"

"Maybe not. Is there really going to be a masque?"

"Great pains have been taken to bring you here," Paien answered obliquely, in his fashion.

In silence they climbed on up the steep muddy path, stepping from one patch of pebbles to another over the trickling water. The hedges grew up green and impenetrable on either side, and trees arched low overhead to complete the green tunnel. Ellen found her breath coming faster, and not only because of the climb: she felt—just the reverse of Bethany's plaint—as though something troubling and irreversible were about to happen, some wonderful secret unfolding that would change who she was forever.

The closed-in secretiveness of the wood gathered her in, all overhanging trees and muddy stones and green growing leaves on every side; somewhere, always, the small quiet music of running water; and no way at all to see where she was. She felt as though she might emerge from this enclosed wilderness into some place completely different from the tidy England of motorways and row houses and shops that she had left behind in the valley: some place still wild with magic, where fairy rings were more than circles of weeds, where the dance of the stars in the sky wrote messages for men to read.

Paien's golden head was slick with rain; how long had he been wandering the muddy lanes? And why? Ellen started to ask, then retreated again into the silence that was gradually easing her anger.

From time to time the hedges parted and Ellen could glimpse a wall of golden stone, head-high, flint-topped. In other places it seemed there was no wall, only the trees and bushes interlaced closely enough to make a living barrier. Some of the plants in the hedgerow had thorns, and others showed the bright toothed leaves of stinging nettles; she decided to restrain her curiosity about what lay on the far side of the hedge. Anyway, the path was leveling now, and when she looked up she saw clouds and sky, not earth and rocks and the trunks of trees. In a few more steps they should be coming out onto the viewing spot Sam had mentioned, and then she'd be able to see clearly all that was now hidden.

Between one step and the next, when only a thin screen of trees still lay between her eyes and the sweep of open space and sky, the fine damp mist thickened all about them until Ellen lost all sense of where she was. She passed what she'd thought were the last trees, and the ground was sloping away gently beneath her feet, and from the feel of it she stood on soft turf rather than stones and mud. She must be standing right on the spot the map called Hackthorn Down, with the open sweep of hill and field and valley falling away before her. But the mist was thick and close, and without quite seeing them, Ellen had a sense of ancient trees clustering close about her, an entangling net that reached from stone to earth to empty sky, root, branch, and green growing leaves. She felt the trees like living presences, a wood much older and darker than the green tunnel she'd climbed through to reach this place.

"Why do you stop?" Paien's voice said softly in her ear, too close; why hadn't she felt the warmth of him behind her? But she was cold with damp and—something else; she knew not what.

"I can't *see*," she said, and her own voice sounded thin and whiny in her ears. "It's gone dark."

"No darker than the dawn," said Paien, and his even voice soothed her unspoken, unnamed fears. "We have light enough, an you know the way."

It seemed to Ellen that her feet moved of themselves, taking a turn away from the path they had been following. Branches bent aside to let her pass, a flowering thorn swung low over a crumbling opening in the golden wall. Paien followed close beside her, so close that when they came upon the others Ellen could not step back out of sight.

They were standing by twos and threes upon the misty grass, slender elegant figures that she could not quite see directly. Around them, like silent guardians, grew the ancient trees Ellen had sensed before. There was an aching in her throat; in another minute she would wilt under the bright incurious glances that had trapped her in front of Paien, disgrace herself and him by breaking into tears. She had to get out, but he was blocking the way.

"Let's go back." Ellen stepped back against Paien but he did not move. The flowering thorny branches on either side of them seemed to bend inwards, tangling themselves in her hair and sleeves.

"Why?" His hands were on her shoulders, holding her without effort to face the crowd—or was it a crowd? Ellen could not count them. The mist eddied and swirled; for a moment she thought she saw nothing but trees, then she heard laughter and the tinkling of music.

"We're—intruding—on a private party."

"Why, lady, these are my friends," Paien said calmly, still holding her, "and you are long awaited in this company. See you no welcome face?"

The mist formed into innocent shapes: trees and golden stones crumbling in the mist, and a bird's whistle high overhead.

Ellen blinked and looked again, and saw as she had seen at first: graceful figures that seemed to burn with their own light, haloed by golden fog. And among those bright alien glances, there was one face that was dark and human and as familiar as her own: the man who came out of nightmares and music and weeping to take away her sanity.

It was the face of the portrait. Wicked Kit Arundel.

If this was a nightmare, Ellen was not sure she wanted to wake up. She wanted to run to him and throw her arms around him. The call was stronger than the pull of the earth on her feet, sweeter than the bird song and trickling water that had been her music all the way up the hill.

And he stared through her as if she were no more than a thickening of the mist. Ellen's throat ached with a grief heavier than she had ever known, an unbearable loss of what she had surely never had. Tears came unbidden to her eyes. She was going mad indeed. She had dreamed herself in love, and had given the face of a man dead four hundred years to the dream she made, and had so confused herself that she would quarrel with Bethany over lies about a dead man, and embarrass a stranger with longing he'd surely never asked for. She twisted free of Paien's light grip and ran blindly, desperate to get free of the mist and the trees, pushing bare-handed through thorns and nettles.

When she finally stopped, Ellen's hand burned as though she'd raked it across a branch of brambles. Somewhere approximately six inches from her left ear, a sheep bawled. Sunlight lanced through the mist; two steps more, and she was out on the clean bare top of Hackthorn Down. There were picnic tables dotting the grass, a busload of tourists reading a map and pointing out landmarks. And there was no ancient grove of towering trees behind her; nothing but the green tunnel and the muddy path she'd walked up to come to this spot. All else had been imagination, or a dream.

Paien was beside her. "What frightened you, Ellen?"

Ellen was too shaken to ask him what he'd seen in the mist. It was all imagination, all her crazy dreaming. It had to be. She couldn't believe it, not now in the plain light of the sun. Paien couldn't have led her into some place that never was, wouldn't have tried to hold her there against her will. She must be going crazy again.

"Nothing," she said shortly, and walked forward to the edge where the smooth grass fell away in a steep sloping curve. From this brink of the high downs she could look out across rolling hills chopped up into fields with neat hedges, old grey stone cottages, occasional trees, down to the cluster of houses and church that was Emminster; then up again, to the hills that rimmed the valley, one shade lighter in the gold-tinged mist, and a sky like smoke.

"You saw someone you knew."

The sun and clouds made a dancing pattern of light and shadow over the distant hills, a flickering light that shifted and changed so that the shapes of things were never quite what they seemed to be. But the iron slab of a map that stood to help tourists find their landmarks told her where all the fixed features of the landscape should be. No matter how confusing things appeared from here, the hills did not move. Emminster was still in the valley below them; and beyond the further hills there was Bridport, and the sea.

Beside her, Paien stirred as if he were about to say something. "Look," she said without turning, "I don't want to talk about it, okay? Just let me enjoy the view for a few minutes."

"What is there to look at?"

"Don't you see *anything* around you? The hills, the sky, the sea."

"You cannot see the ocean from here."

"That's all right. I know it's there." And this childish bickering was infinitely better than—whatever had been in the wood; a memory already blurring, overlaid by the comforting everyday ordinariness of grass and sun and hills.

And not so ordinary, at that, Ellen thought as she stared out over the valley below. Norman knights would have ridden over these hills once. And before them, there had been the ill-fated Roman fort on this very spot. What had happened there, that was so bad the fort was deserted and the very stones taken away from the walls? There was no trace of the Roman presence; only a few words of Latin in somebody's history, and the sense of ghosts and many layers of time laid down over the enduring hills.

And before the Romans, Ellen thought, had there been little blue-painted men who hunted with flint arrows, who worried about wolves hiding in the folds of the hills?

The sense of time passing and time present, all those centuries laid down gently as a cloak over the hills, comforted and calmed her. She tried to tell Paien something of what she felt when she looked over this view, but he seemed not to understand her.

"For one bound by Time, you are strangely enamoured of it."

"I suppose you *aren't*—" Ellen began, and then stopped, reluctant to go on. Paien complained of the stars that they did not move, of feathers and flowers that they would decay. He appeared and disappeared without warning, he could make headaches go away, he would not drive a car. She did not want to think about this logically. An impossible understanding was pressing on her, and she could no longer blur over the memory of the strange faces in the misty wood.

"I don't want to talk about it," she said again, and Paien sighed.

"You have come far to run away at the last." His voice was soft as the blue haze over the distant hills, inevitable as the sea that lay beyond those hills. Here atop the great sweep of the Downs, the double vision that had plagued Ellen for weeks was very nearly cured; there was only a faint shimmering around the cluster of houses in the valley below, a disturbance like heat waves over the thin grey lines of paved roads. All else, grass and sky and clouds and the sea just out of sight, was as it had ever been.

"I suppose Bethany told you everything?"

"Enough," Paien acknowledged.

"Well, I'm not running away. I'm singing again, okay? Isn't that enough?"

"*Is* it?"

Ellen drew breath to say something sensible that would close off the subject forever. The words would not come.

A bird called from the trees below them; a cloud covered the sun; the smooth grassy hill where she stood dipped and swirled like a breaking wave. Ellen's knees trembled.

"You have come so far," Paien repeated. "Why fear to take the last step?"

If she stepped forward, if she moved at all, she would fall into clouds and sky and the reflection of the blue shifting sea. The world tilted around her like a humming top.

"I—don't know—" Her voice was low and halting. Words were heavy as stones, too heavy to lift and offer to anyone.

"Know now what you have always known," Paien said. "Sing for us."

The mist closed in between one breath and the next; the golden slender figures were somewhere in that hazy light, waiting, waiting. "Remember," Paien's voice supported her, "remember now . . ." The words hummed like half-voiced music. "Descend, descend . . ." Now he was singing indeed, and Ellen joined him, leaning on the music as if it were a wave to buoy her up, letting the melody carry her where it would.

Descend,
Descend,
Though Pleasure lead,
Fear not to follow.

The ancient trees were thick and close about her now, and forms moved in the mist that obscured vision; trees dancing, men and women growing from the ground and crowned with leaves and flowers. The logic of dreams turned leaves to fingers and faces to flowers, turned wood to grassy downs and back to forest, sent burning leaves swirling from a green tree in flower. Somewhere a lute of moonlight and silver dropped notes as pure as falling water into the song; Paien's light tenor grew stronger, grew to a voice that supported her and carried her forward through the wood.

> They who are bred
> Within the hill
> Of skill
> May safely tread
> What path they will.

All about her was mist and dreams, clouds becoming chasms becoming level ground that fell away wherever she would step. She left the ground and walked upon air, floated into the bare branches of a winter tree. Stars fell about her and became snow.

"The physics of dreams," Ellen murmured under her breath, as a tenor voice took up the song.

"No ground of good . . ."

The black and barren branches of the tree sprouted green leaves; the snow beneath them melted and became a trickling spring.

"No ground of good . . ." Ellen carried the melody higher, flying on pure sound and song. The running water disappeared between rocks; the trees were all gone now, but she had Paien's hand to hold to, and dry leaves crackled beneath her feet. There was nothing solid under the leaves; the hill was hollow and the water had disappeared; she walked forward through darkness and empty space, following the sound of running water.

"No ground of good is hollow," they sang together, and Ellen stubbed her toe on a rock and the grey sky of a rainy English summer lit the steep muddy path down towards Greenholt. Paien was nowhere to be seen; a stranger held her hand, a dark man in ruff and doublet and jeweled cape, a man out of dreams and imaginations.

"Christopher Arundel," she named the face she'd seen in a painting, in a dream, in the mists of a wood that never grew beneath an earthly sun.

"The same," agreed the man before her.

Ellen felt time shift and stop around her, solid and impenetrable as the wet stones that ground together beneath her feet. This was Kit Arundel, who had been carried away by demons four hundred years ago; and she knew him; and she was—

No. She rejected the alien memories that came thrusting forward out of the shadows in her mind. She did not, could not know this stranger. He resembled a portrait she'd just been looking at, that was all, a picture, a painted canvas.

Painted canvas, and a branching wood. Why did that image carry such pain that her throat ached with unshed tears?

Clouds shifted above them, growling like black dogs. Rain spattered her cheek; not the gentle perpetual drizzling mist of England, but an honest storm that could have come straight out of Texas. A jagged line of pure, pink light seared through the clouds; its noise broke around them, and the man whose hand she held threw back his head and shouted his joy at the rumbling clouds.

"Marry, it rains! No false fogs here, but true falling water!"

"I *know* it rains," Ellen said half under her breath, "your mouth is going to be full of water if you don't close it."

"Blessed water, blessed rain, blessed storm," the dark man cried. His face was pure with a kind of holy ecstasy, a madness of devotion. He fell to his knees in the mud and crossed himself, then scrambled up. "Now, sweeting, will you shelter under my roof?"

Ellen stared at him, taking in all the details she'd managed not to think about up to now: starched white ruff wilting in the rain, short dark velvet cape, puffed trunk-hose and tight fine stockings that sagged wrinkled at knees and ankles.

"Who *are* you?" she said in a whisper that was all but lost in the renewed clashing of thunder all around them.

"Why, know you not your own love? Give over fooling, then. Kit Arundel's alive as ever he was, and all shall yet be well. Be the Queen's men still at Greenholt?"

Ellen shook her head. "Only me and Bethany . . ."

"Well enough, then. Shalt tell me later all that's passed, sweet heart mine. Come now!" And he was pulling her down the muddy path as if that were answer enough, and cause enough for laughter and celebration. A wind from nowhere blew rain straight into her eyes and mouth, tugged her long fine hair loose from its careless plait to plaster over her face. She slipped over rounded, rainwet rocks, scrambled splashing through the muddy rivulet that had taken over the center of the path, and began laughing despite herself. The exhilaration of running through the storm took her over. Just down this steep hill was light and shelter; and the warm living hand that tugged her along was proof that however mad she might be, not all that she'd experienced had been hallucination.

"*Here* we are," said a tenor voice, and they dodged into the forecourt of Greenholt Manor, up the three stone steps and in through the carved wooden door. The door slammed shut behind them and Ellen stood panting in the dimness and blessed silence of the gloomy front hall. Rain spattered against the closed door; the wind was high and menacing at the casement panes.

"Never fear, love," the man called Kit Arundel reassured her, "the house is built strong enough to stand a dozen storms like this."

"Not up under the eaves, it wasn't," Ellen said instead of asking any of the questions she'd meant to ask. "Roof leaked something terrible, didn't it then?" That was more or less a direct quotation from Sam.

"It does?" He yanked off his wet gloves and threw them down on the floor. "By this hilt, I'll have that knave of a builder in the stocks on the morrow!" He looked around him at the gloomy dark Victorian wallpaper that hung in peeling strips of cross-hatched flowers from the walls. "What *is* this trash?"

"I don't much like it myself," Ellen agreed, "but why should you—"

He flung open the door to the front parlor. Bethany, lounging on cushions before a meekly flickering fire, looked up; her pink mouth made a round O of surprise.

Sam was standing behind her. "Fixed the lights," Sam said as they entered, waving proudly at the single dim bulb that glowed weakly in the center of the ceiling. "Found the fuse-box and all."

"*My paneling!*" Arundel howled in tones of purest outrage. "The place is ransacked! What mob of vagrants stripped it?"

"Ellen," Bethany said, "you really must stop bringing strange men home."

"That," said Ellen, "is *completely* unfair."

Arundel advanced three paces and bowed with a flourish of his velvet cape. "Allow me to make myself known to your friend. Christopher Arundel, of Greenholt."

"You do look rather like the picture," Bethany said. "Only I thought the Arundels of Greenholt had died out. That's what the book said."

Kit Arundel drew himself up to his full height. "Not while I live," he said, "and I have every hope to get children after me. Do I seem to you so aged?"

"That you don't," Bethany allowed. "And you do look like an Arundel—at least, if the portrait in the hall is anything to go by." She looked past him at Ellen. "All right, all right, I was just teasing you. I must say, it's about time the rehearsals started. Are you going to introduce this one, Ellen? Is he a friend of the ones who showed up yesterday? Spiffy costume, too," she added, looking Arundel up and down, "but you should be more careful about getting it wet. Do you have any idea how long it takes to make these period reproductions?"

"Eleanor," Arundel said in a low voice, "your friend's manner of discourse is passing strange. Can she be in her wits, do you think?"

Ellen shook her head. "*I* don't know," she said. The strain and grief that had come from nowhere to plague her all her life had vanished; now she felt only confused and possessed of a mad whimsical humor. "We're all mad here," she said at last. "More tea?"

"Tea?"

"Nice cuppa do everybody a bit of good," Sam put in. "I'll see what I can do." He backed out of the room by the door to the kitchen stairs, putting his big feet down lightly, never taking his eyes from Kit Arundel.

"Well, are you a singer or a player?" Bethany demanded as Sam left.

"Madame," Kit said indignantly, "I am a *gentleman*."

"I wasn't asking about your morals," Bethany said. "Can you play a lute?"

"I was indifferent well brought up," said Kit. "*Yes*, madame, I can play the lute. I can also play the virginals and the viol, sing part-songs, trim a fetlock, carve a boar, turn a rhyme, wield a sword, dance a pavane or a galliard, and read my book whether in Latin or Greek or the vulgar tongue. Would there be anything else you wished to know?"

"Er—not at the moment," said Bethany. She looked at Ellen and mouthed silently, *Is he crazy or what?*

"I might point out," Arundel went on, "that I am not accustomed to being served such an inquisition in mine own house, nor have I demanded of *you*, madame, what has possessed you and my dear lady here to put on such a heathenish fashion of dress as I never saw before, save only once in a dream."

"Well, *really*." Bethany looked down at her skintight jeans and fingered the purple T-shirt above them.

She looked at Ellen, muddy in somewhat looser jeans and a once-white shirt of Oxford cloth. "What's wrong with the way we look? Everybody dresses this way nowadays."

"Then have the fashions changed remarkably," said Arundel. He stopped, took a deep breath, and looked round him at the peeling paint, the shabby comfortable room with its faded curtains and soft armchairs. The clock on the mantelpiece took his eye for a long time. "Indeed, all is marvelously different, and were it not that I do see mine espoused wife, and had been assured that the Queen did yet reign—" He caught his breath. "But that was in a dream," he said in an undertone, and his eyes darted from side to side, showing white and frantic in the impassive face. "Of your mercy, madame," he said then, "what is the year?"

Bethany slid to her feet in one fluid motion. "You entertain the gentleman, Ellen," she said, "I'll hunt up a lute for him to rehearse with." As she passed Ellen, she whispered, *Shall I call the police?*"

Ellen shook her head vehemently. "I don't know who he is, but I'm not afraid of him. Anyway, Sam's here."

Arundel looked up, wild-eyed, and the blood drained from his face and left it grey as recycled cardboard. Bethany did not see him; she nodded agreement with Ellen and left the room.

"Did you say truly," Arundel demanded as soon as they were alone together, "that you knew me not?"

"You've got a great look of the first Kit Arundel," Ellen said. "What are you—a distant descendant?"

Kit slowly subsided onto a chair that sagged and gave a protesting creak. "Cursed ensorcelment," he murmured, "that betimes I saw my lady and knew her not, that now she sees me and knows not me. When shall I win free?" He looked up at her, all but pleading. "You truly know me not?"

"I remember . . ." Ellen said reluctantly, and then could not finish the half-begun thought. "I have dreamed . . ."

"Dreams and imaginations!" His fist came down on the slender arm of the chair; the wood broke under his hand. "I pray pardon," he said. "What is this newfangled manner of cabinet-work, that will make chairs and tables so slender, and lamps so brilliant to hang in the air?"

The light from the single bulb was dim by comparison with anything but the candle stubs they'd been using. And if the chair wasn't an original eighteenth-century piece, it was an exceedingly good reproduction. The suspicions growing in Ellen's mind would no longer be denied. She thought with despairing humor that if she was right, the world was mad; and if she was wrong, then she and Kit Arundel could be mad together, and there might be worse fates.

"I should probably break this to you gently," she said, "but . . . you asked what year this was?"

Kit looked up. "I did that. Though I believe I can almost guess at it." He gestured at the room that had been new-furnished long ago. "Much has changed here—though not so much, my love," he added with a tenderness that made Ellen catch her breath with half-remembered pain, "not so much that I should have forgotten you, or you me. Mayhap the same ensorcelment that robbed me of some years in the world has robbed you of your memories."

"Maybe." Ellen was proud that she kept her voice steady.

"'Tis often for a space of seven year, in the old tales, that They keep a man or a midwife," Kit mused aloud. "Or else 'tis seven times seven, or seventy and seven—but so much cannot be, or would you not stand here beside me. Seven year, then." He smiled at her; Ellen could have forgotten everything in the momentary brilliance of that smile. But she began to think she had already forgotten far too much.

"It must be," Arundel announced, "the sixteen hundred and first year since the birth of Our Lord."

Ellen sucked in her breath and bit her lip. The steady brightness of Arundel's smile began to dim as he looked up at her; he was a flame going out.

"A little—more than that," she said carefully.

"Do not cozen me with soft speeches. Say now and have done wi't."

"All *right*, then. It's 1994—all right?"

Kit's smile was all extinguished now; his face might have been one of the carved ornaments on the stone gateposts outside, worn down until all expression was rubbed away by the remorseless passage of time and wind and rain.

"Four hundred years," he said, very slowly and carefully. "Four—hundred— Nay, it cannot be. Eleanor, tell me 'tis but a jest! Sweet heart mine, are you wroth with me that I did tarry so long in that other land? Long and long did I pray to return, but never could find the way until your sweet singing did draw me back into this world. Can you be so cruel, to call me back, and then to deny me so? Call your brother, love, and let him tell me straitly all that has passed."

Ellen shook her head. "I—have no brother," she said, almost whispering.

"You've quarreled?"

"What," Ellen said carefully, "is my brother's name?"

"You seek to test me? To what purpose? Edward, of course," Kit replied at once. "Now leave over fooling, do! Your brother is Edward Guilford, and his wife is Jane."

Edward. Jane. Ellen felt her hands shaking. *Edward would pander his own sister for Master Arundel's delight,* said somebody else's voice in her mind. How had this stranger read her dreams, where did he find the names of her nightmares?

"And they bide here with us," Kit went on, "under the roof of my excellent new-made manor house of Greenholt . . . which is . . . somewhat altered since I dwelt here last. . . ." His voice died away and he looked around the room again. "Much altered," he said.

"Four hundred years," Ellen repeated. She was heart-sore for him.

"Why then, is Edward dead—and Sir Walter—and the Privy Council no doubt thinks me dead too, and hath no more desire to question me! Such safety did the Lady promise me; I see she keeps her bargain well." Kit laughed without humor. "Indeed, might I not as well be dead in truth, that have come into a strange land, and all my friends are dead, and mine own promised wife remembers me not?"

Ellen laid one hand atop Kit's restless fingers. She did not, *could* not know him; but he needed her, and she would give him what little truth she knew. "I think I have been waiting for you all my life," she said. "In dreams half remembered you have come to me. Your music lives, and I have sung it in this world. But I cannot bring back your friends, or make myself remember what passed before I was born." Her voice trembled; it seemed so little that she was offering him in comparison with all he had lost. And shadows crowded about her: Edward, Jane, Sir Walter—but when she tried to look directly at those memories, they disappeared like the flickering lights of a dying fire.

"Why then, I'll make you remember me!" Kit said, and all in a moment she was in his arms.

A door creaked somewhere; Ellen found that she did not particularly care. Certainly not enough to break off this kiss. She put her arms round Kit and kissed him back with enough enthusiasm that whoever stood at the doorway could not imagine she was being coerced.

She never heard the door shut again; she heard very little, for the next few minutes, but the roaring of the blood in her ears and the soft murmur of Kit's endearments, some of which made her want to smile. Finally he felt her quaking with laughter in his arms and released her.

"You find me amusing?"

"Sorry," Ellen said. She was short of breath, and her shirt had come unbuttoned halfway down the front; how had that happened? She straightened her clothes with shaking fingers. "It's—not the custom, anymore—to call your girlfriend a migniard minnikin."

"You truly do not remember me?"

"I dreamed once," Ellen said in a low voice, "that I met you in a garden maze, and we spoke of numbers and sequences; and again, that we sang in a wood where spirits did move." A grief from nowhere tore at her, a sense of loss inexplicable. "Perhaps I knew you once—but I cannot remember, I cannot remember!" she cried.

"Then shall I find the key to your memories, and unlock them," Kit said.

"What if you can't?"

"I must. Eleanor, I must have *something*."

Wheels crunched on the gravel drive outside, and the distinctive wheezing groan of Roger's car came to Ellen's ears through the window. She did not know whether to be glad or sorry that they were about to be interrupted. Kit's last stark, despairing statement was too much; it echoed the emptiness within her, the sorrow that had come from nowhere all her life to drown her in a moment.

Roger's battered car came to a groaning stop in the drive while they watched from the window. "A strange manner of chariot," Kit said, leaning warm and indisputably alive against her shoulder, "and how have they stabled their horses so quickly?"

"A few things have changed in the last four hundred years," Ellen said. "I don't know where to begin."

The problem was deferred by the explosive arrival of Bethany and the English musicians. Bethany introduced them all, looked expectantly at Kit, and went on quickly, and a little nervously, when he bowed and introduced himself as Christopher Arundel. "So we're all ready to rehearse, except we need Paien to sing Actaeon," she finished. "Ellen, do you have any idea where Paien *is*? I thought I heard you talking to him before the storm."

"Paien," said Kit, "has played his part. Do not look for him to return."

Roger frowned. "We need a tenor."

"Aren't *you* singing Actaeon?" Fenella asked Kit. "You've certainly dressed the part."

"I crave your pardon?"

"The costume's smashing," Fenella said. "It's a copy of the Arundel portrait, isn't it?"

"I thought he was one of your crowd," said Bethany.

"I certainly hope he will be," Fenella said with enthusiasm. "Come along, Chris, I want to stand you up against the portrait and see how well your getup matches the original Wicked Kit."

She took Kit's arm and led him to the hall where the portrait hung, followed by Geoffrey and Penny, Roger and Bethany. Ellen trailed along behind, feeling distinctly nervous. Kit was doing very well for someone who'd just lost several hundred years, but what if Fenella asked him a question he couldn't field? She ought to rescue him.

"Ooh, Chris, you *are* so funny!" Fenella screamed in response to an inaudible comment from Kit. Ellen reconsidered. Maybe Kit didn't want to be rescued.

"Look at the two of them, now," Fenella commanded. She posed Kit beside the portrait, touching his shoulder, running one hand along his arm, molding him into the pose of the portrait with what Ellen considered a great deal more touching and patting than should have been necessary. "You've really got an *excellent* copy of the costume there," she told Kit, "only the ruff isn't quite right."

Indeed, his ruff looked much sadder than the starched white frill in the picture. Whole sections had wilted in the rainstorm.

"Otherwise it's a great copy," Fenella said, head on one side. "Who made it for you?"

"My usual tailor," Kit told her.

She shrieked with laughter. "Oh, Chris, you are a card!"

"Never mind the costume," Geoffrey interrupted, "look at the face! He's practically a carbon copy of the first Christopher."

Fenella tilted her head to one side. "Oh, not quite. Chris is taller than Wicked Kit Arundel, and his jaw is firmer, don't you think?"

Kit looked mildly pleased at this bit of nonsense.

"And there's a nasty shifty look in Wicked Kit's eyes," Fenella went on, "you can tell he's the sort of person who'd be plotting to call demons and change lead into gold and all that sort of thing."

Kit looked considerably less pleased.

The other English singers agreed that while the resemblance between Kit and the man in the portrait was quite astonishing, there were nonetheless several distinct differences. While they pushed politely to get a good look at the portrait, Kit somehow maneuvered to get himself to Ellen's side, with the others between him and Fenella. "It must not be as good a portrait as I thought," he murmured in Ellen's ear. "Do *you* think I look wicked?"

Geoffrey interrupted before she could reply. "Amazing resemblance, absolutely amazing," he boomed in his deep voice. "I thought this branch of the family had died out."

"I *wish* people would quit saying that," said Kit irritably. "Do I *look* dead?"

"No offense meant," said Geoffrey equably, "only that nobody around here knew there were any of the Emminster Arundels left alive."

"There weren't," Kit said, "until quite recently."

Geoffrey frowned for a moment. "Oh—you mean you just discovered your connection with the Arundels?"

"I've made quite a number of surprising discoveries recently."

"What are you, a distant descendant?"

"You could say that."

Ellen looked at him and found that she could believe this story far more easily than she could believe an Elizabethan gentleman had walked out of her nightmares to take on living, breathing presence in her world. A distant relation. Of course. Everything made cold and perfect sense. He'd meant to compete at the Renaissance Faire; no, worse, he'd been in the competition the previous day, that's why she hadn't known about him. She'd seen him there, when he tried to disrupt the singing. And after seeing him in the midst of one of her bad spells, then looking at the portrait of Wicked Kit Arundel and hearing Bethany read those stories about him, of course she'd thought his face looked eerily familiar when she saw him in the mist on Hackthorn Down. He was just another musician, a descendant of the Elizabethan Arundels, who'd thought to use the family resemblance to get himself a part in the masque. And if he could make a dramatic entrance already in costume, and fool some crazy girl into thinking he was the reincarnation of the original Kit, why not? She must have given him a great deal of amusement. She moved away from him, backing up the stairs a few steps. He did not notice; the English singers were keeping him quite busy.

"Chris, you've simply *got* to sing Actaeon when we do the masque," Fenella cried.

Kit grew still as the painted canvas. Well, of course, Ellen thought; this was his chance, the thing he'd angled for.

"The masque?" he repeated.

"At midsummer," Penny put in. "Can you sing?"

Geoffrey's booming voice overrode the girls, explaining about the recent discovery of some Elizabethan music for a masque "composed by your distinguished ancestor," Geoffrey said, tactfully omitting any reference to just how Wicked Kit Arundel was supposed to have distinguished himself, and how some anonymous benefactor had donated a sum of money to the Dorset County Council for use in a reenactment of the masque.

"Geoffrey, you leave out all the good bits!" Fenella complained. "'A sum of money' sounds like a bank draft." She put her hand on Kit's arm again, shaking it until he looked at her with an indulgent smile that turned Ellen's stomach. "The money," she announced with a dramatic roll of her eyes, "was *gold coins*. Isn't that romantic?"

"Why?" asked Kit. He looked so perfectly, earnestly confused that Ellen was tempted to believe once again in his whole improbable story.

"Oh, you men, you're impossible." Fenella pouted. "But you will sing with us, won't you? These American girls had a man to sing Actaeon, but they seem to have mislaid him."

"You mean to sing my—the masque," Kit said slowly. "On Midsummer's Eve? Do you think that's wise?"

Fenella giggled, then looked sober. "I say! You *can* sing, can't you, Chris?"

"Of course he can," Ellen said from the landing. "Haven't you heard the resume yet? He can play the lute and the virginals and the viol, can sing part-songs, trim a fetlock, carve a boar, turn a rhyme, wield a sword, dance a pavane or a galliard, and read his book whether in Latin or Greek or the vulgar tongue." She glared at the man who called himself Arundel and turned away before he could reply.

Sir Walter Raleigh to Robert Cecil
17 June 1594
(Cal. State Papers, Dom., 1591–4, pp 698–699)
My very good Lord, and most assured friend—

This night, the 17th of June, we have taken a most notable Jesuit at Arundel House. One of the servants in the house having disclos'd the priest's intent to flee the country by a fishing smack this verie night, we did surround the small cove below Arundel House and so did capture the traitorous priest (hee that did call himself Giles Cavendish, and did pretend to be a simple English gentleman) together with Arthur Arundel, son of Sir John above. The priest brake away from my men and would have given fight, and by most pitiful ill luck was stabbed through the body, himselfe running upon the sword which one of my men did draw in selfe defence and therefore adding the sin of suicide to his other vile and calumnious crimes. Young Arthur I have remanded to Bridport prison, there to be put to the question, but I believe him to be no more than a messenger-boy in this matter; the priest was harbored at Greenholt, the house of one Christopher Arundel who had turn'd aside suspicion, until now, by faining beleef in the true religion. In Arthur Arundel's house we did find letters from the sayde Christopher, requiring of his cousin to send this seminary priest safely from the countrie. As soon as young Arthur shall have been examined I mean to go to Greenholt to question this man, to discover how many notable traitors he hath caused to be brought secretly into the countrie and sheltered within his house.

I have used great diligence in the finding of these notable knaves, and I hope that Her Majestie shall be pleased by this proof that my loyalty to her remains strong though I be still denied her sight, even as the *Ocean* do respond with its tides for love of *Cynthia*[1], that is the *moon*, whether shee be hid by clouds of disapproval or shewing an open radiant face.

Being in haste, I do for the present humbly take my leave. From Chideock, the 17th of June.
Yours at command, and ever to do you service
W. Ralegh

ACTS OF THE PRIVY COUNCIL
1592–95, p. 423
Be it known to all men that a warrant is hereby issued to Mr. Henry Maunder, one of the Messengers of her Majesty's Chamber, to repaire to Greenholt, the house of Mr. Christofer Arundel in Dorset, or to anie other place where he shall understand Christofer Arundel to be remayning, and by vertue thereof to apprehend and bring him to the Court that he may anser such questions as may be put to him concerning atheistical or heretical speeches, forbidden acts of witchcraft or daemonolatry, and other matters which have been rumored of him and his associates. And in case of need to require ayd of all publique officers. Given at the Star Chamber, this 18 day of June the year of our Lord 1594, of our rayne the thirty-sixt.

---

1. Raleigh was referring to his poem *The Ocean's Love for Cynthia*, in which the Ocean stood for himself and Cynthia for the Queen.

11

DAY-BOOK OF CHRISTOPHER ARUNDEL
(HARLEIAN MS. 285, FOL. 31)
20 June 1594—Or rather, I should subscribe this
the 21 day of June; for the sun riseth as I write
this, being new come from Ladyswood with my head
and heart all in such a turmoil as surely never did
mortal man suffer.

Eleanor hath pled herself indisposed these several
days, and kept to her chamber, though I did send
divers messages by her waiting-woman most heartily
entreating her to walk with me. For fear that these
words might be seen by her brother I dared not
write plainly of what had passed between us, but
did in all ways that I might assure her of my true
faith and good will. After supper this night (where
she still did not join the company, but would have
a tray in her chamber) I sent with the wench that
carried the food one last plea that, if she would not
speak with me by day, she would do so this night,
in the place we both did know of. Then seeing that
my guests were well amused, some playing at chess,

the ladies (as ever) talking of dress and stitching at their fine costumes for the morrows masque, I did beg my leave of the company and went alone to Ladyswood.

Here beneath the spreading oaks (whose great age no man now living can tell) the air doth ever seem darker and colder than upon the green hillside where my shepherds graze the flocks. Even as the sun went down, the night mists rose to meet it, swirling and turning among the trees in so uncanny shapes as it did give me to wonder that such a place should have been thought as it were a shrine to Our Lady (for though I be no Catholic, I will not defame Her whom my cousins still revere by such coarse words as the canting Puritan divines do use.)

All alone as I was in the center of the wood, I did think that every whisper of a leaf in the air, every small sound of fox or coney in its burrow was the step of Eleanor comming at last to greet me and to swear she bore me no ill will for our last meeting. Desire for her rose in me so strong at the sweet memory of that night, that I could no longer contain myself. Withouten lute, alone beneath the moon, as any who heard me would surely judge me mad, I did sing all the music that I had made for love of learning and of Eleanor, all the desire that I had to encompass and know the world without and the paradise within her arms. And as I sang it did seem to me that the mist thickened about me, wreathing about mine eyes, and a wind did toss last years fallen leaves about my feet even though the branches above were unstirred.

Of a sudden I felt the certainty of a presence beholding me, and so brake off my song and turned of a sudden, ready to catch Eleanor in mine arms. But she who stood before me was not Eleanor. I could not see her countenance clearly for the mists that did trouble the air; but she was lit all with an unearthly radiance, and it did seem to me that her hair was dressed with pearls and moonlight, and the hem of her farthingale trembling with jewels all of light. And behind her there stood a goodly host of courtiers, both men and women, all so fair as any of the Queen her favorites, and dressed more richly than even my lord of Essex or other such court paycockes.

I made my reverence to this vision of light; she spake not, but regarded me with mocking eyes above a veil of mist that wound about her features. And all her court stood silent as the dead behind her.

Between the leaves of the great oaks overhead there shone a moon that lacked but one sliver to its perfect fullness, and about the moon the stars did move in their eternal dance like courtiers around the Queen. And this double light of moon and stars did give me the words that my wit lacked.

"I see now that Messer Cavendish spake truth," said I, "when he did swear that the stars foretold a Queen would come this month to Greenholt."

The Lady (for so I must name her, having no earthly name for her) moved her head slightly. "I know not this Green Holt," she said, and every word did ring as the chiming of silver bells. "Nor have I come any where. This is my wood; by what right do you disturb us here?"

Then did I know that this place called Ladyswood was not called after Our Lady Mary, but for a Queen both less and more than she; one both earthly and unearthly, the Lady of the Dark Court that doth meet only between midnight and dawn, and that doth carry away mortals betimes with them in their revels. And it seemed to me that nothing could be better than to make one of that shining company; and yet at the same time my heart was full of Eleanor.

I knelt and did most earnestly desire the Lady her pardon for having disturbed her court at their revels. She tapped me on the shoulder with the wand that she did carry in one hand, a slender bow of light from which hung seven silver bells in the shape of apples.

"Thy music were recompense enough, Kit Arundel," she said, and it wondered me that she should call me by my name.

She did laugh, shaking her branch of silver bells, and answered the question I dared not ask. "What is hidden in your world is clear in ours, and what is clear in yours is hidden in ours. These mists that do confuse your sight be light to us, and the sun of your world doth blind us. No man can know all things, save he come from one world to live in the other; and then shall both spheres join as one in his mind."

At this I did startle, for it seemed to me that the Ladys riddling words did offer all that understanding for which Messer Cavendish and I had been working; that which we did painfully attempt by building all our knowledge of the world into one great system of music and signs and seals, she did offer to share with me as a thing natural and easy.

"You are like a child building a tower of blocks, and thinking thereby to reach the Heavens, Kit," the Lady chid me as though mine innermost thoughts were open to her. "Do you really believe that these complications of sign upon seal, of image upon word upon harmonious sound, can ever define all that is and shall be?"

An hour ago I had answered *yes*; now I could but stammer, "I know no other way to learn, Lady, but to proceed from what is known to what is unknown, and to build as goodly an edifice as I may by such means as mortal men possess."

"Come to me," said the Lady, "and you shall not be limited to your mortal toys, and what you have labored to know shall be clear in your sight without effort."

I was sore tempted; but ever the memory of Eleanor was with me, and with her the thought of other things which I did love dearly, yet knew not until this minute that I loved: the strength of my body and the green turf under my feet and the grain growing in the fields and the turning of the seasons in the order that God hath provided.

"If you will not join with us," said the Lady as I did hesitate, "there shall be a forfeit for this nights work. Will you lie with me, or make music for our dance?"

At these words so plainly spoken a hot shame ran through me, for I felt it all unseemly that this Lady should so offer her self to me. And at the same time I did feel angry, for I sensed that 'twas to her no more than as a woman of our world might call her little lap-dog to be petted and rest in her lap awhile.

The Lady laughed again, and the ringing of her branch of bells was as the tinkle of breaking icicles in the winters frosty dawn. "Were I minded to have you, Kit Arundel, you should be mine, body and

soul, and should serve me as faithfully as any little
dog, with never a will of your own to grudge the
service. But I would have you come to us of your
own free will, and so shalt have a day and a night to
consider which offers more—this earthly sun of yours,
or the Light you shall know in my lands. We will
tread a measure together tomorrow night, Kit Arundel;
and tonight you shall make your mortal music for
the entertainment of my gentlemen and ladies."

Then did she put her silver wand into my hands,
or so I thought, but that on the touch I held a lute
all of pale light, the ghost of an earthly lute, and
the strings of silver, and the notes that it played
the most sweetest that ever I had heard; such music
as I would have dreamed the angels do make in
heaven.

The Lady stood in the center of the grassy circle,
and I on one knee beside her did play and sing,
while all in silence her courtiers danced to my music;
with such deep courtly reverences, such graceful
lifting of airy feet, such joyous solemnity and solemn
joy as did make all the court dances that ever I had
seen appear like the cloddish hopping of peasants.
I could have watched with deep delight as long as
they cared to continue; but almost as soon as they
had begun (or so it did seem to me) the stars did
fade into the lightening sky, and the grave stately
gentlemen and the finely dressed ladies did fade
with them.

"Come away, away, away!" cried the Lady. "See
the dawning of the day!"

All in a moment the morning mists did wreathe
about the faery court, and the sun rising through
them did dazzle mine eyes. And an earthly voice,

and one I did love full well, was calling to me from the edge of the wood.

"Kit, Kit, are you within?"

I hastened to where Eleanor stood and did put mine arms round her without waiting for permission. The rising sun was an alchemist to make gold of her loosened hair; she was solid as earth within mine arms; the cool air of the morning played about us, and the dew dampened the hem of her gown. "Oh, Kit," she did say, "I have slept a day and a night, and I dreamed that you were gone away from me forever. Only now did I waken, and reading your letter, did hasten here."

"Fear not, my dearest love," I told her. "I am yours, and you are mine, and no earthly power shall part us."

And I did believe those words as I spake them.

We went lightly down by the meadow path, and I seeing the stone of Greenholt all golden in the morning sun, and the smoke rising from the chimneys, and smelling the earth wet with morning dew, did think no thing better than to live here with Eleanor by my side. And so it doth still seem to me; though 'tis hard to put aside the promise of knowledge which the Lady did make to me.

And my vow could be true in words, yet false in truth; for the Lady is certainly no earthly power.

She did promise to dance a measure with me this night at the masque.

I have sought by the true philosophical method and harmony, proceeding *gradatim* from things visible to consider of things invisible; from things bodily, to conceive of things spiritual; by things mortal, to things immortal.

Is the mystery of infinity solvable by rational means alone?

Is there no middle way, but to live a plain country gentleman with Eleanor, or to forsake her (and in forsaking her, lose also mine honor) for a world where shines no earthly light?

Mathematicks and Musicke cannot resolve all things. *Minimum*: that which will kill men by piercing and running through.

Maximum: that which will presse men to death.

Friday, June 3, 1994

Ellen hid out in her room, pretending to work on the computer, until Bethany dragged her down for a rehearsal. Even then, though she avoided meeting the eyes of the man who called himself Kit Arundel, she was shaken by the old mad sense of double vision, of seeing an England that had been gone for hundreds of years through eyes that had been dead for— No! She *would not* think about it. She clenched her hands tight over a carved chair back and recited mantras of this century under her breath to keep herself sane. "Family values, Bush, Reagan, Desert Storm, ethnic cleansing." Ugh. Why *did* she want to stay in a century like this? She switched to less disturbing incantations, hardly knowing or caring what words she chose as long as they belonged quite firmly to this time and place.

"Ellen," Bethany murmured during a break between songs, "do you have a headache?"

Ellen blinked, caught by surprise in the middle of her current mantra. "Not a bad one, why?"

"Because," Bethany said, "while the rest of us were singing, 'They are here, they are here, here

here here here la la la la la la,' you were singing, "Alka-Seltzer, Aspirin, Benadryl ril ril ril ril ril."

"Oh." Ellen thought it over for a moment. "Perhaps I do have a headache, now that you mention it."

That provided the perfect excuse to slip away while the rest of them took a break to eat. Ellen left Roger explaining the sawdust content of English sausages to Bethany, in a lengthy dissertation that went back to the food rationing of the second World War. It might have been more intelligent to stay and wait for Kit to betray himself by showing some knowledge of this century, but by now tension and fear really had given her a pounding headache. The dim bulbs in the kitchen flickered and glowed with colored lights, and Roger's pleasant, high-pitched, cultured voice made jagged lines of pain through her head.

She went upstairs in her stocking feet, half blindly, wanting only to get away from the light and the chattering voices and the man who had walked out of her dreams, impossibly, unbelievably. "I'll think about it tomorrow," Ellen said under her breath. "Scarlett O'Hara, *Gone With the Wind*, Vivien Leigh, Clark Gable. Sean Connery. Kevin Costner!" She stopped, out of breath, and pushed open the little door that led to the roof.

She felt hot and flustered and untidy; it was soothing to sit in the cool gentle misty air that the rain had left behind, surveying the countryside from this vantage point of rainslick tiles and slanting roofs. Uphill from Greenholt, the dark tangle of trees along the lane to Hackthorn Down glowed with a burnished deep green light; downhill and to the south, the golden stone houses of Emminster town were transmuted to a purer gold by the diffused light of the sun setting through cloud.

After some time there were noisy farewells below, and the sound of a car driving off. Ellen carefully did not think about how many people might have left, or how many she might have to see tomorrow, or how a long-lost descendant of the Arundels could read her mind and pluck names out of her dreams. She sat with her hands folded, thinking about nothing at all in the cool mist until the evening bells of St. Mary's church chimed and the sun sank through the last clouds to blind her with long level rays of reddening light. Then, as the sky behind the Downs dimmed from rose and gold to blue and lavender, she climbed down, carefully closing the trap door behind her, and made her way to her room. She was bone-tired as though she'd walked a thousand miles; she would sleep now, and tomorrow everything would be, somehow, normal again.

No crack of light showed under the door of her room to warn her; but as she opened the door, a dark shape topped with a white ruff and pale face moved to greet her.

"Get off my bed," Ellen said. "Get out of my life! Get out of my dreams! Get out of my head! Dammit! Can't I be let alone for one single solitary moment?" And she burst into furious, shameful tears that washed away all her hard-won calm in a tide of hot salty water.

She had half expected that he would put his arms about her to comfort her; she was braced to push him away. It would be very satisfying to have a good reason to slap his face. But he sat where he was on the bed, plucking at a lute, drawing from the strings the beginning of a quiet lulling tune that crept into and under all her thoughts.

"Eleanor—Ellen, if you will," Kit said presently, "do you know why you are so angered with me, sweeting?"

Ellen gulped down her involuntary sobs, took a deep breath to list the reasons, then let out her breath again in a long hopeless sigh. He reminded her of a bad time in her life; that wasn't his fault. She was afraid she was going crazy again; that wasn't his fault either. He'd insinuated himself into the masque without her permission; well, she didn't own the masque, did she? And Paien had certainly let them down; they needed *somebody* to sing Actaeon.

Sitting on her bed without invitation, on the other hand, was definitely improper. But she should have been perfectly capable of throwing him out without making a scene about it.

"N-no," Ellen admitted finally, while the soft insinuating music of the lute crept through her head. "I d-don't." She sniffed defiantly. "But I didn't invite you here."

"You have called me home from Faerie," Kit said. "The mortal sphere that I did but remember as in dreams is now real to me again, and I do know myself and all our past together." His long dark hands, his beautiful hands, danced over the strings of the lute, plucking at memories and dreams she'd tried so long to bury. No! There were no memories—only dreams. Anything else was crazy. She was through with all that.

"We don't *have* a past together," Ellen said at last, "and I want you to go away. Now."

"*Do* you?"

The faint melody shifted, became stronger, more compelling. Ellen felt weak at the knees. Her heart was beating too hard, too fast. She backed up until she felt the good solid wall behind her. Something real, that wouldn't dissolve into mists and songs and implications; that was what she needed. *Nice* wall, *good* wall. She might possibly be getting slightly hysterical. The music was all around her now, drawing her towards Kit as the moon draws the sea.

"You're trying to put a spell on me," she said, "like Paien. And I won't have it."

Kit sighed and set down the lute. The breaking off of the music was like a sharp edge between them. "At least," he said, "do you admit the possibility of magic. An I were a moderate man, I should be contented with so much, for the first night. But I did warn you once, Eleanor. I am no moderate nor sensible man like your brother—"

"I. Don't. *Have*. A. Brother," Ellen said, a little too loudly and clearly for someone who was not hysterical and not arguing, "and my name is Ellen, not Eleanor, and whatever you're doing, I want you to stop it!"

Kit lifted up his empty hands, pale as moths against the darkness of his velvet doublet. "I have stopped," he said. "An you would let me continue, though, I could cure the headache that pains you."

"Paien did that too," said Ellen, and shrank involuntarily from the memory of a cool inhuman touch, mist passing through her head, and pain lifted away. "Thank you, I'd rather just take two aspirin and go to bed."

Kit gave a sharp sigh. "I'm ill-fated in all my

endeavours," he said, "if all I do or say serves but to make you think me sib to Paien."

"How do you know Paien?"

"Sweet heart, I have known him—by what you say—these four hundred years of wandering in his land."

Ellen thought that over for a while. Her headache had receded on the roof; now it was back again, gripping her temples, biting through her skull like iron claws. It was hard to think of anything through the pain. "I don't understand anything. I wish you would go away," she said.

"Let us make a bargain," Kit proposed. "Lie down—nay, I'll not touch you," he promised, rising from the bed, "but let me play a little, softly, to ease your head. And then I'll go, if it be still your true desire."

Aspirin wouldn't help. It was too late for that. Ellen lifted one hand and let it fall again. She felt helpless, dizzy, and confused by the pounding pain. "This is really, really stupid," she muttered as she crossed the room. "This is Not a Good Idea."

"Does that mean," said Kit, sounding suddenly hopeful and much younger, "you agree?"

Ellen closed her eyes. Sheer bliss to sink back into the soft mattress with its cool uncreased sheets; but the zigzag patterns of light still flashed across her closed eyes, each one carrying its sharp points of pain. "If music be the cure of migraine, play on," she said.

If she listened very, very carefully to the lute, it took her mind off the headache. Kit murmured to her as he played. "The pain comes from fighting the memory of what you were. Long and long have I felt that pain, in the world where time stands still.

Music is the key of memory. Listen, and remember, and be Eleanor again. . . ." Then he was singing very softly to his own accompaniment, a song she had known for so long . . . so long . . . before she was born. . . .

> When love on time and measure makes
>   his ground,
> Time that must end though love can never
>   die . . .

They were walking in the garden . . . no, that was before . . . at the center of the maze . . . "Kit?"

A hand clasped hers, briefly, before returning to the music.

"Rest and remember."

> 'Tis love betwixt a shadow and a sound,
> A love not in the heart but in the eye . . .

Ellen lay unmoving in the center of the bed, while something rose from her body and walked the rooms of Greenholt. Before her closed eyes, now, instead of the zigzag lines of the migraine, she saw the walls and stairs of Greenholt. What was she looking for? She would be late, so late, and Edward would be angered with her.

> A love that ebbs and flows, now up, now
>   down,
> A mornings favor and an evenings frown.

Ah, here it was—the Long Gallery, of course! It must be nearly time for Kit's masque to begin. Eleanor gave a sigh of relief and ran into the empty room to await the rest of the company.

❖   ❖   ❖

The cool silver light of a full moon fell in splintered lines and planes across the Long Gallery of Greenholt. Below, torches blazed where Kit stood at the head of the drive to welcome his guests, men and women dressed as gaudily as the strange plumaged birds of the Indies. Sir Walter Raleigh was not there; but it seemed to Eleanor, glancing through the diamond panes of the gallery windows, that all the other gentry of the West Country had come to witness Kit's midsummer celebration.

The canvas scene-drops at the far end of the gallery stirred as though a breath of wind had come from nowhere to shiver the hanging panels. Painted trees and tinseled branches moved in and out of silver light and black shadow like a living grove. Eleanor was relieved when two manservants entered ahead of the guests to light torches on the walls of the long gallery. The golden, wavering light added its own illusion of movement to the painted wood, but it was a wholly human illusion, made up of all the things she had grown up with: fire and candlelight and the warmth of human bodies coming into the room, and Kit's face alive and real and searching out hers. She let out a breath she had not been aware of holding.

The faint unease was still with her as, after the obligatory greetings and courtesies to Kit's guests, she retired to the robing room behind the scenery to be dressed as Diana. Fine cambric broidered with silver-grey silk next her skin, a wisp of green taffeta shot with silver over that, and finally, the loosely flowing green gown in which Diana made her first appearance as the Huntress. Jane, already garbed in the simpler costume of one of the Nymphs who made up the chorus, combed out Eleanor's long fair hair until it sparkled and crackled over the flowing green, while over her shoulder she chattered to one of the gentlemen house guests who was to sing in Actaeon's chorus of Hounds.

Viols and the tinkling of a harpsichord warned them all to drop their voices. Eleanor left the robing-room and stood watching from behind the painted canvas panels. Kit entered from the far side of their improvised stage, followed by two of his gentlemen Hounds bearing torches to light him for the audience. He had flatly refused any costume other than his customary evening dress; but he carried a bow, and a leather quiver of arrows dangled from his belt, to show the audience that he was the Huntsman. Just in case there should be any doubt, he declaimed in his rich tenor voice, "Hark ye, gentles and nobles all, here is poor Actaeon to lament his sorrowful state. Hunt as I may, the hind escapes my reach; search as I may, I cannot discern the light for which my soul longs. This forest of dark error and false prophecies . . ."

A stir at the far end of the gallery distracted Eleanor from the rest of Actaeon's richly symbolical speech. She tiptoed to the wall and peered along the line of sconces, trying to make out who had broken in so rudely upon their entertainment. She heard rough raised voices, and Edward expostulating in learned tones while the leader of this new group kept interrupting him.

Eleanor threw on her own dark cloak over the green gown and slipped along the wall to discover what was the matter.

"See here, Maister Gull-ford or whatsoever your name be, we bear warrant of arrest for one Christopher

Arundel of Greenholt, and the order of the Privy Council to summon such aid as we may require!" said the red-faced man whose voice was loudest, shaking a parchment in Edward's face.

Behind him were more men, looking like soldiers in their jacks of boiled leather. One of them pushed forward slightly, so that the light from the nearest sconce lay across his face, and Eleanor felt cold amid all the heat and light and press of folk. She knew that face. It was Topcliffe the priest-hunter, one of Raleigh's men. *Thanks be to our Lord that Mr. Cavendish is safely away!*

"Why, Richard Topcliffe," she said, as sweetly as she might, "what do you here? We harbor no priests at Greenholt, as y'are welcome to prove by searching every room of the house at your leisure. But pray, does your warrant include a command to disturb these gentlemen in the midst of their entertainment?"

"The warrant's for Arundel himself, and not for priest-harboring, but for heresy plain spoken before witnesses," growled the red-faced man who held the papers, "and Sir Walter has but lent me his men to escort Arundel under close arrest to London, as is but his right and duty as Sheriff of the West Country."

On the raised dais among the painted trees, Kit as Actaeon began his first song.

> *No grave for woe, yet earth my watery*
> *   tears devours;*
> *Sighs want air, and burnt desires kind*
> *   pitys showers:*

In a moment Eleanor would have to make her entrance as Diana. She must say something to calm these angry men first—but what? Raleigh. Heresy.

London. Here was some trap for Kit, something graver than the Queen's possible displeasure.

The masque, with its endless dances and songs, would give her and Kit time to think what this might mean. Somehow she must persuade these men to wait—and not, Eleanor thought impatiently, just so that Kit could complete his midsummer magic. It was all very well to speak of drawing the power of the stars from their courses, of joining the human and angelic spheres by the magic of music and the word. Such things did well enough to amuse philosophers. But they had a *real* problem now.

"Why, sir, if it is Master Arundel you desire, there he is in plain view," Eleanor said sweetly, pointing out the torchlit stage where Kit was finishing his first song. "But will you come so rudely upon us as to break up the entertainment which he has planned for all these gentry? Do but wait until this little, little masque be finished, and he shall go with you of his own good will. Force an end now, and those who have labored to make the masque will be sore displeased with such overzealous servants."

The man with the warrant hesitated. Topcliffe was about to speak.

Sir Walter's man. "Even now," Eleanor added quickly, "it is time for us to sing a poem of Sir Walter's own making, in praise of the Queen as Diana. Neither she nor he would be well pleased to hear that you put a stop to such an entertainment."

Even Topcliffe was thinking now. *Pray God he thinks slowly!* Eleanor slipped back along the way she had came, dropped her cloak in a dark puddle behind the scenes, and whispered to the musicians, "Remember the song of Sir Walter's that we cut from the masque? We're to sing it after all. Now. Find you the music!"

She conveyed the same message to Jane and the other Nymphs while, on stage, Actaeon ended his song.

> *Stars hold their fatal course, my joys*
> *   preventing:*
> *The earth, the sea, the air, the fire, the*
> *   heav'ns vow my tormenting.*

On the last word Kit sank down against a "rock" of wood and plaster, conveniently facing away from the side of the stage where Eleanor made her entrance, followed by her chorus of Jane and the other Nymphs with torches to light the way.

> *Praised be Diana's fair and harmless light;*
> *Praised be the dews wherewith she moists*
> *   the ground;*
> *Praised be her beams, the glory of the*
> *   night;*
> *Praised be her power, by which all powers*
> *   abound.*

After the first quavering start, the other Nymphs joined in the song with Jane, circling Eleanor with a slow, graceful swaying step. She stood in the center of the dance, looking regal and thinking furiously.

> *Praised be her nymphs, with whom she*
> *   decks the woods;*
> *Praised be her knights, in whom true honour*
> *   lives;*
> *Praised be that force, by which she moves*
> *   the floods;*
> *Let that Diana shine which all these gives.*

She had never cared for this song of Sir Walter's, but it had seemed politic to let him insert his own poems into the masque, even at the cost of some slight disruption to Kit's original plans. Now those plans were as nothing. Eleanor found, when it came right down to it, that she could not *really* believe Kit's music and Edward's poetry and their acting out of gods and mysteries could lend men the power of angels. If only it were so! Then might Kit fly right out of the reach of Topcliffe and this damnable warrant. But right now Eleanor would have traded all the philosophical enlightenment in the world for a good, fast horse ready-saddled behind the house; or for a private word with someone in the Privy Council. No—that would do no good. Now, why was she so certain that Kit must not answer the warrant, that the questioning in London was not the real danger he faced?

A knowledge pure it is her worth to know;
With Circes let them dwell that think not
    so.

The song was over. Eleanor dipped her knees in a graceful flowing bend and curtsey, turned half a step, and faced the audience so that her first speech might be heard clearly.

"Ladies mine, the summer days are long and warm, even in this Arcadia of ours. I would bathe in yon crystal fountain; do you dance and shield me from the prying eyes of the curious while I refresh me."

Now they could return to the original plan of the masque. A lingering, melodious music rose; the Nymphs set their torches in the wall brackets and joined hands to circle round Eleanor while

she went through the gestures of disrobing as if
to bathe in the painted waterfall behind her.

Shake off your heavy trance,
And leap into a dance
Such as no mortals use to tread,

Eleanor sang to the Nymphs. They imitated her
gestures, gathering round to conceal her while Eleanor
made a graceful dance of discarding the outer layers
of her costume. First the green gown flowed loose,
falling from shoulders to waist to hips to lie in a
velvet pool about her feet while she thought furiously.
The warrant was to question Kit about his heretical
talk before witnesses. What witnesses? That night when
Parson Hensley came to dinner? Yes, he might well
have made the mischief for them. But Raleigh had
been there too; he'd spoken as wildly as any of them.

Fit only for Apollo
To play to, for the moon to lead,
And all the stars to follow,

Eleanor sang while her wits were elsewhere. The
Nymphs chimed in, "Follow . . . follow."

The red-faced man from London might serve
the Privy Council, but the others with him were
Raleigh's men. Raleigh sending his men to bring
Kit for questioning on a matter that implicated
Raleigh . . .

The green taffety floated away from Eleanor's
shoulders, borne out of sight by invisible hands,
and she stood in her shining robe of silver-threaded
cambric. The painted water was so real, it seemed
to ripple in the uncertain light of the torches; she
could almost fancy that she heard the quiet sound

of running water. The canvas forest on either side of her was closer and denser than she had imagined. And the gentry who crowded the gallery were far away, little white blotches that were faces and starched white ruffs, jeweled clothes winking like stars in the torchlight.

Actaeon's full chorus of Hounds leapt onto the stage, five gentlemen baying most realistically and brandishing their torches. For a moment of panic Eleanor was a hunted thing, goddess or hind, a creature of the forest which these rude men had violated. She shrank back most naturally while Kit, alerted at last by his Hounds, leapt up and peered in amazement at the vision presented by Diana with her Nymphs.

A hunted thing . . . The hunt was up, but she was not the quarry. Why would Raleigh send his men to aid in Kit's arrest, when he would hardly wish Kit questioned about his own careless table-talk that night? An accusation of heresy was not a hanging matter, not in the England of Elizabeth; but neither was it a road back to the Queen's favor.

A year ago this spring, Edward's friend Marlowe had been arrested on very similar charges. Or would have been, save that—he died first. He died in a tavern brawl with some gentlemen who were friends of Sir Walter Raleigh's.

She was about to have a long spoken dialogue with Actaeon. She would have to find some way to change the words, to warn Kit without letting the watchers at the back of the gallery know that was what she did.

First, though, the Nymphs had to overcome Actaeon's doubts. While he wondered aloud whether he had intruded on matters meant for no mortal to learn, and contemplated flight, they danced towards him seductively, pale hands outstretched, silvery hair floating about their shoulders. There seemed to be more of them than Eleanor remembered; they moved and twined about one another in a complicated, dizzying pattern so that she could not be sure, between torchlight and moonlight, whether there were five or seven or nine dancers between her and Actaeon, all tall and slender and more graceful than ever they had seemed before.

> *Descend,*
> *Descend,*
> *Though Pleasure lead,*
> *Fear not to follow,*

she sang, and the Nymphs echoed again, "Follow, follow." The sound of the singing was rich and true, the mingling of many sweet voices; they had never sung so finely in rehearsal.

> *They who are bred*
> *Within the hill*
> *Of skill*
> *May safely tread*
> *What path they will;*
> *No ground of good is hollow.*

"Hollow, hollow," the Hounds joined in, and their deep voices sounded like the belling of hunting hounds upon a scent. The Nymphs and Hounds blended and parted, gliding gracefully through a dance that by insensible degrees brought Diana and Actaeon closer and closer to one another, until at last both groups of choral dancers slipped away to leave the principals gazing at one another.

Kit's face was alive with love and delight. Eleanor knew that her own was stiff. Diana was supposed to be angry with this mortal who had intruded. What—what—*what* were her first words? The player at the harpsichord tinkled forth a musical phrase, paused a moment, then repeated the introduction. The music brought back her memory and she began the speech upbraiding Actaeon for his intrusion upon her privacy. "My sacred groves . . . mortal presumption . . . a Light to blind thine eyes . . ." The phrases came easily to her now. The lines written by Edward to lead into Actaeon's next song served equally well to conceal the very real warning that she must give him. "This place holds dangers unsuspected," Eleanor improvised, "and enemies unseen. Who tarries here shall swiftly prisoner be." Would Topcliffe guess what she had added? She could not see his face from here; he and Raleigh's other men and that one from the Privy Council must be waiting quietly at the far end of the gallery. She caught at Kit's wrist as if to strike him; the movement allowed her to draw closer, facing him and away from the audience. "There's warrant to bring you before the Privy Council for questioning," she whispered. "You must flee at once."

Kit's answer was in the lines already written for him. "How can I leave the light that illumines my soul? Ask me to die for you, gracious Queen of all that lives and moves, but not to leave you."

"No man may enter in my sacred sphere," Diana responded, and Eleanor used the pause after this warning to whisper in her own voice, "Are you mad, Kit? Raleigh's men to bear you to London for questioning on Raleigh's heresy?"

His face had gone as still as her own. Please God,

the watchers would think this only good acting on both their parts. "You *must* go," Eleanor whispered under cover of the music introducing Actaeon's next song. "Remember what happened to Marlowe? You'll never reach London alive."

Lady, death were sweeter far,
Than to leave so bright a star,

Kit sang, and followed in an undertone, "Canst not feel the deep magic working, Eleanor? To break off now were more danger than to go on."

Hardly pausing for breath, he launched into the song written by Philip Sidney and set to music by Christopher Arundel.

Who hath his fancy pleased
With fruits of happy sight,
Let here his eyes be raised
On Nature's sweetest light;
A light which doth dissever
And yet unite the eyes,
A light which, dying never,
Is cause the looker dies.

Even as he sang, the light itself seemed to dance and twine about them, now golden as torches, now silver as the moon; a pattern of brightness and shadow that was like a maze upon the floor. Eleanor felt herself and Kit tangled within that labyrinth of light.

She never dies, but lasteth
In life of lover's heart;
He ever dies that wasteth
In love his chiefest part;
Thus is her life still guarded
In never-dying faith;

> *Thus is his death rewarded,*
> *Since she lives in his death.*

The painted forest was a thicket enclosing them, and the shadows where neither torchlight nor moonlight fell were alive with half-seen shapes, a thickening of the air. Eleanor felt a childish panic, fear of the dark, the unknown. But it was only painted canvas. Kit was the one who faced a real danger.

"Kit, you must vanish in the transformation scene," she whispered between verses. They had planned the staging of this part carefully; the Nymphs and Hounds who were waiting behind the canvas panels were to come swirling back on in a mad dance, then draw the audience in to dance with them. During that ritual of "commoning" everybody would be too taken up with the antics of the vizarded masquers to notice that Kit had slipped out of sight to put on the horns and furry mantle of Actaeon's stag costume— or to find a fast horse.

A tight-lipped shake of the head, barely perceptible, was Kit's answer. "I'll finish what we have begun," he muttered, hardly moving his lips, and the next moment launched into the last lines of the song.

> *Look, then, and die; the pleasure*
> *Doth answer well the pain;*
> *Small loss of mortal treasure*
> *Who may immortal gain."*

Anger burned through Eleanor; the silver light of the moon pouring down upon them was a cold fire within her. Someone put Diana's silver wand into her hand. She raised it, surprised by its lightness; the branch of apple-shaped bells made for this scene seemed to have no more weight than a skein of

moonlight. The bells rang out a mocking echo to
Kit's music as she struck him across the face. It was
supposed to be only a mimed blow, but she struck
out with her full strength, hardly caring if she ruined
the play by giving Actaeon a bloody nose and a bruised
lip. It was time for Kit to come out of his philosophical
dreams and understand that real danger awaited
him; as real as a blow across the face.

But the branch of bells seemed to glide across
Kit's face like nothing more than a stream of silver-
white moonlight; and in that cold radiance he began
to change. His face grew still and remote, and the
labyrinth pattern of light and shadow masked him
more effectively than any vizard, changing the stillness
of his face like ripples across icy water. Kit, a stranger,
Actaeon, Kit lit from within by one of his joyous
moods, Kit still as death, Kit/Actaeon intent on the
hunt . . .

Had he grown taller, too? Eleanor felt overshadowed;
where the pattern of moonlight and torchlight and
writhing shadows fell upon her, she felt a net of
fire and ice. Raising her eyes, she saw what sense
could not comprehend, nor sight take in: the branching
horns that crowned Kit's head, silver and glimmering
with light like the apple branch within her hand.

A murmur of pleased amazement rose from the
audience, who took Kit's transformation for one of
his mechanical marvels. They had expected no less
from the man who made candles to dance in the
air, and sent wine sailing down his dinner table in a
ship of silver. If their appreciation was mixed with
a frisson of fear, it was no more than might serve to
intensify the pleasure.

The musicians struck up the lively tune that was

the prelude to the interlude of commoning. Eleanor's
fingers opened, let the silver bough fall. No sound
of ringing bells followed; she looked down and saw
the branch falling down into a mist that had risen
above the floorboards—and farther down, into stars
that swirled and danced in dizzying patterns beneath
her feet. She looked up, and the same stars danced
above her head, as though the roof of the Long Gallery
were no more than a whisper of summer breezes.
Lights above and lights below drew closer, joining
here on this stage the spheres that had been so long
apart.

"A dance, a dance!" cried a boy's shrill piping
voice, and all at once the whirling lights were the
jewels on the masquers' vizards, and the stage was
filled with the Nymphs and Hounds—too many of
them, far more than there could possibly have been.
Eleanor could not recognize Jane's merry smile beneath
any of the Nymphs' glittering vizards.

They were like a rushing stream of stars between
her and Kit. Eleanor stepped back, behind the painted
scenes. She did not fall into the skies that glittered
above and beneath her; here, in the center, the natural
sphere of mankind still kept its shape.

Or did it? The painted trees about the gallery
trembled in the darkening air, now that the masquers
had carried all the torches into their wild leaping
dance. Eleanor laid her hand on a canvas scene-
cloth. It was rough as bark, cold as night air, and it
seemed to curve in the shape of a tree trunk under
her fingers. Beside the rough rounded bark, her
questing fingertips found only air and darkness, then
another green growing tree springing to life where
there should have been only painted canvas. She

reached forward and felt only air and darkness. She could still see the stage and part of the hall, but they were like a distant image, a painted picture that moved by unknown art.

While Eleanor watched from her starry prison, the two choruses of masquers, Diana's Nymphs and Actaeon's Hounds, set their torches in the wall brackets and mingled with Kit's nobly-born guests. Beneath the jeweled vizards their faces seemed pearl-pale, unfamiliar, and their eyes glinted brighter than jewels in the torchlight. A cool shadowless light of their own, like the brightness shared between moon and sea, illuminated the hall where they drew the visiting gentlefolk of the West Country into a stately pavane. The pure sexless voices of children, or angels, or spirits, sang what Kit had written for the masquers. The Nymphs and Hounds took hands with the gentry and danced in silence through the high clear words and their answering echo from the far end of the gallery, where no singers should be.

> *Circe bids you come away,*
> *Echo Come away, come away.*
> *From the rivers, from the sea,*
> *Echo From the sea, from the sea.*
> *From the green woods every one,*
> *Echo Every one, every one.*
> *Of her maids be missing none,*
> *Echo Missing none, missing none.*
> *No longer stay except it be to bring*
> *A med'cine for love's sting;*
> *That would excuse you and be held more*
>   *dear*
> *Than wit or magic, for both they are here.*
> *Echo They are here, they are here.*

It was Eleanor's cue to enter as Diana, but she could not move back into that world of light. Darkness surrounded her, and the cool damp air of a night wood. The moon that had shone so brightly to welcome Kit's guests to Greenholt gave no light to this wood of troubled air and spirits. An owl hooted, and leaves brushed her cheek, invisible fingers of darkness and mist. Where was the crescent moon now?

That question was answered as she gazed at the distant figures dancing in the hall. One moved among them crowned with moon and stars. It was she— the Dark Lady of the wood. She had taken Eleanor's place in Greenholt, and Eleanor was trapped in the Ladyswood. She had taken all the lamps of the night to light her dance. Kit had claimed he would join the spheres of this world and the next, would draw down spirits with his music. Was this his success?

Eleanor could not even call to them; her throat was filled with darkness. She could only watch as the dancing came to its ceremonious end and the masque resumed.

Where she should have appeared as Diana, the Lady clothed in pearls and moonlight stepped forward to meet Actaeon, and the vizored nymphs welcomed her. Kit came forth, his lean dark face cast half into shadow by the high branching horns that crowned his head: Actaeon made less than man by Diana's retribution and the relentless pursuit of his own hounds.

The chorus of Hounds followed him, fantastically prancing masked dancers in close-fitting doublets and hose of white with red spots, feet shod in soft white felted boots and hands covered with felted mittens. They leapt and howled around Actaeon, now on four legs, now on two, menacing him with the painted teeth of their pointed masks. The Dark Lady watched unmoving, a shadow surrounded by the moon's radiance, as the Hounds that had been Actaeon's own now hunted him up and down the narrow stage. From where she stood in the dark treeshade of Ladyswood, it seemed to Eleanor that there were too many Hounds, and that some of them had tails and claws, and their opened jaws moved and slavered like no masks ever devised. Their savage ballet coursed back and forth in dizzying, narrowing spirals that kept Kit—Actaeon—trapped in their midst. His face was streaked with sweat, and the turmoil of shadows thrown by the horns rising above his head was a network of lines like wounds, grey and black and red, over the sober plainness of his hunting costume.

The myth we told was true, Eleanor thought. *Diana is real, a Goddess older than ever we prayed to in church, and she will kill him like Actaeon for intruding. Oh, Kit, where has Philosophy led you?* She strained unsuccessfully at the invisible bonds that held her, mute and unmoving, within a dark wood that somehow was, and yet was not, the same as the lighted space of the stage.

The Dark Lady moved the fingers of one hand, and the silver branch appeared within her grasp. The bells danced in an ever-mounting spiral of high clear notes that floated above the frenzied cry of the hunting hounds. The chorus of Hounds parted, leaving a clear path between Kit and the Dark Lady, and sank down upon their haunches.

Kit took three steps forward. His eyes were wide and dazzled, like those of a man gazing too long

into the sun. Did he see clearly what it was he knelt
to, what received the homage of his song? Eleanor
could not guess. She only knew that his eyes were
all upon the radiant shadow where the Dark Lady's
face should have been, and that he had not a glance
to spare for her in the Ladyswood.

The musicians had been whispering among
themselves while the wild music of the Hunt played
itself out without their aid. Now, pale and shaken,
they took back the music and the masque. The
measures Kit had written for this song began,
wavering at first, then steadier as the musicians
played on. And whatever the Lady had made of
Kit, there was enough left of his mortal mind to
hear and respond to that cue. He dropped to one
knee before her and sang while she gazed above
him with lifted head.

> *The Fire to see my wrongs for anger*
>   *burneth,*
> *The Air in rain for my affliction weepeth,*
> *The Sea to ebb for grief his flowing*
>   *turneth,*
> *The Earth with pity dull his center keepeth;*
> *Fame is with wonder blased,*
> *Time runs away for sorrow,*
> *Place standeth still amazed*
> *To see my night of evils, which hath no*
>   *morrow:*
> *Alas, alonely she no pity taketh*
> *To know my miseries, but, chaste and*
>   *cruel,*
> *My fall her glory maketh;*
> *Yet still her eyes give to my flames their*
>   *fuel.*

By the end of the song he had recovered the memory of his lines. He spoke his piece as Edward had written it, sueing for pardon and pleading that a man ought not to be punished for loving the light. It was a most excellent philosophical piece of pleading, and Jane had always complained that it was too long by half; the audience would grow bored. And so they might have done, but the Dark Lady raised her silver wand of bells and interrupted Kit in midspeech.

"Choose now," she said in tones so sweet that she might have been singing. "Will you belong to me and be of my sphere, will you live in light and hear the music of the spheres and see all things plain; or will you remain to the mortal death that awaits you here?"

Those words were no part of the masque. *Oh, Kit*, prayed Eleanor hopelessly, *do not take her bargain!*

The Hounds leaned forward, long red tongues drooping, slavering about their sharp white teeth, as though they too prayed that Kit would refuse the bargain. And suddenly Eleanor remembered Raleigh's men in the back of the gallery, waiting for the masque to end that they might arrest Kit and ride with him for London.

"Lady, you do me too much honor," Kit improvised. Eleanor thought that some sanity returned to his face. But the gleaming branch of horns still crowned him, casting its skein of shadows as though already marking him for the Dark Lady.

"Honor," said the Dark Lady, "or death?"

The musicians began playing Kit's next song, as if trying to get the masque back to its planned course. A song, Eleanor realized with sinking heart, that could be taken as acceptance of the Lady's bargain.

Lady of light, revive my dying spright,
Redeem it from the snares of all-confounding
night.
Light me to thy blessed way;
For, blind with worldly vain desires, I
wander as a stray,
Sun and Moon, Stars and underlights I
see,
But all their glorious beams are mists and
darkness, being compar'd to thee.

As the last notes of music died away, the Dark Lady raised her branch of silver apples over Kit's head. The crown of horns dissolved into a dazzling mist that drifted slowly downwards, transforming Kit as it moved. Instead of Kit's lean intelligent face, his sober black doublet and trunk-hose, Eleanor saw a form made all of moving shadows like the Dark Lady's own. And like her, he now gave off his own ghost-pale radiance, as if the two of them burned in a cold fire impalpable to mortal touch.

Kit's voice mingled with the clear purity of the Dark Lady's song and the cold music of her silver bells. Together they sang the words that should have been his duet with Eleanor.

A day, a night, an hour of sweet content
Is worth a world consum'd in fretful care.
Unequal Gods, in your Arbitrement
To sort us days whose sorrows endless
are!
And yet what were it? as a fading flower;
To swim in bliss a day, a night, an hour.

What plague is greater than the grief of
  mind?
The grief of mind that eats in every veine,
In every vein that leaves such clods
  behind,
Such clods behind as breed such bitter
  pain,
So bitter pain that none shall ever find
What plague is greater than the grief of
  mind.

It was Kit's voice she heard, somehow stripped
of earthly feelings until the perfection of his clear
tenor matched the purity of the Lady's song. He
knew no more "the grief of mind," thought Eleanor.
What had made him human was lost, or frozen
by the same magic that had trapped her in this
wood beyond the world. That dark wood held her
mute, a spiderweb of branches and leaves that
had never flourished under any earthly sun, and
Kit knelt to sing his worship to the Lady whose
face was a shadowed mist behind her dazzle of
moonlight radiance.

Time stands still with gazing on her face,
Stand still and gaze, for minutes, hours
  and years to her give place.
All other things shall change, but she
  remains the same
Till heavens changed have their course,
  and Time hath lost his name.
Cupid doth hover up and down blinded
  with her fair eyes.
And Fortune, captive at her feet,
  condemned and conquered lies.

Then they were gone, and never a hint of the creaking ropes and pulleys that should have managed their magical ascent into Diana's starry heaven: only two cold pale flames that burned a moment beside Eleanor, amidst the trees of the Ladyswood that had against all reason replaced the painted scenery of the hall. And then—nothing, no trees, no flames; only the waves of human voices murmuring, shouting, crying aloud in surprise, crashing against Eleanor's ears, and drawing her back into the room full of guests and masquers.

The dark wood was only painted canvas again. She could not find her way back into the place where Kit had disappeared to; she was fixed in the hall again, locked in mortality. The smell of burning tallow and bodies crowded into a small space and rushes too long unchanged assaulted her. Kit's guests stirred and muttered, and a man pushed forward from the back of the gallery. It was Raleigh's pet priest-hunter, Richard Topcliffe. "An end, an end, an end!" he shouted, brandishing the warrant from the Privy Council.

The Nymphs surrounded Eleanor. They were warm and human and stank reassuringly of sweat and paint, and there were only the three of them, not the multitude of inhuman masquers who had commoned with Kit's guests. Jane smiled tremulously at Eleanor and attempted to lead their final chorus.

Come away, away, away,
See the dawning of the day,

she sang, before Topcliffe's voice overpowered hers. "The villain's 'scaped us! Search the house!"

The other two Nymphs tried to lend their voices

to Jane's, to bring back the pretense that everything was normal.

The morning grey
Bids come away;
Every lady should begin
To take her chamber, for the stars are in.

A mocking voice, pure as moonlight and accompanied by a chime of silver apples, rose over the shouting of Topcliffe and the other men come with their warrants for Kit.

Live long the miracles of times and years,
Till with this hero you sit fix'd in spheres.

12

Ellen woke to sunlight, stretched, and smiled lazily and lay in the high soft bed, floating perfectly balanced between past and present. Something stirred on the floor; she looked down and gasped. Unshaven, his fine Elizabethan clothes in disarray, Kit looked indisputably real, and masculine, and somehow more solid than he had been yesterday.

Of course, today she knew who he was, this man who'd slept on the floor all night to guard her dreams and memories. Ellen laughed aloud. The grief was still there, but now she knew whence it came; and the time for it was over. She had her life in a world where she needed no man to give her permission for learning. And now, it seemed, she had Arundel as well.

"What *am* I to do with you?" she said aloud, and Kit opened his eyes.

"An 'twould not affright you, I could make some suggestions," he said. He stretched and sat up. Half his points were untied.

"I just bet you could." Ellen wrapped the sheet around her.

"An I were not an honorable man," Kit said in hurt tones, "would I have spent last night upon the floor? The boards of Greenholt are grown no softer since my father laid them down. And I a poor old man, hundreds of years now, by thy accounting. Of your mercy you might have offered me a softer resting place."

Ellen laughed again. "I'll find you a bed today. There are lots of rooms here."

"What a pity." Kit leaned his elbow on the bed, inches from her knees. "This lodging would suit me well."

"But not me," Ellen said, and then, thoughtfully, "not yet."

"What, sweeting, no longer afeard?"

She shook her head. Memory had banished the shadows; she stood in the sun now. "I know who I am," Ellen said slowly. "And I know who *you* are. And I can sing without fear now."

Sitting up with the sheets tumbling about her, she demonstrated with an arpeggio of high sharp notes that brought a furious thumping from Bethany's room next door.

"Why should you fear?" Kit asked.

"I began to remember quite a long time ago," Ellen said. "In a music class at the university."

Kit frowned sharply, but she was lost in memories wrapped in memories. "Some of your songs survived," she said, "not from the masque, but the others . . . They'd been attributed to Dowland, I think. I sang one in a music class and . . . I thought I was going mad." She laughed softly. It was sweet to sit in the sunlight and remember, as if reading a story, the pain and fear of that dark winter when she had tried to run away from music, from the ghostly memories that overlaid her present vision, from her self. "I gave up music, it frightened me so," she said. "Can you imagine?"

"I cannot imagine or understand *anything*," Kit said plaintively. "What had you to do at Oxford?"

"It wasn't Oxford, it was the University of Texas," Ellen said without thinking, and then realized how much more was needed. "Texas is a state in the United States of America," she explained rapidly. "That's a different country—well, it used to be a colony of England, but we had a revolution—oh, dear. This is going to be more complicated than I realized."

"Later," Kit said. "I was ever a quick scholar at the book; I shall find my way around this world in time. But I still do not understand how a woman came to study at any university."

"Things have changed a bit since your time," Ellen said. She did not think that Kit would grasp the magnitude of the changes by sitting in Greenholt and reading books; nor would he be content for long with such a restricted world, not her Kit. She looked down at his long form with a smile, thinking how truly she knew him, had always known him, if she would but have listened to the music he wrote to unlock the doors of memory.

"How much *do* you remember?" Kit asked then, as if he'd been following her unspoken thoughts.

"Everything." Ellen shivered. The midsummer magic of that four-hundred-year-old masque was still with her, far more chilling than the more distant memory of her breakdown six years ago. "We came to visit you at Greenholt; you and Edward were working on a masque that was to call down spirits and give you the knowledge of the universe."

That quick frown slashed across Kit's face again. "And the masque?"

"You . . . vanished," Ellen said. Across the years, that memory still felt like ice in her heart. "I could not move or sing; another took my place; the Fair Folk were all about the hall, and then you burned like a flame of darkness and there was nothing there but the air."

"I know what happened to me," Kit said. His fingers encircled her wrist. "What of *you*?"

Oh, I died. One couldn't say such words. Ellen covered Kit's tense fingers with her own hand and felt the reassuring double beat of their two pulses. She was alive, and Eleanor was alive in her with all her memories; but the body that had housed Eleanor had been dust hundreds of years ago.

"Eleanor fainted—"

"*You* are Eleanor."

"Yes and no. Eleanor died."

The pressure on her wrist increased until Ellen felt faint with the pain. "Kit, give over, pray!"

"I'm in no mood for mazes and puzzles," he said between clenched teeth, but he released her.

"Tough shit," Ellen said, rubbing her arm. "*Yes*, I am partly Eleanor; I remember all that she lived through. . . . She was ill for several days; wandering in her wits, or so Edward said when she . . . I . . . woke." She shivered at the recollection of that other awakening, so close in memory, so distant in time. "There were wild tales told in the village, Kit; some would have it that Raleigh's men had murdered you in secret, some that the Devil snatched you like Doctor Faustus in Germany."

"Which did *you* believe?"

"Neither," Ellen said simply. "I knew who had taken you, though Edward thought I'd run mad. I had to slip out of the house by night, when no one was watching me." She shivered again. "The Ladyswood was very dark. I had your lute. . . . The moon was past the full, waning towards the quarter. I did play and sing your songs of magic until I could see the other sphere of the wood, not clear, but as a misty dimness. There did I see you wandering therein, did call to you, but you could not hear me. Then *she* came—the Lady of the Wood. And even she could not quite take human form in our sphere; there was the light of Faerie about her, and times she did seem to be a tree, or a wisp of cloud. She said I had missed my day; their sphere and ours had drawn too far apart, and you could not return to me in this time. Then did I recall Mr. Cavendish's prognostication that the spheres should not draw so close again these four hundred year, and so did I pray the Lady of her mercy—"

"That one has none," said Kit, "you had better have prayed to Our Lady."

"But she did grant it me," said Ellen. "That I should sleep until the spheres drew close again, and should awaken in good time to bring you back into the mortal world. And so . . . Eleanor caught a chill from wandering in the damp wood in her night rail, and she had no more strength or desire for this world. . . ."

"*No.*" Kit was pale. "Eleanor was not such a ninny as to die for love of any man."

"Edward," Ellen said, "had taken away the books you gave her, calling them devil's work."

"Oh . . ."

"She went home, and fell asleep, and . . . I do remember nothing after; but there is a book in this house that tells how she—her mortal part died then, and her spirit . . . my spirit . . . slept until now. Only, I did not remember properly what it was that I must do, or who I had been."

"Such is ever the Faerie way," said Kit grimly, "to make fair promises and withal to cheat you of the truth."

"But they helped me to remember," Ellen protested. "Paien brought me here to sing in the masque. Why would he do that, if he did not mean that they should keep their bargain in sense as well as words?"

"That I cannot guess," said Kit, but his gaze was too steady, his face too still. He was keeping back some thought, she could tell. "But for me it is enough to have you back, Eleanor."

It would have to be; what more did he have now? Even Greenholt was no longer his. She hated to contradict him. "Not . . . entirely," Ellen said. "I do remember all that Eleanor lived, but . . ."

"And what but memory makes the man?" Kit demanded.

"I don't know. But . . . Kit, Eleanor died at nineteen. I have lived twenty-six years as Ellen Ainsley from Baytown, in a world you know nothing of, and that life is just as real to me as Eleanor's. I need *time*," she said.

"You are my Eleanor."

"I have lived her life. But it is also true that Eleanor caught a chill and died in 1594—and if you can't believe both those things," Ellen said, "I wonder how you manage to believe in the Holy Trinity, not to mention the resurrection of the body and the communion of saints."

Kit laughed under his breath. "A hit, my lady! Truth to tell, the Trinity was ever a difficult theological point for me."

"As I recall," said Ellen, marveling at all that was implied in those three simple words, "as I recall, that got you into some trouble last time."

"No more," said Kit with heavenly simplicity. "I've no need to play at theological quibbles now."

Ellen looked at him suspiciously. "Indeed! Why not?"

"I understand everything now. Such was my bargain with the Dark Lady, love. My soul and body to Faerie, and the understanding of the spheres for me: the whole sacred chain that links stones with animal nature, animal life with human soul, and man with the angels."

"How very convenient," said Ellen. "Do you suppose we could interface you with the KNEE data base?"

"What is a day too base? Hmm, it sounds like the first line of a song. I wonder what I could do with that?"

"It's computer stuff. I thought you knew everything."

"In principle only. I must learn the facts of this new world like any boy at school. Where shall we begin?"

Bethany banged on the door then, and reminded Ellen that Sam was waiting to take them down to the Emminster Fete, and that provided the answer.

"Not," said Ellen anxiously, "that I'm quite sure what a Fete is. But I *am* sure that you can't go to it in those clothes." Kit's ruff had lost most of its starch in the rain; it was a limp puddle of white under his chin. His short velvet cloak was spotted with water and crushed from having been rolled up for a pillow, and his fine linen hose were stiff with dried mud. "I wonder if they sell jeans and sweaters in Emminster?"

"Have to go to Bridport for that, won't you?" said Sam when Bethany relayed the question to him. "I'll pop on back home and get some spares."

When Ellen tried to thank him, he waved away thanks and payment together with one big hand, mumbling some words about the honor of supplying one of The Family.

"Feudal," said Ellen while Sam was on his errand of supply.

"Useful," Bethany said.

Kit had to be introduced to the mysteries of the zipper, and that delayed them still further; so that it was nearly noon before Sam's van bumped down into Emminster and came to a halt before the little stone shelter in the center of the triangular market space.

"Okay," Bethany said, looking around at the stalls and booths and amusement stands that had sprouted overnight, covering the market space right up to the verges of the two-lane highway that ran through the center of the village. Ladies in flowered dresses and children in shorts were offering to sell enamel frog pendants, folded star pin cushions, Toby jugs, used books, and cheese sandwiches. "At least now I know what a Fete is. It's a village-wide garage sale." She eyed Kit and added to Ellen, under her breath, "But I still don't know what *he* is. What's come over you?"

"I'll explain everything later," Ellen promised, and hoped that when the time came she would be able to think of some acceptable explanation. *He's an old friend. How old? Oh, very old. You wouldn't believe me if I told you. How come I never mentioned him all the time we've lived together? Well, um . . . look, Bethany. I don't interrogate you about Paien, do I? What do you mean, that's different?*

Ellen shook her head and gave up on the unprofitable imagined conversation. She could only hope that it would go better in reality. Meanwhile, Kit was wandering through the crowded market square and about to step out in front of a moving car.

Abandoning Bethany and Sam in their study of the used books, she ran after Kit and grabbed his hand just in time to yank him out of the car's path. A red-faced man stuck his head out the window and shouted, "Bloody tourists, can't you look where you're going!" before vanishing in a puff of exhaust fumes down the A3044 towards Mosterton.

"What," said Kit carefully, "is a *tour-ist?*"

Ellen laughed. "He thinks you're a visitor from foreign parts." She stopped laughing at the sight of Kit's set face.

"That I be, in truth," said Kit, "and my own land drowned beneath the seas of Time, that I wander ever here exiled."

Ellen thought of various comforting, untrue, or useless things to say, and said none of them. *It's not that bad. You've got me . . . sort of. You'll get used to it.*

"Let's go see the church," she said at last, thinking that Kit might welcome a respite from the relentless modernity of Emminster during a Saturday Fete.

"The sixteenth-century west front is supposed to be very fine."

Not to Kit's eyes, it wasn't.

"What have they *done* to my fine new stonework?" he howled. "That thief of a mason swore he'd carve the church front in Ham stone, but from the looks of it he must have used nothing but soft chalk. It's worn away like an iced cake in the rain!"

"*You* paid for the church?" Ellen asked. "I thought—"

"I know what's due to my position," Kit said. "Parson Hensley's a prating fool, but as the chief landowner . . ." His voice trailed away into a whisper. "Hensley's dead," he said with finality.

Perhaps it hadn't been such a good idea after all, visiting the church. Ellen led the way into the interior, which had been rebuilt and restored several times since Kit's day and should awaken no such painful memories.

The church was filled with flowers: blue and white sprays of delphinium shooting out of a tall Chinese vase, an armful of blowsy overblown pink roses nodding over the tall carved pulpit, daisies and ferns beneath each commemorative marble plaque along the north wall.

"What," said Kit, "is this a pagan festival for Flora?"

"I think," Ellen said doubtfully, "it's an old English custom."

"Nay, some newfangled flummery." Kit dismissed the floral tributes with a disdainful flip of his hand.

"Shh! You'll insult the ladies who decorated the place." The old woman in the horrible green overshoes was waddling down the center aisle, almost within earshot. She seemed to take no notice of Kit's comments, but when she reached them she stopped and looked Kit in the face, intent, searching. Then, as if satisfied, she nodded once.

"So, Arundel. Reckon 'twasn't true, all they wrote about you, if you can come into church all peaceable."

"I should be able to," said Kit, wounded, "I paid for its building."

"Needs a new roof on the vestry, doesn't it?" She glanced at Ellen. "Seems well enough, love, but I'd have parson to bless him, to see does he fly out of window at the Name."

"I don't think I need do that," Ellen assured her.

"No? Well enough," the old lady repeated. "As well he's come back, then. He'll be some company for the other one there." And with a nod of her head towards the vestry curtain, she stumped on out of the church, green overshoes flapping and squelching around her ankles.

"What a monstrous old beldame," murmured Kit, staring after her.

"What do you suppose she meant about you being company for the other one?" Ellen asked, but the last half of her question was drowned out by the rising music that she'd heard once before; a breathy singing of many voices, loud and almost tuneless. Her palms felt cold and clammy. Kit was staring at the faded red velvet curtain, head slightly on one side, intent as a cat waiting for the first twitch of a mouse's whiskers.

The curtain stirred, and Ellen felt the fine hairs on her forearms separate and stiffen. The air smelled wrong: not the still coolness of damp stone, but the rush of a rainwet breeze through growing leaves and dry leaves.

There was a boy before the curtain, where a moment earlier there had been only air shaking the faded reddish brown folds. His long, coarse coat did not belong to this century. There was a white cloth around his left hand. Ellen catalogued details, frantically, in an effort to avoid looking at the eyes that stared through her, unseeing, exactly as Kit had done when she first saw him in a wood that was no longer there.

"Mam," the boy said on a long questioning note. "Mam?"

The church door swung open, and a group of people came in, all talking at once and exclaiming over the floral decorations. Between, "Lovely, my dear," and "Smashing roses, Mrs. S.," the music died away and Ellen saw the vestry curtains where the boy's head had been.

Beside her, Kit gave a long trembling sigh. "Poor John, could you not find your way?"

Ellen let go Kit's hand. Suddenly she felt that one of them was an alien. Perhaps, she thought wildly, the old lady's advice to sprinkle him with holy water had not been so bad after all. "You talk to ghosts?"

"I *was* a ghost," Kit said. "Would still be, had you not called me from the wood. Poor John Daniel has no one in this world to call him, and he has all but forgotten the way."

"I think," Ellen said slowly and carefully, "you had best explain."

"Yes . . . but not here." Kit looked balefully at the twittering couples who had interrupted them.

They walked hand in hand through the graveyard with its tilting, moss-green gravestones, and then on down Church Lane. Kit did not speak, and Ellen was half afraid to hear what he might say; silence felt safer. Beyond St. Mary's, Church Lane straggled downwards, narrowing, losing its paving, changing its name to Shorts Lane and then all but disappearing. Where it became no more than a narrow muddy lane under an arch of green leaves, a signpost read, "DORSET COUNTY COUNCIL BRIDLEWAY."

"What's happened to the path?" Kit demanded in disgust. "It did lead straight through the open fields here."

Now the trees grew up tall and shady, and the path itself was a well-worn track several feet below the level of the adjoining field. On either side they were walled in by vertical banks, solid green with ferns, grass, nettles, bracken, and the roots of trees that grew up and arching over the path to make a green tunnel.

"Annihilating all that's made To a green thought in a green shade," Ellen murmured.

"That's a pretty conceit," Kit said.

Ellen thought briefly of the centuries of English literature that waited Kit's discovering, and then of the years of feet walking this path to wear it down so far below the fields, while the saplings grew up and entangled their branches overhead to make the tunnel; and where had Kit been all this while? The strangeness of the day took her again between one breath and the next, and she felt as cold as if they stood in the ghostly mists of Ladyswood again.

"You were going to tell me about the—what we saw in the church," she said.

"I was?" Kit sounded first evasive, then resigned. "Yes, I suppose I was."

It was like probing a sore tooth; painful, but one could not resist. "You knew him? You knew who he was." *Little John Daniel. They thought he drowned in the creek, but no one ever found the body.*

"Certes I did know him," said Kit. "Think you I was the only mortal man or woman ever to be taken into Faerie? Many and many a one of us have they brought into their own sphere. For a time they do grieve—*we* do grieve," he corrected himself with a catch of his breath, "for our own kind, for true sun and wind and candlelight and all that we have lost. But we forget—we forget. Him that you saw, he stepped over the running water and into Ladyswood on a day when the spheres were close together, and for that trespass was he forfeit to Faerie."

No one ever found his body. Ellen shivered in the green twilight under the overarching branches. Pigeons cooed in the sunny field beyond the line of trees; some other bird that she could not name burst out with a sudden call, sharp and rasping and startled, like a sentinel in the high branches.

"Is that what all ghosts are, then?" she asked. "Wanderers like you, lost in Faerie and seeking the way home again?"

"Nay, there be divers kinds of ghosts, as there be of spirits and men," Kit said absently. "The Wanderers be not evil intentioned towards the living, as might be the unquiet spirit of one who died by violence. But in time do they forget their mortal lives, and then they become the ghosts of Faerie, and can no longer walk this earth even in dreams."

He comes back—he comes back, every so often.

"*You* did not forget," Ellen said, "and you have been gone more years than John Daniel." There was a riddle here that she must read; but puzzle her head as she might, she could not crack the shell.

She could not even think directly on it, or not for
more than a few moments at a time. Why did it
matter how one was saved and another lost? Kit
had been brought again alive to her, and in coming
he had brought back all her memories so that she
need never more fear her own madness or her own
music. Was not this enough to content her?

"Having you to call me back, I could not well
forget," said Kit.

"And John Daniel? Why does he come back after
so many years?"

"How should I know? Why waste our days in pointless
questions?" Kit embraced her suddenly, and the mud
of the lane was slippery under her feet, so that she
leaned against him to keep her balance, and his kisses
took the breath and sense from her but left behind
the troubling sense of questions unanswered, perhaps
the right question still unasked.

They came to the sunny bank at the end of the
bridle path, with high woods of oak and beech on
one hand and a hedge of brambles on the other,
and the land falling away below the hedge in gentle
green folds and ripples like a cloak cast down carelessly.
Incurious cows grazed in the shadow of the hedge,
and did not look up when Kit wove a garland for
Ellen's head and sang to her, both songs of his own
composing and the strange minor melodies of Faerie
that had no more tune than the rippling of water
over rounded rocks. Ellen drifted in the peace of
those timeless songs, content in the softening air
of the summer day, until the church bells rang for
noon and called her back to the times and rhythms
of the mortal world.

"We'll be late for rehearsal," was all she said, but

Kit stopped his singing on a word, and the silence was broken only by the last humming echo of the bells of St. Mary's church.

"Is it so important to you," he said, "this masque?"

"*Your* masque," said Ellen. "I should think you'd be happy to hear it sung once again."

"I doubt it is not wise to meddle with such powers as I raised upon the first time," said Kit slowly. "In very truth, I know 'tis not." A cloud passed over the sun; the birds in the wood fell silent, and he shivered. "I can see it now, Eleanor, the bones and frame of magic that music can build, calling the spheres together that should be let drift apart again. I should not have written that music; I shall not sing it."

"Well, somebody will," Ellen pointed out. "After what's been spent to bring us to this place, they're not likely to forget about the masque just because it makes you nervous."

"Faerie gold," Kit said.

"Oh. I didn't think. Of course." Ellen frowned. "But if my singing brought you out of Faerie, why would they *want* me to sing and free you? They went to some trouble to take you; why would they want you brought back now?"

"Who can say?" And Kit became amorous again, so that Ellen had enough to do to scramble to her feet and remind him of their promise to gather for rehearsal at one o'clock, and she quite forgot that once again he'd evaded her questions. Another thought preoccupied her as they made their way back along the path through the woods and fields south of the village.

"If the masque makes a dangerous magic," she

said at last, "cannot you change the music so that it will be safer?"

Kit brightened at that suggestion, and while they walked through Emminster and up the narrow paved road to Greenholt Manor he was so occupied with humming new measures, and beating time with his hands, that all conversation died a natural death, and Ellen's questions remained unanswered.

A group of schoolchildren picnicking on the grass at Hackthorn Down fled the viewing point where once a Roman fort had stood, shrieking about the metal man with feathers on his head. Their teacher told them to for God's sake sit quietly in the omnibus while she investigated.

Sunlight pierced the clouds and blinded her for a moment with the flash of polished metal, and for a moment she thought she saw what the children had been screaming about: a figure standing half in and half out of a gentle rise in the land, with a breastplate of metal and a crest of red horsehair on its helmet. The air smelled hot and strange, full of ozone, and it crackled around her when she moved. "Lightning," she thought. "And now the thunder . . ."

The thunder seemed to be asking a question of her, low rumbling words that almost made sense in another time, another language. Then the strange image burned into her eyes by the sudden flash began to fade. Some impulse made her speak. *"Vale,"* she said, and she had the illusion that a hand was raised to match her own; then there was only turf, and the birds crying overhead, and a sense of oppression in the air like a thunderstorm about to break. She went back to her charges and told them firmly that they were not to make up foolish stories again, and said nothing to anyone about the bright silver coin she had picked up from the ground where the image had appeared. "A penny for the ferryman," she thought, for she had had a classical education, and then, "But I could never explain finding it, and so it's best to say nothing." And so there was nothing about that strange occurrence in the Emminster papers.

The Long Gallery still had its chequerboard of black and white floor tiles, and the sun still broke into rainbows where it shone through the diamond-shaped panes in the casement windows. As she stepped into the room, Ellen felt as though she were walking through two times at once. She could remember being Eleanor, standing in this very room and peering through these tall windows at the guests arriving by torchlight. And she knew that she was Ellen, with a mortal body that was hungry enough to appreciate Geoffrey's offer of a cheese and chutney sandwich. And presently her two selves would become one, and she would sing for the first time with all her self poured into the music—without fear or ghosts or shadows stalking behind the measures.

She was eager for the masque to begin, impatient to try herself on Kit's music. He wanted to put off rehearsing to another day altogther.

"Why?"

"But we're all here now; why not get on with it?"

"We haven't that long before the real masque," three outraged English voices said all at once.

Kit gave Geoffrey, Penny, and Roger a level stare. "The music needs changing."

"You *can't* change the music!" Roger howled.

"This is Kit Arundel's *original manuscript*, don't you understand?"

"Over my dead body . . ." Bethany started.

"Look," said Geoffrey, more reasonably, "we're all putting our spare time and effort into this thing, because we live here and we love Emminster, understand? This is Arundel's music, and no matter how much you've got the family face, the music is ours—not yours to fiddle with."

"Little you know," Kit began indignantly, and Ellen seized his arm and drew him aside.

"Let's sing it as it stands today," she whispered. "We don't have time to make up a good explanation, and they're eager to start rehearsal. And you *can't* tell them the truth—they'd never believe it."

"And what if . . ."

"If anything at all looks the least bit strange," Ellen said, "I promise to give a piercing shriek and interrupt the masque with seven kinds of fits. But I don't think it will. Remember how often we rehearsed last time?" Last week, last year, last century . . . farther back than that, and closer than last month in memory. "It's not midsummer yet, and it's broad daylight. Surely there can't be that much danger?"

"Let's hope not," said Kit gloomily. He nodded to the chorus and went off to make his entrance as Actaeon. And Ellen remembered, too late, that she'd been unable to do anything at all last time. If they called the deep magic of Faerie today—

They wouldn't. Not by the earthly sun that shone in at the windows.

Kit strode to the center of the stage. "Speech as Actaeon, peer around stage, song. Music?"

Roger picked up his lute. "We'll have to do the

Chorus bits *a capella* for now, though," he warned them. "Mrs. Edwardes has a church picnic today."

"Who's Mrs. Edwardes?" Ellen whispered to Geoffrey.

"Church organist," he whispered back as Kit launched into Actaeon's first song. "Plays the virginals, too. Remember, we're having some of the choir to be extra Nymphs and Hounds."

Once again Ellen reflected that this masque seemed to be organizing itself—or had Paien worked on the villagers as he'd worked on Bethany and her? And if so, why? No time to puzzle it out now—it was almost time for her entrance as Diana, with Bethany and Penny singing the parts of the Nymphs.

As she moved towards the stage, Fenella took her place beside Geoffrey. "I don't understand anything," she complained. "What's he singing about?"

"It's Actaeon and Diana," Geoffrey answered, eyes on the stage where Kit finished his opening song. "Just listen to that! We've got to keep him for Actaeon, even if he does give us trouble over the music. He fits the part as if it had been written for him."

Ellen coughed and tried to compose her face.

"So who's Actaeon, when he's at home?" Fenella persisted.

Geoffrey looked down at her. "My God," he muttered, "where *were* you educated, my child, at a Young Ladies' Finishing Seminary? Look here. You know who Diana is."

"The Moon Goddess," said Fenella. "I'm not *totally* ignorant."

"And the Huntress," Geoffrey said, "and the goddess of knowledge and enlightenment, and in the Renaissance mind she symbolized Hermetic knowledge—oh, never mind," he stopped himself, "let's not get into all that. It's a very simple story basically. See the stage? That's a valley sacred to Diana, all right? Private property. No trespassers. There's a fountain—"

"Where?"

"There will be," said Geoffrey patiently, "when we've made the scenery. Look, just *imagine* a fountain, okay? Now one day when Diana had been hunting, she stopped off to wash in the fountain. . . ."

"Praised be Diana's fair and harmless light," sang Bethany and—not Jane. The other girl was Penny, and she belonged to this century; but as Ellen stepped out onto the stage, her feet walked both ways together, and she heard Jane's sweet, pure contralto behind Penny's thinner voice. As their song drew to a close, her feet and voice carried her into Diana's part without conscious memory. Bend and curtsey and turn, all as part of the dance with the Nymphs, but end facing the audience.

"Ladies mine, the summer days are long and warm, even in this Arcadia. . . ."

"Holy Christ! Where'd she learn to speak like that?" Roger's penetrating whisper startled Ellen, and she heard her own voice—*Eleanor's* voice— clear and carrying, but with the long pure vowels and measured cadences of Elizabethan stage-speech.

"And so forth and so on," she gabbled, trying to remember how to talk like an American again, "song . . ." She nodded at Roger, and hoped he would be too busy to notice her accent. Because the music was taking her now, Kit's music, with all the magic of memory flowing through the perfectly crafted measures, and she was Ellen freeing herself from fear and Eleanor awakening from her long sleep, singing to break the chains of all the spells that had been wound about to keep her from full knowledge of herself.

"Shake off your heavy trance," she sang, "and leap into a dance such as no mortals use to tread . . ."

Then Roger and Geoffrey put their instruments down to act the part of the Hounds, gamboling around Kit to make him notice Diana. They weren't half the dancers the first Hounds had been, Ellen thought absently; but then, it was no longer part of a gentleman's training to dance a pavane or a galliard, make a leg or fence in the Italian style . . .

She had to sing again. And the music carried her through the masque without thought or fear until the rowdy dance of Nymphs and Hounds let her and Kit retire offstage.

"What comes now?" panted Roger after a lively attempt at singing "Circe bids you come away," while dancing with the Nymphs.

"Commoning. We descend into the hall and dance with the guests," Geoffrey prompted him. "Gives Actaeon and Diana time for their costume changes." He peered out across the black and white tiles of the Long Gallery. "Granted we're a bit thin of company at the moment . . . Come on, ladies; we'll have to mime it." He leapt from the stage with a Hound-like manic jump and began energetically "dancing" with an invisible partner.

"The music needs work," Kit said while Geoffrey and the Nymphs mimed their dance.

"I told you," said Roger. "We don't muck around with the music."

Kit nodded. "Yes, but there *are* places where it could be better. Perhaps an error in transcription. Look at this passage here. It should be played faster

than the rest, then slow down again when the men's
voices join in. . . ."

Roger bent his head over the music and grunted.
"Mmm. I see what you mean."

"And this should all be pitched a half-tone higher
to better fit Eleanor's—Ellen's—voice," Kit went
on. "Otherwise will the joining of melodies fail, and
so is all brought to ruin."

"That *is* better," Roger allowed after trying a few
notes. "Fits better with the rest, somehow. Damned
if I know how you got on to it so quickly, though."

"I was used to be reckoned a musician of some
note," said Kit absently. "Ficino saith that music
unlocks the keys of memory and animates the
imagination; and according to the Nolan, it is
imagination joined with the cognitive power that
is the source of all energy. But memory is the
key—music and memory. See you, thus shall the
notes recall the words to your mind, the words
the images, and the images linked one with another
by the power of association. . . ."

"Semantic data bases," Ellen said.

Both men turned and looked at her.

"Semantics?" said Roger.

"What?" said Kit.

"Data bases," Ellen repeated. "Not the kind banks
and insurance companies use. The super-flexible
ones people are building for AI—artificial intelligence,"
she translated for Roger, "and language processing.
The company I work for, we write software to help
people create semantic data bases." And she loved
her work; only now, when she wasn't using it as a
hiding place, could she remember the exultant joy
of bending her whole mind to a complex problem

whose elegant solution presently would scroll across her screen, a piece of the world's inherent structure translating into graphs and links and moving images.

Such work as I could never do in Kit's world, lacking Latin, being despised of the scholars. That was Eleanor's memory; it was also hers. "It is all," she said slowly, "about patterns; patterns in words or sound or sense." Eleanor had known that, four hundred years ago, but she'd lacked the learning to build on her intuitions. "You see, instead of tables or hierarchies—"

"The universe is a hierarchy of powers," Kit interrupted, "from sense to elements, from elements to daemons, from daemons to stars, from stars to gods, and thence to the very spirit of the universe. So saith Messer Giordano Bruno in his great work *De Magia*, and so have I proven in mine own experience."

"Where in this hierarchy is the sphere in which thou'st dwelt these four hundred year?" Ellen demanded.

Kit stopped, his mouth slightly open. Roger retreated to where Geoffrey and Fenella sat talking, shaking his head. "I can't understand a word those Americans are saying," he told them.

"Chris isn't American," Fenella pointed out.

"Must be," said Roger, "he makes no more sense than the other one."

Kit finally closed his mouth.

"The model of the hierarchy is *inadequate*," Ellen insisted. "What you need is a network. See, you let each element define its own set of links. Then if you define Faerie and our world as subsets of data . . ."

Words weren't enough. She wanted to show Kit

the dance of the interlocking nets which she had created by changing one rule in KNEE's knowledge structure. She knelt on the floor and drew pictures with one finger in the film of sawdust left by Sam's carpentry work. Kit dropped to his knees beside her and studied the graphs with mounting excitement.

"Using the nature of the divine universe to organize the mind, which then reflects the universe in itself . . ."

"Modeling mental processes by neural networks . . ."

"But the system must be complete. So could I never do, by any piling of seal upon seal or sign upon sign, until music and the daemons of Faerie opened my mind."

"Yes. A total world-knowledge data base is the key. But what I never could see . . ."

"Signs, notes, characters, seals . . ."

"Object-oriented programming, search strategies . . ."

They both halted and stared at one another.

"Eventually," Ellen said.

"The mind cannot hold so vast a store of knowledge."

"The system gets too complex."

"Memory fails."

"Yes, memory's been the problem up to now," Ellen agreed, "but it's so cheap nowadays, you can't blame that. The problem is with the model—we haven't been working with the right model; so things get more and more complicated. It's like trying to do chemistry before people figured out about atoms and molecules. There is a structure underlying the universe, but we don't know what it is. We still aren't using the right paradigm."

"I know," said Kit, and suddenly his voice sounded so hollow that Ellen looked at him sharply, frightened. No—there was no glimmer of magic about him; it was only that he looked desperately tired. "With the right—paradigm, you say? it all falls into place. Look—I know not how you call these signs," he said in frustration, tracing over the diagram Ellen had made in the dust.

"Nodes," Ellen said under her breath. "Links. It doesn't matter. Go on." The new structure made a new kind of sense, one that held Newton's common-sense physics together with the dream-physics of Faerie, that allowed both and neither to be true.

"I do not *know* enough," Kit said. "There is more, is there not?"

"Inferencing rules. Basic axioms . . ."

"Had I time to learn these mystical seals of *inference* and *axiom*, then should you design this *data base* anew and aright. All shall be known now, all the secrets laid bare."

Ellen felt a wild longing to dash to her notebook computer. Kit's understanding of the universe was beginning to mesh with hers; but it was fuzzy, uncertain. She needed to get it down in the words and symbols of predicate calculus; then it would make sense, it would be testable, it would be part of her world . . . and that thought, suddenly, was very frightening. As if by changing the symbols in the computer, she could somehow change the reality they represented.

"After the masque," she said at last, with some relief. "I can't *think* about this stuff without writing programs to test it on the computer. Then if I could get a decent phone connection without too much line noise and upload the model to GIC's mainframes . . ." She shook her head. "There's not *time*. One thing at a time. We'll talk about it later."

"Talking," said Kit gloomily, "will serve no manner of purpose."

In any case, there was no time left even for talking. Roger was pushing them back into the rehearsal, shouting at Geoffrey to quit explaining Greek mythology to Fenella and get onstage for the mime of the Hounds pursuing Actaeon.

Ellen took her place at stage left. She had nothing to do but stand and wait and look like a moon goddess while the Hounds pursued Actaeon up and down the stage, driving him at last to fall exhausted at her feet. Then she spoke the words written for the original masque, Diana demanding an apology from Actaeon for his intrusion upon her. Actaeon pleaded his desire for enlightenment—another most cleverly philosophical piece; it could be read as Raleigh trying to get reinstated in the Queen's grace, or as the philosopher demanding enlightenment of the gods, or—as the magician calling upon the great chain of being. "From sense to elements, from elements to daemons, stars, gods, thence to the very spirit of the world," Kit had said to Roger. But last time, no such speech had been wanted; the daemons had come of their own will and desire.

Now Kit dropped to one knee before her for his last song. "Lady of light, revive my dying sprite," he began, to the soft accompaniment of Roger's lute, and then broke off. The lute played the next phrase alone.

"What the hell are you playing at?" Roger shouted.

"We shall omit this song," Kit said.

In the hall of memory Ellen heard the song and saw Kit's gradual transformation, the light of Faerie that had glimmered about him in place of earthly

sun and moon. "He's right," she said before Roger
could gather his arguments. "This ending bit is too
long. We can't do the whole masque, not for a modern
audience. They'll get bored. Look at Fenella."

Fenella was eating apples, noisily, and leafing through
a romance novel.

"Hardly a fair example," said Roger, "m'sister's
illiterate. But I do see your point—though I'd rather
cut the speech . . . well, no, then it won't make sense,
will it? All right, you two, how about the duet?"

Ellen and Kit sang "A day, a night, an hour of
sweet content," and then Kit suggested that they
could vanish more effectively if his last song also
were cut. Instead, let the Nymphs and Hounds rush
onstage with their ballet and song to end the piece,
while Diana and Actaeon quietly slipped behind
the scenes.

"Unless you wish to recreate the ropes and pulleys
of the original, for their ascent among the stars?"

"Umm." Roger rubbed his chin. "I do see your
point. Wicked Kit Arundel" —Kit winced slightly—
"could hire all the carpenters and builders and stage
designers he wanted; besides, he was an expert at
tricks like that. I'm no expert, and all we've got is
Sam. He said he'll knock up some scene flats for us
in his spare time, but I don't think he'd be willing
to construct a flying machine."

"And you can be damned sure," said Kit, "that
I'm not willing to trust my life to the original ending."

"Sam's a good carpenter," Roger said. "Oh, well.
It's your own songs you're cutting; anybody object?"

No one spoke up except Fenella, who'd dropped
her romance novel to gaze at Kit when he came
forward and started talking. "*I* think it's a *pretty*

story," she said enthusiastically. "I don't see why you told me it was a gruesome myth, Geoff!"

"Well, you see, the way the myth originally went, Actaeon turned into a stag and was torn to pieces by his own hounds," Geoffrey explained gently.

"But Wicked Kit Arundel changed it around," Roger chimed in. This time Kit managed to control his wince. "In this version, Actaeon is rewarded for his love of enlightenment, symbolized by Diana, by being removed from the earthly plane to dwell with her."

"Oh, that's ever so much nicer," Fenella enthused.

"*Is* it?" Kit muttered under his breath. "You know not whereof you speak, my girl. I just hope to—whatever Gods may be," he said, bowing his head slightly, "that this production ends not as did the first one."

"It won't," Ellen said with more confidence than she felt. "You were sent back from Faerie. Whatever they wanted with you, they're through; otherwise Paien wouldn't have gone to so much trouble to bring me here to you." She held his arm, mortal bone and flesh and muscle warm and strong under her hand, and the sun was bright in the windows.

"All the same," said Kit, "I pray you will excuse me that last song. You'd love a song about Time standing still as little as do I, had you been where I have spent the last age."

Ellen could not help herself; she *had* to see if her new vision of the universe could be stated in KNEE's terms. During the next tea break she slipped away to her room and brought up the temporo-spatial model. Before she'd just deleted one rule, the sequentiality of time; now she added ambiguities.

Because KNEE was intended to handle the notorious ambiguities of natural languages, it was possible to qualify rules as simultaneously true and not-true, depending on context. She did that to the sequentiality rule, then stared for a while at the resulting rule set. It wasn't enough. You had to add something. *Kit.* She created an atom and called it KIT_STRUC_KB and added a rule which said that the presence of KIT_STRUC_KB in any net would cause the sequentiality rule's truth value to change. It was a crude approximation, but she needed *some* way to factor in the presence of someone whose brain held all the understanding they were trying to give to KNEE.

This time, the simulation program did not produce the old elegant dance of interlocking and unfolding, overlapping and separating spheres, that Ellen had produced every other time she altered the temporal rules. Instead one sphere folded and collapsed as if it were being drawn inside out.

"Where did I go wrong?" Ellen muttered. "This *can't* be right. It looks as if time were collapsing in on itself, as if all times were becoming one. And that is obviously *not the case.*"

A brief paragraph in the Emminster paper deplored the recent outbreak of petty vandalism. John Daniel's marble plaque in Saint Mary's Church had been defaced—the verger saw a short person, probably a boy disguised in his father's coat, pounding it with a stone; but when he ran to catch the child, it disappeared into streaks of shadow and light and left behind only a fist-sized stone on the ground.

On the same day, a sheep belonging to Furze

Farm had been killed and half butchered before
the shepherd frightened the miscreants away; he
hadn't seen them, but a flint arrowhead was found
in the sheep's corpse, so the paper blamed this too
on the destructive pranks of schoolchildren.

After that first long slow rehearsal the masque
and the plans for the masque seemed to take on a
frenetic pace of their own. The County Council had
money for costumes but no one to sew them; here
Penny had pitched in, bringing up her mother's sewing
machine to Greenholt Manor and borrowing a battered
black treadle machine from a friend in the village.
Bethany and Roger made an expedition to Dorchester
and returned with yards of billowing gauze for Nymphs,
dark brown felt and tights for Hounds. Ellen sang
the new settings that Kit had devised for his songs
and watched Bethany slashing through gauze with
her heavy shears and tried not to remember Jane
Guilford's dark head bent over Greene Taffety at
four nobles the yard—Jane who was still alive and
near in one set of memories, four hundred years
gone in another.

While Fenella and Bethany sewed and Ellen
sang, Kit plucked at his lute and irritably changed
metre and key until Roger declared that he meant
to drive them all mad. Twice a week the church
choir came up to Greenholt to shuffle about the
Long Gallery and sing the parts of Nymphs and
Hounds. Ellen found her double memories sharper
when she sang with Kit than at other times, which
was only natural; but his altered masque did not
change the quality of the light about them or bring
a troubling of the air that turned shadows into

faces. Four times in two weeks they went all through the masque with the choir in rehearsal, and then it was almost midsummer and the performance was scheduled for the day after tomorrow and the costumes were being hemmed.

"You see," Ellen said to Kit that night, "everything will be all right."

"I do most heartily pray it may end no worse than it has begun," said Kit. "Is it too late to stop the masque, do you think?"

"Much too late," Ellen said. "And you see, we have been rehearsing and nothing's happened."

In the shady lanes around Greenholt, gravel and asphalt disappeared in some places to be replaced by deep muddy ruts. The neat fences of a neighboring farm were overgrown all in a night by white-flowering brambles that smelled sweet and winey. Clouds and sun made a patchwork of light and shadow over the high grassy Downs, and in the shadows there were forms of air blurring together, and in the golden sunlit grass there were twisting lines of sharper, clearer light.

A milk van making deliveries to outlying cottages was lost for half a day and reappeared near Chideock, miles south of the route. The driver told a story of flashing lights and roads that turned in upon themselves like the branches of a maze; he was sacked for drunkenness.

13

Monday, June 20, 1994

Ellen and Kit and all the principal masquers spent all day before the masque rehearsing and drawing chalk lines on the floor of the Long Gallery and struggling in and out of costumes and taking long frantic stitches in the hems of skirts that had suddenly turned out to be six inches longer than intended. By the time it came to the sewing, to be accurate, the girls were alone. Roger and Geoffrey had gone off to the village with some vague promise about bringing back beer and sandwiches for everybody, and Kit was ensconced in the window seat at the end of the gallery with a pile of Roger's old schoolbooks. As far as Ellen knew, he had not explained to Roger why he wanted to study physics and chemistry from the grammar-school level on up, and Roger hadn't asked. Kit devoured the books like a lumberyard saw going through fresh timber, crunching up facts and absorbing them through half the night and emerging bright-eyed and sparkling with new words every morning. In the ten days since he'd begun his reading project he had advanced from awed discussion of the structure of the atom to forbidding tomes in cosmology and biochemistry.

"The labor of learning is, in nine parts of ten, the task of creating the true structure of the universe within the mind," he told Ellen once when she commented on the speed with which he absorbed new facts. "The structure is mine, I have only to add the facts. Did you realize that this substance called DNA builds in spirals like unto the spirals of the whirling stars—"

"Yes," said Ellen happily. "Is it not marvelous?" She scarcely knew, these days, whether she was Ellen or Eleanor; both sets of memories had flowed together in a seamless unity, and Kit was the joining-place. The music she had loved to make, the work she had learned to love—she could share both with him. They went from song to science and back again twenty times in the day, and she had never been so content.

Bethany called her now to help untangle a twisted mass of spangled gauze, and she left Kit to his studies. While she folded and tugged and pinned and cut, her mind wandered to a tangled wood and an arrogant young man with a very bad reputation. He had declared that she must wish to marry him, and not for his house and lands—such self-doubt had never crossed Arundel's mind—but because he was the only perfect match for her. Where, he had asked, would she find another man whose mind was in such harmony with hers?

"Where indeed?" Ellen said under her breath. She looked fondly at Kit where he sat amid a tumbled heap of books. She would really have to teach him about computers when they got back to America; he'd love them.

"What?" Bethany asked without really listening for an answer. "Have you got the pincushion? Fenella! Ellen's hoarding all the straight pins over here."

Fenella had proved surprisingly useful in the last-minute rush to have costumes together and the Long Gallery decorated for the masque; more useful, really, than Penny, who tended to stand empty-handed and hum her music with a soulful look while the rest of them were working on lights or cutting lengths of gauze. Now, though, instead of taking the pins, Fenella stood up and stretched. "I'm perishing with hunger," she declared. "Where's that worthless brother of mine when we need him? They should have been back with food *hours* ago."

Ellen looked up at the fading sky and realized she was right. The long summer twilight of England sometimes fooled her into thinking the afternoons could last forever; but the sky was pale and cool now, and her watch said that it was after seven o'clock.

"I'll walk down and meet them," Fenella announced. She whisked herself out of the room before anybody could quarrel with her decision.

"She doesn't have to run away," Bethany said ruefully, "it's not as though she were under any obligation to help us put things together."

"Mmm." Ellen's mouth was full of pins; she removed them one by one and thrust them through the spangled gauze, holding it in place like a butterfly mounted for scientific study. "I think their parents are some sort of local gentry. Noblesse oblige and all that. Didn't she say Mummy and Daddy were coming tomorrow night?"

"*Everybody* is coming tomorrow night," Bethany said, seizing two handfuls of her curly hair and yanking them away from her head. "These English, I *don't* understand them! Our lead tenor disappears into thin air and *he*"—she jerked her head towards Kit, rapt in his books—"shows up as if he were the designated understudy all along. Nobody knows who's paying for the masque, there's money but nobody to organize it, but every living soul in Emminster stops me when I go marketing and asks how we're coming and if we really mean to perform tomorrow night. They're incurably vague," she ended, "and if it weren't for the fact that I know it's been over a hundred degrees in Austin for the last two weeks, I'd go—*what's that?*"

Ellen heard nothing. She glanced at Kit; his head was still bent over a back issue of *Nature*. But Bethany was already on her feet, and after a moment Ellen followed her.

On the landing she could hear the sound that had alarmed Bethany: a faint sobbing shriek. They skidded pell-mell down the steep narrow stairs and reached the front door just as Fenella collapsed in a heap on the steps.

"What's the matter?" Bethany demanded.

Fenella gulped, swallowed, rubbed the back of one hand across her eyes, and shook herself all over, like a dog coming out of water. She looked much younger than she had ten minutes earlier. "N-nothing. I got lost—it's getting dark—I was frightened, that's all."

"On the way down to Emminster?" Bethany demanded. "And you living here all your life? Come on. What happened?"

"Nothing," Fenella repeated. "I—got turned around somehow; the road tilted uphill, and—the light was all wrong."

Ellen sat down on the steps beside her while Bethany shook her head. "Mist?" she inquired gently. "And trees where there should be none?" Bethany might think the land could not change underfoot. Ellen remembered better.

"There were lights among the trees," Fenella said. "Flowers of light, moving, lifting. And mist around them like puddles of water, and—all right. Laugh at me if you want to. I'm not leaving this house again tonight."

"I wasn't planning to laugh," said Ellen, just as Bethany announced that there was nothing wrong with the road down to the village and she'd be happy to prove it. She started down the gravel drive and Ellen felt an irrational leap of fear for her.

"Don't leave me," Fenella begged, clutching Ellen's hand. "I don't want to be here alone."

Bethany was alone, though; and as Ellen watched unbelieving, her dark head moved through the solid trunk of a tree; the ground shifted under Ellen's feet, not shaking as in an earthquake, but slipping and sliding away like the tilting landscape of a dream, and Bethany walked on, becoming transparent, an outline, a shadow among shadows.

"Bethany!" Ellen shook off Fenella's damply clinging grasp and ran through shadows, through impalpable quicksand, through air as thick and heavy as mud. The small cleared space of drive and garden stretched out forever, like elastic, and the dark trees that had taken Bethany receded. Flowers of light bloomed within the shadows, cold light that rose and swelled like music, but she could not reach them.

Ellen stopped and found herself still on the steps, the road and the trees still as far away as ever. But a chord of music hung on the air where the lights flowered, and that gave her the key. The opening song of the masque came to her lips, and she walked forward slowly singing, and the steps of the house fell away beneath her and she moved into the mist where Kit's beloved laws of physics had no rule.

"Praised be Diana's fair and harmless light," she sang, and the flowers of light swayed aside and let her pass. Singing, she went forward through mist and stars.

> Praised be the dews wherewith she moists
>   the ground;
> Praised be her beams, the glory of the
>   night;
> Praised be her power, by which all powers
>   abound.

The music slowed and twisted about her in random discords. The tree before her opened to show her Bethany in an oval of light, eyes open and unseeing. Briars were entangled in her skirt and sleeves, holding her prisoner. A slender tree swayed in the wind with a shower of golden leaves, bending branches across her path. Ellen struck at the branches and they became solid flesh, a man's arms in full white sleeves. Paien's hands caught and held her, and his breathless laugh interrupted the lingering discordant echoes of the song.

"Softly, softly, fair trespasser!"

"Bethany," Ellen said. She felt stupid, as slow in her head as her legs had been when she tried to run through the deep magic of Ladyswood. "Bring her back."

"She is lost," said Paien, softly but without any

trace of human sorrow, "and so shall you be, do you linger here."

Ellen set her teeth. The wood around her became a chaos of flying dark leaves that shrieked in the wind. She held to Paien's arm. "I don't leave without Bethany."

The flying leaves fell in green showers about them, turning to the burning hues of autumn as they fell, and the radiance about Bethany died away. "Lost," Paien repeated, and the leaves cried, "Lost, lost, lost!"

A chorus of birds with silver wings and human voices drowned out Ellen's furious reply. *"Come away, away, away,"* they sang, echoed by bells that seemed to ring from very far away. Trees and leaves and birds became cold mist, and mist became the cloudy evening sky outside Greenholt. Paien still held Ellen's wrist loosely in one hand, looking as much flesh and blood as any other man. The bells of St. Mary's danced their evening chimes through the brightening sky, as clouds thinned and a pale sun suffused the hills with a misty glow. And Bethany was nowhere to be seen.

Ellen turned to face Paien. She took his hands in hers. They felt almost like any mortal hands; she could feel the intricate network of bone and flesh and muscle all alive beneath her fingers. But he had neglected to give his human shape the warmth of living flesh, and there was no fluttering of blood pulsing through his wrists.

"Bring her back," she repeated.

"Too late," Paien said.

Ellen held tighter. "I won't let you go until you bring her back," and saying it, she knew it was an empty threat. How could she hold the mist and the wind?

Paien's features melted and ran into one another, and his arms shrank back into his trunk. Ellen threw her own arms around the changing form; a serpent's head reared back, and the flickering tongue touched her face. She remembered the old songs.

"And they shall change me in your hands
Into a burning brand,
But hold me fast and fear not . . ."

she whispered as the serpent's head became a pair of open jaws that could have swallowed her alive, as the scales changed to fur and the fur to something slimy that smelled of rotting wood and things too long beneath the water.

For a moment Paien's human shape reappeared. "You are thinking of the wrong charm," he said with a smile, "it only works to hold those who began as mortals."

And then she could see the trees and hills through his face, and a wind blew through her empty arms, whipping up the leaves and whirling them about her in a mocking dance.

"Damn you!" Ellen shouted at the spiraling leaves.

"Theologically impossible," a black crow cawed at her ear. She snatched at it and caught one wing feather, iridescent with green and purple, black as the darkness where no sun rose; it melted in her hand like a black snowflake, and the crow flapped above her, its wings growing and spreading and their edges softening until it was a black thundercloud to blot out the twilight.

"You owe me an explanation!" Ellen shouted at the cloud.

The cloud filled all the air about her, a dark mist

sparkling with its own interior lights; mist became droplets of water, each drop a light in shadow, and the individual drops coalesced and ran down an invisible plane of air like raindrops trickling together on a windowpane, tracing out fantastic shapes: scrolls, rivulets, birds in flight, the figure of a man. One last shimmer of light and water, and then Paien stood before her again.

"No debt unpaid, save one," he said, "and in the hour when that last debt is to be paid shall the celestial spheres forget their motions, the moon wander from her beaten way, the times and seasons of the year blend themselves by disordered and confused mixture."

His voice was a rolling of thunder pronouncing doom. Ellen shrank before it, and then felt Eleanor stiffening her spine.

"Says who?" she demanded.

Paien sank down cross-legged on the grass, graceful as a dancer. "One of your wise men. The scholars of Kit's age called him Hermes Trismegistus, and studied his writings for a key to our world. But the preconditions must be satisfied, Ellen Ainsley. If by mortal reckoning we owe you a debt of explanation, then allow me to pay it."

"First," said Ellen, "we have to go after Bethany."

"You cannot follow her," Paien said. "Not until you understand what is happening."

Ellen knelt on the grass beside him. "All right, but make it quick."

"Do you understand the doctrine of the spheres?"

"No . . ." Ellen began, and then Eleanor's knowledge joined with her own. "From sense to elements, from elements to daemons, from daemons to the stars . . ."

"Aye, so your mortal philosophers would have had it, some time past," Paien murmured. "But they were wrong; and this new world has all but forgotten what fragments of the truth they did grasp. Pythagoras did say that numbers have more reality than magical things; Bruno understood that they were the same. The images of numbers are intermediary between the celestial reality and the common one. If one can create a pattern corresponding with both at once, then can the inferior world be changed with the changing of the patterns. Such was his attempt; but lacking the thinking-machines of your day, he was doomed to failure."

"But it doesn't *work* that way," Ellen cried. "Computer simulations are just that. *Simulations*, images, not the real thing."

"The patterns of line and number are perfect, and therefore closer to the celestial reality than these physical shadows in the lower world."

As he went on, images began to form in Ellen's mind, shifting and uncertain, but as much of the truth, perhaps, as any mortal mind could encompass. The "erroneous" simulation she'd created by changing a single rule in KNEE was in fact exactly correct in what it showed: two spheres, one of mortal men, bound by time and logic, space and causation; the other one of Faerie, timeless, where illusion and reality, past and future, dream and waking mingled in an ever-shifting dance. A time before time, when both spheres were one; a time before language and law. Then Paien showed her the eternal dance of the spheres, their gradual separation as a gracious galliard in which the partners now drew apart, now clasped hands again. When the spheres overlapped,

Faerie could move in the world of mortal men, and men dwelt in the timeless sphere of Faerie. When they were close, mortals and those of Faerie could call to one another, and momentary shiftings and illusions could take place.

"Hence," Ellen said slowly, "witchcraft and magic, raising demons, people disappearing into the fairy hill . . ." *Bethany.* Fear choked her.

"Just so," said Paien. "But with each step in the dance, the time of separation is longer, the time of joining is less, and the spheres come never so close as in the beginning."

"Farewell rewards and fairies?"

"We did not truly understand the matter either, once," Paien said, "and most of my fellows still do not grasp it, for we do not think in terms of time and space. As we began to understand, though, so did we begin our plans to link the spheres again. Again and again have we offered mortals life in exchange for coming into our sphere."

"John Daniel," Ellen said slowly. "And all those stories about fairy hills . . ."

Paien nodded. "But ever have we failed. Those who came back were those we had stolen without their consent, so was no bargain broken. Those who came consenting did forget their mortal selves and become as ghosts of our sphere. Until Kit. Love of you has drawn him back across the years and the spheres, Ellen."

"So Kit's return was your planning. You made the masque again that I might call him back with the same magic he used before. You *wanted* him to come back."

"His bargain was not for life, but for knowledge,"

Paien said, "and ever did he long to return to this mortal sphere. But he could not find his way until you drew him like a lantern in the mist. Now he has brought that which he learned in Faerie into the mortal world."

"And all the strange things around here lately— are they because of Kit's return? Or would they have happened anyway? I think the spheres are drawing closer, not apart. As Master Cavendish did predict." That was Eleanor's memory, now hers also.

"The spheres are close now, and now is our time to join them forever. All debts but one unpaid," said Paien. He stood up; he seemed taller now, tall as a tree or a cloud; solid as stone, insubstantial as mist; part of the world as he said it was in the beginning, when there was no separation of light from darkness, of time from eternity. "Yes, Ellen, the spheres draw closer now, and soon they will be one again. Bethany has but gone before you a little way. By bringing back his knowledge into the mortal world, your Kit has broken his bargain with us," Paien said. "A little thing, perhaps, but enough to tilt the balance of the spheres. As water will run down the gentlest slope, so our sphere will be drawn again to yours, until finally all is one world again, as it was before history began: one unchanging sphere whose center is everywhere and whose circumference is nowhere, where your mortal time and space and logic hold no power. And there is nothing you can do to stop it."

Ellen wanted to ask why Paien was so intent on convincing her of this. If all he'd said of symbols influencing the mortal world were true, she could think of one thing at least that she might be able to do. But he was gone with that last sentence, dissolving into a trembling of the air, leaving only the echo of his voice behind like ripples across still water: "Now have I given my explanation, and thus is my debt to you paid, Ellen Ainsley!"

"Wait—wait!" Ellen scrambled to her feet and followed the shadow of movement, the wind that tossed the dry leaves, the mist that swirled among trees. Was she following Paien, or only her imagination? She could not tell; she had no way of knowing. But there was dark green grass under her feet where there should have been the muddy path up to Hackthorn Down, and the trees whispered secrets above her head, and somewhere far ahead of her she thought that she could see Bethany wandering among flowers of light. White flowers bloomed like candles on trees that had never grown under an earthly sun, and even as the flowers blossomed and the green leaves unfurled the same trees dropped tempestuous whirls of dried autumn leaves about her face. Brown and gold and rust flicked past, whipped her face until she closed her eyes, tangled in her hair; and when the gusts of wind ceased battering at her, she opened her eyes again and found herself in the heart of the Ladyswood. The trees were close about her, filling all the world with shadows of green and brown; and those who dwelt here were moving shadows compounded of the same shapes, shifting and changing until she became dizzy with trying to make sense of the patterns they made: now faces, now flowers, now the swirling grain of wood and the stark lace of naked branches against the sky. Chaos and shadow surrounded her, and there was no earth beneath her feet.

"Bethany!" she called, and the wind blew her voice to tattered shreds. "Bethany!"

She could not feel the ground, but she could move, and as she moved the Ladyswood transformed itself; a chasm opened at her feet, a waterfall plunged from nowhere to nothingness, thorny hedges sprang up wherever she looked. Neither sun nor moon gave light to this place; she could see, but there were no shadows to the things she saw, and no certainty to their shapes. How had Kit survived four hundred years in Faerie? *Music*, Ellen thought, and on the thought she remembered the last song of the masque, the song that was to end the time of magic enchantment and return the audience—and the players—to the mortal world.

"Come away, away, away," she sang, and from somewhere beyond mountains and rivers Bethany's contralto answered: "See the dawning of the day."

There was a thorny hedge between them. Ellen broke off a branch; the thorns pierced her palm, and became a snake with fangs sunk in her flesh. No, not a snake; now it was a silver wand that burned with the cold of Thule's ice.

"See the dawning of the day," she repeated Bethany's line, "risen from the murmuring streams."

Was there a cloudy light around her now, a light that cast the faintest of shadows, like the sun through mist and fog? The hedges between her and Bethany writhed like a mass of serpents and became an ordered labyrinth, clipped and neat as the maze-garden of Greenholt in another time. Ellen walked forward, still singing, as her feet retraced the pattern that Eleanor had divined. First turn to the left, second to the right, third left, fifth right . . . "Some stars show with sickly beams," she sang, and Bethany's voice twined about hers in the next line, "what stock of flame they are allow'd."

There were stars above and beneath her now, and between them a glowing sun haloed by the mist. "Stock of flame," Ellen sang, high and pure.

"Stock of flame," Bethany echoed.

"They are allowed," both voices joined in close harmony, and they were standing in the center of the maze, and the hedges writhed again to become a wall of thorns about them.

"Bethany? Are you all right?"

Bethany's eyes were wide and blank, unseeing. She sang as if by rote, but she did not look at Ellen. She shivered incessantly.

"You're cold," Ellen said. That, at least, was something she understood and could deal with. She struggled out of her denim jacket. The sleeves caught on her wrists. She pushed them inside out in her haste to cover Bethany, who stood unmoving while Ellen wrapped the jacket around her with all its ragged inside seams showing. As soon as her shoulders were covered, Bethany gave a start of surprise and grabbed Ellen's hand.

"What are *you* doing here? How did they take you?"

"I followed you," Ellen said.

Surprise and doubt clouded Bethany's eyes. "But it's been so long . . ."

Now Ellen felt the cold striking inward. "How long?"

Bethany looked vague. "Oh, years and weeks. Months anyway, or days . . . I forget . . . Ellen, what exactly is a day? Oh, well, never mind. Let's go inside."

"Where?"

"Into the *house*," Bethany said impatiently. "Right *there*." She strode forward, straight at the hedge of thorns; no, there was a little indentation at one side of the perfect circle. Was that what she called a house? Ellen followed her; the thorns somehow were not where Bethany stepped, although they were everywhere else. The memory of an old story came to her.

"*Wait* a minute, can't you?" she called.

"What?" Bethany was too far ahead of her now, lost amid stars and cloud.

"*The morning grey,*" Ellen sang, her voice muffled as she pulled her T-shirt over her head, "*bids come away . . .*"

"*Come away . . .*"

The mist swirled thick about her, condensing into tiny glittering droplets on her bare skin. Ellen turned the T-shirt inside out and pulled it on as quickly as she could.

And there was Greenholt, solid golden stone upon the solid earth, and the clear sky of an English summer evening still bright with the ending of the day; and Bethany a few steps ahead of her, half turned with one hand outstretched.

"Every lady should begin," Ellen finished the song in a whisper, "to take her chamber, for the stars are in."

Paien stood beside one of the stone pillars that flanked the front door of Greenholt, one hand on the worn carving of a crescent moon. Fenella was still crouched on the front steps, shaking. And the chimes of St. Mary's bells were still hanging in the air. The last humming vibration died away as the gravel of the drive crunched under Ellen's shoes, only to be replaced by other sounds: feet pattering down the inside stairs, the grumble of a car laboring up the steep road from Emminster.

Ellen watched Paien's face. She would have to pass by him to bring Bethany safe into the house. And how long the house itself would be safe— She dared not think about that. Not now; not yet.

As they came closer, Paien spoke. "I have seen a brave thing done this day." And he bowed to her, so deeply that the tips of his outstretched fingers brushed the grass. Where they touched, small flowers like stars sprang out, deep pure blue and pale lavender and twinkling white. "My reverence to you, Ellen that is, Eleanor that was. The pity is that such bravery will serve no earthly use."

"Why not?" Ellen demanded.

Kit burst out of the house. "What's amiss? Did hear someone scream—"

"That was me," Fenella said.

Paien answered only obliquely. "None come out of Faerie but with wit and grace and courage. How thought you to turn your shirt?"

"It's—in our stories," Ellen said.

Kit's face grew white with fury. "You ventured yourself in Faerie, and without my consent?"

"Bethany," Ellen said. "She was lost."

"Could have asked *me* to save her!"

"Oh, stop being such a macho pig," Ellen snapped, "there wasn't time to take a vote on what to do. Time's different, where she was; she might have been too far in Faerie to bring back. You should know that."

The groans of a straining engine had been growing louder for several minutes. Now a prolonged, metallic moaning like the last cry of an ancient dragon overrode everybody's voices, and clouds of black smoke shot across the drive. Roger brought his car to a steaming halt and jumped out, talking before he even closed the door. Geoffrey followed more slowly, burdened with sacks and cardboard boxes that smelt of hot fat.

"—and I hope we never have to go through *that* again," Roger said as though finishing an argument begun in the car.

"Wasn't my idea to take a detour through South Perrott," Geoffrey said mildly. He handed a sack to Paien. "Here. Chips."

"If you hadn't suggested that lane to nowhere—"

"Used to be the lane to Muchhay Farm." Geoffrey shook his head in sorrowing wonderment. "It'll be all that new building down around the industrial estate, they've been mucking round with the roads again."

"I *live* here!" Roger exclaimed. "I should know the way down to Emminster and back!"

"So you should," Geoffrey agreed. "Me, too. So we got lost. Embarrassing, but you don't have to keep going on about it."

"Did the road twist and turn back on itself?" Fenella asked. "And were there lights?"

"Damnedest streetlights I ever saw. And the mist—"

"But that's exactly what happened to me!"

"Couldn't have," Geoffrey said. "You weren't with us. Here's the fish. Didn't you get any vinegar, Roger?"

"I thought *you* were getting the vinegar."

"You put vinegar on fish?" Bethany demanded. "What's wrong with ketchup?"

"An American abomination," Roger said.

"There's some in the kitchen," Kit announced.

"Some what?"

"Vinegar. Go and eat, all of you. I have to talk to Paien." He made shooing motions with his hands. Fenella seized the chips, stacked them on top of the fish, and marched into the house. The others followed the lingering aroma of burnt grease and fried batter.

"You too," Kit said to Bethany and Ellen.

Ellen urged Bethany to go on in and eat. "You'll feel better. I'll be there in a minute."

"I seriously doubt that," said Bethany. But she drifted on into Greenholt, and Ellen felt free to devote her attention to Kit and Paien.

They might as well have been speaking in a foreign tongue for all the sense she was able to make of their conversation.

"Is it beginning, then?" Kit demanded of Paien.

"It has been beginning for some time," Paien said.

"Because of me?"

Paien inclined his head slightly. "It seems the masque was not necessary. We had thought that magic might work again to remind you who you were in mortal life, to make you remember one you had loved."

Kit drew Ellen towards him, his left arm encircling her waist. "I never forgot," he said. Then he tried to laugh. "How could I? Your folk gifted—or cursed—me with infinite memory. How could the man whose immortal mind holds the mortal spheres forget aught of earth?"

"There was a price to be paid, a bargain struck," Paien said. "We gave you knowledge—"

"I never asked to be burdened with it!" Kit cried.

"Did you not? Forgive me," said Paien with elaborate

humility, "then was this masque of yours nothing but a device to gain favor with Raleigh? You did seem to seek earnestly enough after truth; do not blame us now, if the taste of it lingers bitter in your mouth. We did but give what was asked."

"'Twas not your sphere I sought," said Kit, "but who seeks to undo a bad bargain is a knave and no gentleman. Very well. Can I not undo what has begun here?"

"Can you untwine the roots of knowledge from your mind?"

"Can I not at least keep *her* safe?"

"There will be no place that is not ours and part of us," said Paien.

"If I return?"

Paien's features blurred, as though he had called the mist of Faerie to conceal him. "To serve the Lady in our sphere, through eternity? Would you return to what you hated so?"

"Not for my life," said Kit. "But for hers, and to keep safe all she loves—"

"*No*, Kit," Ellen interrupted. "I've seen—I know—" She could not speak of what she had seen; there were no words, nor was there any need. Kit knew that land of dreams and illusions too well already. "You *can't* go back," she said, "I won't let you."

"Sweet, Paien is in the right. My debt unpaid will bring Faerie into and over and through the mortal sphere."

"As water will run down the gentlest slope," Ellen whispered, looking at Paien. Had he delighted in explaining and not explaining, in telling her all she asked while withholding the one thing that would have made sense of the puzzle?

"Then you understand. There is yet one way to restore our world for mortal sight," Kit said. His voice was calm and level as ever, but Ellen could not look at his eyes: blank and dull, they reminded her of the blind Kit who had wandered, bereft of memory and mortality and all but the ghost of longing, in the wood where his own songs gave her the key to him.

"No," said Ellen, but her voice was a thread as fine as spider-spinning, as weak as winter sun in falling snow.

Kit took her in his arms, and she thought her heart would break at the warm and living touch of him. "Sweet heart mine, why think you I dared not think overlong on this before, nor would speak of it to you? There is but one way. Since my coming home has made this debt, I can but pay it by returning. It will not be so bad," he said, like one comforting a crying child, "remember that I have dwelt in Faerie many and many a year already. I should be somewhat used to it by now," he said with a wry grin that tugged at the living heart of her.

"You can't go," Ellen said. "I won't let you." But she knew, with sick despair, that she had no right to keep him. His life for hers, that was a trade she could not let him make; but if what Paien said were true, all the natural world poised insecurely on Kit's decision.

"There is none other choice," he reminded her. "Should I stay, what would it profit us? *A day, a night, an hour of sweet content*—and none so very sweet, methinks, knowing as we should the price that all must pay—and then would we all, you and I and this house and the village and all the mortal world, be trapped as was Bethany. You have seen that world of dreams for yourself now, sweet Eleanor; is it right that such a vile sphere should replace the goodly earth and the brave sun and the strong tides of the sea?"

Paien made a small noise, almost like clearing his throat, save that one of Faerie could not have made so ungracious a sound. "It is," he said apologetically, "my world of which you speak."

"I have miscalled you and your world by ruder names before," said Kit.

"As may be," Paien admitted. "Yet it is unwise to speak so now, when the Lady of the Wood is very close to all of us. She has held you in high favor for a mortal, Christopher Arundel; will you forfeit her good will now, when she shall soon be high Queen of the joined spheres?"

Kit made a gesture with his thumb and clenched fist. "That, and a rotten fig, for your Lady! Let me but have one last taste of your lips, Ellen," he said, "and I shall go singing into the mist."

"I wish you two would stop talking like third-rate Renaissance poets and musicians!" Ellen cried.

Kit's stern set face showed a flash of very human anger. "I crave your pardon, dear love. A second-rate poetaster I may have been, but I was a musician of the very first rank indeed, as doth my success in this matter prove."

"Success? *Success?*" Ellen shouted. Rage warmed her, consumed her, fought the chill mists of Faerie that seemed so close around them. "I call that a damn poor success, to get yourself lost in Faerie all these hundreds of years, and only coming out again long enough to break my heart all over again!"

"I pray you, Eleanor," said Kit, "do not again fall into a decline, or seek to bargain with those more clever than all of us poor mortals. You have done enough in trying this once to save me; now is it time for you to find happiness in this your new world."

"Damn right I'm not falling into any decline," said Ellen. "If you're set on this, I'm coming with you."

"*No,*" said Kit. He glanced at Paien; a heartbeat later Ellen felt hands stronger than any mortal man's upon her shoulders. She stood unmoving and furious under Paien's hands, while Kit cast one last look upon the golden stone and glittering windows of Greenholt, then at her. "Mistress mine, well may you fare," he whispered, "kind be your thoughts and void of care . . ."

And before she could think of one more protest to keep him in this world, he was gone; still mortal, still walking the mortal earth, but his back turned upon her and his velvet cape swinging jauntily from his shoulders as he stepped up the steep muddy track between the trees that led to Hackthorn Down, or to the wood between the worlds that folk called the Lady's.

"*I will go with him,*" she said between her teeth, but Paien's hands on her shoulders were hard as the roots of ancient trees. "Roger! Geoffrey! *Bethany!* Isn't anybody awake in there?"

The windows of Greenholt flashed back the evening sun, and only silence answered her call.

"They sleep, and it would be no kindness to wake them now," said Paien. "Do not tempt me, lady."

"I wish I knew how!" Kit's dark head was blending with the deep shade under the overhanging trees; his velvet cape was the shadow of night in twilight.

A few steps more, any moment at the whim of those like Paien, and he would be lost to her like Bethany, wrapped in a light that was not of the earthly sun.

"And do you think," said Paien, his lips close to her ear, "that I am not tempted to bring such a brave lady into Faerie to dwell with the Immortals? I could warm myself forever at the fire of your mortal life."

"Then let me go!" As well fight a tree growing around her living body as struggle against the inexorable, inhuman will of Paien's hands keeping her rooted to this spot. But words she still had, and a tongue, and a voice to work what magic she could against him. "We have to stop him before it's too late. You can't stay here," Ellen guessed from what he'd said already. "With Kit returned, the debt paid, our spheres will drift apart again; you will fade from this realm, and we from yours." *And Kit from mortal knowing.* But that thought hurt too much for her to rest her mind upon.

"So be it," Paien said. "I will save your world, though your Kit be lost for it."

"*Why?*"

"I have passed among mortal men too long," Paien said, "and have become infected with their nature. And you are much to blame for that, Ellen! You have shown me a blue feather and a white flower and the thing called laughter, which we do not hear in the sphere where I have my being. Faerie is finer than this world, as a king's palace to a peasant's hovel; but it has come to me," he said with wonder in his voice, "that this muddy world full of death and blood, which you call home, has its own grace; and I would not see it vanished into Faerie. Perhaps in another thousand of your years the spheres may near conjunction again, and I may walk again beneath

the earthly sun. I would not see it spoiled. And so
I have made the debt clear to your Christopher,
that he may pay it, and the spheres separate again."

"You're not going to be popular at home for this,"
Ellen pointed out. Kit was entirely gone now, but
she could hear the high notes of his singing uplifted
to the wind; that much of him, then, remained in
this world.

"I think I shall survive the Lady's displeasure this
once," said Paien gravely, and Ellen wondered in
the midst of her grief and fear just how high Paien
stood in the councils of that other world where all
was at once inconstant and eternal.

"Think how much pleasanter it would be to be
out of favor if you had me for company, and all my
gratitude," she suggested.

"No, your heart is given already; I have no wish to
see you twined with Kit, two poor ghosts instead of
one. I love you too well to let you go to such a fate."

"Then God preserve me from such love as yours,"
Ellen said between clenched teeth, and brought the
heel of her sandal, with the nails half sticking out
of the shoddy stuff, down full upon Paien's foot.

His cry of pain was like a bird's shriek, or a cat in
the fire; and she could smell burning behind her.
So it was true about the faerie folk and iron things!
Ellen fell forward in the instant when Paien's hands
released her, and turned the falling into a running
step, another and another, until the dark green tunnel
of the trees above Greenholt shadowed her and she
could just see another shadow moving ahead. Kit
must have been walking very slowly; he should have
all but reached the top by now, with the time she'd
wasted arguing with Paien. Heart bursting, throat

raw with gasping breath, she scrambled up a path grown impossibly steep. The rocks bruised her hands and knees and all the muscles in her legs quivered like running water, but Kit was before her, his cloak swinging free, and with the last of her strength she caught at the jeweled hem and fell, bringing him down beside and over her in a tangled heap. Something crunched beneath them, and splinters of wood jabbed into Ellen's ribs.

"Pox and plague! You've broken my lute!"

Ellen sat up and tugged her short denim skirt over her knees.

"That," she said between gasps for air, "is one hell of a way—to greet—somebody who's going into exile with you."

"Go away."

"And that's worse. I'm not going away, Christopher Arundel, so stop swearing at me and let's get on with it. You despoiled my maidenhead and you owe me a marriage, remember?"

"That was some time past," Kit said gravely.

"Debts are always to be paid. I've just had a lesson in it. Now shall we go on to—the place," Ellen said, finding herself strangely reluctant to say the name of Ladyswood here where brambles grew green over the stones and the sound of running water was always close at hand, "or do you propose to waste your last chance at saving the world by sitting here in the mud and arguing metaphysics with me?"

"Contentious woman!" But he gave her a hand up, and Ellen managed not to wince when he grasped her scraped palm. "Why couldn't you stay where you were safe?"

"Safer with you than any other where," said Ellen,

and it was almost true. She would not look back through the trees for one last glimpse of Greenholt's golden walls, nor up for a sight of the sun; she had said her farewells when she stamped on Paien with her iron-nailed shoe. No more stones or sun or moon for her; only Kit. "Perhaps arguing will keep us sane," she said with a grin she did not feel. "How much farther is it to—the place?"

"God knows," said Kit in an odd tone, "or the Lady. It did seem to me that I had been walking a very long while when you came and dragged me down in the mud—as," he added, "is ever the way with women."

The last words were shouted into the wind that was rising all about them, plucking at the edges of Kit's short cloak and pulling with little sharp pinpricks on Ellen's hair as it whipped about her face.

"Is She coming for you?" she cried back while the wind moaned louder, and dry leaves crisped and rattled about them.

"How should I know? Before, the air was still, and the world of Faerie compounded of mist and pale light. Storms are a mortal thing." But Kit's face was white in the pallid storm-light, and he clutched the broken pieces of his lute too tightly. "Mayhap she seeks to keep me from climbing on; they are not overeager to see this debt paid, I think."

An ancient tree groaned and tilted sideways with deadly slowness; the roots tore through mud and rock, and the earth made smacking sounds around it. But Kit was on the uphill side before the tree fell, and Ellen was with him; one cheek scratched, and the sleeve of her shirt flapping loose where a branch had reached to tear the seam with almost animal viciousness. It was a winter landscape they faced, pale as cloud and snow, with the muddy path frozen as hard as any rock beneath their feet. The trees were bare, black lace against the silver sky, and no birds sang.

Ellen glanced over her shoulder. The barren branches of the tree that had come down bore fiery autumn leaves on the far side, and below that, as Time ran downhill like the trickling of a spring, she could see an arch of summer's green framing the golden house where roses spilled out of every corner in the garden.

"My way lies uphill," said Kit.

"Mine too," Ellen said, and to give them both heart she found from somewhere the breath to sing as they struggled up the icy slope.

Descend,
Descend,
Though pleasure lead . . .

The path was not so steep now, and the twining branches of thorny bushes on either side showed hints of green pricking out.

Though pleasure lead,
Fear not to follow,

Kit's voice rose to support hers.

There were pale flowers among the leaves now, creamy white and palest pink, and somewhere Ellen heard the trickling of water. Together they sang on, walking without looking back.

They who are bred
Within the hill
Of skill

May safely tread
What path they will . . .

"Would that were true!" Kit interpolated under
his breath. But Ellen thought that it might be. The
path was smooth and easy now, a green lane sloping
ever so gently downwards, and the high green hedges
on either side were green with summer flowers, lacy
white heads and thorny sprays of blackberry flowers
and purple thistles. She sang on alone.

May safely tread
What path they will,
No ground of good is hollow.

The path dipped down into a muddy hollow churned
by the feet of many cattle, and a five-barred gate
interrupted the hedge. Kit set down the splintered
remains of his lute on the gatepost, very gently, and
swore under his breath. "Furze Farm," he said, "and
the churl's let his cattle into the road again. We've
come through the hill and out the other side."

The homely smell of manure was thick in the air,
and on the far side of the gate was a very earthly
fence of barbed wire. Ellen leaned on the gate and
looked across the field and through the barbed wire
fence. The land rolled on, one noble sweep of valley,
field, hedge and farm and field again, up to the
darkening line of trees on Hackthorn Down and
the white mist settling gently as feathers falling on
the hills. Bethany had disappeared at eight o'clock,
when the bells of St. Mary's drove back Faerie with
their music dancing upon the cloudy evening sky,
and now it was still just light. The clouds had blown
away; an even grey-blue radiance filled the sky, and
the trees along the high edge of the Down were

sharply etched blue-black silhouettes against that calm passionless light. A bird startled from the hedge beside them with a sudden ruffling flutter of wings, and Ellen remembered all the ravens and spying birds and crows of ill omen: *one for sorrow*. A black and white milk cow ambled to the gate and put her head over it to inspect them, blowing out a friendly, warm, breathy *chuff* of grass-scented air.

"We'll have to go back," Kit said. His shoulders were drooping. "But may ten thousand fiends fly away with me if I know how we could have come over the Downs without knowing it. . . . That storm must have been worse than I thought."

They went up and down lanes and byways Ellen had never guessed at, cutting across fields where the folk of Emminster had walked to church or village before the first Elizabeth sat the throne or Greenholt Manor was built, and Kit sang his throat raw with the music of the masque, and all to no avail. The hedges and lanes were closed to them now, doubling back upon themselves so that they could reach any place except the high hollow in the Downs. No winds rose about them, no mists thickened into the formal courtiers of Faerie, no birds sang to guide the way. They were turned and turned again in a maze built of roads and paths and fields, until under the rising moon Kit sank down wearily beside the new-paved road to South Perrott and confessed defeat.

"They will not have me again," he said. "It suits them well enough to leave me here, and the debt unpaid, and their world running into ours as water will run down the gentlest slope. It will have been simple enough for them to turn the paths of my own country into a maze, for already is it half theirs."

He shook out his cape, now bristly with the leaves and prickly seed heads of the hedges they'd broken through, and looked upon it doubtfully. "Shall I turn my coat, do you think? That served you well enough, as I recall."

"To leave Faerie," Ellen said, "not to find it." She felt bone-weary and hopeless, but Kit sprang up with the light of new hope in his eyes.

"Well, then, perhaps 'twill lead us back to Greenholt," he said, "and there's one hope left." He put on the cloak wrong-side-out, suppressing a wince at the prickling of the rough seed heads caught in the velvet, and pulled Ellen to her feet.

"What hope is that?"

He walked briskly now, and only shook his head when she questioned him. "Better not to speak o't. But if this world holds another day and a night . . . The eve of Midsummer is a time of old magic."

"Oh. Yes. I see." Ellen saw more, she thought, than Kit wished her to understand. He would repeat all as it had been done before. What the songs of the masque could not do, sung out of their proper time and order by two voices without lute, the whole masque enacted on the solstice night might yet achieve. And if it did—if he disappeared again, leaving her alone? She could not let him do that; for his sake, if not for hers.

There was no magic to their path now; they took the straight way back to Greenholt, and the road lay still beneath their feet, with no sudden turns or changes of view. Up a long gentle hill they went, past a farmhouse with some lights in the upstairs windows; from this high point they could look down to see the lights of Emminster as a golden cluster in the valley, between them and the rising ground on which Greenholt Manor stood.

"We shall have to leave the music of the masque as it was in the beginning," said Kit as they started down into the village. "Can you find the originals again?"

What would happen if she said no? Nothing, Ellen concluded wearily, except that Kit would stay up all night writing the deleted songs out again from memory. If Faerie did not cover the mortal world before then, they would sing the masque tomorrow night; and if it served Kit's purpose, he would disappear into endless exile without her, and if it failed, all the world would become part of the shifting mists of Faerie. There was no good ending to this story.

"Yes," she said, and left it there. They walked in silence through the outskirts of Emminster, where new houses filled solid blocks of stone and asphalt, jammed wall to wall with only a few postage-stamp gardens to break the monotony. Ellen looked at her watch. She felt as though she had lived a hundred years since Bethany's disappearance, certainly as though she had walked from Land's End to John O'Groats and back; but by mortal time it was only half past nine. These suburbs were eerily silent for such an early hour: no children playing, no lights on in the houses, no teenagers making obnoxious noises under the lampposts. Her skin prickled and she began surreptitiously looking for signs of habitation: here was a car, there the blue-white light of a television flickered behind sheer curtains. The enchanted suburb: were they all inside behind their curtains, sitting inside and watching television for a hundred-years' waking sleep? Had the timeless mists of Faerie already swallowed their minds?

14

Tuesday, June 21, 1994

Ellen rose early on the morning of the masque, when the sky was still dark outside. Moving very quietly, so as not to disturb anyone else, she set up her notebook computer and began copying certain files. There wasn't time to do the job right; but she could write a driver for the display she wanted. . . . She kept looking over her shoulder, knowing Paien's tendency to appear out of nowhere; but wherever he was this morning, it seemed he slept too. She was able to finish her work in time to join the others for breakfast and a last rehearsal.

The morning that had begun with mist and clouds grew darker, not lighter, until by midafternoon Greenholt was an island in the fog. Ellen was depressed and desperate because Paien had not appeared, and without showing him her work she had no hope of stopping what had been set in motion. Kit looked like a man going to his execution. And everybody else was miserable because of the English weather.

"I don't see the *point*," Fenella whined for the

hundredth time, "of even *having* the masque if nobody can even *find* Greenholt in this mist." She pointed at the windows, where a white swirling fog pressed against every diamond-shaped pane, obliterating the view of field and hedge and stream and lane and whatever else had once been visible from Greenholt Manor.

"Fret you not, sweet, shalt have spectators enow," Kit said. He was very white in his costume of black velvet and jeweled cloak and starched ruff, and his eyes seemed to look beyond Fenella, beyond the mist that blanketed the windows, as though he were already more than half returned to the sphere of Faerie. His hands roamed restlessly up and down a lute, producing a tinkling shower of discords that were a musical echo of Fenella's high monotonous whine.

"I'd like to know where they're going to come from." Fenella pouted.

"I very much doubt that," said Kit gravely. A flicker of amusement lit his eyes; he was just marginally more present with them than he had been any time since he and Ellen had returned to Greenholt the night before. "Now don your robes, Fenella. Should be dressed to greet our guests."

Fenella flounced and muttered off to the little room at the far end of the Long Gallery—the same one, Ellen remembered, that she and the chorus of Nymphs had used as a robing-room on the night of the first masque. Bethany was already in there, pinning up a hem that had come loose at the last minute. Roger and Geoffrey were presumably changing into the costumes of Hounds. For this one moment she and Kit were alone in the long room with its diamond panes. Ellen put one hand on his shoulder; he started like a man expecting an enemy to creep up on him.

"Do you think *they* will come, then? The . . . Paien's people?"

"I would not call them *people*," said Kit, "but yes. I think we shall see them tonight."

"They'll try to stop you."

Kit's hands swept over the lute, sending out a strumming sequence of melodies: from a dance tune to a country song to the heartbreaking bars of his final duet with Diana. "They have their magic," he said, "and we have ours. And on this night of all nights are the spheres in equal balance one with the other. Do you sing your part, sweet love, and I shall sing mine."

"And go back to *them*?" Ellen cried. "Without me?"

"How else?" Kit put down the lute, took Ellen's hand in his, and laid it against his cheek. "I do love you too well to see you there. In memory of me, live again in this mortal world, Eleanor, and love it for me."

"There must be some other way!"

"Debts must be paid." Kit took up the lute again and began playing mechanically, a complex jigging tune with no more heart to it than the silver ship and the hooting brazen owl and the other mechanical marvels he had once loved. "I did bond my self to Faerie for the freedom of their sphere and for the knowledge which they did offer me. It seemed none so ill a choice at the time," he pointed out without losing control of the complex musical game he was creating. "A better bargain than any Raleigh's men would have offered."

"But now—"

"But now," Kit went on steadily, "there is no way to unmake the bargain, nor dare I leave that debt unpaid. They did tempt me with you to return into this world; do not you tempt me anew."

"There must be some other way," Ellen said in despair.

"Sweet love, no mortal man can untwine the roots of memory, un-know what has been known. Could you forget our love?"

"Never. Never again," Ellen amended, and felt a moment of hope. "But I *did* forget, once, Kit; I slept, and woke again, and knew not what dreams did plague me. If you could so sleep—"

"Your sleep was the gift of Faerie," Kit pointed out. "Think you they will so easily give me the means to escape them? And even then, Ellen, you did not forget entirely. A little thing, as little as a song—"

"A *magical* song. That's not fair."

"This is not," said Kit, "about fairness."

"What then?"

"Justice. An eye for an eye, but no more. My mortal self for their immortal knowledge, *but—no—more*. If I do return, they cannot bind this world to theirs."

"Come *on*, Ellen," cried Fenella, erupting from the dressing room in a cloud of green gauze and silver spangles. "People are coming after all. Don't you hear them? You'd better get into costume."

Ellen moved to the windows. She looked down through the diamond panes and saw the silver moonlight at war with golden lamps. Visitors were arriving—but what were they? She saw battered cars that she recognized from the parking squares around Emminster marketplace, ladies in flowered

dresses and men in sagging tweed suits. But she
also saw shadows costumed in high starched ruffs
and jeweled doublets or flowing brocaded skirts.
And when she looked slantwise through the beveled
edges of the panes, a pale rainbow of moonlight
danced before her eyes and showed her other figures,
tall and slender, their faces covered with fantastical
beaked and winged and gilded masks.

The spheres were very close together, now.

Behind her, Roger and Kit were not quite having
an argument over the score of the masque. "All *right*,"
she heard Roger say, "you want your songs back in,
they're back. I only wish you'd made up your mind
sooner."

He probably thought Kit was giving in to vanity.
Ellen knew better. She remembered Paien saying,
"It is most important that everything be done as it
was in the first performance of the masque."

The painted scenes behind the stage moved as if
a breeze from the Ladyswood breathed through them.
Ellen looked on the stage with two visions, present
and past together, and did not know in which one
the pictured forest sighed like a living wood.

Electric lights came on, making all things flat and
common again under their unmoving yellow glare,
and the twittering of women's voices drowned out
the whisper of leaves stirred by a cool wind.

"Mrs. Edwardes!" Roger greeted one of the ladies.
"I was afraid you wouldn't make it through this fog."

Mrs. Edwardes patted Roger's hand. "Dear boy,
of course I wouldn't fail you. Has the choir arrived
yet?"

"There've been some last-minute changes in the
music," Roger informed her. "We're putting back all

of Actaeon's original songs." He drew Mrs. Edwardes over to the virginals to show her the amended score, and Ellen reluctantly went into the dressing room to put on her costume as Diana. It seemed that nothing was going to stop this performance, after all.

But something was blocking the deep magic of Faerie; that grew more and more evident as they sang through the first half of the masque. Always there was the troubling sense of things unseen, of a true eternal wood behind the painted trees, of guests who were no mortal gentry of this or any other century. But the sense of magic remained at that level; no other voices joined the choruses of Nymphs and Hounds, and the flat painted panels of forest and fountain remained as they had been made by mortal hands.

Kit was safe; the world of Faerie would not receive him again. Ellen tried to give herself entirely to the music, and not to think. She could not be glad that Kit was safe, knowing that the price of his life was the very world in which they all lived. But neither could she truly wish in her heart that the Dark Lady would choose to take her place in the masque again, to make Kit vanish without hope and without reprieve into that world where he had wandered already through so many misty years.

She gave all her mind to the singing; and it was not until the Nymphs and Hounds came onstage for their song before the commoning that she saw how the chorus had grown. The ringing chimes of Faerie sounded from Nymphs who seemed to have stepped directly from their trees; Roger and Geoffrey led a chorus of Hounds whose masks were fiercer and more real than anything concocted by mortal craft.

And as they ended their song and swung out to draw the guests into the dance, Ellen put her hand on the last Hound, tall and slender, with hair like pale gold beneath his mask.

"Paien."

"Lady." He bowed, all serious grace, and kissed her hand.

How could she make him stay and talk?

"Someone must lead the dance," she said. "The mortals of this time do not know our measures." And indeed, the flowers-and-tweeds set were making a poor job of following the dancers of the Chorus.

Paien and Ellen moved to the center of the stage. She dipped her knee and swayed in the steps of the pavane Eleanor had learned as a little maid of seven; Paien bowed and stepped back from her advance, forward to her retreat. The confused medley of guests and chorus began to take shape around them, now that they had a model to follow.

Two steps forward, two back, turn, and curtsey.

"You are blocking the magic," Ellen whispered as Paien advanced towards her in time to the tinkling music of the virginals.

"Not I." He retreated, turned, and took her hand.

"Your kind, then. Can you say a debt's unpaid," Ellen whispered under her raised arm, "if you'll not give the debtor a chance to pay?"

They stepped down from the low stage and proceeded across the black and white floor of the gallery, letting the other couples pass awkwardly or gracefully under the arch of their joined hands.

"Is it your will that he pass again into Faerie?"

Ellen blinked back tears, turned, and made a deep curtsey at the end of the gallery. "It is *his* choice.

But he must not. You have erred, you and your kind. If he does return to Faerie, you will be the losers as greatly as we."

"Yes," said Paien. "I have grown to love this mortal world. But I dare not disobey the will of the Lady."

"And if her will were to destroy her own sphere as well?" Two steps to either side; she followed his movements without conscious thought, extended her left hand to him, and turned to proceed back towards the lighted stage.

"This is not possible. We know the laws of Faerie."

"But now," Ellen said, "you mingle them with the laws of the mortal sphere, and you have erred greatly. I can show you what will become of it, if you stop Kit from passing, and also what will come if you take him. You must do neither."

Again the assembled guests passed beneath the arch they made. Ellen and Paien stepped upon the stage again, parted with curtsey and bow, joined hands again to step the last measure of the pavane.

"One or the other must be done," Paien murmured as the virginals ended their sparkling tune and the Chorus withdrew, taking him with them. Ellen followed, leaving Kit to sing his solo lamentation upon being transformed into a stag. The virginals rippled, Geoffrey and Roger picked up their lutes to join the accompaniment, and Kit began his song.

> *The Fire to see my wrongs for anger*
> *   burneth,*
> *The Air in rain for my affliction weepeth,*
> *The Sea to ebb for grief his flowing turneth,*
> *The Earth with pity dull his center*
> *   keepeth . . .*

The music he had composed four hundred years ago drew out the wraiths of the elements he invoked; the stage was lit now with the ruddy glow of fire, now with shimmering pearlescence of air, now with rippling waves of pale green and blue. The audience murmured their admiration of what they took to be clever lighting; Ellen saw the failure of mortal magic. Each of the elemental lights rose and died down again; Kit's singing could not bring them together in their magical sum.

"You will find another way," Ellen whispered to Paien in the wings.

"Why?"

"Because of *this*." She drew him aside to a dusty corner behind the curtains, where she had left the notebook computer up and running. The display was dimmer than it had been; batteries were failing, or perhaps something deeper. "This," Ellen said, "is a computer simulation of the mortal sphere and that of Faerie in their dance, as you have explained it to me. Do you understand?"

Paien peered at the screen, at the lines of green that curved out to trace webs within the yellow net, then passed and repassed in a stately, curving, repeating pattern like the dance they had just finished. "A marvelous toy," he said. "Fain would I learn the secrets of such mortal games. But . . ."

"It is more than a toy," Ellen blazed with triumph, "it is a *pattern*, Paien, a perfect pattern of the celestial reality. Do you know what I can do with this pattern? You yourself have told me. Look!"

She tapped a single key and the display changed. The sphere on the right shrank and collapsed in on itself. As it atrophied, Paien seemed to grow pale and unsubstantial. He reached towards the computer, but Ellen struck his hand away and touched another key, halting the display.

"You were wrong," she said. "You folk of Faerie were all wrong. You did not understand how the mortal world interacts with yours. We are stronger than you, Paien, because we are weaker. Because we are bound to time, we love life; because we must die anyway, we are willing to die before time when the cause is just. Your sphere will not conquer ours; ours will destroy yours, if you do not find some other way to cancel the debt."

For the blink of an eye Paien was gone; then he reappeared, looking as pale and shaken as it was possible for such a perfect beauty to look. "I have spoken with the Lady."

"Oh, come on. You didn't have time!"

"Time," Paien said, "works differently with us. Remember? Allow me to assure you, I have had quite as much time to convey your information to the Lady as anyone could want. And to hear her instructions. All shall be as you wish."

The music onstage was dying away. "Why should I trust you?" Ellen demanded of Paien as Kit concluded his song.

"Because you've no other choice, and no more mortal time. And because we of Faerie also have no other choice."

"Ellen!" Bethany whispered urgently. "What are you *doing* back here?" She looked from Ellen's flushed face to Paien's pale one. "Oh, never mind, I can guess. Really, couldn't you wait until after the masque? You're on now." She pinned a crown of rhinestone stars on Ellen's head and threw a gauzy silver-trimmed

veil over all. Through the veil, Paien's features were dimmed; she could not read his eyes. She never had been able to.

The music that was Diana's cue began, paused, trembled, repeated; Mrs. Edwardes tinkling at the virginals with emphatic fingers.

"There is another way. The Lady has told me what to do." Paien shivered slightly. "She has told me . . . many things." He took her hand for a moment; she could almost feel a mortal pulse beating in his fingers. Or was it the beating of her own heart reflected back to her? The music grew staccato, emphatic, plucking her forth without time to discover Paien's meaning.

"My oath by fire and air, by sea and earth and iron," Paien said rapidly, "I mean no harm to you and yours, Ellen Ainsley. And if I fail this oath, then am I forsworn, and my debt to balance Kit's. *Follow as I lead.*" The last words were an urgent undertone as she stepped away from him, into the welcoming song of the Nymphs.

> *Welcome to this flowery place,*
> *Fair Goddess and sole Queen of Grace,*

Bethany and Fenella sang. A chorus of higher, purer voices rang behind theirs like a mocking, laughing chime of silver bells: "Queen of Grace—of Grace—Fair Goddess and sole Queen of Grace."

Kit dropped to one knee before her, awkward in his overbalancing crown of papier-mâché horns.

> *Paradise were meeter far,*
> *to entertain so bright a Star.*

He drew breath to continue, and was interrupted by Paien's voice, taking up the tune where Kit paused.

"But why errs thy folly so?" All in shades of green, from deep mossy green to the bright springing green of new leaves, Paien moved between Kit and Ellen like one of the painted trees come to life. The stage lights played in the burnished gold of his hair. Mrs. Edwardes drew in one deep breath of pure pleasure and, miraculously, played on while Paien turned to Ellen and sang the rest of Kit's lines.

> *Paradise is where you are:*
> *Heav'n above, and heav'n below.*

And on the words, the stage and the rafters above shimmered translucent, now cloudy, now clear as glass, and the starry spheres danced below Ellen's feet and above her head.

"It is as it was," she whispered, sick with memory of that other masque and with foreknowledge of what was to come.

"It is, and it is not," Paien replied, and launched into another song.

> *Sleep is a reconciling,*
> *A rest that Peace begets,*

Paien sang without accompaniment, save for the furious rustling of pages as Roger and Geoffrey hunted through the score for music they'd never heard before.

Paien gestured to Kit; the crown of antlers was gone as though it had never been. And through the gasps of amazed delight in the audience, Kit followed Paien's words line for line.

> *Doth not the sun rise smiling*
> *When fair at e'en he sets,*

Paien sang, and Kit echoed, "fair at e'en . . ."

It was a bargain of some sort between the two of
them, with no place for Ellen in their duet. And if
she interfered, would Paien's oath be void? She stood
mute, while the subtle interplay of Kit's and Paien's
voices wove into and around and under and through
her thoughts until she could scarcely remember what
was to do here, or why they had held the masque
on this night of all nights.

> *Rest you then, rest, sad eyes,*
> *Melt not in weeping,*

Paien sang, and Kit's own eyes closed.

> *While he lies sleeping,*
> *Softly, now softly lies*
> *Sleeping.*

And on the last note, there was only a dark flame
where Kit had been; a light that burned briefly and
without giving light to anything save itself; a light
that vanished even as Mrs. Edwardes cried out in
alarm and let her hands fall across the keys of the
virginals. A tinny discord sounded, drowned almost
at once by cries from the audience.

Ellen grasped Paien's arm, and felt only the
rough bark of a tree beneath her hands; the living
face that looked at her disappeared even as she
looked behind swift-growing briars that wreathed
about Paien's form. Then there was only the green
of new leaves, and then nothing; her hand grasped
emptiness.

"*What happened?*" Roger whispered, suddenly
beside her, and then, "Never mind. We're nearly at
the end; let's finish it."

He gestured urgently to Bethany and Fenella.

Their voices rose in the Nymphs' last song, sounding thin and weak without the chorus of Faerie.

Come away, away, away,
See the dawning of the day.

After the first couplet Mrs. Edwardes recovered herself and picked up the accompaniment.

Risen from the murmuring streams,

Fenella sang, and Bethany's alto came in strong and sure on the next verse.

Some stars show with sickly beams
What stock of flame they are allow'd,
Each retiring to a cloud.

Ellen stood in the shadow of the painted scenery, numb with grief and despair. All had been as it was; Kit was gone, and she had no way to follow him. No magical lights bathed the stage now, no strange forms mingled among the guests. The sphere of Faerie was separate again from that of Earth—and Paien had lied to her, and then vanished himself.

What had he promised? "No harm to you and yours . . . And if I fail this oath, then am I forsworn, and my debt to balance Kit's."

The memory blended with Paien's singing voice, taking up the last lines of the chorus with Bethany and Fenella.

The morning grey
Bids come away;
Every lady should begin
To take her chamber, for the stars are in.

For a moment Ellen thought she had gone mad indeed, for Paien's voice was coming from the image of Kit; lean dark face, dazzling white starched ruff, velvet doublet, and jeweled cloak.

And yet, as she looked, she saw that the semblance was not quite perfect. This shape was taller than Kit, and the face was too smooth; Kit as he might have been without the lines of laughter and living, without the small scar that tilted one eyebrow at the corner.

Was this how Paien meant to keep his promise? To send Kit back to Faerie, and to give her in his place this smoothly polished simulacrum? To act the part of Kit Arundel for her?

The singers were trooping forward to bow to their audience. Roger grabbed Ellen's wrist and propelled her to the center of the stage. The thing that was not Kit put out its hand to her; she held cool fingers without the warmth of mortal blood, bowed and curtsied and retired without letting go of the simulacrum.

Behind the painted scenes some careless person had left a tack hammer lying on the floor. Iron. Ellen stooped to take it up, whirled in one quick motion to strike the Kit-thing with iron. Perhaps that would make it reveal its true nature; perhaps she would only hurt it. Either would serve.

But the semblance of Kit was now no more substantial than a thickening of the air, and the iron passed harmlessly through the shadow of a man. Cool air and a whisper of falling leaves whirled about her head.

"I think that went off rather well, don't you?" Roger said with satisfaction. "Wish I'd known Chris was going to pull that vanishing trick, though. How'd you do it— Chris?" He stared, puzzled, at the empty space beside Ellen.

"He—he was called away," Ellen said. "Go and talk to people. They want to congratulate you. It was—" Her throat closed for a moment. "It was," she said slowly, tasting bitterness, "a most successful masque."

"You should come too."

"I'm afraid of tearing this gauzy stuff," Ellen improvised. "Go on. I'll just slip into my other costume and be right out."

And so she would—but not into the Long Gallery. Four hundred years ago, when first Kit was taken, she had been a fool who allowed herself to faint and waste precious moments. This time she would not lose a minute of this night. The spheres were still close together; she might still be able to bring Kit back. No. Bring him back this time, and she doomed them all to wander in the timeless, formless world of Faerie. But perhaps she could—

"Ellen Ainsley."

Ellen stopped, half in and half out of her shimmering dress of gauze and silver threads, and glared at Paien. He had resumed his own form, or at least, the form by which she had first known him in this world. "You lied to me."

"I saved you."

"I don't want to be saved. And if you think I was fooled for one moment by that pretty-boy image of Kit—"

"Oh, maybe for two or three moments," Paien said lightly. He shimmered, insubstantial as a breeze.

"Don't you *dare* disappear!" Ellen cried. "You have to take me to Kit. You owe me that much, at least.

And don't ever—ever borrow his face again." She was so close to tears that her throat ached with holding back. There was no time for tears, now; no time for anything but Kit.

Not even time to say farewell to Bethany. Ellen suppressed a stab of anguish, one brief flare of memory over all she had known and loved in the world.

"I cannot disappear," said Paien, and his voice was hollow as the wind in the trees. "I am bound to this world now, Ellen Ainsley; no more can I pass in the changing ways of Faerie. Such is the Lady's punishment on me for my failure in this great matter. So am I trapped helpless in this world, with no friend nor function."

"All right, all right, I'll get you a programming job," Ellen promised. "You'll like it. I think. Now *where is Kit*?"

Paien sighed. "Go to the top of Hackthorn Down, Ellen Ainsley, and find what you will find and do what you must do. And take with you these things."

He handed her a pile of incongruous objects. Ellen stared at them for a moment, then gave one choked sob and scooped them up into her arms. She had no better chance than to follow Paien's instructions, no better guide than the words of something immortal that had already forsworn himself to her. And the back stair that led from the Long Gallery was her surest and quickest way outside. . . .

Moonlight painted the path up to Hackthorn Down with silver light; the trees broke the light with patches of blackness. But there was no magic in this moonlight, and no mist obscured the path. Ellen, arms full, trudged steadily upwards. Sometimes she slipped on muddy patches; once she stubbed her toe against a lumpish root disguised by shadow. The path was as steep as it had always been. She counted under her breath, lips moving steadily, making hopeless wagers with herself and losing every one. If she could look only at the moonlight on the path for ten steps, all right, *twenty* steps, then when she looked up she would see the Ladyswood about her and Kit waiting there. . . . No. If she could think only of the steep climb for the next fifty breaths, then she would hear the music of Faerie mingling with the trickle of running water and the breath of the wind in the trees. . . . *No*.

She passed the trees and came to the top of Hackthorn Down without ever reaching the older, darker trees of the Ladyswood. The green slope was empty as ever it had been in this century: Ellen counted three picnic tables, the bronze map at the edge of the cliff, a crumpled bag that some careless picnickers must have left. . . .

A cloud passed over the moon; wind brushed her cheek, blowing her long loose hair over her eyes. She turned to face into the wind and saw what she had been sent to find: a naked man sleeping in the shelter of the hawthorn hedge.

"Kit, Kit!" Ellen was on her knees, shaking him; the things she had brought lay scattered over the grass.

He opened wide blank eyes and stared at her without understanding, and her heart sank. "Don't you know me, Kit?"

"I did dream of fair ladies," he mumbled, and fell back again, one arm crooked over his face.

"Kit, *please*! Wake up!"

"Who is Kit?"

"Don't you remember any—" Ellen stopped and
bit her tongue. Remember? *No mortal man can untwine
the roots of memory, un-know what has been known.*
Had this been Paien's gift to her? Kit stripped of
all he had brought into this world, from the clothes
on his body to the deepest memories of his own
life?

She looked over her shoulder at the things she
had dropped when she saw Kit sleeping. Their purpose
was clear now. Paien, stripping Kit of his memories
to cancel the debt, had known what she would find
here and what she would need. The cloak from Kit's
stage costume, to cover him while he slept. The
borrowed jeans and shirt, to clothe him when he
woke. And the lute—

Carefully Ellen spread the cloak of imitation
velvet and acetate satin over Kit's sleeping body.
Then she sat back against a tree trunk that grew
out of the hedge, took the lute, and began trying
to do for Kit what he had done for her. All the
songs that he had composed, all the music that
carried within it the keys of memory, flowed through
her fingertips; and she sang with the lute in a
breathy whisper that was not quite enough to
awaken a sleeping man or alarm any midnight
travelers.

> Who hath his fancy pleased
> With fruits of happy sight,
> Let here his eyes be raised
> On Nature's sweetest light . . .

That song finished, she chose another by chance,
paying no attention to the order of the masque or

the secret keys of the songs, only to the even rise
and fall of Kit's breathing.

> *No longer stay except it be to bring*
> *A med'cine for Love's sting;*
> *That would excuse you and be held more*
> *   dear*
> *Than wit or magic, for both they are here.*

Light was creeping over the eastern hills when
she came to the end of her music, voice cracking,
fingers aching with weariness. From where she sat
beside Kit she could look into the valley that cradled
Emminster like a jewel in a green bowl, then up
again to the rim of high ground on the far side.
Beyond those ridges there was a glitter to the air,
the promise of light, and the knowledge of the sea.

And if this sun did not wake Kit to himself, what
was she to do?

She swept her fingers over the strings and began
one last song, the one she had saved to greet this
new day.

> *Fair in a morn, o fairest morn,*
> *Was ever morn so fair,*
> *When as the sun but not the same*
> *That shined in the air,*
> *But of the earth no earthly Sunne,*
> *Nor yet no earthly creature . . .*

Ellen sang, while all around them the sun of this
earth gilded grass and trees and clouds with its own
mortal magic.

A wind that carried a handful of dry leaves whirled
past her, and voices clearer and purer by far than
hers finished the verse, then died away.

There stood a face, was never face
That carried such a feature.

For a moment the dried leaves danced in a pattern that might almost have been a mask, or a face; tilted eyes and curling lips and a shimmer of silver light. Then they whirled away, and with them the music of the other sphere. There was only the grass touched by the rising sun, and a little pile of clothing, and Kit opening his eyes on the new day. And this time he looked on her with recognition.

"Eleanor, dear heart," he said, and reached out to her, "I have dreamed such visions!" He sat up and looked about him in amazement. "But what is this strange dress of yours? And who has cut down the wood? And what be these great houses sprung up over night?" He gestured towards Emminster, the cluster of golden stone houses in the heart of the valley.

"You know me?"

"How should I not? But all else is strange to me."

Ellen saw the truth of it in his eyes; he gazed wondering around him as though he saw a village of stone and brick in the valley where there should have been only a scatter of wooden huts and some cattle grazing. She remembered that double vision all too well. And as she remembered, understanding came to her.

Paien must have taken all Kit's memory; and the music that he had written four hundred years ago was sufficient to restore his memories of the Kit Arundel who had lived then, but not of all that had passed since he returned to the mortal sphere in this century. Ellen suppressed a tear for Kit, who would have to learn all over again that he had left the world he knew four hundred years in the past, kissed him, and concentrated fiercely on practical things.

"There have been," she said carefully, "a few changes in the world. Dress you in these garments, and come with me; I will explain as we go along."

Appendix

Ellen's attribution of songs by Dowland and Campion to Christopher Arundel is not as unreasonable as it may seem in the era of copyrights and mass publication. Walter Davis, editor of Thomas Campion's poems, warns the reader:

"While attribution of unsigned poems is a difficult matter always, in the case of songs with music it reaches almost unsurmountable difficulties. In the published songbooks, most lyrics are unsigned, and the reader has no way of knowing whether they are to be taken as the composer's own lyrics, or lyrics written for him by another, or common property. Furthermore, practices such as composing a new body and ending for the beginning of another's lyric, setting a lyric to new music and altering it slightly to fit, and merely taking a suggestion for one's own song from an old song were so widespread among both amateurs and professionals that what may seem a variant or first draft of a published lyric may well be merely someone else's 'poetical descant' upon it."

This must serve as my excuse for borrowing the works of other poets and lending their glory to a fictional gentleman. Below are the texts of the songs quoted and the names of the authors.

When love on time and
  measure makes his ground,
Time that must end though love can never die,
'Tis love betwixt a shadow and a sound,
A love not in the heart but in the eye,
A love that ebbs and flows, now up, now down,
A morning's favor and an evening's frown.
              —Attributed to John Lilliatt

Praised be Diana's fair and harmless light;
Praised be the dews wherewith
  she moists the ground;
Praised be her beams, the glory of the night;
Praised be her power,
  by which all powers abound.

Praised be her nymphs,
  with whom she decks the woods;
Praised be her knights,
  in whom true honour lives;
Praised be that force,
  by which she moves the floods;
Let that Diana shine which all these gives.

In heaven queen she is among the spheres;
She mistress-like makes all things to be pure;
Eternity in her oft change she bears;
She beauty is; by her the fair endure.

Time wears her not; she doth his chariot guide;
Mortality below her orb is placed;
By her the virtues of the stars down slide;
In her is virtue's perfect image cast.

A knowledge pure it is her worth to know;
With Circes let them dwell that think not so.
              —Sir Walter Raleigh

Shake off your heavy trance,
And leap into a dance
Such as no mortals use to tread,
Fit only for Apollo
To play to, for the moon to lead,
And all the stars to follow.

—Francis Beaumont,
in *The Masque of the Inner Temple*

No grave for woe,
  yet earth my watrie teares devoures;
Sighes want ayre,
  and burnt desires kind pitties showres:
Stars hold their fatal course,
  my joyes preventing:
the earth, the sea, the aire, the fire,
  the heav'ns vow my tormenting.

—Attributed to Thomas Campion

Descend,
Descend,
Though Pleasure lead,
Fear not to follow;
They who are bred
Within the hill
Of skill
May safely tread
What path they will;
No ground of good is hollow.

—Ben Jonson,
in the masque *Pleasure Reconciled to Virtue*

Follow thy fair sun unhappy shadow,
Though thou be dark as night
And she made all of light
Yet follow thy fair sun unhappy shadow.
Follow still since so thy fate ordaineth:
The sun must have his shade

Till both at once do fade
The sun still priz'd, the shadow still disdained.

—Thomas Campion

Who hath his fancy pleased
With fruits of happy sight,
Let here his eyes be raised
On Nature's sweetest light;
A light which doth dissever
And yet unite the eyes,
A light which, dying never,
Is cause the looker dies.

She never dies, but lasteth
In life of lover's heart:
He ever dies that wasteth
In love his chiefest part;
Thus is her life still guarded
In never-dying faith;
Thus is his death rewarded,
Since she lives in his death.

Look, then, and die; the pleasure
Doth answer well the pain;
Small loss of mortal treasure
Who may immortal gain.

—Sir Philip Sidney

Circe bids you come away,
Echo Come away, come away.
From the rivers, from the sea,
Echo From the sea, from the sea.
From the green woods every one,
Echo Every one, every one.
Of her maids be missing none,
Echo Missing none, missing none.
No longer stay except it be to bring
A med'cine for love's sting;
That would excuse you and be held more dear

Than wit or magic, for both they are here.
Echo They are here, they are here.

—William Browne,
in the masque *Ulysses and Circe*

The Fire to see my wrongs for anger burneth,
The Ayre in raine for my affliction weepeth,
The Sea to ebbe for griefe his flowing turneth,
The Earth with pittie dull his center keepeth;
Fame is with wonder blased,
Time runnes away for sorrow,
Place standeth still amazed
To see my night of evils, which hath no morrow:
Alas, alonely she no pitie taketh
To know my miseries, but, chaste and cruell,
My fall her glory maketh;

Yet still her eyes give to my flames their fuell.

—Sir Philip Sidney

Welcome to this flowrie place,
Faire Goddesse and sole Queene of grace:
All eyes triumph in your sight,
Which through all this emptie space
Casts such glorious beames of light.

Paradise were meeter farre
To entertaine so bright a Starre:
But why erres my folly so?
Paradise is where you are:
Heav'n above, and heav'n below.

Could our powers and wishes meete,
How well would they your graces greete.
Yet accept of our desire:
Roses, of all flowers most sweete,
Spring out of the silly brier.

—Thomas Campion

Author of light, revive my dying spright,
Redeeme it from the snares
  of all-confounding night.
Lord, light me to thy blessed way;
For, blinde with worldly vaine desires,
  I wander as a stray,
Sunne and Moone, Starres and underlights I see,
But all their glorious beames are mists and
  darknes, being compar'd to thee.

—Thomas Campion

A daie, a night, an houre of sweete content
Is worth a world consum'd in fretfull care.
Unequall Gods, in your Arbitrement
To sort us daies whose sorrowes endles are!
And yet what were it? as a fading flower;
To swim in blisse a daie, a night, an hower.

What plague is greater than the griefe of minde?
The griefe of minde that eates in everie vaine,
In everie vaine that leaves such clods behind,
Such clods behind as breed such bitter paine,
So bitter paine that none shall ever finde
What plague is greater than the griefe of minde.

—Thomas Campion

Time stands still with gazing on her face,
Stand still and gaze, for minutes, hours and
  years to her give place.
All other things shall change, but she remains
  the same
Till heavens changed have their course, and
  Time hath lost his name.
Cupid doth hover up and down blinded with
  her fair eyes.
And Fortune, captive at her feet,
  condemned and conquered lies.

—John Dowland

Come away, away, away,
See the dawning of the day,
Risen from the murmuring streams;
Some stars show with sickly beams
What stock of flame they are allow'd,
Each retiring to a cloud.
Bid your active sports adieu,
The morning else will blush for you.

—James Shirley,
from the masque *The Triumph of Peace*

The morning grey
Bids come away;
Every lady should begin
To take her chamber, for the stars are in.

Live long the miracles of times and years
Till with those heroes you sit fix'd in spheres.

—Thomas Middleton,
from *The Masque of Heroes*

Weep you no more, sad fountains:
What need you flow so fast?
Look how the snowy mountains
Heaven's sun doth gently waste.
But my sun's heavenly eyes
view not your weeping
That now lies sleeping.
Softly, now softly lies
Sleeping.

Sleep is a reconciling,
A rest that Peace begets.
Doth not the sun rise smiling
When fair at e'en he sets.
Rest you then, rest, sad eyes,
Melt not in weeping
While she lies sleeping,

Softly, now softly lies
Sleeping.

—John Dowland

Fair in a morn, O fairest morn, was ever morn
*   so fair,*
When as the sun, but not the same, that shined
*   in the ayre,*
But of the earth no earthly Sunne, and yet no
*   earthly creature,*
There stood a face, was never face, that carried
*   such a feature.*

—Nicholas Breton

MERCEDES LACKEY

The Hottest Fantasy Writer Today!

URBAN FANTASY

Knight of Ghosts and Shadows with Ellen Guon
Elves in L.A.? It would explain a lot, wouldn't it? Eric Banyon really needed a good cause to get his life in gear—now he's got one. With an elven prince he must raise an army to fight against the evil elf lord who seeks to conquer all of California.

Summoned to Tourney with Ellen Guon
Elves in San Francisco? Where else would an elf go when L.A. got too hot? All is well there with our elf-lord, his human companion and the mage who brought them all together—until it turns out that San Francisco is doomed to fall off the face of the continent.

Born to Run with Larry Dixon
There are elves out there. And more are coming. But even elves need money to survive in the "real" world. The good elves in South Carolina, intrigued by the thrills of stock car racing, are manufacturing new, light-weight engines (with, incidentally, very little "cold" iron); the bad elves run a kiddie-porn and snuff-film ring, with occasional forays into drugs. *Children in Peril—Elves to the Rescue.* (Book I of the SERRAted Edge series.)

Wheels of Fire with Mark Shepherd
Book II of the SERRAted Edge series.

When the Bough Breaks with Holly Lisle
Book III of the SERRAted Edge series.

HIGH FANTASY

Bardic Voices: The Lark & The Wren

Rune could be one of the greatest bards of her world, but the daughter of a tavern wench can't get much in the way of formal training. So one night she goes up to play for the Ghost of Skull Hill. She'll either fiddle till dawn to prove her skill as a bard—or die trying....

The Robin and the Kestrel: Bardic Voices II

After the affairs recounted in *The Lark and The Wren*, Robin, a gypsy lass and bard, and Kestrel, semi-fugitive heir to a throne he does not want, have married their fortunes together and travel the open road, seeking their happiness where they may find it. This is their story. It is also the story of the Ghost of Skull Hill. Together, the Robin, the Kestrel, and the Ghost will foil a plot to drive all music forever from the land....

Bardic Choices: A Cast of Corbies with Josepha Sherman

If I Pay Thee Not in Gold with Piers Anthony

A new hardcover quest fantasy, co-written by the creator of the "Xanth" series. A marvelous adult fantasy that examines the war between the sexes and the ethics of desire! Watch out for bad puns!

BARD'S TALE

Based on the bestselling computer game, *The Bard's Tale.*℠

Castle of Deception with Josepha Sherman

Fortress of Frost and Fire with Ru Emerson

Prison of Souls with Mark Shepherd

Also by Mercedes Lackey:

Reap the Whirlwind with C.J. Cherryh

Part of the Sword of Knowledge series.

The Ship Who Searched with Anne McCaffrey

The Ship Who Sang is not alone!

Wing Commander: Freedom Flight with Ellen Guon
Based on the bestselling computer game, *Wing Commander.*™

Join the Mercedes Lackey national fan club! For information send an SASE (business-size) to Queen's Own, P.O. Box 43143, Upper Montclair, NJ 07043.

THE SHIP WHO SANG IS NOT ALONE!

Anne McCaffrey, with Margaret Ball, Mercedes Lackey, and S.M. Stirling, explores the universe she created with her ground-breaking novel, *The Ship Who Sang*.

☐ **PARTNERSHIP by Anne McCaffrey & Margaret Ball**
"[*PartnerShip*] captures the spirit of *The Ship Who Sang* to a surprising degree . . . a single, solid plot full of creative nastiness and the sort of egocentric villains you love to hate."—Carolyn Cushman, *Locus*
0-671-72109-7 • 336 pages • $5.99

☐ **THE SHIP WHO SEARCHED by Anne McCaffrey & Mercedes Lackey**
Tia, a bright and spunky seven-year-old accompanying her exo-archaeologist parents on a dig is afflicted by a paralyzing alien virus. Tia won't be satisfied to glide through life like a ghost in a machine. Like her predecessor Helva, *The Ship Who Sang*, she would rather strap on a *spaceship*.
0-671-72129-1 • 320 pages • $5.99

☐ **THE CITY WHO FOUGHT by Anne McCaffrey & S.M. Stirling**
Simeon was the "brain" running a peaceful space station—but when the invaders arrived, his only hope of protecting his crew and himself was to become *The City Who Fought*!
0-671-72166-6 • 432 pages • Hardcover • $19.00

And don't miss The Planet Pirates series:

☐ **SASSINAK by Anne McCaffrey & Elizabeth Moon**
0-671-69863-X • $5.99

☐ **THE DEATH OF SLEEP by Anne McCaffrey & Jody Lynn Nye**
0-671-69884-2 • $5.99

☐ **GENERATION WARRIORS by Anne McCaffrey & Elizabeth Moon**
0-671-72041-4 • $4.95

Above three titles are available together as one huge trade paperback. Such a deal!

☐ **THE PLANET PIRATES** • *72187-9 • $12.00 • 864 pages*

If not available at your local bookstore, fill out this coupon and send a check or money order for the cover price to Baen Books, Dept. BA, P.O. Box 1403, Riverdale, NY 10471

Name: _____

Address: _____

_____

I have enclosed a check or money order in the amount of $ _____